T0362997

WESTERN

Rugged men looking for love...

Her Son's Faithful Companion
Jill Weatherholt

Sunflower Farms Redemption
Stacie Strong

MILLS & BOON

HER SON'S FAITHFUL COMPANION
© 2024 by Jill Weatherholt
Philippine Copyright 2024
Australian Copyright 2024
New Zealand Copyright 2024

First Published 2024
First Australian Paperback Edition 2024
ISBN 978 1 038 91053 0

SUNFLOWER FARMS REDEMPTION
© 2024 by Stacie Butts
Philippine Copyright 2024
Australian Copyright 2024
New Zealand Copyright 2024

First Published 2024
First Australian Paperback Edition 2024
ISBN 978 1 038 91053 0

MIX
Paper | Supporting
responsible forestry
FSC® C001695
www.fsc.org

Published by
Harlequin Mills & Boon
An imprint of Harlequin Enterprises (Australia) Pty Limited
(ABN 47 001 180 918), a subsidiary of HarperCollins
Publishers Australia Pty Limited
(ABN 36 009 913 517)
Level 19, 201 Elizabeth Street
SYDNEY NSW 2000 AUSTRALIA

Cover art used by arrangement with Harlequin Books S.A.. All rights reserved.

Printed and bound in Australia by McPherson's Printing Group

Her Son's Faithful Companion

Jill Weatherholt

MILLS & BOON

Weekdays, **Jill Weatherholt** works for the city of Charlotte. On the weekends, she writes contemporary stories about love, faith and forgiveness. Raised in the suburbs of Washington, DC, she now resides in North Carolina. She holds a degree in psychology from George Mason University and a paralegal studies certification from Duke University. She shares her life with her real-life hero and number one supporter. Jill loves connecting with readers at jillweatherholt.com.

But as it is written, Eye hath not seen,
nor ear heard, neither have entered into the heart of
man, the things which God hath prepared for them
that love him.
—*1 Corinthians* 2:9

DEDICATION

To Suzanne, for over fifty years of friendship
and laughter.

CHAPTER ONE

INHERITING HER CHILDHOOD home along with a valuable piece of land might be the answer to Caitlyn Calloway's prayers. Selling the property could hold the promise of some financial relief, allowing Caitlyn to provide her son with the care he deserved. Last year's epilepsy diagnosis had buried her under a mountain of bills, pushing her months behind on the rent for their cramped Wyoming home. Selling might even free Caitlyn from the turbulent memories associated with the death of her parents, casting a shadow over her adult life.

"Let's go inside, Mom."

Caitlyn glanced at her seven-year-old son, Henry. At the rate he was growing, he'd surpass her five-foot-four-inch frame by the end of next year. His sandy-blond hair desperately needed a cut, as evidenced by the tousled wavy locks practically covering his ears. Signing his adoption papers two years earlier, after fostering Henry for a year, had been the best day of her life. Henry's kind heart and dimpled smile were the reasons she got out of bed each morning. She slid her phone from her bag to double-check the text message from the estate attorney. "The caretaker should be here soon, but we're a couple minutes early. Let's wait until he gets here before going inside." With no updates to the first text, Caitlyn tucked the phone away.

Late May thunderstorms had extended the drive from Wyoming to Bluebell Canyon, Colorado. The weather had forced them to stay overnight at a motel outside of Denver. An unexpected expense that added pressure on Caitlyn's already strained finances.

Henry's gangly jean-clad legs took the stacked stone steps of the farmhouse two at a time. At the top, he spun on his heel. "I can't believe you lived here. This house must be really old… like you." He giggled while gazing at the large two-story home with a steeply pitched roof. The painted trim underneath the gutter appeared chipped and peeling. "Cool! It's got a real fireplace—not like our fake one!" Henry pointed to the weathered red-brick chimney on the end of the house.

It was nice to see him so happy. Lately, the stress of Henry's diagnosis of epilepsy had taken a toll on Caitlyn. She felt as old as the restored eighteenth-century home she'd inherited. A place that had once provided a carefree childhood had developed into a tumultuous environment the year she'd turned seven.

"Funny guy, now come down and wait with me."

"Look!" He jumped and snatched hold of a weathered cord hanging from a cast-iron bell. Two quick pulls sparked a vivid memory of Caitlyn's mother. Ringing the bell meant dinner was on the table.

"Henry! Down here, now," she snapped.

"But I want to try this cool swing." Henry's tennis shoes whacked against the cedar porch as he sprinted toward the old two-person swing hanging from the ceiling by frayed rope. The splintered wooden seat appeared it would collapse even with the weight of a child.

"Stop! It's not safe." Caitlyn's sharp tone cut through the air. She bolted up the stairs and toward Henry to prevent him from climbing on the rickety swing.

Henry stopped short and turned with a puzzled expression. "What's wrong? I just wanted to play on it."

Caitlyn couldn't blame Henry. As a child, she'd had many fond experiences on this porch swing. She pulled her dark brown ponytail over her shoulder, knelt and took Henry's hand in hers. "I'm sorry, sweetie, but the swing is too old and it could break if you sit on it. You might get hurt."

Henry glanced over his shoulder before turning back to his mother. "Yeah, it looks kind of old, like the rest of the house."

Caitlyn stood and guided Henry to the top step of the porch. "Let's sit."

Henry followed her lead and sat down. "Has the swing always been here?"

"Shortly after my parents were married and moved into the house, my dad built the swing for my mom. In the evening, when my dad would come in from working in the field, he liked to relax out here." Caitlyn's heart squeezed as a vivid picture of her dad crossing the field and waving filled her mind. With a pitcher of lemonade on a nearby table, Caitlyn's bare feet had swung back and forth over the wooden floor while she'd anxiously waited for her father. "When I was not much younger than you are now, in the summer, I'd always wait for him with something cold to drink. He'd climb the steps, take off his cowboy hat and always say with a smile, 'Hey there Katydid. How was your day?' before he took a seat next to me."

Henry giggled. "That's a bug! Why did he call you that?"

"Once I was old enough, my father told me when I was around two years old, I started to giggle each time we'd hear the Katydid chorus during the summer. Anyway, I'd snuggle beside him, and we would enjoy the soothing motion swinging back and forth while we watched the sun set over the Rocky Mountains. He'd tell me stories about when he was a little boy."

Sounds of a diesel engine rumbled. Caitlyn peered over her shoulder and spotted a blue extended-cab pickup truck heading down the dirt driveway. "There's the caretaker. Let's go." She pulled her hands from the back pockets of her jeans and motioned for Henry to follow her down the steps.

Adrenaline coursed through her body. In a matter of minutes, she'd be inside the home she'd run away from a month before her seventeenth birthday.

With Henry at her side, Caitlyn squinted into the bright sun and wished she hadn't forgotten her sunglasses at the motel this morning. She watched as the truck pulled around to the side of the wraparound porch.

Seconds passed before the door slammed and gravel crunched.

Caitlyn placed a hand over her eyebrows and spotted a tall, ruggedly muscular outline approaching. A stray cloud drifted across the sun, finally revealing a face. Memories flooded her mind. Her breath caught. *Logan*.

"Caitlyn?"

The crinkled brow and stunned expression proved her presence had equally surprised Logan Beckett. Surprised or not, Caitlyn clearly remembered the piercing green eyes that always remained focused on whoever was in his presence. His neatly cut black hair with flecks of gray around the temples highlighted his firm jawline. The two had met during her years on the rodeo circuit as a professional barrel racer. Logan's brother, Luke, a professional bull rider, had been a good friend to Caitlyn.

She blinked rapidly to will away the butterflies flitting in her stomach. "This is a surprise." Her voice trembled.

A slow smile that could make friends in an instant crossed his face. He tilted his head to one side, sending a shiver down Caitlyn's back. In Logan's company, she'd always had this reaction, but her desire to be the best barrel racer had kept her focus off of Logan and on the sport.

"Hi! I'm Henry. Who are you?"

"It's nice to meet you, Henry. I'm Logan. Your mother and I are old friends."

Logan moved closer and gave Caitlyn an awkward hug, pulling her closer to his broad shoulders. His six-foot-two-inch frame towered over her. He smelled nice, reminding her of the spicy nutmeg she used to make Henry's favorite pancakes. Still trying to understand Logan's presence, Caitlyn pulled away from his muscular arms and took a step back. "Are you the caretaker for this property?"

"No, I lease several hundred acres of land, but Joe Lucas has taken care of the house since the owner, Martha Williams, moved to Florida. She recently passed away and Joe has left Bluebell. I got a voice mail from him about an estate attorney needing the key to the property," Logan explained. "Did you know Martha?"

Caitlyn remained confident her parents

wouldn't have chosen Martha as her guardian if they had foreseen the eventual downward spiral of her life. "She was my mother's best friend and my guardian after my parents died."

"I remember Luke mentioning the car accident. I'm sorry."

Caitlyn nodded. "It's been a long time." She turned and focused on the farmhouse. "This was my home for almost seventeen years." Following the death of her parents at seven years old, Caitlyn had no other choice than to place her trust in Martha. Years later, when Martha had brought her boyfriend into the home, Caitlyn had realized what a mistake she and her parents had made for trusting the woman. "At the time of the accident, except for me, my parents didn't have any living relatives, so they willed the home and property to Martha. Until recently, I didn't know my parents' will stipulated everything would go to me upon Martha's death, as long as I was of legal age. I haven't spoken with her since I left for Wyoming when I was a teenager."

Caitlyn forced the ugly memories of why she left into the back of her mind. "So, is Joe returning, or do you have the key?"

Henry bounced on his toes. "Yeah, I want to see my mom's old bedroom."

Logan grinned and ruffled the top of Henry's sandy-blond hair. "I don't have the key, but Joe told me where Martha stashed a spare. I'll run around back and grab it."

Caitlyn watched Logan round the corner of the porch.

"Was he in the rodeo with you, Mom?"

"No, but his brother Luke was a professional bull rider." Although she and Luke were closer in age, back then, she'd carried a secret crush on Logan.

"That's so cool! Maybe if the doctors find a cure for epilepsy, I can be a bull rider, too."

Caitlyn prayed for a cure. Since the diagnosis over a year ago, she'd tried to stay positive and encourage Henry. She never wanted Henry to feel limited. "Maybe so, sweetie. Let's go up on the porch while we wait for Mr. Beckett." Caitlyn took her son's hand and headed up the front steps. A loose board rattling underneath her foot caused her to question exactly how long Joe, the caretaker, had been out of town.

Grateful for a moment to calm her nerves after the surprise appearance by Logan, Caitlyn scanned the expansive green pasture then looked down at her son. "You like it here, don't you?"

Henry's head bobbled up and down. "If this is your house, why can't we move here?"

"Our home is in Wyoming. Plus, your friends are there." If moving to Colorado would make the pile of past-due bills waiting on her desk disappear, Caitlyn would move in a heartbeat. By summer, using the proceeds from the sale of her inheritance, Caitlyn hoped to have Henry's medical bills paid off, as well as the overdue rent to her landlord. Then she'd expand the size of the barrel racing classes she taught and extend the hours. One day, she dreamed of having schools across the state of Wyoming that offered specialized boot camps, along with private lessons. Maybe even offer an all-inclusive camp where the girls could stay for a week. Caitlyn had always believed a solid foundation was the key to excellence in the arena.

Henry struggled to sit still and squirmed on the porch step. "But if we moved here, no one would know I have epilepsy. I could have more friends. Back home, lots of the guys are afraid to play with me now."

Caitlyn rested her arm around Henry and pulled him closer. After a recent seizure he'd had at school on the playground, she'd noticed many of Henry's friends wouldn't come by the house anymore. She'd talked to some mothers who'd explained witnessing the seizure had frightened their children.

"Give them time. They'll come around."

Footsteps rustled in the grass. "Are you ready to see the inside?" Logan bounded up the steps two at a time, flashing the key.

Henry jumped from the step and followed Logan to the front door. "I am!"

Logan slipped the key into the lock and turned it.

There was no turning back. Caitlyn inhaled deeply. In the weeks leading up to the night she'd run away from home, Caitlyn had kept a close eye on her bedroom door. For more than half of her life, she'd avoided coming home, but now, for the sake of her son, she had no choice but to face her past.

"It looks old," Henry noted as he shadowed Logan inside.

Caitlyn's heart thumped in her chest when she stepped over the threshold and into the front room, or the parlor, as her mother had called it. Instantly recognizing the peeling gold wallpaper, she pressed her damp palms against her legs. Caitlyn's father had hung the paper as a birthday surprise for her mother.

Logan flipped the light switch and moved toward the front windows. "Let's bring in a little daylight. It might brighten things up a bit." He drew the curtains. Particles of dust swirled in the sunlight that came streaming through the window.

"I think it was better without the light." Caitlyn scanned the room. The once-luminous hardwood flooring was now dull and covered with black scratch marks. "When exactly did Joe leave town?"

Logan rubbed his neck. "It's kind of hard to tell. He's never had a steady job, but he goes off for long stretches in search of work as a ranch hand. I tried to help by offering him temporary jobs here and there, but he was never reliable."

Caitlyn tilted her head. "It's obvious he didn't take his job as caretaker seriously. Martha couldn't have been aware of this or she wouldn't have continued to pay him."

Logan closed the space between himself and Caitlyn. He glanced toward the kitchen where Henry had wandered, but was still in sight. He whispered, "You must know about Martha's drug and alcohol problem."

Caitlyn nodded. "Yes, but like I said, I hadn't spoken to her in years." After Caitlyn had left Colorado, she'd prayed that one day Martha would reach out to apologize. Perhaps even share if she'd overcome her addiction.

"Before she left town, my brothers and I tried to help her, but by the time she left for Florida, she was in terrible shape. It was a shame. She'd once been a gracious lady, but seemed to get mixed up with the wrong company."

When Caitlyn was around twelve, Martha had turned to alcohol following a nasty breakup. The woman her parents had entrusted to care for their daughter had morphed into a different person. "I suppose Joe and Martha both weren't too concerned about the property...that explains why the place is in much worse shape than I expected."

"Mom! Come look! There's a mouse back here," Henry shouted from the kitchen.

"Why am I not surprised?" Caitlyn scurried to the rear of the home. Loose floorboards rattled underneath her boots. Another expense.

Logan followed. "By the look of things, there's probably more than a few mice running around the place."

Shelling out money for a motel room last

night was already more than Caitlyn could handle. She didn't have the funds to stay anywhere while in Bluebell, so the plan had been to remain in the house while she addressed any necessary repairs. But with mice—and anything else—creeping around the home, the dilapidated floorboards, the peeling wallpaper, and who knows what other problems, she might have to come up with another solution. But what other option was there?

"Are you sure you saw a mouse?" Caitlyn immediately noticed the kitchen was in no better condition than the front room.

"Yeah, look over there." Henry pointed.

Logan chuckled as he looked in the critter's direction and turned to Henry. "You must live in the city in Wyoming. That's a chipmunk."

Caitlyn's shoulders relaxed. "I suppose a chipmunk is better than a mouse, right?"

"Not necessarily." Logan moved to the walk-in pantry, pulled out a broom, and headed to the door leading from the kitchen to the back porch. "These little guys might be cute, but similar to a squirrel, they can be quite destructive. If they chew on the wiring, that could create a fire hazard. Plus, they can burrow holes in the backyard. The last thing you want is to break your ankle walking around in the yard.

My guess is the enormous chestnut tree along the fence line is the primary food source." He opened the door before walking over to the chipmunk, who appeared too interested in his chestnut stash in the corner to notice anyone.

What if there was already damage to the wiring? Caitlyn bit her lower lip. Electricians cost a fortune. "So, how do I keep them from coming inside the house?"

Logan used the broom and guided the critter across the kitchen floor and out onto the back porch. He closed the door and squatted. "First, I'll need to seal entry points, crevices and gaps, similar to this one." He pointed to the gaping hole at the baseboard.

Was Logan offering his services for free? She'd learned the hard way not to depend on a man. Her skills with a hammer were better than most. Caitlyn scanned the room and spotted two more holes in the kitchen. "That could be an extensive project." Visions of her bank account balance depleting played in her mind.

"Probably so, but I can get it knocked out in no time. We don't want any snakes to find their way inside."

"Cool! I always wanted a pet snake," Henry cheered.

Logan stifled a laugh.

A shiver traveled up Caitlyn's back. She could handle most creatures, but she drew the line with snakes. This wasn't good. The rooms downstairs required significant attention. Martha had left a small amount of money to cover household repairs, but not nearly enough for all the issues Caitlyn could see. Concern rolled around in her head. Caitlyn couldn't help but wonder what they'd find on the second floor...

CAITLYN WAS AS cute as Logan remembered, with her heart-shaped face and the light brown freckles across the bridge of her pert nose. Although still petite, she'd grown up from her early competitive barrel racing days when he'd first laid eyes on her. Back then, she was barely out of her teen years. Now she could turn every man's head in a packed stadium. And she had a child.

"Do you think there are snakes in the house?" Caitlyn gnawed on her thumb while her hazel eyes shifted around the kitchen.

"It's a little early in the season, but you could have a problem this summer if I don't get the house sealed properly." Logan closed the door and returned the broom to the pantry.

"Henry and I will be long gone by then. The

new owner will have to deal with any unwelcome visitors."

It surprised Logan to hear Caitlyn could so easily sell her childhood home. If he had kids, he'd love for them to grow up in the house where he'd lived as a child. Maybe her work kept her busy in Wyoming. "Do you still compete? You were pretty good." Logan knew she had exceptional talent. He'd followed her career closely for several years. There was a time when Caitlyn Calloway had been the most successful barrel racer on the rodeo circuit.

Caitlyn laughed. "No, I retired a few years ago. The sport is for the younger generation." She reached down and rested her hands on Henry's shoulders. "These days, this guy keeps me running in circles."

Overhead, a loud thump sounded.

Logan peered up at the ceiling. "I'm not sure what that noise was, but I guess we better go check out the upstairs. It's probably nothing." Old houses often made unexplained noises.

Henry jumped up and down. "That sounded like a bear or something! Let's go see!"

Logan laughed when Caitlyn rolled her eyes. "I'll go first. I've had a little experience with bears out in the woods." He winked at Caitlyn before heading toward the front staircase.

With every movement, the wooden steps creaked under their feet. When they reached the top, the last stair popped and cracked.

"I can't believe the steps still make noises. It used to annoy my mother, but my father refused to fix the problem."

Outside of the first room, Logan turned to Caitlyn. "Why didn't your dad have them repaired?"

Caitlyn wrapped her arms around her waist. "He said it would come in handy when I became a teenager and tried to stay out past my curfew."

Logan half smiled, believing the steps may have stirred up painful memories from Caitlyn's past. He couldn't imagine how difficult it must have been for her to lose both parents at such a young age. "The noise might have come from this room." He reached for the doorknob and turned.

"That's the main bedroom. I'm hoping it's in decent enough shape for Henry and me to sleep in while we're here."

Henry's eyes widened. "I'm not sleeping in a room with a bear."

Logan laughed. "I promise there are no bears in this house."

They moved inside the bedroom. Logan spotted the source of the sound. "I think the barnyard cat decided he wanted to upgrade." The animal sprinted across the room and into the bathroom.

"Cool! I always wanted a cat. Can we keep him, Mom?"

"I thought you wanted a snake?" Logan glanced at Caitlyn.

Henry shrugged his shoulders. "I don't care which one. Mom has never let me have a pet."

Dogs had always been a constant throughout Logan's childhood. Now, as an adult, he trained service dogs. "Well, cats are pretty low maintenance, so maybe she'll change her mind."

"I doubt a stray cat would enjoy the car ride back to Wyoming. He belongs here." Caitlyn paused. "Well, not here exactly. We'll have to take him outside and figure out how he got in."

Logan moved inside the bathroom. "I don't think you'll have to worry about the cat. It appears he found the escape route." He pointed to the window, open enough for the animal to come and go. With some force, Logan pushed the window closed and attempted to secure the lock. "It's broken. I'll have to change the lock."

If Caitlyn planned to sleep in the house, he'd have to do a thorough search of the property. But, even then, it wasn't a good idea for them to stay here alone. Hopefully, he could convince her to settle at his brother's place. Luke and his family lived in Whispering Slopes, Virginia, so his house in Bluebell sat vacant most of the time.

Twenty minutes later, Logan had taken Caitlyn and Henry on a tour through the entire house. Henry went outside in search of the stray cat while Caitlyn ran out to her car. She returned with a red journal and pen in hand. While moving around the kitchen, she began furiously scribbling page after page of notes.

"Are you making a to-do list?" Logan broke the silence, filling the room.

Caitlyn dropped her hands to her sides but continued to clutch the journal and pen. "It's becoming more like a book than a list." She blew a stray piece of hair away from her face. "I'm pretty good with do-it yourself projects, but I don't think I'll be able to put the house on the market as soon as I had hoped."

Logan couldn't help but wonder if someone special was waiting for her back in Wyoming, but he didn't want to pry. "What's the big rush?" Or did he? "Don't you want to spend time with your son in the town where you grew up?"

"Wyoming is our home."

He was still unsure of her reason for rushing, but it seemed best not to pressure Caitlyn. It appeared she had things on her mind that she'd rather keep private. He could respect that. Logan was a private man himself. "You could always cut the price and sell the house as is. The repairs on the first floor alone could take weeks."

"Time is something I don't have," Caitlyn snapped. "I'm sorry. I didn't mean to be rude."

Logan considered Caitlyn's response. Something wasn't right. Was she in some sort of trouble?

Caitlyn moved to the window over the kitchen sink and whirled around. "Cutting the price isn't an option. Many of the repairs I can do on my own, but I'll need to hire an electrician and plumber."

"I can recommend a few."

"I'd appreciate it." She took a peek inside the journal then closed it shut. "Martha left around fifteen hundred dollars in her will for home repairs."

Logan didn't want to alarm Caitlyn, but given the problems they'd uncovered during their tour, the repairs would eat up the allocated funds in no time. Money could be an issue, or lack of, in Caitlyn's case. He couldn't let his brother's friend make the repairs herself. "I can help you with most of the projects."

"That won't be necessary."

Caitlyn repositioned her stance. It wasn't Logan's imagination. She'd planted her feet against the floor, ready for a fight. Luke had always said Caitlyn was stubborn. His brother hadn't been joking. The woman didn't want his help, but she was kidding herself if she believed she could do everything on her own.

A crack of thunder sounded outside.

"We better get Henry inside. These storms can pack a punch." Logan headed to the front door. Caitlyn tossed the journal as they moved past the dining room table.

"Wow! It's pouring!" Henry flew in through the door the moment Logan pulled it open.

"You're soaked," Caitlyn said.

"I saw some towels in the upstairs hall closet.

I'll run and grab some," Logan offered, running to the stairs, taking them two at a time.

Once at the top of the steps, the overhead lights flickered at the same time thunder rattled the walls. The surrounding space went dark. Rain pounded against the roof. A window at the end of the hall provided no outside light. No surprise there. From what Logan had seen during their walk-through of the farmhouse, every window needed a thorough cleaning.

He opened the closet door. A musty aroma shot up his nose. Logan fumbled in the dark space and snatched two bath towels before heading downstairs.

The entire first level of the house was as dark as the upper floor. "Here you go." Logan handed off the towels to Caitlyn. "I better look around for some candles. There's no telling how long we'll be without power, so we don't want to only rely on our phone flashlight."

Inside the kitchen, Logan checked each drawer. Martha appeared to be a packrat. Every drawer was overflowing with odds and ends. Who needed four pairs of scissors? He threw them back and continued to work his way around the room.

"Have you found any candles? It's getting

darker outside." Caitlyn entered the room with Henry at her side, swaddled in a towel.

"Not even a flashlight. But if you need any scissors, there's no shortage of those."

Caitlyn moved into the dining room and opened a drawer in the breakfront. "Here they are." She pulled out a handful of tapered candles in a variety of colors.

"How did you know to look there?"

"Some people use their dining room table a couple times of the year for holidays or family gatherings. Usually, they'll light candles for the occasion." Caitlyn stuck one candle in each holder on the tabletop. "Now, if we can find some matches, we'll be good to go."

"I saw one of those long plastic lighters in the drawer beside the stove." Logan scurried to the kitchen and grabbed the lighter. Seconds later, the candles' warm glow softened the room.

"That's much better." Caitlyn pulled out a chair at the table and took a seat. She snatched the journal and scribbled inside.

"You must go through a lot of those," Logan laughed.

Caitlyn's face flushed. "I'm a little obsessed with notebooks and journals, so I stay well-stocked."

"Mom plans everything," Henry shared.

"Well, I hope you leave a little time for unexpected events. Sometimes they make the greatest memories." Following the sudden loss of his fiancée, Logan had quickly learned that every day was a gift that no one should take for granted.

"I'll keep that in mind." Caitlyn wiped her cheek and shook her head. "Something dripped on me?"

Logan looked up and spotted a large water stain on the ceiling. "That's coming from the guest bathroom."

"You didn't leave the water running when you used the restroom, did you?" Caitlyn asked Henry.

"I don't think so." Henry took off up the stairs.

"Wait, you need some light." Logan slipped his cell phone from his back pocket. He turned on the flashlight and chased after the child. Caitlyn followed, clutching her journal.

Inside the bathroom, water spilled over the top of the toilet, covering the floor.

"I didn't mean to break it." Henry blew out a sigh.

Logan squatted and reached for the valve to shut off the water flow. "It's not your fault. The pipes in this house are old."

Once again, Caitlyn put pen to paper, scribbling in her notebook. "Do you think every pipe will need to be replaced?" Her eyes darted around the room before focusing in Logan's direction.

Logan stood and dusted off his jeans. "Of course, an inspection needs to be done, but my guess is yes. If you want to sell the property for a good price, new piping would be a wise investment."

Henry moved to Logan's side. "My mom doesn't have any money."

"Henry!" Caitlyn slammed the journal shut. "Please, if it's okay, take Mr. Logan's phone and go back down to the kitchen and wait for me."

Logan nodded and passed the device.

Henry obeyed his mother's command and scurried down the steps.

Years ago, Logan had his own financial struggles. Keeping them private was understandable. "My offer still stands. I'm sure you can handle some repairs on your own, but getting this place ready to list on the market is going to be a huge undertaking. There's no way one person could do everything, especially if time is an issue. Please, let me help you."

Caitlyn took a shuddery breath. "But I can't pay you."

Without a mortgage on the property, the proceeds from the sale could pay for the repairs and more, unless Caitlyn was flat broke and carrying debt. Her reaction to Henry's comment caused Logan to believe that could be the case. An idea percolated in his mind. But would she go for it? He wasn't so sure. Something told Logan that Caitlyn might have more than financial struggles hidden in her closet.

CHAPTER TWO

MONEY. EVEN WHEN Caitlyn had it, she'd didn't care to discuss it, especially with a total stranger. She inhaled sharply. But Logan wasn't a *complete* stranger. Still, she had no intention of building any relationships during her time in Bluebell. That rule applied to the hunky older brother of a dear friend whom the younger Caitlyn had fallen head over heels for the first time she'd laid eyes on him.

An hour later, the storm had passed and the gusty winds were now nothing but a midafternoon gentle spring breeze. A cardinal chirped outside on a nearby branch. With the electricity restored, pen poised over the open journal, Caitlyn made some quick calculations at the dining room table. Henry and Logan were outside cleaning up tree limbs on the driveway and in the front yard.

Her mind drifted to what Logan had said.

Who was she kidding? He was right. She'd never be able to complete the repairs on her own. The material alone would eat up every dollar Martha had left in her will. With a firm grip on the pen, she scratched through the numbers on the page. Tears threatened, but she swallowed hard to tamp them down. A couple of hours earlier, she had believed the house was the answer to her prayers, but the fact remained it was doing nothing but adding to her debt.

"Mom! Come quick!"

Outside, Henry's cry for help sent Caitlyn's protective-momma-bear's instincts into overdrive. She pushed herself away from the table. The chair legs screeched across the wooden floor. She slammed the journal closed and raced outside.

The dilapidated screen door closed with a bang behind Caitlyn. From the porch, she scanned the property and spotted Henry and Logan across the pasture. She bolted down the steps and across the muddy grass. Pumping her arms, her favorite leather boots sunk into the ground, kicking up clods of mud against the back of her pink button-up blouse.

"Look! The fence is totally smashed." Henry

pointed to a portion of the split-rail fencing surrounding the property.

Caitlyn skidded to a stop and attempted to catch her breath. "You scared me," she sputtered. "I thought you got hurt."

Logan rested his hand on her arm. "He's fine. He got a little excited by the fallen tree, that's all."

"Sorry. I didn't mean to scare you, but look! The tree is gigantic!"

Neon dollar signs flashed in Caitlyn's mind. To remove a tree that size would be another major expense. She'd used a chain saw a few times, but with other projects on her ever-growing list, it would take her until next spring to get the house ready to sell. She inhaled a calming breath. "Yes, but I'll get it taken care of. I'm sure there are plenty of tree services in the area." She turned to Logan for confirmation.

"Of course, there are. But why would you want to hire someone when there are plenty of able-bodied men ready and willing to do the work for free?"

Confused, Caitlyn tossed Logan a questioning look.

"My brothers and I can get it out of here in

no time." Logan slipped his hands into the back pockets of his jeans as he assessed the damage. "Besides, this would make great firewood. The temperature here drops pretty low in the winter months."

"I appreciate the offer, but I wouldn't think of imposing on you or your brothers."

Logan crossed his arms over his chest. "Since you used to live here, you probably remember what it's like in Bluebell. We help others in their time of need. That's what being a tight-knit community is about. We don't pay to have work done when we can do it ourselves with the help of a neighbor or two."

Caitlyn had no intention of becoming part of this community for a second time, so accepting the help from the residents wouldn't be right. "That's great for you, but I don't live here anymore. And I don't plan on ever making this my home again, so accepting help isn't an option."

Logan laughed. "Boy, my brother Luke was right."

"About what?" Caitlyn questioned.

"You are stubborn."

"No, I'm being realistic. I won't be around to return the favor," Caitlyn stated.

"Fair enough, but what if we made a deal?" Logan's left brow arched.

Dealmaking wasn't Caitlyn's style, but neither was carrying a heap of debt. Prior to Henry's medical issues, she'd never owed a dime to anyone. She'd even had the suggested six-month reserves saved in her bank account. That was long gone now. "I'm not sure. What did you have in mind?"

Logan cleared his throat. "For a couple of years, my livestock have grazed on the land I've been leasing from Martha. However, I have a new idea for the property that I'm currently working on. I had planned on making an offer to purchase the acreage, but she never returned my phone calls. I assumed since she didn't respond to my voice mails, she wasn't interested in selling."

Caitlyn wasn't sure what this had to do with her dire situation. She continued to listen while keeping a close eye on Henry as he skipped rocks in the creek that meandered through the property.

"Since the land is yours now, I thought I could make you an offer."

Hope bubbled. "You want to buy the land? What about the house?" If Logan purchased the property along with the farmhouse, perhaps she and Henry could head back to Wyoming sooner than expected.

Logan shook his head. "I don't have a need for another residence. The couple of hundred acres I've been leasing is all I'm interested in owning."

Caitlyn's heart sunk. Her chance for a quick exit out of town slipped away. "I don't plan on splitting up the property. I'm sure I could command a larger price by selling the house and the land together."

"That's true. But think about the money you'll save on repairs."

"I'm not sure I'm following you."

"You didn't let me finish," Logan continued. "If you allow me to purchase the land I've been leasing, I'll help you get the house and the remaining property ready to sell. You'll have little out-of-pocket expenses."

"With so many repairs needed, I can't take your time. It's as valuable as my own." Caitlyn's suspicions rose. Logan was Luke's brother and she could always trust Luke, yet something didn't sit right with her. Who works for free?

"I'm a rancher, so I'm not on anyone's clock. My brothers and I also train service dogs. I choose how I want to spend my time. The land is important for the growth of my business. If a new owner takes over, he or she might not allow me to continue with the lease, much less buy the property. That's a risk I can't take."

Caitlyn considered Logan's argument.

"Plus, you're my brother's friend. Luke would never let me live it down if I didn't come to the aid of his old friend. You'll be helping me as much as I'm helping you. I can't afford to lose the land."

"Your time may be free, but what about the electrical work and the plumbing? You said yourself a professional would be required for those jobs. I can't let you cover those expenses."

Logan nodded. "As I mentioned, this town is full of people who live to help their neighbor. We have retired folks with great trade skills. Many worked as plumbers and electricians. They love to keep their hands and minds sharp by helping others."

"Thanks, but I don't accept charity. I won't have strangers working for free."

Caitlyn couldn't wrap her head around the idea of people working for no pay. Lately, she hadn't had time to make friends within her community. She worked long hours to keep up with Henry's medical bills. Most of the people she knew were the parents of Henry's classmates, and they were merely acquaintances. Most of the girls enrolled in her barrel racing classes weren't local thanks to some savvy online marketing that had proved beneficial. Many parents drove a couple of hours round-trip for their child's once-a-week class. Apart from her neighbor, Caitlyn didn't have many people she could call if she needed help. But that was okay, at least for this season in her life. She and Henry managed.

"They wouldn't exactly be working for free."

Caitlyn's guilt eased. "I would never expect someone to do that."

"A homemade pie or a plate of cookies is all anyone would accept as payment. Well, maybe old George Dunaway might order up a meat loaf." Logan rubbed his stomach.

Caitlyn laughed and rolled her eyes. "You're kidding, right?"

"I never kid about food. George doesn't either," Logan laughed.

Chewing on her lower lip, Caitlyn's mind raced while she considered her options. But what were they? Earlier, she'd tried to make a list in her notebook, but the page had remained blank because there were no options. Either she made a deal with Logan, or she'd go deeper into debt trying to repair the old house. There wouldn't be any money from the proceeds of the sale to pay the medical bills or her back rent. Her inheritance would end up costing her money. As much as she wanted to handle the situation on her own, she couldn't.

"What do you say?" Logan waited for an answer.

Caitlyn looked up at the house in defeat. She remained silent for a moment before slowly extending her hand. "It's a deal."

LOGAN GRIPPED THE wrench to tighten the doorknob on the kitchen door leading to the back patio. Since getting Caitlyn to agree to his deal, everything he touched in the house seemed to break, fall off, or didn't work at all. Before he could begin making phone calls to recruit help, he'd need to make a master list of things that required immediate attention. Logan laughed to himself. Maybe he should check with Caitlyn. She may have already created that list.

The front screen door slammed.

"What should I do with the suitcase, Mom?"

"You can put it in the main bedroom."

Logan leaned toward the voices and shook his head. When Caitlyn mentioned staying in the house, he'd thought she'd been joking. He'd been wrong. Logan slid the wrench into his back pocket, readying himself for a disagreement once he reminded Caitlyn the house was in no condition for overnight guests.

Logan stepped into the dining room and found Caitlyn. Once again, she sat hunched at the table, writing in her notebook.

Henry stepped onto the stair landing.

"Hold up, buddy."

Henry stopped and put the suitcase down.

Logan approached the table. "Why don't I drive you into town so you can get checked into the hotel? Kathleen Kilby owns the Sleep Inn. She'll take good care of you and Henry."

Caitlyn lifted her head and held a strong posture. "We plan to stay here."

Exactly the response he'd expected. "I don't think it's a good idea. You'd both be more comfortable and safer staying in town."

"All we need is a bed to rest our heads. Besides, I can easily replace the lock on the main bathroom window."

"What about meals?" He clasped his hands behind his back. "We haven't checked the stove. I doubt anyone has used it since Martha left town."

"The refrigerator seems to work fine. I'm sure the stove is okay, too. We aren't going to a hotel, so let's drop the subject."

It appeared hopeless. No matter what he said, Logan would not change Caitlyn's mind. But he had to try. "Okay, no hotel. How about you stay at Luke's place? His primary residence is in Virginia, but he has a place here. If I called him now, I'm sure he'd offer it to you."

"That won't be necessary." Caitlyn turned to Henry. "Take the suitcase upstairs."

Henry took off before Logan could say anything more. It was just as well. He'd be wasting his breath. Caitlyn was adamant. "At least let me drive you into town to pick up some sheets for the bed and some groceries."

Caitlyn smiled. "I'd appreciate that, but I thought maybe Henry and I could drive to Denver to get what we need."

Logan glanced at his watch. "It's getting a little late to make that drive. By the time you made it home, it would be dark."

"That's what headlights are for," Caitlyn laughed.

He liked her quick wit. "I suppose you're

right, but there are tons of critters on the roads at night. I wouldn't be comfortable with you and Henry traveling alone." It wasn't the wildlife Logan worried about. The city was full of dangerous people. Something he'd never thought much about until his fiancée hadn't returned from her trip.

"Okay, you win." Caitlyn held up her hands. "The last thing I need is a car repair bill on top of everything else. Let me run upstairs and get Henry. I want to change into something a little more presentable, if you don't mind."

"Of course, but I think you look great the way you are." Logan noticed Caitlyn's cheeks redden. "I'm sorry. I didn't mean to sound forward. It's just—we're pretty casual around here."

"I'll keep that in mind." She turned and headed up the stairs.

Logan watched until she rounded the corner. The woman would look great dressed in a potato sack.

A few minutes later, Logan opened the passenger door of his truck for Caitlyn. She climbed aboard wearing a pair of khaki pants and a yellow blouse. A shiny gloss highlighted her naturally pink lips.

"I'll get Henry fastened in the back seat,"

Logan offered. "Don't worry. I have booster seats for my niece and nephew."

"I can do it myself." Henry jumped once and then again.

"It's a little too high for you, buddy. Let me help you." Logan hoisted Henry into the truck and buckled him in.

"Do you remember Garrison's Mercantile Company?" Logan asked, turning on the main road into town.

"It's still open?"

Logan nodded. "It sure is. The place is a historical landmark. Hank and Nellie are both pushing eighty, but they're still going strong. They plan to pass the store on to their son if they ever decide to retire."

"I remember my mother taking me every Saturday for an ice cream cone before we'd shop for groceries," Caitlyn remarked, gazing out the window.

Logan hoped he'd sparked a fond memory for Caitlyn.

"One time, Mr. Garrison gave me two extra scoops after my mother told him the next day was my birthday. My small hands could hardly hold on to the cone. One scoop rolled off the top and hit the floor. When I started crying,

Mr. Garrison ran to me carrying a bowl with four scoops."

"That's Hank all right." Logan was relieved the memory was a good one.

"Do you think he'll give me some ice cream?" Henry called out from the back seat.

Logan chuckled. "I'm sure he will."

Caitlyn slipped the ubiquitous journal from her bag and began writing. "I'll make a grocery list."

"Make sure you include a couple of flashlights and batteries. We could have more storms, like earlier today," Logan said.

"I sure hope not. The last thing I need is for another falling tree to damage the fencing."

"Try not to worry so much. Cleaning up the tree and repairing the fence won't be a big deal." Logan hit the turn signal and pulled into Garrison's gravel parking lot. "We're here."

"The place hasn't changed a bit." Caitlyn unfastened her seat belt and exited the vehicle.

Logan stepped out of the truck, helped Henry from the back seat, and they headed inside.

The bell over the front door jangled, and the aroma of freshly baked cookies filled the store.

"Nellie must be baking this afternoon." Logan inhaled the sweet scent.

"Oh, my goodness." The petite, gray-haired woman scurried from behind the counter with open arms. "Caitlyn Calloway, I knew you'd come home one day."

"Hello, Mrs. Garrison." Caitlyn closed the distance and wiped a tear.

Logan watched while the women held each other.

"You're grown up now. Please call me Nellie." The woman pulled away, her eyes damp with tears. "You look just like your mother." Nellie moved her gaze to Henry. "And who do we have here?"

Henry grinned and stepped forward. "I'm Henry. Did you know my mom when she lived here?"

"I did." Nellie reached out her hand. "It's nice to meet you, Henry. I've got cookies fresh from the oven." She turned to the counter and picked up a yellow plate. "They're still warm." She held the cookies in front of Henry.

The boy's eyes widened and he helped himself. "Chocolate chip are my favorite." Henry took a big bite and reached for a second.

"Caitlyn and Henry plan to stay at Martha's place for a while. We need to pick up some groceries and other supplies." Logan looked around. "Is Hank here or at the house?"

"He's in the office on the phone." Nellie quickly turned to Caitlyn. "From what I hear, the farm is yours now. I think it's wonderful that Martha left the house and land to you. That's where you belong."

"My mom wants to sell it, but I think it would be cool to live here."

"Sell? But it's your home, dear." Nellie flashed a look of concern.

Caitlyn shifted her weight. "Our home is in Wyoming now. I came back to sell the property. Unfortunately, it needs a lot of work before it's ready to go on the market."

Logan knew Nellie would do everything in her power to convince Caitlyn to stay, but from what he could tell, that was going to be a losing battle. "That's what I wanted to speak with Hank about. I had hoped he could round up some of his ranch hands to help with the repairs."

"I'm sure they'd be happy to lend a hand. Nelson Whitfield was here last week to replace our hot water tank. Let me run back and see if Hank's off the phone."

Nellie shuffled toward the office but stopped

short and turned. "Henry, you help yourself to more of those cookies on the counter."

"Thanks!" The boy ran to the plate.

Logan followed and snatched one. "You better grab one for yourself before Henry devours them," he said to Caitlyn, who had her face buried in her journal.

She looked up. "Is Nelson a plumber?"

Logan nodded. "Yes, but he's also a wiz with appliance repairs. He retired about ten years ago, but he keeps busy helping others around town with their plumbing issues. So you can check 'find plumber' off of your list." He winked.

"Mom, don't forget to get some cereal for my breakfast."

"I've got it on my list. Pick out an inexpensive box with little sugar." Caitlyn marked her sheet.

"Hold up, Henry. I know chocolate-chip cookies are your favorite, but have you tried chocolate-chip pancakes?" Logan asked.

"I've never had that. Mom always makes blueberry pancakes. They're okay." Henry shrugged his shoulders.

"I make pancakes on Saturday mornings. Growing up, it's something my mother did for me and my brothers, so I've held on to the tradition." Logan glanced in Caitlyn's direction and she smiled. "If it's okay with your mom, maybe I can come over tomorrow morning and make you chocolate-chip pancakes." Logan had concerns about the safety of the stove and other appliances in the house. This would give him the opportunity to check them out. "I have the ingredients, so you won't need to purchase anything."

Henry bounced on his toes. "That sounds awesome! It's okay, right, Mom?" Henry waited for a response.

Caitlyn twisted a strand of her hair and watched her son's excitement. "Well, we don't want to inconvenience you, but the pancakes do sound delicious."

Logan had expected Caitlyn to decline the offer, but perhaps she didn't want to disappoint Henry. What if she'd said no? Logan wondered if he would have been more disappointed than Henry.

CHAPTER THREE

WHY HAD SHE agreed to Saturday-morning pancakes with Logan? Caitlyn stood in front of the bathroom mirror and secured the loose bun with a claw clip. She had agreed, for Henry's sake. Everything she did was for her son. But, she had to admit, she was excited to see Logan for breakfast as well.

Caitlyn glanced at her reflection and blew out an exasperated breath. Concealer. The dark circles beneath her eyes were proof of a restless night. Caitlyn wasn't frightened to sleep in her childhood home, but the squeaks and creaks throughout the night had kept her tossing and turning. The sagging-middle mattress hadn't helped either. Of course, Henry was out the moment his head hit the pillow.

Caitlyn fumbled through her cosmetic bag and eyed her watch. Logan would be here in ten minutes, and she still resembled a raccoon.

"Mom, there's water on the floor," Henry called out from downstairs.

Caitlyn dabbed two dots of makeup under each eye and blended it into her skin. "I'll be down in a second." She zipped the bag closed, grabbed her journal off the vanity, and headed downstairs to investigate.

The hardwood at the bottom of the staircase was dry. With a quick scan of her surroundings, she spotted wet shoe prints outside of the doorway to the kitchen. She moved closer and found Henry stomping his new tennis shoes in the puddles of water that covered the floor. "Henry! You're making a mess."

"It's not me. It's that white thing." Henry pointed to the mudroom off the kitchen.

"That's the hot water heater." That would explain the cold shower she'd endured this morning and probably the hissing and knocking she'd heard last night.

"Don't worry, Mom. Mr. Logan can have that guy Nelson come and fix it."

Caitlyn relaxed her shoulders. Sometimes Henry knew exactly the right thing to say to calm her nerves. "You're right. Thank you for reminding me."

A knock at the front door sounded. Caitlyn had her hands on the mop inside the pantry. "That must be Mr. Logan. Can you go let him in?"

"Sure!" Henry shot out of the room, leaving behind a path of shoe prints through the kitchen.

Within seconds, Logan ran into the kitchen and stopped short of the water covering the floor.

"The water heater is leaking," Caitlyn shouted from the pantry.

"Have you turned off the shutoff valve?"

"No, I was upstairs when Henry yelled." Caitlyn glanced over her shoulder before continuing with the mop.

"Don't panic. I'll take care of it." Logan moved into the mudroom.

Forty-five minutes later, Nelson had come by to assess the problem with the water tank. He replaced a corroded valve, but recommended replacing the tank to prevent further issues.

Settled at the kitchen table, Caitlyn clenched her teeth in frustration as she reviewed her list of repairs. On a positive note, with Nelson's help, Logan had completed the inspection of the stove and everything seemed to be in working order.

"Grab a plate, Henry." Logan stood at the stove with his broad back to her. He flipped the pancake and called over his shoulder.

The sweet aroma of the milk chocolate chips melting inside the skillet calmed Caitlyn's nerves. "Those smell delicious."

Logan piled two more cakes on Henry's stack. "Okay, let me get some ready for your mom." He passed the plate to Henry before turning to pour three circles of batter. The oversize skillet sizzled. "Yours will be ready in a couple of minutes." He tossed a grin at Caitlyn before wiping up a dollop of batter he'd dripped on the counter.

Caitlyn admired Logan's cooking skills. He followed the clean-as-you-go method to avoid dealing with a big mess after the meal, something she remembered her mother had done.

"Oh man! These are so good." Henry shoveled another bite into his mouth. "Can I come over to your house next Saturday?"

The last thing Caitlyn wanted was for Henry to break her own rule to not get attached to anyone or anything in Bluebell. It would make it that much harder on him once she sold the house and they headed back to Wyoming. Caitlyn picked up the napkin and wiped the melted chocolate from Henry's chin. "Sweetie, it's not polite to invite yourself to someone's house."

Logan ferried Caitlyn's serving and placed it on the table. He ruffled the top of Henry's hair. "You're welcome to come over anytime. Sometimes it gets a little quiet for me and Rocky."

"Who's Rocky?" Henry asked.

"He's my German shepherd." Logan settled into the empty chair across from Henry with a cup of coffee.

Henry's eyes widened. "Wow! I've seen those dogs before. He must be huge."

Logan beamed. "He's seventy-five pounds."

Caitlyn nudged Henry's shoulder. "Rocky weighs more than you do," she laughed.

"Maybe I can meet him tomorrow." Henry sat up straighter in his chair.

"Henry! What did I say about inviting yourself to Mr. Logan's house?" Caitlyn shook her head and looked at Logan. "I'm sorry."

Logan smiled at Henry. "I'll be at church in the morning, but you and your mom are welcome to come over in the afternoon for lunch. Rocky is only a year old, and he's still growing. He's got a lot of energy and loves to meet new people."

"Can we go, Mom? Please." Henry pouted adorably.

Against her better judgment, Caitlyn nodded. "Okay."

"Great, you can meet Rocky and Sophie."

Caitlyn's ears perked up. Sophie? Logan didn't wear a wedding ring. Perhaps Sophie was his girlfriend.

"Who's Sophie?" Henry asked, finishing the last bite of his breakfast.

Caitlyn opened her mouth but quickly pressed her lips together. It was natural for kids to be inquisitive. At least, that's what she told herself. Besides, she couldn't deny she was a little curious about Sophie, too, so she held her peace.

"Sophie is a rescue dog I'm training. She's a Labrador retriever."

"Cool. What are you training it to do?" Henry eagerly waited for Logan's answer.

"She's being trained to become a service dog."

Intrigued, Caitlyn settled back against her chair. "You mentioned you and your brother's train service dogs. We'd love to hear more about it. Right, Henry?" She glanced at her son.

Henry quickly nodded and leaned in, placing his elbows on the table.

"My brothers and I started Beckett's Canine Training. Our goal is to improve the quality of life for individuals with disabilities and other physical impairments. We specifically train each dog to meet the exact needs of its master," Logan explained.

"So what will Sophie do?"

Logan glanced at Caitlyn before answering Henry's question. "Sophie is being trained to be a seeing-eye dog."

"What's that?" Henry's face scrunched.

"They are service dogs trained to help people who can't see. The animal becomes their owner's eyes and helps them to navigate a world of darkness. They help to keep them safe."

Henry's eyes popped. "Wow! That's what you do?" Henry placed his hand over his eyes. "Not seeing anything must be hard. I'd be running into everything."

Logan nodded. "It is difficult. Our eyes are one of the many blessings God has provided, unfortunately not everyone can see, so we train the dogs to take over."

Caitlyn's heart warmed at Logan's sweet explanation. From what she'd seen so far in his interactions with Henry, Logan was great with children. Of course, that's what she'd believed about her ex-boyfriend. She'd trusted him and, as their relationship had grown, she'd allowed the man to be a part of Henry's life. That had proved to be a grave mistake; one that had caused her to question her judgment in men. Caitlyn wouldn't allow her painful history to repeat itself. Protecting Henry was her job. Allowing him to form an attachment to Logan was a risk she couldn't take. Maybe accepting Logan's lunch invitation hadn't been such a good idea.

SUNDAY MORNING, FOLLOWING a period of fellowship in the hall, Logan stepped outside the church and breathed in the fresh, sun-drenched air. He moved across the gravel parking area with an extra spring in his step. Sure, the sermon this morning had been uplifting, but his heightened mood was present the moment he'd planted his feet on the floor upon waking up. Caitlyn and Henry were coming over this afternoon. He couldn't deny the excitement he felt about their impending visit.

Last night, a few buddies had invited him to a baseball game in Denver. Logan had declined the invitation and stayed home to prepare for his lunch guests. He'd used his mother's family recipe to make extra-crispy fried chicken and cheesy scalloped potatoes. For dessert, Logan planned to serve German chocolate cake from Garrison's market. Since Nellie didn't bake on Sunday, she'd taken his order late yesterday and made the cake last night. Nellie brought the treat to church, saving him a trip into town.

Logan climbed into the truck, placed the cake on the floor of the passenger seat and removed his cell phone from his glove compartment. He'd made a habit of keeping the device outside of church after an embarrassing incident a couple of months ago. During the benediction, his phone, which he'd thought was on vibrate, blasted the sound of various farm animals. Unbeknownst to Logan, his brother Jake had playfully changed his ring tone the day before, never imagining it would go off in the middle of church services.

"Hey, buddy." Nelson approached the open window of Logan's truck.

Logan turned the engine off and exited the vehicle. "Thanks again for taking care of the water heater yesterday. I'm sorry if I interrupted your Saturday."

"The only thing you interrupted was a chance to chip away at Thelma's never-ending honey-do list," Nelson laughed.

Logan's expression wavered as he looked at his friend. He had longed to have such a list. Marriage and family were things he'd always wanted and assumed one day he would have. The years had passed quickly without meeting the right person—until Melody. With her, Logan had found a love to last a lifetime. So why hadn't he protected her? He should have been there in her last moments. It should have been him. *Throw it into the air. Let God deal with the questions of why.* That's what Pastor Kidd had told him to do, but the guilt and regret remained.

"I know Caitlyn was thankful you could make the repair."

"That's what I wanted to talk with you about. Like I mentioned yesterday, the repair was a temporary fix, so it's probably a matter of time before the tank fails. When that happens, it could create substantial water damage." Nelson frowned.

Logan nodded, and a muscle in his jaw knotted. "I think Caitlyn is hoping to sell the house before that happens. With the cosmetic repairs alone, she's overwhelmed by the potential costs involved." The constant scribbling in her journal was proof the house was causing anxiety.

Nelson reached inside the jacket of his Sunday suit and pulled out a package of chewing gum. He held it out to Logan.

"Thanks." Logan removed the foil and popped the piece into his mouth.

Nelson did the same before tucking the pack away. "I have some news that might ease Caitlyn's worries a bit. I got a text last night from a buddy over in Mineral Springs. He's always buying the latest and great appliance. A couple of days ago, he bought a tankless water heater."

Logan had considered purchasing one for his house since his tank was up in the attic. If it ever went out, he could imagine the mess it would create. "I hear those are great, but probably out of Caitlyn's budget."

"That's the good news. Jeb offered me his existing heater for free. And the best part is, it's a significant upgrade from what she's got now, since his tank is shy of three years old."

Logan was delighted at the blessing. Caitlyn could check "addressing the water heater" from her list without spending a penny. "That's fantastic news. Caitlyn will be thrilled."

"I told Jeb I'd come by in the morning and install his new unit, so I'll have Caitlyn's on my truck whenever she's ready."

"That sounds good. She's coming by for lunch this afternoon, so I'll let her know."

Nelson grinned. "Oh, really?"

Logan knew Nelson's mind was churning with possibilities. He and his wife were the ones who'd introduced Logan and Melody. Three years earlier, the matchmaking couple had invited them to Sunday dinner. Thelma had known Melody since she was a child, and believed she was perfect for Logan. Thelma had been right. After that dinner, Logan and Melody had practically been inseparable.

Logan held up his hand. "Hold on. I see you're going into matchmaking mode. It's not what you think. The main reason I invited Caitlyn over was for Henry to meet Rocky and Sophie. The boy was curious yesterday when I mentioned I'm training Sophie. I thought it might be good for him to see firsthand how a seeing-eye dog can change a person's life for the better."

"Okay, whatever you say." Nelson chuckled. "When Caitlyn brings Henry over to meet the dogs—" Nelson threw in a wink "—you can ask her when it's convenient for me to install her new water heater."

There was no changing his mind about a love connection. When an idea planted into Nelson Whitfield's head, it took root. "I'll do that." Logan extended his hand in gratitude. "Thanks again for everything. And please, tell Jeb I said thank you as well."

Nelson nodded and turned on his heel.

For the second time since church had ended, Logan climbed back into his truck. More excited than he'd been when he'd first woken up this morning, he glanced at the time on his dashboard. Caitlyn and Henry weren't due to arrive at his house for three hours. No doubt she was home worrying and adding items to her to-do list. Energized by Nelson's surprise, Logan couldn't wait to share the good news with Caitlyn and hopefully calm her nerves. He'd pop by her house on his way home.

Ten minutes into the drive, Logan had the windows down and his favorite country station playing. Before church, he'd met up with a few fellas who'd offered to help with the exterior repairs. Since the extended weather forecast showed no chance of rain, tomorrow was a good day to start the work. Everything was falling into place. Caitlyn would be pleased.

Logan turned the wheel of his truck onto the gravel driveway. He spotted Caitlyn's SUV in front of the house. A faint aroma of smoke filled the cab of his vehicle as he unfastened his seat belt. Once outside, his eyes popped when he spotted flames shooting from the roof of the old farmhouse. He sprinted toward the front door, knowing Caitlyn and Henry were inside.

CHAPTER FOUR

CAITLYN STOOD IN the front yard after the Bluebell Canyon Volunteer Fire Department extinguished the flames. As she assessed the damage to the home, questions swirled in her head. Should she abandon her plan to make improvements and instead sell the house in its current state? Was the fire an ominous sign to reconsider her idea of using the money from the sale of the property to pay her debt?

"Thanks for saving us, Mr. Logan!" Henry fixed his eyes on Logan.

Earlier, while in the kitchen with Henry, she'd heard Logan pounding on the front door and yelling for them to get out of the house. Caitlyn didn't have a clue what was happening up in the attic. "Yes, thank you, Logan."

"I know what I want to be when I grow up." Henry tugged on his mother's arm.

Caitlyn's eyes were gritty with fatigue,

but she managed to raise a curious eyebrow. "What's that?"

"A firefighter. Mr. Jack told me they really need more people. Maybe if we stayed here, I could work for them. Do you think I could?" Henry looked up at Logan.

"Sure, but you need to wait until you're eighteen. Keep in mind, everyone who showed up today is a volunteer."

"What's that mean?"

"They don't get paid. Some leave their full-time jobs in town when there's a fire, while others are retired."

Henry's eyes widened. "Wow! They do all of that work for free?"

Caitlyn admired the commitment the volunteers had for their community. She also had a great respect for the business owners who allowed their employees to leave their job whenever called to assist. It takes an exceptional person to make such a commitment. From what she'd seen so far, this town was full of special people ready and willing to help others. The number of townspeople who'd come to her aid today was overwhelming. They weren't even part of the fire department.

"They love their community and the people.

Most have lived here their entire lives, along with past generations," Logan explained.

"That's pretty cool. Mom's my only family. Before her, I moved around a lot," Henry said before he dashed toward a group of volunteers talking on the front porch.

"I adopted Henry two years ago, after being his foster parent for a year. He lived the first four years of his life shuffled from one foster home to the next," Caitlyn told him.

Logan shifted his weight. "I didn't want to pry into your business. My brother never mentioned you'd gotten married, so I kind of wondered about Henry. But like I said, it's not my business." Logan glanced up at the front porch before turning his attention back to Caitlyn. "You're doing a wonderful thing—Henry is a terrific kid. Few people would make the sacrifices you've made."

"Henry had a rough start in life. I wanted him to feel safe. That's why it's important for me to sell this property and get him back to Wyoming as soon as possible. I want him to have stability in his life." Caitlyn couldn't let her son down. Yes, the house she rented in Wyoming was old and had a tiny yard, but it was the only true home Henry had ever known.

"Fortunately, there was only fire damage inside the attic. It could have been a lot worse if it had spread downstairs," Logan noted.

Caitlyn shuddered at the thought. "That's a relief. So what's next? Is it safe for me to go up there and clean?"

"Absolutely not. You need to leave that to the professionals."

Another expense. Caitlyn wasn't seeing a light at the end of this costly tunnel.

"Don't worry. Lester has a buddy in the fire restoration business. He'll come out to remove the smoke and ash properly. Prolonged debris presence amplifies the damage potential because of the acidic nature of the ash. We don't want the smoke to stain the walls."

A chill traveled down Caitlyn's spine. What if the fire had started at night while she and Henry had been sleeping? With so many repairs necessary, she'd neglected to consider whether the smoke detectors worked properly. "If you hadn't shown up, I'm not sure what would have happened."

"It's best if you don't let your mind imagine the worst. According to Lester, faulty wiring caused the fire. He's an electrician by trade, so he can fix the issue that started the fire. He'll also do a complete inspection of the entire house."

Caitlyn crossed her arms. "Yes, definitely. I can't sell the property if there's any risk of this happening again. Have Lester do whatever needs to be done. When it comes to safety, I won't cut corners."

"You can trust Lester." Logan turned his focus upward and pointed. "As for the hole in the roof, I'll take care of that."

"Was the hole caused by the fire?"

Logan shook his head. "No, that was how the squirrel or a chipmunk got into the attic to chew the wiring. Lester has flagged all the wires the critter had sunk its teeth into. He'll be back tomorrow to fix those and to inspect the rest of the house."

After escaping the home and watching flames shoot from the top of the house, Caitlyn realized Logan was right. It wasn't safe for her and Henry to remain in the house. "I suppose Henry and I need to head into town and book a room at the motel for the night." What choice did she have? If it were only her, maybe she'd stay, but she had Henry's safety to consider.

"I hope you don't think I'm out of line, but a motel could end up costing you a lot of money."

Logan's words rang true. It was an added expense she couldn't afford. Addressing the wiring issue would most likely take more than one day. Caitlyn had an emergency credit card with a zero balance tucked away in the side pocket of her wallet. This would definitely fall under the emergency column of her budget.

"Last night, I spoke with Luke. I mentioned you were in town and some issues with the house you've inherited. Before I even asked about you and Henry bunking at his place, he extended the offer." Logan reached out and placed his hand on Caitlyn's arm. "It would make Luke feel good to know he was helping an old friend. Besides, Henry will have a lot more fun exploring Luke's property than hanging out in a motel with a paved parking lot as the front yard."

Caitlyn considered Logan's offer. As much as she wanted to do things on her own, she had to put Henry's safety first.

"Come on. What do you say?" He smiled into her eyes.

She hesitated then smiled back. "Okay. But only until Lester gets the wiring situation repaired."

"Great. I'll shoot a message to Luke and let him know. He'll be thrilled."

"I'd like to send him a thank you text." Caitlyn pulled her phone from the back pocket of her jeans. "I'm sure the number I have for him is outdated."

Caitlyn edited her contact information while Logan recited the numbers. She'd send Luke a message tonight and thank him for his generosity. The years may have passed, but she could tell Luke hadn't changed. A sense of calmness covered her like the first warm blanket of winter. "Thank you. By the way, you know I'm grateful you arrived when you did, but what brought you by? Did you see the smoke from the road?"

"Actually, I didn't see the fire until I arrived at the house. I came by to share some good news with you. Of course, I could have waited until you and Henry came over for lunch, but I suppose I got a little overexcited."

Caitlyn could use some good news. Since her arrival in Bluebell, one expensive problem after another had overwhelmed her. "What's the news?"

"After church service this morning, I ran into Nelson in the parking lot. He's got a practically brand-new water heater whenever you're ready."

This wasn't exactly the good news Caitlyn

had hoped to hear, but she didn't want to appear ungrateful. "I appreciate your and Nelson's concern. Since the heater isn't leaking anymore, I should spend my money on repairs that need immediate attention, so I'm able to put the house on the market. Please tell Nelson I said thank you, though."

"I should have made myself clearer. The water heater won't cost you a dime. Nelson's friend purchased an upgraded model, so he has no use for two tanks. Nelson will have it on the back of his truck tomorrow whenever you're ready for him to install it for you." Logan pushed his hands into the front pockets of his jeans.

Caitlyn chewed on her lower lip.

"Look, I know how you feel about accepting charity. But you'd be doing Nelson a favor by getting it off his truck."

Caitlyn listened as Logan explained the history behind the new heater. She glanced over at Henry on the porch, swinging and laughing with Mrs. Garrison. Something he hadn't done a lot of lately. Maybe it was time to check her pride at the door for the well-being of her son and accept the generous offer. Her shoulders relaxed and she took a breath. "I'm sorry if I appeared ungrateful. Replacing the water heater would be one less thing for me to worry about. So yes, tell Nelson he can do the installation whenever he has the time."

Logan sighed silently with relief. "I'll do that—and one more thing."

Caitlyn gave him an assessing look. "What's that?" She couldn't imagine what more good news Logan had for her.

"Don't forget to scratch off replacing the heater from that to-do list of yours," he quipped.

Across the front yard, several men congregated around the cars parked in the driveway. "It looks like the rest of the crew is getting ready to head out. I'm going to go talk with the guys who plan to come by this week to get started on the repairs. Why don't you and Henry pack up your things? You can follow me to Luke's place and we'll get you settled. Then we can head to my house for that lunch I promised. You're probably starving."

Several hours had passed since Caitlyn had cooked waffles for Henry's breakfast. She'd opted for a cup of coffee and a piece of toast. "I am kind of hungry," she conceded.

"Great. We can eat lunch and, after, Henry can meet Rocky and Sophie."

Caitlyn loved dogs. She'd thought about

getting a puppy for Henry, but her plans had changed following Henry's diagnosis. Bringing an untrained dog into their home required time and patience—two things she was short on these days. Truthfully, the added expense of welcoming a pet into their home was the main reason she'd frequently had to tell Henry that it wasn't the right time. She glanced up at the farmhouse with the gaping hole in the roof, and her stomach twisted. With so many repairs to be done before she could think about putting the place on the market, Caitlyn wasn't sure how much longer she and Henry would even have a home.

"YOU PROBABLY THINK I'm just trying to be polite, but honestly, this is the best fried chicken I've ever eaten in my life." Caitlyn sank her teeth into the half-eaten breast, devouring it as if she hadn't had a meal in days.

Logan chuckled and pushed himself away from the solid oak kitchen table. The afternoon sunlight streamed through the oversize windows of his recently renovated farmhouse kitchen. "There's plenty more." He moved to the stainless-steel, six-burner stove and opened the oven door to remove the remaining pieces of chicken.

"I'll have another leg, please," Henry requested.

Logan placed the serving dish on the table. "You got it, buddy." Logan grinned at Henry, and his heart gave a tug.

Henry snatched the piece the second it landed on his plate. His eyes popped when he took a bite. "Why doesn't your chicken taste like this, Mom?"

Caitlyn frowned. "It's healthier when it's baked." She turned her attention back to her meal.

"But not as good. Right, buddy?" Logan winked at Henry.

Henry licked his fingers. "No way."

"Okay, you guys are right," Caitlyn said before reaching for a wing. "Who taught you how to fry chicken like this?"

"It's my mom's recipe. It's been in the family for years. Mom taught all of us Beckett boys to cook. She said it was the best way to win a woman's heart."

Caitlyn wholeheartedly agreed. "I think she might be right."

Logan considered Caitlyn's response while

an awkward silence hung in the air. He noted her cheeks turning red.

"I didn't mean… I…um… I mean, it's good for a man to know how to cook."

Logan laughed. He was pretty confident Caitlyn wasn't about to allow any man into her life. He'd sensed her guarded heart since their first meeting. That was one thing they had in common. "I know what you meant. Yeah, my mom was afraid all of her sons would end up starving bachelors."

"Your mom sounds like a smart woman to teach her sons how to be independent. I hope I'm able to do the same with Henry."

Henry jerked his head up. "I don't want to learn to cook. I'll just order takeout like David's dad does."

"Is David a friend from back home?" Logan asked.

"We're not really friends." Henry's smile slipped away. "I don't have a lot of those. He's just a kid in my class. His parents live in different houses now, so his dad orders out when David spends the night."

Henry was a likable kid. Why wouldn't he have friends?

"Knowing how to cook can save you a lot of

money. Ordering out can be expensive. Besides, you might enjoy hanging out in the kitchen cooking with your mom. I know I did." Logan would give anything to cook a meal with his mom. Shortly after her Alzheimer's diagnosis, she'd lost the ability to even put together the simplest meal.

Caitlyn dabbed her mouth with the napkin. "Do your parents live in the area?"

Logan felt a stab of sadness. "Actually, my mom is in a memory care facility in Denver."

"I'm sorry to hear that," Caitlyn responded.

"Thanks. My brothers and I helped my dad care for her at home as long as we could. He did an amazing job as her full-time caregiver for several years. As the disease progressed, my dad believed Mom needed specialized medical professionals. That wasn't available here in Bluebell. We're all at peace knowing she's getting the best care. They still have their home here on the family ranch, but my dad stays in a condo in Denver most of the time, so he's able to visit with her every day." Logan admired his father's dedication to his mother. He longed for a relationship like theirs and had thought he'd found it with Melody...until he'd made the worst decision of his life.

Caitlyn looked up at Logan. "Your dad sounds like a wonderful and selfless man."

"I could only hope to be half as good of a man." Logan took a drink of his iced tea.

"When do I get to meet Rocky and Sophie?" Henry downed the last of his drink.

It thrilled Logan to see Henry so excited about the dogs. After hearing his comment about the lack of friends, Sophie and Rocky might be just what he needed. "Well, we can either head outside now or after we've had dessert." Logan glanced in Caitlyn's direction. She was leaning back in her chair with her hands splayed across her stomach.

Caitlyn released a heavy breath. "After all of this delicious food, maybe a nice walk outside would be a good idea. What do you think, Henry?"

"I want to see the dogs!" Henry jumped out of his chair.

"Okay, the German chocolate cake can wait until later." Logan stood up and retrieved the plates from the table. He ferried them across the kitchen and placed them in the sink.

"I can help with those." Caitlyn grabbed the dishtowel from the island and moved toward Logan.

"Thanks, but that's unnecessary. I make a point of not putting my guests to work. I'll take care of this later."

Outside, the brilliant afternoon sun ignited the landscape. Its warmth provided the perfect late springtime temperature.

"Is it always so beautiful this time of year?" Caitlyn gazed up at the cumulus clouds painted across the crystal-blue sky.

"We can have fantastic weather in late May, but it can quickly change. It's good to check your weather app before planning your day."

Caitlyn slid her hands into the back pocket of her jeans. "You're right. I remember as a child wearing a short-sleeved shirt one day and building a snowman the next."

The trio strolled across the grassy field. A gentle breeze moved through the vibrant and colorful wildflowers, creating a soothing rustling sound. A sweet fragrance filled the air.

"Is that water over there?" Henry pointed to the pond on an area of the land Logan currently leased from Martha.

Logan loved the property, particularly the pond. Once he's started leasing the land, it had become his mother's favorite place to sit and spend time with God, which was one of several reasons it was important for him to take ownership of the property. "It sure is. Do you like to fish?"

"I don't know. I've never fished, but I'd sure like to." Henry bit his lower lip. "My mom doesn't like me to get near water since I don't know how to swim."

Logan's father had taught him and his brothers how to swim almost as soon as they'd learned how to walk. In Whispering Slopes, where he grew up, Logan and his siblings could never wait for that first swim of the season. Against their mother's advice, they'd often jump into the pond on their property in early May. Sometimes the water was so cold he thought his head would freeze. "I don't recall not being able to swim. My father practically threw me and my brothers into the pond and told us to sink or swim."

"Cool! Why can't I do that?" Henry stopped in his tracks and turned to his mother.

"You need to be taught to swim by a professional." Caitlyn rolled her shoulders. "I plan to sign him up for swimming lessons this summer."

Logan nodded. It wasn't his place to interfere, but a boy his age should go fishing. "Maybe if it's okay with your mom, you and I can fish at the pond sometime." Logan eyed Caitlyn with hopes he wasn't overstepping her boundaries. "I'll make sure he doesn't get too close to the water's edge."

Henry ran to his mother's side. "Oh, can I please go fishing with Mr. Logan?"

Caitlyn chewed on her thumbnail, contemplating Henry's request.

"You can come along and supervise. We could have a picnic. Maybe make an afternoon out of it," Logan suggested.

Henry's eyes widened with excitement before he jumped up and down. "Please—can we, Mom? I never get to do anything fun like that at home."

Caitlyn dropped her hands to her sides and looked down at her son. She hesitated before turning to Logan. "That sounds like a wonderful idea and a perfect way to spend an afternoon."

"Awesome!" Henry did a fist pump. He skipped off ahead of the adults.

Out of earshot, Logan stepped closer to Caitlyn. "I didn't mean to overstep my bounds. I thought it might be something fun for him to do. One of my greatest memories when I was his age was spending the afternoon fishing with my dad."

Caitlyn tipped her chin. "I'm sure it was. But you're not his father. I don't want Henry to get wild ideas into his head."

"I understand your concern. Please know that I'll respect your boundaries. I only want the boy to have a little fun, that's all." Logan turned, and they walked the rest of the way in silence.

Upon arriving at the barn, Logan placed his thumb and index finger into his mouth and whistled.

"Cool! Can you teach me to do that?" Henry asked.

Caitlyn pressed her hands to her ears and chuckled. "I'm not sure that's a good idea."

The dogs responded to the whistle. Both the German shepherd and yellow Labrador ran from inside the barn, across the grassy area, to the fence circling the structure. As they peeked through the split-rail, their tales moved back and forth like windshield wipers in a summer rainstorm.

Logan placed his hand on the top of the shepherd's head first. "This is Rocky." Next he introduced the Lab. "And this is Sophie."

"Is it okay for me to pet them?" Henry squeezed his hands together.

Logan turned to Caitlyn. "Sure. If it's okay with your mom, you can go inside."

"Why don't we all do that?" Caitlyn suggested.

Logan led the way and unlocked the gate. He opened the door to the paddock. Both dogs ran to the opening. "Stay," he commanded. The animals obeyed and sat at the gate.

"That's so cool. It's like they understood what you said." Henry continued to observe the dogs.

"I taught them how to obey commands." Logan fished inside the pocket of his jeans and pulled out a treat for Rocky and Sophie. "I try to keep a few in my pocket." He extended his hand to reward each dog.

Logan stepped inside. Caitlyn followed. "Come on in." Logan motioned for Henry to join them, but his earlier excitement appeared to have disappeared.

"They're pretty big." Henry's eyes widened. He kept his arms pinned to his sides and stood rooted in place.

"They won't hurt you. I promise," Logan said in a calm and reassuring tone.

Henry slowly stepped inside the gate before Logan closed it behind him. The dogs remain seated, but their tails continued their rapid movement.

"Don't they like me?" Henry asked.

Caitlyn rested her hand on Henry's shoulder. "Why would you ask that?"

"They aren't coming to me." Henry's lower lip rolled.

Logan squatted in front of Henry. "Do you see their tails moving?"

Henry nodded.

"They are both excited to see you, but they're obeying my command to stay. I've trained them not to move from that position until I give them permission." Unlike some dogs Logan had worked with over the years, Rocky and Sophie had been quick to learn some of the basic commands.

"I wish this little guy would listen that well." Caitlyn ruffled the top of Henry's hair.

Logan stood and clapped his hands. "Okay, guys, you're free." Both animals jumped to their feet and immediately ran to Henry, covering his hands with wet kisses. Henry dropped to the ground, giggling as the dogs shifted from his hands to his face.

Caitlyn moved closer to Logan. Her hair

smelled like honeysuckle. "I can't remember the last time I've seen Henry laugh that hard. Thank you for inviting us today."

"It's been my pleasure. You're both welcome to visit the dogs anytime. They're always ready to go for a walk. We've got some fantastic trails that go around the property." Logan loved his quiet time walking outdoors.

Henry lifted his head off the ground while the dogs discovered his ears. "Can we take them for a walk now?"

Logan snuck a quick glance in Caitlyn's direction.

"It couldn't hurt to walk off some more of that delicious meal." Caitlyn rubbed her stomach.

Henry bounced up and down on his toes. "Can we take them down to the pond? I see some ducks down there."

Logan waited for Caitlyn to answer.

"Lead the way. It looks like there's a walking trail that circles the pond," Caitlyn said.

"You're right. There's over a mile of trail around the water. Sophie and Rocky love it. They like to chase the geese and ducks. Let me grab their leashes." Logan jogged inside the barn and returned with two leather straps.

Ten minutes into the walk, Henry held tight to Rocky's leash while the animal forged ahead. Caitlyn did her best to keep pace with Sophie. The animal moved swiftly, her nose buried in the trampled grassy path, eagerly sniffing every scent. Purple wildflowers lined both sides of the trail, providing a splash of color to the otherwise green-and-brown landscape.

"Isn't this cool, Mom? If we lived here, we could do this every day." Henry's eyes were bright with enthusiasm as he daydreamed out loud.

Caitlyn remained silent.

"Look at the ducks! They're swimming closer to the edge." Henry pointed to the water.

"Those are mallards. The one with the glossy green head and white collar is the male, or often referred to as a drake. The other one swimming along his side, streaked with shades of brown, black and buff, is a female." It pleased Logan to see Henry's interest in the birds.

"How do you know so much about ducks?" Henry asked.

"When I was little, back in Virginia, my dad had a boat. We'd spend hours fishing in the pond on our property. He taught me all about the birds and waterfowl we'd see in and around the pond. The female, referred to as a hen, is the one you hear quacking. Male ducks don't quack."

"I never knew that," Caitlyn mused.

Logan watched Henry keep a close eye on the water. "Look at that one over there all alone. How come he looks so different? His face has red bumps on it."

"That's a good observation, Henry. The duck you noticed isn't native to this area. She showed up last spring and set up residency in the pond. It's possible she was someone's pet."

Henry continued to eye the duck. "What kind is it?"

"Donald is a Muscovy."

Caitlyn raised an eyebrow. "You named her Donald?"

Logan laughed. "Well, when I first spotted her, she seemed large. I assumed it was a male, so I named her Donald. Several months after she was here, she built a nest and laid some eggs. By that time, it didn't feel right to change her name." Logan reached down and released Rocky from the leash. The dog took off toward the water. Sophie pulled on her restraint.

Caitlyn turned to Logan. "Is it okay if I let her go?"

"If you don't, she might pull your arm out of the socket." Logan smiled.

Henry jumped up and down. "Can I go down and see Donald close up?"

"Why don't we all go?" Caitlyn reached for Henry's hand.

At the water's edge, Logan took notice of how Henry kept a watchful eye on Donald. He seemed to ignore the other ducks and the larger Canadian geese that circled the pond, honking and flapping their wings.

"Do you like Donald?" Logan asked Henry.

Henry placed his finger to his lip and nodded, and kept his gaze fixed on the duck. "The others stay away from her because she's different," he murmured softly. "Like me." Henry turned and moved from the bank. His enthusiasm for the pond seemed to fade.

Logan spun on his heel to face Caitlyn. His heart raced with worry. "Is he okay?"

A heavy silence hung in the air until a fish splashed in the water. A breeze created a soft rustle of leaves in the trees.

Caitlyn's nod was barely noticeable before she turned and hurried after Henry.

Logan's chest tightened with concern as Caitlyn caught up to her son and knelt in front of him. He strained to hear the conversation, but the murmur of their voices was too soft to discern. Caitlyn took Henry into her arms. Something was troubling him. The incident left Logan with a sense of unease and a nagging feeling that something was terribly wrong.

CHAPTER FIVE

CAITLYN STEPPED INSIDE one of the four bed-rooms in Luke Beckett's cottage-like house.

A colorful mural of a rodeo with a bull rider in the ring filled one wall. The two adjacent windows had curtains covered with pictures of horses. Caitlyn laughed to herself. Luke had definitely had a say in decorating the room.

Not paying for an expensive motel eased her mind somewhat, but it couldn't erase the look on Henry's face yesterday at the pond. Her heart pounded as she recalled his meltdown. The poor boy had barely mustered the energy to climb onto the top bunk in one of the kid's rooms, where he remained sound asleep.

It was still early. The soft light of a new day filtered through the curtains. Maybe she'd let him sleep a little longer while she spent some time planning the hours ahead. Caitlyn tiptoed toward the door and reached for the handle.

The aroma of the freshly brewed coffee she'd prepared earlier drifted into the bedroom, inviting her to the kitchen.

"Can we go to the pond and visit Donald after breakfast?" Henry sat up in the bed and rubbed his eyes.

A part of Caitlyn had hoped that after Henry had a good night of sleep, he would have forgotten about the duck. But she knew better. Henry saw himself in Donald. With her red, bumpy face the complete opposite of the beautiful and iridescent mallard ducks, Donald was different. Caitlyn tried to convince her son that he was special, not different. But Henry felt like he didn't fit in with his friends. Each time he'd experienced a seizure in front of his classmates, it became harder for Henry to believe his mother. Yesterday, while Caitlyn watched the other ducks exclude Donald, she understood why Henry felt an attachment.

"I thought you were still sleeping."

Dressed in his superhero pajamas, Henry climbed down the ladder as if he did it every day.

"Be careful, sweetie," Caitlyn cautioned Henry.

"This is easy. Can we get a bunk bed in my room?"

A few seconds ticked by. Given her current

financial situation, Caitlyn questioned if she and Henry would still have a home once they returned to Wyoming. Last night, she'd received a text message from her landlord asking her to call him. Until she had a better idea on the timeline of the repairs, she planned to try her best to avoid talking with him. "We'll see."

Henry shook his head and frowned. "That means no."

Caitlyn moved across the bedroom and drew the curtains. She squinted as a stream of bright morning light radiated through the window. "Not necessarily. We have a lot to take care of here first." Caitlyn's heart rate increased.

"What about Donald? Can we go see her? That doesn't cost any money."

Caitlyn didn't want Henry to start his day with two disappointments. She glanced at her watch. Logan mentioned a training session he and his brother Jake had this morning. After, Logan planned to get started on the house. "We'll have to make it a quick visit. Mr. Logan and his crew are going to begin repairs today."

"At Last Dollar?" Henry asked.

Caitlyn blinked rapidly. "What are you talking about?"

"Our house—I saw the sign. It's on Last Dollar Road. Isn't that a cool name?"

With everything going on, the street name of her childhood home had slipped her mind. No surprise there. Over the years, it had been easier for Caitlyn to push aside the negative memories. The only problem was that before her parents' accident, there'd been a lot of wonderful memories. She chuckled at the coincidence. Henry's name described the home perfectly. The way things were going, it would probably take her last dollar to get it ready to sell.

Caitlyn reached out and ran her hand across Henry's cheek. He always liked to name things. Moving from one foster home to another, Henry had slept in a lot of beds. After she'd signed the adoption papers, as she'd tucked him into his bed that night, he'd told Caitlyn he'd never felt this way in a bed. The next day, he'd told her he'd named his bed "Mr. Cozy." After that, he'd named her SUV "Lucy." Caitlyn smiled at the memory and laughed. "I don't think I could have come up with a more perfect name for the house."

Caitlyn extended her hand. "Let's get you cleaned up and dressed. I'll make some toast and fix you a bowl of cereal. I'd like to go into town and pick up some additional cleaning supplies." This morning, while logging into her online banking, she'd noticed a deposit for her monthly cash reward from her credit card. The money would come in handy for her trip to the store.

"What about Donald? You said we could go see her."

"We'll stop by the pond on our way back from town. Go wash your face and put on the clothes I laid on the vanity in the bathroom. I'm going to get breakfast ready."

"Yes!" Henry ran to the bathroom at the end of the hall.

Caitlyn watched until he slammed the door closed. If seeing Donald made her son smile, then she'd have to put aside her worries. As long as Henry spent time with the duck when Logan wasn't around, she could avoid answering questions like he'd asked yesterday. Caitlyn appreciated Logan's concern for Henry. But sharing the reason for Henry's attachment to Donald would only open up the possibilities of more questions. Keeping Henry's health and her dire financial situation private was a priority.

Forty-five minutes later, they were ready to head out. With Henry securely buckled in the booster seat of the SUV, Caitlyn was prepared to begin a long day. She pushed the ignition button but the engine didn't start. A second attempt gave the same result. This time, she sent up a silent prayer before trying it. Still nothing. A pain throbbed in her left temple.

"Why aren't we going?" Henry called out from behind.

Caitlyn was asking the same thing until she remembered canceling the five-thousand-mile checkup with the car dealership. Prior to learning about her inheritance, she had scheduled service for the vehicle. The same day she'd made the appointment, came a surprise bill from Henry's trip to the emergency room the prior month. She'd added finding an independent mechanic who charged less to her list of things to do and canceled the service appointment. After, she'd gone online and paid one fourth of the balance owed to the hospital. "The car won't start."

"Maybe you should call those people that come to help?" Henry suggested.

Something else Caitlyn had canceled while evaluating her monthly budget was the auto club membership. She'd never used it last year. It was money down the drain. Or so she'd thought. When the renewal notice arrived in the mail along with a hefty increase in the annual fee, she'd opted not to renew and shredded the notice. She released a heavy breath. "That's not an option since I canceled my membership."

"Because of me?"

Caitlyn looked into the rearview mirror. "What makes you say something like that, sweetie?"

"All the bills are because of my epilepsy."

Caitlyn tried her best to protect Henry from knowing about her financial struggles, but as he grew older, he became more perceptive. It hadn't helped that recently he'd overheard her on the phone with their landlord. She'd explained the medical debt and promised to do her best to catch up on the rent. Two days later, he'd heard her talking with the billing department at Henry's doctor's office. "No, my canceling the service had nothing to do with you, sweetie. It made little sense to renew since I never used it the year before." Caitlyn eyed Henry lovingly in the rearview mirror.

"I sure wish we had it now. I really wanted to see Donald."

"Donald isn't going anywhere. You'll have plenty of time to visit her."

"It looks like we aren't going anywhere either," Henry sighed.

Henry's words sounded more like a teenager's than a seven-year-old's. He was growing up much too fast for her.

"We'll be on our way before you know it." Caitlyn unbuckled her seat belt, popped the hood and exited the vehicle. She knew a little about cars. Thanks to the internet, she'd recently saved herself over sixty dollars by watching a video on how to do an oil change. It was a messy job. But using the extra money to cover the water bill provided breathing room on her budget, not to mention the satisfaction she'd gotten from doing the job herself.

"Are you going to fix it?" Henry removed his belt and jumped down to the ground. He rounded the SUV and joined Caitlyn at her side. "I can help you." He looked up and squinted into the sunlight.

Caitlyn looked down at Henry. "You just being here helps, sweetie. I have a feeling the car probably needs a new battery."

Henry's eyes brightened. "My Game Boy is in the house. It has a battery. I'll get it for you."

Caitlyn laughed and placed her hand on Henry's shoulder. His heart was always in the right place. Caitlyn was proud of the little boy who was too quickly growing into a young man. "Your Game Boy takes a different type of battery, but I appreciate your generous offer."

Henry chewed on his lower lip and studied the open hood. "Maybe you should call Mr. Logan. He probably knows a lot about cars. I'm sure he can fix it fast. Then I can go visit Donald. Maybe Mr. Logan can come with us? He knows a lot about ducks."

Since Caitlyn's arrival in Bluebell Canyon, Logan had already gone above and beyond to help her get the property ready to put on the market. She'd like to believe it was out of the goodness of Logan's heart, but her experience with men had made her suspicious. Logan was probably only interested in taking possession of the land she'd agreed to sell.

"Come on, Mom. Call him. I think Mr. Logan knows a lot more about cars than Mr. Jeffrey did. He couldn't fix anything. Remember when the wheel came loose on my scooter? He didn't even know a screwdriver from a hammer." Henry rolled his eyes.

Caitlyn stifled her laugh. Henry was right. Her ex-boyfriend had been all about the money. Creating wealth by refinancing homes was his top priority. If something broke, you hired someone to fix it. Learning how to do menial tasks wasn't worth his time. Toward the end of their relationship, Jeffrey had resented Henry because of his medical condition. It had consumed her attention and the one thing she'd learned about Jeffrey was that he enjoyed being the center of attention. Henry had sensed the resentment, which had made it easier for Caitlyn to deal with the breakup. In the end, she'd repaired Henry's scooter herself.

As much as Caitlyn hated to, she really had no other choice but to call Logan for help. She and Henry could hike over to Last Dollar, but that would waste time she couldn't spare. How would it look if she showed up late when so many kindhearted people were offering their time and help? She pulled in a deep breath and took out her cell phone.

To say it surprised Logan to receive a call from Caitlyn asking for help would be an understatement. It was the last thing he'd expected from Caitlyn, who seemed fiercely independent and didn't need anyone's help, especially a man's. Perhaps someone had betrayed her in the past, causing her to be cautious and not rely on anyone. Or maybe it was because she'd lost her parents early in life. As tempted as he was to learn more about this intriguing woman, Logan refused to pry into her personal life. Keeping things on a business level was the safest way to protect his heart. Yet despite his curiosity, he couldn't help but feel a sense of duty and determination to be there for her and Henry in any way he could.

Logan headed up Luke's driveway and spotted Caitlyn in front of her SUV with her journal in hand. She wore faded blue jeans, a green-and-yellow top, along with a tan cowboy hat, and boots that gleamed. He couldn't ignore the fact that she looked beautiful.

Caitlyn never looked up as his pickup approached. She scribbled inside the pages of her journal. Henry busied himself twirling with his arms extended, occasionally losing his balance while staring up at the sky.

Logan parked and stepped out of the truck.

"Mr. Logan!" Henry ran toward him while his mother finished her thought and closed the journal.

"Hey, buddy. How'd you sleep last night?"

"Great! I love the bunk bed. If I had one in

my room, I'd never argue with Mom about my bedtime."

"I had a feeling you'd like the bed." Logan patted Henry's shoulder.

Henry's smile quickly faded.

"What's wrong?" Logan asked.

"I'm kind of bummed out. The car won't start. I wanted to go see Donald before we go to Last Dollar." Henry frowned.

Logan scratched his head and turned in Caitlyn's direction. "I understand going to visit Donald, but I'm a little unclear about the last dollar part."

Caitlyn rolled her eyes. "He's named the house. He always likes to give everything a name."

Logan laughed and ruffled the top of his head. "I get it now. The house is on Last Dollar Road. That's pretty creative."

Caitlyn placed the journal on the roof of her SUV before turning to face Logan. "As much as the house is going to cost me to get it ready to sell, I think Henry's name describes it perfectly."

If Caitlyn would let go of her stubborn ways, the kindhearted people in Bluebell Canyon could prevent her from spending money on repairs. "Well, right now there are ten volunteers working hard to put a new roof on your house."

Caitlyn stood speechless. Her arched brow carried surprise.

Logan had a feeling his change of plans about the roof might upset Caitlyn. As she stood wringing her hands together, he knew his assumption had been correct.

"I didn't give the go-ahead for a new roof. It was my understanding that you would make repairs to the existing structure."

Logan offered an understanding nod. "I know what we discussed, but George, the inspector, didn't feel the integrity of the roof was worth repairing. A new roof would make better use of the donated materials."

Caitlyn shook her head and kicked the tip of her boot into the ground. "I can't cover the cost of a new roof along with fixing all the other problems with the house. It's just not in my budget."

"You probably have your journal filled with funds allocated for the repairs that need to be addressed." He tilted his head toward the roof of the SUV. "But whether you repair the roof or do a complete replacement, it won't cost you anything. The men have donated their time, along with the material, out of the kindness of their hearts. They want to help you. Besides, selling a home in pristine condition versus patchwork repairs can benefit the community in the long run. It can raise the comparable sales in the area. If anyone sells their home, your sales price could increase their property value."

"I don't feel comfortable being the town charity case," Caitlyn said.

"Relax, Mom. I think it's pretty cool people want to help you. It's like Mrs. Wilson taught us in Bible school. She said you have to be good to your neighbor. It's what God wants us to do."

Logan watched as the tension appeared to subside.

Caitlyn's shoulders relaxed. A smile traced her lips. "You're right, sweetie, that's exactly what God wants us to do. Thanks for reminding me."

"Now that we have that straightened out, let me look." Logan rubbed his hands against his pant legs and stepped closer to the open hood.

Caitlyn summarized what had happened when she'd tried to start the vehicle. Logan tinkered underneath the hood before attempting to get the vehicle going. He agreed it was most likely the battery. "I'll get my jumper cables. If it is the battery and we get it started, I'll follow you over to Last Dollar and then run out and get you a replacement. It's easy to install, so I can pop it in and then we can get to work on a few of the interior projects."

"What about Donald? Mom said we could visit with her." Henry gave Logan a hopeful look.

"If it's okay with your mother, you can ride along with me to get the new battery. On the way back, we can stop and say hello to Donald if you'd like."

Henry bounced on his toes. "Can I, Mom? Please!"

"Let's wait until Mr. Logan determines what's wrong with the car. If it is the battery, we can all go together to pick it up so I can pay for it myself. Plus, I wanted to pick up a few cleaning supplies. If there's enough time after, we can make a quick visit with Donald. Remember, we have a lot of work to do if we want to get back home."

"But I'm not in a hurry to go home. I like it here. Why can't we keep Last Dollar house and just live there? I like this town. Plus, Mr. Logan and Donald are here," Henry pleaded.

For the second time in five minutes, Logan

watched Caitlyn's shoulders stiffen. It was obvious she wanted no part of making her childhood home a place for her and Henry.

"Let me get those cables." Logan spun on his heel and headed to his truck. The longer those two stayed in Bluebell, the more of a challenge Caitlyn would have with Henry.

An hour and a half later, Logan found himself at the pond once again with Caitlyn and Henry. He'd wanted to bring the dogs along for Henry, but Caitlyn had insisted this would be a quick visit. She was eager to get to work.

"Thank you again for taking me to pick up the battery. That's an enormous weight off my mind." Caitlyn gave Logan a warm smile, causing his pulse to tick up a few beats.

"It was no big deal. Glad I could help." Assisting others came naturally to Logan, but it also served as a reminder of the one time he hadn't been there for the person he'd loved the most. His fiancée had needed him, and he hadn't been there. The guilt gnawed at him every day, every moment.

"It surprised me how inexpensive a new battery could be." Caitlyn tossed him a questioning eye.

"Let's just say I'm a long-time customer of

Gary's shop. I've done a few favors for him, so he was just paying it forward."

"Look!" Henry pointed out to the water. "A couple of gigantic birds are swimming toward Donald. We saw those before. Aren't they from Canada or some place? Maybe they want to be friends with her."

Logan looked out across the pond. "They're Canadian geese."

As the geese drew closer to Donald, their honking grew louder and more aggressive. They spread their wings and puffed up their chests. Donald continued to paddle, unfazed by the commotion surrounding her.

Henry kept his gaze fixed on the water.

The geese were relentless. They formed a semicircle around Donald and honked in unison.

"Why are they doing that?" Henry asked.

Logan slipped his hands into his back pockets. "This is their pond. Geese aren't always welcoming to other types of waterfowl. They know she's different."

Donald continued to paddle around, occasionally flapping her wings in defiance.

Henry stomped his foot into the dirt. "They're being so mean. Can't we help her?"

"Donald can take care of herself." Logan rested his hand on Henry's shoulder.

Henry continued to study Donald's reaction until the geese finally won the battle and Donald swam away, defeated and alone. "I wish we could build Donald her own pond and bring other ducks like her to live with her."

Logan looked down at Henry, pleased. "That sounds like a good idea. Maybe if everything works out with the sale of the property, I can do that."

Henry's head cocked to one side. "Really? That would be so cool!" He turned to his mother. "If Mr. Logan builds a new pond for Donald, can we come back and visit?"

Caitlyn tossed Logan a look of displeasure about his idea of building a new home for Donald and a few friends.

"I think we'll have to wait and see what happens, buddy. I could always email you some pictures and videos," Logan offered.

Henry looked down at the ground. "That's not really the same. I don't understand why we can't just move here. You could have your school here, couldn't you, Mom? There's lots of land."

Logan was unclear of what Henry was alluding to. He looked at Caitlyn but she avoided his gaze, staring at the grass.

"Don't you think so, Mom?"

Logan was relieved when Henry pushed his mother. Caitlyn did her best to keep her life in Wyoming to herself, but he wanted to know more about her.

"With all the property around Last Dollar, you could get more horses. Then maybe more girls could sign up for your class." Henry appeared excited by his own suggestion.

It was then Logan remembered. His brother had mentioned Caitlyn's dream to start a school to teach barrel racing.

"Owning more horses requires a bigger expense, sweetie. It's not as simple as just having the property to board them," Caitlyn explained to Henry.

"Yeah, but wouldn't you make more money if you had a bigger class?"

Logan concealed a grin with his left hand. Henry might be seven years old, but he had a pretty good business head on his shoulders.

"If we moved here, I could help you more. I promise. Please, Mom."

Caitlyn rubbed her hand down the front of

her jeans. "I think we need to discuss this another time." She glanced at Henry.

"Your mom is right, buddy." Logan noted the time on his watch. "We better get going. It's past the lunch hour. I still need to install the new car battery and then we've got a lot of work to do."

"I don't want to leave Donald. She'll be lonely without me." Henry gazed out at the water.

"Donald will be fine. Don't worry. If we don't get to Last Dollar, everyone's going to think we're goofing off. Knowing those guys, they've probably already finished putting on the new roof." Logan looked at Caitlyn and grinned. This time, she returned his gesture with a smile. But this one was different, and it ignited warmth in him like a cozy fireplace on a cold winter night. For a moment, Logan felt he could brave any storm as long as he had Caitlyn's smile to light his way.

CHAPTER SIX

CAITLYN DIDN'T LIKE this one bit. But she had to admit the mix of experienced carpenters and enthusiastic volunteers brought new life to the sagging and dilapidated roof. Sounds of hammers and saws echoed across the open field. Men worked steadily, hoisting heavy bundles of shingles onto their shoulders and carrying them up to the roof while others nailed them down in place.

The sense of camaraderie among the men as they laughed and joked with each other captivated Caitlyn. "What they're doing is amazing." She turned to Logan, who stood by her side.

"It's great, isn't it?" Logan waved at his neighbors. "They're standing in the gap. It's what being a part of a community is about."

Caitlyn's eyes welled with inexplicable tears. Why was she so emotional watching these men?

"Are you okay?" Logan asked.

Get a grip.

This reaction was so unlike Caitlyn. Her decision to be independent and to not rely on others had worked fine throughout her life. She'd let down her guard with her ex and look where that had gotten her. Yet, as she observed the progress being made, even though there was still much work to be done, she knew doing it on her own wasn't possible. If she wanted to get back to Wyoming and mend her broken life, maybe setting aside her ego was the only option. "I'm fine. It's all just a little overwhelming."

"Mom! Come inside and see what all they've done," Henry called from the front porch.

Logan placed his hand on Caitlyn's lower back. "I told you they'd have a full day of work conquered by the time we got here. They are a determined bunch. Let's go check it out."

Caitlyn climbed the front steps and rubbed the wetness underneath each eye with her index finger. She'd never met such generous people in her life. Once inside the home, the smell of freshly squeezed lemons teased her senses. "It looks so much brighter in here." She scanned the parlor, thinking that first a coat of fresh paint had brought additional light into the room. But upon further inspection, the original beige color that had been there when she'd moved out remained, only more faded and dingy.

"A few of the ladies from church came by early this morning, loaded down with sponges and squeegees to clean the windows." Nelson stepped forward, wiping the sweat from his forehead with a handkerchief he had pulled from his back pocket. He unscrewed the cap from a bottle of water in his hand and took a long swig. "They thought it would be easier for us to see what needs to be done once they scrubbed away years of grime and dirt that had accumulated on the windowpanes."

"They did a fantastic job." Caitlyn looked around the room. "The place desperately needs a new paint job," Caitlyn added.

"I can help paint!" Henry offered.

Caitlyn eyed the black outlines going up the staircase where family pictures had covered the walls. The first outline was where her parents' wedding picture had once hung.

"After we get the floors done in here, we'll take care of the paint. Don't worry," Logan reassured Caitlyn.

"Jeb came by at the crack of dawn with the

new hot water heater. I've got it installed, so you're good to go. You can take as many long, hot showers as you'd like." Nelson drained the last gulp from his bottle.

Logan glanced at Caitlyn. "Did you hear that? Something else you can check off from your list. Everything is moving right along, so you can relax. You and Henry will be back in Wyoming before you know it."

Nelson cleared his throat. "Unfortunately, you won't be able to check off the wiring issue today."

Caitlyn's joy over the water tank slumped.

"Why is that?" Logan asked.

"Lester came by earlier this morning. Becky's mother is ill, so they're driving to Memphis. He hopes to be back by Friday, but nothing is definite," Nelson explained.

Caitlyn was sorry to hear about Lester's mother-in-law and sent up a silent prayer. This wasn't good. "Maybe I better hire someone."

"I know you're in a hurry to get back to Wyoming, but it might be in your best interest to wait for Lester. If this turns out to be a bigger job than he expects, hiring an electrician could eat away at your budget," Logan said.

As much as Caitlyn wanted to hurry and get

the house sold, she had to be realistic. Logan was right. Given the age of the home, she had to be prepared that the entire place might need new wiring. That was a cost she could never afford without maxing out her emergency credit card. She'd opened that line of credit after Henry's diagnosis—just in case. "I suppose waiting a few more days won't hurt. In the meantime, there are other projects to address." Caitlyn's eyes locked on Logan.

He rested his hand on Caitlyn's arm. "You've made the right decision. In the long run, waiting on Lester will save you a lot of money."

"The good news is, before he left town, Lester contacted his fire restoration buddy, Jacob. He said Jacob and his crew will be out tomorrow afternoon to begin the cleanup of the attic," Nelson confirmed.

Caitlyn considered Nelson's report and gazed out the window of the farmhouse. The vibrant greens and golden yellows of the rolling field sparked memories of her childhood. For a moment, a twinge of sadness filled Caitlyn's heart. There wouldn't be any hot showers or leisurely evenings spent on a renovated porch swing with Henry. She shook off the thought. Bluebell wasn't her home. Not since the death of her parents. There were too many sad memories buried inside this old house.

Nelson glanced at his watch. "If you two are ready to get to work, Charles dropped off several gallons of paint for the main bedroom. You can get started up there, if you'd like."

Caitlyn chewed her lip. "What about the flooring in the room? It seemed in rough shape."

"There was nothing that a few nails and a little sanding couldn't fix. After that, the ladies polished the wood. It looks fantastic. We thought you'd want to get that room finished up first, in case you planned to stay in the house, but it sounds like you'll be heading back to Wyoming soon." Nelson paused and glanced between Logan and Caitlyn. "Then again, you might change your mind. I can't count the number of folks who visited Bluebell over the years but ended up making this wonderful town their home. You and your son might be next."

"That would be awesome!" Henry cheered and looked up at Nelson. "I sure hope my mom changes her mind."

Nelson smiled at Henry. "I hope so, too. Why don't you run back to the kitchen? School had an early release today, so there are a few kids devouring a plate of homemade cookies my wife made. After they finish their snack, they're going to help clean up the garden and the barn."

Henry turned to his mother. "Can I?"

Caitlyn hesitated for a moment.

"Don't worry. The children will have some adult supervision." Nelson rested his hand on Caitlyn's arm. "He'll be fine."

Nelson was a kind man. It was as though he'd read her mind. "Have fun." Caitlyn nodded at Henry. "You haven't had lunch yet, so don't eat too many cookies."

"Thelma also fried a ton of chicken, so help yourself, son." Nelson extended the offer before turning to Caitlyn and Logan. Henry took off in a hurry. "Maybe you two should eat before you get started upstairs."

Logan rubbed his stomach. "Let's go grab some lunch. I'm starving." He nudged Caitlyn's arm.

"That sounds good to me." Caitlyn's stomach had been growling for the last hour.

"The fellas set up a couple of picnic tables in the backyard," Nelson said.

Logan patted Nelson on the shoulder. "You thought of everything. Thanks, bud."

Nelson focused his attention back on the loose floorboards as Caitlyn followed Logan to the kitchen.

Minutes later, Caitlyn sat at a rickety table nestled beneath the giant weeping willow tree. Henry had grabbed a chicken leg and headed to the barn. Apparently, one kid had told him there were a couple of stray cats inside. Logan offered to bring out the food and asked that she grab a spot to sit down. She looked up at the sprawling branches rustling in the breeze and draping down around her like a protective canopy.

Caitlyn inhaled a deep breath and relaxed for the first time since discovering her car wouldn't start. She scanned the property filled with gorgeous blue and white columbine. Not much about the landscape had changed since she was a young girl, but she couldn't say the same about herself. The carefree child who used to sip a cold beverage on the porch swing with her daddy no longer existed.

As much as she tried to focus on her blessings, Caitlyn couldn't shake the feeling of despair that had settled over her like a dark cloud. She was on the verge of losing her home and, with each day that passed, the weight of her financial burden threatened to drown her. It left her feeling like she was treading water in the middle of the ocean with nothing but a deflated raft. But then, at her lowest moments, she'd think of Henry. He was the best thing that had ever happened to her.

Despite the mounting obstacles, Caitlyn had no other choice but to continue working hard and get the house ready to sell. It was the only way to keep a roof over their heads and pay off her debt, and then maybe she could focus on her dream of expanding her business.

But convincing Henry that they didn't belong in Bluebell was becoming more difficult. Caitlyn couldn't deny the allure of the small town with its friendly people. But the costs of moving there permanently would send her further into debt, and she couldn't bear the thought of putting her son's future in jeopardy.

Caitlyn's head whipped around at the sound of the screen door slamming. Her heart rate quickened as she caught sight of Logan. His muscles rippled beneath his white T-shirt as he juggled two plates of food, piled high with fried chicken, mashed potatoes, corn on the cob and biscuits.

The flutter in her stomach caught her off guard when she met his warm, inviting smile. Caitlyn couldn't deny the attraction. She tried to shake off the feeling and focus on the task at hand, but she couldn't help but steal another glance in Logan's direction.

Logan carefully placed the plates on the table.

"Should I run inside for some drinks?" Caitlyn asked.

"Nope, I've got them right here." Logan reached behind his back. "I hope you like grape?" He grinned and pulled two cans of soda from each back pocket.

The memory of sipping icy grape soda on the porch swing with her father played through her mind. "It's my favorite." She accepted his offering and popped the top. The carbonated fizz tickled her nose.

"Mine, too." Logan opened his beverage, took a drink, and placed the can on the table. "Hold on one second. I'll be right back." He spun on his heel and sprinted back inside the house.

Caitlyn eyed the extra-crispy piece of chicken on her plate. Her stomach rumbled in response to the delicious aroma, but she waited for Logan to return.

Moments later, Logan strolled to the table with a water glass filled with freshly picked vibrant blue forget-me-nots. He set the glass between their two plates. "I thought you'd like these while we enjoy our meal."

Caitlyn's heart warmed. "Thank you for this." She traced her finger down the side of the glass. "That's very thoughtful of you. When I was a little girl, I used to pick forget-me-nots for my mother. She told me they reminded her of me." Caitlyn remained quiet and stared out over the open countryside. She glanced at Logan, who appeared to be saying a prayer over his food.

Logan lifted his head. He picked up his napkin and placed it on his lap. "I saw you noticing the flowers out front earlier," he admitted.

Caitlyn couldn't ignore the pang of sadness. Maybe if she was at a different place in her life, Logan could be the prince she had dreamed of as a little girl. But the pain and suffering she had endured earlier in life had left her feeling lost and alone, trapped in the wilderness of her own heart. Caitlyn yearned for the love that would make her feel whole again, but the scars from her past ran too deep.

CAITLYN LEANED FORWARD and held her stomach. "I don't remember the last time I've eaten such an enormous meal."

"You really packed it away," he teased. Logan liked a woman with a healthy appetite.

Caitlyn reached over and gave Logan's arm a playful swat. "Thanks a lot."

Amusement tugged at his mouth. "I'm only joking. It's nice to see a person enjoy their meal." Logan ran his eyes over her empty plate. "You really did a number on that corn cob."

She dabbed the napkin against her lips. "It's always been a favorite of mine. But you didn't do so bad yourself. You looked like a beaver going to town on the last tree standing by a lake."

Logan laughed and glanced at the gnawed cob. "You got me there. I saw some of Nellie's famous homemade brownies in the kitchen—if you're interested." Logan's brow arched.

"Honestly, I can't eat another bite, but I'll take a rain check for later." Caitlyn pushed a strand of hair blowing in the gentle breeze away from her face. "I don't know how you expect me to paint after this big lunch. I feel like I could curl up and take a nap."

While enjoying their meal, Logan couldn't ignore how Caitlyn's serious demeanor had softened. A more playful and easygoing side had blossomed. He found himself drawn to her even more, both intellectually and physically. He couldn't deny the attraction he felt. Despite knowing Caitlyn valued her privacy, Logan wanted to learn more about her and the life she lived in Wyoming. "I hope you don't mind me asking, but I'm curious about your school. I'd love to hear more about it."

A peaceful smile appeared. Caitlyn's hazel eyes shimmered in the sunlight. "If there's one thing I'll talk nonstop about, it's my barrel racing school. It was a dream I had for many years. In fact, I'm sure your brother got sick of listening to me ramble on about it." She chuckled.

"Back in the day, when I asked Luke about you, he mentioned how excited you were about your new venture. But he never said he was tired of hearing about it. He was proud of you," Logan told her.

Caitlyn tilted her head and her eyes grew bigger. "You asked Luke about me? I didn't think you knew I existed." She gave a nervous laugh and squirmed on the bench.

Logan remembered how his heart had rattled inside his chest the first time he'd met Caitlyn. She'd worn tan, formfitting riding pants that had hugged her athletic physique in all the right places. A white button up shirt highlighted her hazel eyes. The high-heeled Western boots and the dark brown cowboy hat had completed her attire. She was a knockout. He'd realized then that there was more to her than beauty after she'd taken first place in the women's championship barrel racing competition. He swallowed the lump in his throat. "Oh, trust me. I noticed you. How could any man with a pulse not?"

Caitlyn tipped her chin down and her face flushed.

"I'm sorry. I didn't mean to embarrass you. My mother taught me to always be truthful— especially to a lady."

The sound of hammers pounding nails and whirling power tools echoed through the air.

"So tell me about the school." Logan needed to get his focus off of Caitlyn's stunning good looks. Or at least to try to.

"Over the years, I had a few injuries. Thanks to the aging process, with each injury came longer and more difficult recovery times. During those periods when I had to take a break from competition, I kept a journal to plot ideas to achieve my dream of opening a school. For six months, I mentored a few girls in between competitions." Caitlyn's eyes lit up with excitement. "I loved to see their enthusiasm for the sport, especially when I taught them something they never believed they could do. I realized that was the path I needed to follow. Once I had my plan in place, I announced my retirement and adopted Henry."

"That's quite a story. But you left out one of the best parts." Logan placed his elbows on the table and leaned forward.

Caitlyn grinned widely. "No. I don't believe I did. Adopting Henry was the best part of it all." Her face was a canvas of emotion while her voice conveyed tenderness.

"I don't doubt that. What I should have said was you left out the best part of your career. The recognition your school has received is impressive. Being voted number one in the country is a major achievement. That's incredible. I'm proud of you." Logan's eyes sparkled with admiration.

"How did you know about that?" Caitlyn asked.

Busted. He'd have to come clean. He put his hands up. "Okay, I confess. After we first met, I followed your career for a while, but then life got busy. Until last night, it had been a long time since I went sleuthing. It's amazing what you can find on the internet." Logan's face felt like he'd just stepped inside a sauna. The last thing he wanted was for Caitlyn to think he was some sort of creepy stalker who trolled the web late into the night.

Caitlyn straightened her shoulders. "As long as we're making confessions, I've done a little sleuthing myself and searched for your name online a few times." Her cheeks blushed when their eyes briefly connected.

Logan laughed. "You're just saying that so I don't feel like a silly high school boy."

"I promise." Caitlyn put up her right hand. "I know you have a few service training accolades to be proud of yourself."

Logan ran his finger down the side of his soda can. "I can't take all the credit. My brothers play a huge role in the success of our school."

Caitlyn nodded. "I'm sure you work just as hard as they do. What I was referring to was the article I read about the dog you rescued and trained for the little girl who lost both of her eyes in that tragic accident. What you did was incredible."

Logan preferred to stay out of the limelight, but he understood that as a business owner, sometimes he had to step out of the shadow and into the light. "Thank you. When a neighbor of the little girl, who was a reporter from a Denver newspaper, called me for an interview, I was hesitant at first. But the reporter was persistent. He shared with me how he had witnessed the remarkable transformation the dog had brought to the little girl's life and her family's. When I realized telling the story could help others understand the power of service dogs, I agreed to the interview."

Caitlyn brushed away a tear that ran down her cheek. "I can't imagine how grateful her parents must have been. What a magnificent gift you gave to the family."

"Seeing the impact the animal had on the family was actually a gift to me," Logan shared. But deep down, Logan couldn't help but feel that he didn't deserve it. He had failed to protect the person he'd loved the most.

"I'm sure it was. You should be proud," she stated.

Logan wanted to share more with Caitlyn, but he thought it was best to keep it to himself.

After losing Melody, Logan had made two promises to God. One was to spend the rest of his life training dogs. He wanted to make a positive impact on as many lives as possible. His second promise was to use some of the property he'd been leasing from Martha to establish a rescue organization. Logan's love for dogs was the driving force behind his dream to start the organization. But a part of him hoped that by rescuing these dogs it would somehow lessen the pain and guilt of not being able to rescue his fiancée.

CHAPTER SEVEN

Early Saturday morning, Caitlyn eased her SUV into the gravel lot in front of Garrison's Mercantile. She parked in an open spot and removed the list she'd prepared earlier of ingredients to bake her mother's German chocolate cake. Whenever Caitlyn was nervous, her antidote was to bake. A text message from her landlord late yesterday had her rattled. She'd gotten up before dawn and downed half a pot of coffee before rousting Henry out of bed.

"The sign says closed." Henry poked his head up from behind his Game Boy and studied the front of the market.

Caitlyn eyed her son in the rearview mirror. He'd obviously decided against picking up a hairbrush this morning. She glanced at the time on the dashboard and reached inside her purse. "They should open up any minute. Here, take my comb and run it through your hair before we go inside?"

Henry followed his mother's instructions and combed his unruly hair. "Why did we have to come so early? I didn't even get to watch the Saturday cartoons."

Poor Henry had to suffer the consequences of his mother's nervous tendency to bake following a surprise invitation yesterday. After she and Henry had spent all day at Last Dollar, Logan had stopped by to check on the attic. Lester and his wife were still in Memphis, tending to Becky's mother, but Lester had wanted Logan to make sure the fire restoration project was being addressed. After Logan had conducted his inspection, he'd invited Caitlyn and Henry to a Memorial Day cookout tomorrow.

If Caitlyn hadn't been so exhausted from removing the grungy wallpaper from the kitchen, she might have declined the invitation. But she was so tired she'd been unable to come up with a fast excuse. Of course, Henry had been so excited by the offer, he'd accepted on her behalf immediately. "I told you I need to get the ingredients to bake a cake to take to the town cookout tomorrow."

"Oh, yeah. That's the party at Mr. Logan's

brother's house that's making you nervous." Henry pushed the bill of his hat up from his eyes. "Do you think there will be a lot of kids there?"

"I'm not nervous. There's just a lot on my mind." According to Logan, the party was an annual event held the Sunday before Memorial Day, immediately following church service. This year, it was to be hosted by his brother Jake and his wife, Olivia. "I'm sure there will be a lot of children attending. I believe Mr. Jake has three kids."

"That will be fun. But what about today? It won't take you all day to bake a cake. It's Saturday. We always do something fun at home on Saturday," Henry pleaded.

Henry was right. Following the adoption, Caitlyn had made sure that Saturdays were their day. No matter how busy she was with teaching or managing the business, she always set aside the day for Henry. Each week, she would allow Henry to make up the itinerary for the day. Caitlyn had to admit, putting a squiggly worm on a fishing hook wasn't at the top of her list of things to do. But as long as she was with Henry and he was happy, she really didn't care what they did. "Let's get what we need in the store, and then we'll make a plan for the day."

Henry unbuckled his seat belt. "Okay. Maybe we can go see Rocky and Sophie today? Mr. Logan might let us take them to the pond. Then we can see Donald, too. Or maybe we can go fishing like he talked about."

With Logan being so involved with the repairs on Last Dollar, it was increasingly more difficult to limit the time Henry spent with Logan. Although his heart was in the right place, Caitlyn feared too much time with Logan couldn't be a good thing for her son. If she was being honest, it probably wasn't such a good thing for her either. Logan's handsome good looks were consuming more of her thoughts lately. It didn't help either that since their private picnic last Monday, Logan was giving Caitlyn fresh forget-me-nots each time he came to the house. It was a sweet and kind gesture, but not the best way for her to maintain her focus on getting the repairs done, selling the house, and leaving town.

"Why don't we see what the day brings?" Caitlyn exited the vehicle and opened the back door.

Henry bounded to the ground and pointed. "Look, that place over there has a ball pit outside."

Caitlyn glanced down the street. As far as she could see down the sidewalk, each lamppost had a flower basket filled with colorful petunias. She spotted what had captured Henry's attention. The Hummingbird Café. It appeared to be a quaint bistro-type establishment. A place she'd like to spend a lazy Saturday afternoon with her journal and a cup of strong coffee. It probably wasn't the best environment for a rambunctious little boy. Then again, the ball pit could keep Henry occupied. "Maybe we can go there for lunch sometime."

"Or we could go there?" Henry shouted and turned his attention across the street. "They probably have good pizza."

"With a name like Mr. Pepperoni, I have to agree with you. Let me take care of my errands. After that, we could explore the town a little and maybe get a pizza for lunch." Making plans with Henry was settling Caitlyn's nerves about accepting Logan's invitation. After all, it was only a cookout.

Caitlyn locked the door of the SUV and glanced at the front window of the store. She noticed the Closed sign had been flipped and now read Open. "Let's go inside." She took Henry's hand and they climbed the steps of the clapboard building. The bell over the door jingled as they stepped inside. Last week, the sweet smell of freshly baked cookies greeted her, but this morning coffee and cinnamon rolls caused her empty stomach to growl.

"Something smells yummy." Henry looked up and grinned.

"Good morning. It's nice to see you two again." Nellie scurried from behind the counter wearing a yellow apron. Smears of flour dotted her face. She gave Caitlyn a hug before turning to Henry. "I've just taken a fresh batch of cinnamon rolls out of the oven. Would you like one?"

Henry turned to Caitlyn. "May I?"

"Of course, you may," Caitlyn answered.

"They just need to sit a minute or two. So, what brings you two out so early? I thought Saturday mornings were for watching cartoons in your jammies and eating sugary cereal." Nellie ruffled the top of Henry's hair.

Caitlyn slipped her grocery list from her crossover bag. "I need to pick up some ingredients to bake a German chocolate cake. It's my mother's recipe," Caitlyn noted.

"Mom likes to bake when she's nervous," Henry added.

Caitlyn shot Henry a look.

"What? That's what Mr. Jeffrey used to say." Henry shrugged his shoulders.

Caitlyn's ex used to say a lot of things in front of Henry that he shouldn't have said. "I'm baking the cake for the Memorial Day cookout tomorrow."

Nellie clapped her hands together. "I'm so happy to hear that you and Henry are planning to attend. You'll have a wonderful time. It's a special day of fellowship to honor the brave individuals who've served our country."

"We are both looking forward to it." Caitlyn caught a whiff of the freshly brewed coffee. "I'd love a cup of that coffee. It smells delicious." Caitlyn inhaled the rich scent and took in her surroundings. Seeing the store aisles her mother had once roamed every Saturday triggered bittersweet memories. The heaviness of the realization settled upon her. She almost couldn't breathe.

Nellie stepped closer and placed her hand on Caitlyn's arm. "Are you okay, dear? You look a little pale."

Caitlyn glanced at Henry, who had wandered over to the enclosed glass cabinet at the back of the store. The shelves housed nostalgic candies, giant jawbreakers, colorful lollipops, and classic candy bars. Her heart squeezed as she watched Henry's eyes fixate on the jawbreakers. He leaned in closer to the cabinet, examining the candies with intense curiosity. It was exactly what she had done many years earlier. Caitlyn swallowed the lump that had formed deep in her throat. "Being here—it's a little overwhelming."

"Let's have a seat." Nellie guided Caitlyn to the corner of the store. Four small round tables were arranged beside a window overlooking a courtyard filled with flowers and trees. "I'll get your coffee. Wait right here." Nellie pulled out the chair. It screeched across the hardwood floor.

Caitlyn sat down and inhaled three deep breaths. What she'd thought was a negative reaction to her surroundings had somehow turned into a calm delight. She felt as though she'd come home. Of course, Bluebell wasn't her home. It had so many bad memories. But for every negative memory, Caitlyn could remember good ones.

Nellie approached the table with a tray. She placed the bone-china cup, hand-painted with yellow daisies, along with a saucer, pitcher of cream, spoon and bowl of sugar in front of Caitlyn. "Here you go, dear."

"Thank you." Caitlyn poured a dash of cream into the cup and stirred. "I was just thinking about my mom."

Nellie slipped into the empty chair. "She was a special lady."

Caitlyn nodded. "I remember my first day of second grade. I'd had a horrible day.

Someone had taken my lunch box from the coat closet and filled it with sand from the playground. The teacher discovered it was a classmate who'd snuck into the room during recess to carry out the prank. His name was Joey Littleton. He had a crush on me and thought that was a way to get my attention. All the kids in my class teased me. My mom brought me here for ice cream. She thought it would make me feel better."

"And did it?" Nellie reached across the table and placed her hand on Caitlyn's wrist.

Caitlyn brushed the tear that raced down her cheek and nodded. "She always made everything better. That afternoon was the last time she was there to comfort me. She and my dad died in the car accident two days later."

"I remember when I first heard. It was such

a shock. Your parents were pillars of the community and loved by everyone," Nellie said. "I know you don't plan to stay in town forever, but while you're here, I'd be happy to share stories about them, if you'd like." Nellie squeezed Caitlyn's hand.

"I'd like that." Caitlyn took a sip of her coffee and smiled. A part of her wished she could stay in Bluebell long enough to hear every story Nellie had to tell about her parents, but that wasn't possible. If she lingered, she would get stuck and wouldn't be moving forward toward her dream and what was best for Henry.

Lingering wasn't an option for Caitlyn.

NEXT TO THE annual Fourth of July celebration, the Memorial Day picnic held a special place in Logan's heart. It was a time to honor and remember those who had given their lives fighting for the country's freedom, but it also carried a bittersweet memory. Two years ago, after the last fireworks had faded into the darkness, Logan had taken Melody for a walk under the stars. With only the sound of crickets filling the night air, Logan had felt a sense of contentment wash over him when he dropped to one knee and asked Melody to be his wife. Wide-eyed and glowing underneath the full moon, she'd said yes.

Logan neared his brother's house. The farm field to his left was now a makeshift parking lot. Three dozen parked cars flattened the grass, leaving behind tire tracks that looked like a maze. A few members from church still jostled for positions. Logan navigated his vehicle to the front of the residence and parked.

"Uncle Logan! Uncle Logan!"

Logan pulled himself back into the moment and glanced out the window of his truck. He spotted his adorable twin niece and nephew, Kyle and Kayla, running through the field toward the gravel driveway in front of Jake's house. Their arms pumping them forward as the sound of laughter filled the air. Logan's brother had lost his first wife and their unborn child. God had carried him through the challenging season and blessed him with a loving woman who'd given him a third child, Maddie.

Logan unfastened his seat belt and jumped from the truck. Rocky let out a bark from the back seat. "Hold on, fella. I haven't forgotten you."

"Can we take Rocky for a walk?" Kyle reached the truck first.

Logan attached Rocky's leash to the leather collar. Still kneeling, he turned to the breathless children. "Don't I get a hug first?" Having seen Rocky grow up from a puppy, the twins loved the dog especially.

Kayla was the first to fling her arms around Logan's neck. "Sorry! We're just excited to see Rocky. Miss Myrna brought Callie, too. She said we could take her for a walk once she asks Daddy for permission. We thought we could take both at the same time."

Jake had trained Callie to assist his dear friend, Myrna Hart, following a diagnosis of macular degeneration. "Do you think you can handle both dogs?"

Kayla pulled away from Logan and Kyle stepped up to give his uncle a quick hug. "Sure we can. Kayla can walk Callie, since they're both girls. I'll take Rocky. He's bigger and I'm stronger." Kyle stated his case and squared his slim shoulders.

"That sounds like a plan." Logan passed the leash to Kyle. "You hang on to Rocky while I get the hamburger and hot dog rolls out of the back. Kayla, you can help me."

"Sure, Uncle Logan." Kayla rounded the vehicle.

Logan opened the back of the truck and

turned to the sound of tires crunching on loose stones. He peered over his shoulder and smiled when he spotted the familiar SUV. *Caitlyn*. His pulse increased. When he'd extended the invitation the other day, he'd sensed a bit of hesitancy, so he wasn't sure if she'd definitely show up. Logan was positive if she'd had a moment of hesitation, Henry had changed her mind.

"Who's that?" Kayla asked.

"That's a friend of your uncle Luke's, but now she is also our friend. She has a son named Henry who is just about your age. He's a little shy, so let's make him feel welcome," Logan instructed the twins, even though both Kayla and Kyle always treated other children with respect.

"Cool!" Kyle sang out. "Maybe Henry can go for a walk with us."

It hadn't taken Logan long to learn Caitlyn was protective with her son. He didn't want her to feel in an uncomfortable position by having the children ask to whisk her son away. "Why don't we get to know each other first? Then maybe later you can go for that walk."

Logan unloaded the bags of groceries from the truck, along with a tank of propane for Jake's grill. He placed the tank on the ground as Caitlyn rolled up behind him.

"Hi. Should I park over there?" Caitlyn stuck her head out the window of the SUV and pointed toward the parked cars.

Caitlyn's eyes gazed into his, causing warmth to course through him. Maybe she wanted to attend the picnic. "No, you can stay right where you are." Logan motioned with his hand for her to pull up a few feet before he halted. "Perfect." He returned his focus to unpacking his truck.

Moments later the SUV's doors slammed. Logan glanced over his shoulder. When he spotted Caitlyn walking toward him, the warmth he'd felt a couple of minutes earlier suddenly turned into a raging inferno. And it wasn't the late May sun beating down on his face, creating this reaction. It was all Caitlyn. Wow! She wore a floral, cotton sundress that billowed in the gentle breeze, paired with pink, strappy sandals. Her hair flowed loosely over her shoulders. She looked incredible. Logan used his left hand to steady himself against the truck as she approached.

Caitlyn's attire differed from what Logan had spotted her wearing in church only hours earlier. Five minutes into the service, wearing black slacks and a light blue blouse, Caitlyn and Henry had slipped into the back row. Henry had dropped a hymnal that had prompted Logan to turn toward the rear of the church. For a second, Caitlyn and Logan's eyes had connected before she'd picked up the hymnal and sang along with the congregation. He had hoped to catch up with her after worship. Instead of going to the fellowship hall with Henry, Caitlyn had scampered out of the building like a sandpiper.

"Hi, Mr. Logan!" Henry was the first to speak while Logan tried to get his tongue unraveled.

"Hi!" The twins stepped up and greeted the twosome.

Logan's mouth felt like he had ten large cotton balls stuffed inside as he took tentative steps toward Caitlyn. His eyes locked on her demure smile. She looked nothing like the woman who furrowed her brow while poring over her journal filled with endless lists and thoughts.

As he drew closer, Logan could not keep his reaction to her presence to himself. "You look beautiful," he finally breathed, his voice barely a whisper. Caitlyn's cheeks ignited with a rosy blush and he couldn't help but feel a twinge of doubt. Was he wrong to admit to the effect she had on him? Right or wrong, he spoke the truth.

"Thank you." Caitlyn glanced down at her outfit. "I hope I'm dressed appropriately." She tucked a strand of hair behind her ear.

"I told her she should wear jeans in case there's a potato sack race or something," Henry stated.

Logan ruffled the top of Henry's head. "Your mom made the right choice."

"She sure took long enough to decide. I thought we'd never get out of the house." Henry rolled his eyes.

Logan faked a cough to hide the humor he found in Henry's words. "How are you doing today, buddy? Are you ready to have some fun?"

"I sure am! We don't get to do stuff like this much at home. Mom is always so busy with her school and worrying about stuff," Henry lamented.

Logan noticed Caitlyn's earlier expression had faded. "Well, I can guarantee both of you will have a great time today." Logan turned to the twins and Rocky. "First, I want you to meet my niece and nephew. This is Kayla and Kyle." Logan placed a hand on each child. "They'll both make sure you enjoy yourselves today. Of course, you already know Rocky."

"It's nice to meet you." Caitlyn smiled.

"Hi," Henry chirped and knelt to the ground in front of Rocky. "Hey, Rocky—remember me?"

Rocky's tail wagged with rapid, frenzied movements. Without hesitation, the dog jumped to greet Henry, smothering his face with sloppy kisses. As Rocky continued to shower Henry with affection, Henry giggled and rolled over on his back, finally giving in to the dog's relentless attention.

Kyle dropped to the ground alongside Henry to join in the fun. "Rocky really likes you."

"You think so?" Henry wiped away the dog drool from his cheek.

Kayla joined the boys. "Yeah, he doesn't act like this with just anyone."

Logan turned his attention from the children to Caitlyn. Not that his awareness had faded since she'd stepped out of her truck. "Did you enjoy Pastor Kidd's sermon this morning?" The message on worry couldn't have come at a more perfect time. Since Caitlyn's arrival, Logan worried he'd lose the land along with his dream of creating the dog rescue organization. The pastor's words reminded him not to be anxious and to continue to let his requests be known to God. In the end, it would all work out. Of course, some days not allowing his mind to follow the worry trail was easier said than done.

Caitlyn nodded. "I did. He even captured Henry's attention. He kept nudging me. And on the way home, he reminded me I was wasting too much time worrying." Caitlyn touched her throat. "Sometimes it's hard for me to believe he's only seven years old."

Logan glanced at Henry, chatting with Kayla and Kyle as though they were lifelong friends. "Yeah, I've learned a lot from those two." Logan tipped his head toward the twins before he turned his attention back to Caitlyn. "I tried to catch up with you after the service. I wanted to grab a cup of coffee with you in the fellowship hall, but you ran out like the church was on fire," Logan joked.

Caitlyn dug the toe of her sandal into the gravel. "I wanted to have plenty of time to run back to Luke's house to change and pick up the cake that I baked."

"I'm glad I didn't catch up to you then. You really look great."

"It's been a while since I've worn a dress. Back home, jeans and T-shirts are my go-to attire," Caitlyn said.

Logan watched as Caitlyn fingered the silver necklace with a hummingbird pendant. "Well, no matter what you wear, I'm sure the guys in your town would walk on hot rocks for a date with you." Logan waited for Caitlyn's response and it was worth the wait. Her eyes sparkled and a playful smile danced across her lips. In the time they'd spent together, he'd never heard her mention a husband or boyfriend. There was a part of him that wanted to know so much more about Caitlyn, but he didn't want to scare her away. Perhaps today would be the day she might open up and reveal a secret or two.

CHAPTER EIGHT

SOMEWHERE ALONG THE LINE, Caitlyn's plan to keep her focus on revitalizing the farmhouse and off of Logan had flopped like a cake removed from the oven too soon. Something stirred inside and had come alive when he'd told her she looked beautiful. Caitlyn couldn't remember the last time a man spoke those words to her. Was that why she was reacting this way, because no man had paid her a compliment in forever? Or could it be because Logan was the one who'd paid the compliment, and he was the most gorgeous man she'd ever known?

"Thanks for carrying the grocery bags for me," Logan called out over his shoulder. "Don't worry about Henry. The kids will be fine walking the dogs. Kayla has already developed that motherly instinct. She's great with her baby sister, Maddie."

Caitlyn had had reservations when Kyle had

suggested Henry join him and Kayla while they walked Rocky and the other dog, Callie. But when she'd noticed the excitement in Henry's eyes, she couldn't say no. He longed to do things on his own, like other children.

Caitlyn trekked across the well-manicured lawn to the patio with the cake carrier in her hands and two bags hanging from each wrist. Logan led the way, carrying the propane. He placed the tank on the oversize patio.

"Wow, that's an impressive outdoor kitchen." The stainless-steel cabinets next to the six-burner grill gleamed in the sunlight.

"Yeah. Jake built it for the family to enjoy. In March, when Pastor Kidd announced the town was in search of a venue for the Memorial Day picnic this year, Jake was the first to raise his hand. Let me introduce you to him." Logan placed the backup propane tank off to the side of the patio.

Caitlyn's heart raced with anticipation as she realized she was about to meet Logan's older brother. She already knew Luke, Logan's younger brother, so why did she feel nervous now? She bit her lip to calm her nerves.

"There he is." Logan pointed.

Jake stood over the grill, flipping burgers

with a practiced ease. From behind, he appeared tall and muscular, dressed in jeans, a white shirt, along with a brown cowboy hat.

"Hey, buddy," Logan called.

Jake turned and displayed the same chiseled features as an older version of Logan. Salt-and-pepper hair peeked out from underneath the hat. He looked over and threw off a wave, the spatula in his hand, as they approached.

"Hey there." Jake placed the utensil on the side table and extended his hand. "You must be Caitlyn. I'm happy you came today. Logan's told me all about you and the farmhouse renovations."

Caitlyn's cheeks flushed under his intense gaze as she greeted Jake. His grip was firm. "I've heard a lot about you as well. I made a German chocolate cake." She handed off the dessert.

"That's a favorite around here. Thank you very much." Jake placed the cake on the table behind him.

"Thank you for welcoming me and my son to your beautiful home." Caitlyn smiled.

"Any friend of Logan and Luke's is a friend of mine." Jake scanned the area. "I wanted to introduce you to my wife, Olivia, but she must be inside with Nellie getting the side dishes together."

"Hosting a large function like this is a lot of work. I'll look forward to meeting your wife later when she's not busy. Your children are delightful. We met earlier. You should be proud," Caitlyn said.

Jake tipped the brim of his hat. "Thank you. I could say the same to you. I had a brief introduction to Henry before he headed off with the kids to walk the dogs."

"Thanks, I appreciate the twin's hospitality. Henry can be a little shy," Caitlyn explained.

Logan patted his brother on the shoulder. "We better let you get back to work. Looks like a sizeable crowd, which means a lot of hungry mouths to feed."

Caitlyn's attention turned to the growing commotion near the beverage table. A line snaked around the table like a ribbon. Laughter filled the air as more guests gathered, shaking hands and welcoming one another. Caitlyn couldn't think of any place she'd rather be. "Would you like for me to help you serve?" she offered.

Jake shook his head. "No way. I appreciate the offer, but I want you and my brother to relax and enjoy the day. He doesn't slow down too often, so I'm hoping you can show him how." Jake winked.

"Thanks, buddy. I'll try. But you know me," Logan drawled.

"Why don't you grab some food and take Caitlyn up on the swing? I've placed a couple of tables up there." Jake glanced at the few fluffy clouds drifting lazily across the vibrant blue expanse. "With a sky like this, the view should be nothing short of spectacular."

Logan tipped his chin. "I was thinking the same thing." He turned to Caitlyn. "Let's eat."

A few minutes later, Caitlyn spotted the oversize swing underneath the towering Douglas fir tree. She splayed her fingers across her chest. "This view is absolutely breathtaking. I don't think I've ever seen the Rocky Mountains this clearly."

As she and Logan approached, the tree's sheer size left her in awe. The thick trunk and sprawling branches seemed to reach endlessly toward the sky. Suspended by sturdy chains, the swing creaked in the gentle breeze that rustled through the trees.

Caitlyn couldn't resist. She plopped down on the wooden bench and extended her legs out in front, kicking her feet like an excited child. "I could stay here forever." She inhaled a deep breath of the crisp mountain air.

Logan laughed as he took a seat next to Caitlyn. "That's exactly what my sister-in-law said the first time Jake brought her here."

"Really?" Caitlyn rested her head on the plank.

"She sure did." Logan stood, holding both plates of food. "We could eat our burgers here, if you'd like."

"That sounds perfect." Caitlyn accepted her plate as Logan settled in.

"Yeah, when Jake tells the story, he likes to say this swing is the reason Olivia made Bluebell her permanent home. She worked as an ER doctor in Miami." Logan laughed and started a forward motion of the swing.

The wood squeaked softly beneath them as they ate their burgers and munched on potato salad. An aroma mixed with sweet onions and meat drifted from the patio. Sounds of children laughing and adults chattering filled the air.

"Actually, this is where he proposed to Olivia."

Caitlyn closed her eyes for a second and tried to picture the scene. She couldn't think of a more romantic place to ask someone to spend the rest of their lives together. It was something she'd dreamed of, but as the years slipped away, and after the breakup, Caitlyn accepted the fact that it would be her and Henry. "I can't imagine any woman saying no to a proposal made here. This is like a setting for a romance novel."

"I'll make a note of that," Logan responded before tasting his burger.

"So you've never brought a girl up here to propose?" Caitlyn joked.

Logan swallowed. "Not here." He took another bite.

Wait. Logan wasn't married. Did that mean he was engaged? If so, why hadn't he mentioned a fiancée? Where was she? Or maybe, like she and Jeffrey, they'd parted ways.

"I can hear the questions rolling around in your head," Logan quipped.

Busted. She was breaking her own rule. No exchanging of personal information. By keeping things all business, there would be no emotional attachment. Well, maybe this one time wouldn't hurt.

"So, are you engaged to be married?" Caitlyn nibbled on her burger and peered at Logan from the corner of her eyes.

"I was. In fact, Lester and his wife introduced me to Melody. Thelma had known her since she was a little girl."

Maybe Melody had dumped Logan like Jeffrey had ditched her? Was that even possible? The woman would have to be an egg short of a dozen to break up with Logan. From what she'd seen, he was exactly like his brother Jake— sweet, kind, great with children, and gorgeous.

"Melody died over a year ago," Logan stated and stared straight ahead.

Caitlyn gasped and covered her mouth with her hand. "I'm so sorry." Thoughts swirled in her head. How? Why? But Logan said nothing more. They continued to eat their meal in silence while swinging and looking out onto the sweeping mountains stretching across the horizon.

LOGAN WASN'T ABOUT to allow his past mistake to ruin Caitlyn's day at the picnic. Today was her first day off since arriving in Bluebell and working nonstop on the farmhouse. The second he'd mentioned Melody, regret numbed his mind. Pain and shock reflected in her eyes. Logan wanted to keep the mood more lighthearted, but he had opened the door to his past.

He prepared himself to answer Caitlyn's questions, but for the past ten minutes, she had remained quiet.

"A couple months before the wedding, Melody and I had an appointment in Denver to meet with the wedding photographer." Logan remembered how he'd felt that morning. He'd woken up the day of the appointment drenched in sweat. Then a sudden chill had run through him, causing him to convulse. His body had felt heavy and nonresponsive until a deep hacking cough had erupted in his chest, igniting waves of pain through every bone and muscle in his body. "That morning, I woke up with the worst case of the flu I'd ever had."

Caitlyn remained silent.

Logan inhaled a deep breath and continued. "When I phoned Melody to tell her I was sick, she wanted to reschedule the appointment. I knew how important getting the right photographer was to her, so I insisted she take my new Range Rover to the city to meet with the photographer without me. Her car was older, and it had been in and out of the garage for repairs. I thought my vehicle would be safer. I was wrong." Logan looked up toward the sky and prayed silently for the strength to continue recalling the worst day of his life.

"You don't have to say any more. I know how difficult it can be to talk about a car accident that takes away a loved one," Caitlyn said.

Of course, after losing her parents in a car accident, Caitlyn would assume that was how Melody had lost her life. Especially based on what he'd told her so far. Logan shook his head. "No, Pastor Kidd told me I should talk about it. The thing is Melody didn't die in a car accident. She died because of me. I wasn't there when some guy with a gun approached her in the parking garage and wanted my fancy new car. If I'd let Melody take her beat-up clunker, she'd still be alive."

Caitlyn gasped. She reached out and placed her hand on Logan's arm. "Oh, Logan, I didn't know. I'm so sorry."

Logan shook his head. His eyes brimmed with tears. "When I got the call from a Denver state trooper, I thought I was delirious from the fever. At first, I didn't believe him. I wanted it to be a bad dream. But when I had to call her parents, it all became real. Telling her mom and dad that they'd lost their baby girl was the hardest thing I've ever had to do."

Caitlyn moved her hand slowly up and down Logan's arm.

"You're a good listener. Thank you." Logan's brothers were constantly telling him to get past it, to move on. Not that easy when it should have been him.

"I'm here whenever you want to talk. It's not good to keep things bottled up inside," Caitlyn said.

"I appreciate that." Logan didn't see a need to go into the worst details of the dreadful day. "I hadn't planned on unloading all of this on you, today especially." Caitlyn's touch provided comfort, but it didn't stop the guilt that he carried daily. He just had to keep putting one foot in front of the other and trust that God would one day heal his wounds. But today wasn't about wallowing in his grief.

Logan straightened his shoulders. "What I'd really had in mind when I brought you to this special place was to learn more about you."

"Oh, really?" Caitlyn grinned.

"So—are you seeing anyone?"

Caitlyn jerked her head in Logan's direction. Logan laughed and Caitlyn joined in.

"You don't beat around the bush, Mr. Beckett." Caitlyn chuckled, shooting him a sly look before turning her attention back to the view.

"We have been spending a lot of time together. It's only natural for me to wonder if there is someone waiting for you back home in Wyoming." Logan couldn't imagine Caitlyn didn't have men lining up to date her. She was charming and beautiful, plus she had a quick wit, something he always found attractive in a woman.

"Let's see, the guy who runs the local tack and supply shop is always waiting for me to come in with my horses to have them re-shoed." Caitlyn twirled a strand of her hair around her finger.

"And?" Logan leaned in and noticed her familiar honeysuckle-scented shampoo.

"He replaces the shoes for my horses and then I go home," Caitlyn answered.

"So you're not dating him?"

Caitlyn giggled. "He's nearing eighty years old and has been married since he was sixteen."

Logan's eyes danced in amusement and a small smile parted his lips. The playful banter was a welcome reprieve from the seriousness of the previous conversation. "Let's forget that guy. Is there anyone else in the picture?"

Caitlyn's smile faded and her shoulders

dropped. "There was someone a while ago—but it's over now."

Logan waited for Caitlyn to expand a little on the relationship that had ended, but she remained quiet, examining her fingernails. "I'm sorry. I shouldn't be prying into your personal life. Just because I spilled my guts doesn't mean you have to do the same."

"There's no need to apologize. In hindsight, the breakup was probably for the best. Jeffrey, that's his name, and I wanted different things." She leaned back against the swing.

"Relationships can be hard enough without having common goals. How did Henry take it when things ended?" Logan wanted to know more, but he didn't want to push Caitlyn. Then again, when would they have time alone like this? "Did he like the guy?"

"When Jeffrey and I first started dating, I was already fostering Henry. I kept those two parts of my life separate, but I made sure Jeffrey was aware of my plan to one day adopt Henry. Once the adoption process was complete, the three of us spent more time together. Jeffrey was good to Henry. He liked to buy him things and take him to fun places, but there was never an emotional connection between the two of them. Henry is an intuitive little boy. I think he sensed Jeffrey preferred when he wasn't around." Caitlyn picked at the hem of her sundress.

"I didn't mean to upset you." Logan shifted closer to her. It had to have been difficult for Caitlyn to keep two parts of her life separate and then gradually join them together.

Caitlyn rolled her shoulders. "No, you didn't. I should have ended things before he did. In fairness to Jeffrey, circumstances in my life changed dramatically after the adoption, so I can't put all the blame on him."

Logan admired Caitlyn. When relationships fail, it's easy to put the fault on the other person. "Well, Jeffrey is missing out. Henry is a great kid."

Caitlyn rested her head against the swing and glanced up to the sky. "I can't imagine my life without him."

Enjoying the sounds of nature and the gentle motion of the swing, Logan wasn't quite ready for his alone time with Caitlyn to end. A part of him wanted to stay and watch the sunset with her, but Logan knew they couldn't ignore the fact that there was a community picnic happening. "Do you think we'd better head back and be social?" Logan asked.

A low rumble sounded in the distance.

"What was that?" Caitlyn turned to Logan.

"Maybe it was someone's truck."

"Look!" Caitlyn pointed to the dark clouds gathering on the horizon, their edges illuminated by the last rays of the sun. "I think a storm is coming."

Logan looked up and spotted ominous clouds, lightning flickering inside, moving in their direction. Gusts of wind whipped through the trees. Logan sprang from the swing and grabbed Caitlyn's hand. "We need to get back to the house as fast as we can." Running across the open field during an electrical storm was too dangerous. They had to outrun the storm clouds and take shelter before the storm hit.

"Henry!" Caitlyn cried out.

"He's probably back at the house. We need to hurry." Logan shot glances at the clouds.

"I can't run in these sandals." Caitlyn shouted as she bent over and stripped the shoes from her feet.

"Hold my hand and run as fast as you can," Logan instructed her.

Splat. A fat raindrop hit Logan's cheek, followed by another. Seconds later, the storm clouds above opened, stinging their bodies like a swarm of bees, soaking their clothes. The ground beneath their feet shook as the thunder grew louder. It was too late. The storm was right over top of them. Logan and Caitlyn were in the most dangerous place to be—a wide-open field.

CHAPTER NINE

"GET INSIDE, QUICK!" Logan called out when they finally reached Jake's house.

Caitlyn's bare feet skidded across the slick stone as she felt Logan's hand strong against her back, guiding her through the open patio door. Safe from the elements, but not knowing whether Henry was still outside with the dogs, she scanned the family room area. People packed Jake's house, seeking shelter from the storm. Her eyes ran over the area a second time. There was no sign of him. Her heart pounded in her chest. "I have to find Henry!" she cried out to no one in particular. Her voice filled with worry.

Logan stepped closer. "He could be inside. There's Olivia." Logan pointed to the tall, slender woman speaking with Nellie. "Olivia!" Logan motioned her over.

Caitlyn couldn't stand still so she met the

woman halfway. "Have you seen my son? He's with your children."

Olivia placed her hand on Caitlyn's arm. "Jake went out to look for the kids. Don't worry. He'll be back with them any minute."

Caitlyn's heart sank. Her worst fear had come true. The entire time she'd raced through the open field, running from the storm, she had prayed that Henry and the twins were safe in the house. She should have never allowed him to go off for a walk without adult supervision. How could she be so irresponsible?

"Kayla!" Logan shouted.

Caitlyn turned to the open patio door and spotted Kayla. Her hair was soaking wet. The denim shorts she wore dripped water like a faucet onto the hardwood floor.

Caitlyn sprinted toward Kayla. She dropped to her knees in front of the child and placed her hands on her forearms. "Where are Henry and Kyle?" she asked, foregoing her inside voice.

"I don't know," Kayla cried.

The piercing sound of cell phones blaring storm warnings filled the room.

Caitlyn's heart raced.

Olivia joined her daughter's side. "Sweetie, where did you last see them?"

Kayla's lip quivered. "Henry wanted to walk on the trail at the pond, so he could visit Donald, the duck. We kept telling him we shouldn't go that far, but he said he had to see him."

The hollow pit in Caitlyn's stomach widened. Henry didn't know how to swim.

Nellie approached the group with a large bath towel and draped it over Kayla's head like a wedding veil. "Here, sweetie, try to dry off a little."

"Thank you, Nellie." Olivia used the end of the towel to dry Kayla's face.

"Did you make it to the water?" Logan asked before taking a quick glance at Caitlyn.

Caitlyn used her hand to cover her mouth. The look in Logan's eyes told her he remembered Henry didn't know how to swim. Swimming lessons. It was on her list of things to do.

Kayla nodded. "When we got closer to the pond, Kyle let Callie off her leash so she could run down to the water. I told him not to, but he didn't listen. Then we heard the thunder, and it started raining. Kyle couldn't get Callie back on the leash. I think the storm scared her because she took off running toward Uncle Logan's house. I came back here as quick as I could. Are they going to be okay?" Kayla looked up at the adults with tears streaming down her face.

Caitlyn heard the rain pounding against the roof. The muscles in her legs tightened, readying herself to run out the door. She turned to Logan. "How do I get to the pond from here?"

"No, the storm is right over us. I can't—" Logan hesitated for a second and drew in a breath "—I won't let you go. It's too dangerous out there. We need to wait for the storm to pass."

Allowing Henry to go off with Kyle and Kayla had been a big mistake. Caitlyn knew better than that. She was his mother—his protector. Under normal circumstances, she would have never allowed this. She'd let down her guard. For what? Time alone with Logan? Was that the reason Caitlyn had given Henry permission? Her mind reeled with possibilities. What if his anxiety from the storm triggered a seizure? Who will help him? "My son is out there. I can't leave him alone. He doesn't know the property. He'll never be able to find his way back."

Olivia stepped closer to Caitlyn. "I know we've never met and I hate that it's happening under these dreadful circumstances, but I want to reassure you that Kyle knows every inch of this property. We've taught him what to do if he's caught in any type of inclement weather, particularly thunderstorms. Please wait here. It won't do anyone any good if you go out in the middle of the storm and get hurt."

Caitlyn felt an instant bond with Olivia. She knew Jake's wife was right, but how could she just stand there and do nothing?

Caitlyn walked to the window, but the blinding rain didn't allow her to see beyond the glass. A few seconds ticked by before little balls of ice pecked against the window. "It's hailing!" Suddenly, tiny pellets grew to the size of golf balls and knocked against the glass. A memory flashed in her mind from last summer. While transporting a new horse from Montana back to Wyoming, Caitlyn had gotten caught in a horrible hail storm. Thankfully, she'd made it to an underpass where she'd rode out the storm that had produced hailstones the size of softballs. Caitlyn had witnessed the aftermath. Dented cars and trucks littered the highway with front and rear windshields shattered, the roofs smashed like tin cans. Glass and other debris had cluttered the asphalt. Caitlyn had spent the entire ride home thanking God for providing a refuge from the fierce storm.

"Everyone move away from the windows and skylights!" Logan instructed the crowd.

Overhead, the roof sounded as though it were being pummeled with rocks.

Caitlyn's knees felt locked as she forced herself to step back from the glass. She noticed Logan and Olivia exchanging glances. Their concern was palpable. "We can't just stand here! Our children are in danger!" Caitlyn directed her words toward Olivia. She hoped another mother would understand the hopelessness she felt. But Olivia only moved away from the window with no sign that she planned to head outside and look for the children.

Moments later, as suddenly as the hail arrived, it departed as though someone had turned off a switch. The banging on the roof subsided, replaced by the sound of heavy rain.

Caitlyn rubbed the back of her neck and turned to Logan. "Since the hail has passed, can we at least get in your truck and drive to your house? Kayla mentioned they went in that direction." If Logan said no, Caitlyn was ready to jump in her own SUV to look for Henry.

Logan nodded. "We can."

Caitlyn pressed her hand to her stomach and released a sigh of relief.

"I need to call Jake with an update. Let me check the weather app to make sure the worst of the storm has cleared before we venture outdoors."

"Jake was in such a hurry, he ran off without his phone. It's still in the kitchen," Olivia said.

Logan pulled his phone from his pocket, swiped and tapped. "The storm is moving east, so we should be okay." He returned the device to its original spot. "I'll pull my truck around front. If you'd like, you can wait for me on the porch," Logan instructed Caitlyn before he jogged out the door.

"I'll get you a pair of tennis shoes. You can't be traipsing outside in your bare feet with all the mud and debris on the ground. Can you wear a size eight?" Olivia asked.

"That's exactly my size." She watched Olivia move swiftly out of the room. Caitlyn rubbed her hands up and down her arms to warm the sudden chill.

As quickly as Olivia left the room, she returned carrying a pair of neon-green tennis shoes. "Logan won't lose sight of you in these." She laughed and handed the shoes to Caitlyn.

"I have the same color at home." Caitlyn examined the footwear. Under different circumstances, Caitlyn and Olivia could be good friends.

"I brought you a sweater, too. Following a hailstorm, the temperature drops," Olivia explained.

"That's very kind of you. Thank you."

"Don't worry, Miss Caitlyn. My brother Kyle will take care of Henry. He's really good with outdoor stuff. He's a Cub Scout."

Caitlyn looked down at the drenched girl and smiled. "Thank you, sweetie."

"Here's the sweater." Olivia moved closer and placed the pale yellow cardigan over Caitlyn's shoulders.

Logan's horn honked out front.

"Thank you." Caitlyn slipped on the garment and headed out the door.

Olivia was right about the weather. The sweater did little to protect Caitlyn from the arctic blast of air. A chill ran through her body the second she stepped outside. The temperature must have dropped over twenty degrees. She noticed the blue flax that had once lined the sidewalk leading to the front porch was flat on the ground from the hailstones.

Logan jumped from the truck and rounded the vehicle. Rain splattered against Caitlyn's face as he opened the door and she climbed inside. She didn't see any hail damage on Logan's truck, but sometimes it was more visible depending on how the sun hit the vehicle. Caitlyn gazed up at Jake's roof, looking for any visible damage. Thoughts of the new roof on her farmhouse entered her mind. Had it remained unscathed? Right now, that was the least of her worries. Finding Henry safe was her top priority.

LOGAN BUCKLED HIS seat belt and jammed his foot down on the accelerator. The rear wheels of the truck spun, kicking up clumps of mud and gravel.

Caitlyn remained quiet, staring straight ahead while smoothing her sundress.

"My brothers and I have talked about paving a road to connect our properties. But the estimates we've received from asphalt companies in Denver were outrageous." Logan hoped to squash the silence inside the cab. Caitlyn blamed herself for Henry getting lost in the storm. Logan understood the burden of carrying guilt.

Several minutes later, Logan released a sigh of relief when they arrived at his house. The storm had passed and the late-afternoon sun filtered through the cirrus clouds drifting overhead. He navigated the truck up the gravel driveway and parked in front of the home.

Caitlyn didn't wait for Logan to come around and open up her door. She flew out of the vehicle before he turned off the ignition. She scanned the property with her hands on her hips. "Where should we look?"

"Kyle knows where I hide the spare key. If the boys made it this far, they would have gotten inside the house with no problem. Let's go see." Logan motioned for her to follow.

They ran up the four brick steps leading to the front porch. Outside the door, Logan fumbled for the house key in his pocket. He slipped it into the lock and turned the knob. "Kyle! Henry! Are you in here?" Logan's shoulders dropped. They hadn't been able to seek shelter in his house.

"What do we do now?" Caitlyn's voice echoed in the foyer.

"Kayla mentioned Henry wanted to see Donald. We can start here and follow the trail to the pond. We've walked the path so many times, Kyle could probably find his way blindfolded."

Caitlyn squeezed her eyes shut and then opened them. "After that violent storm, I can't imagine they would still be down there—unless they're both hurt," she whimpered.

Logan reached for Caitlyn's arm. "You've got to trust me. I know Kyle. He wouldn't stay out in the weather we just experienced. I've taught him to respect the power of Mother Nature. My thought is since the storm has passed, the boys might have headed back to the pond to make sure Donald is safe."

Caitlyn's shoulders relaxed slightly. "You're right. That's exactly what Henry would want to do."

"Let's get going," Logan said.

Minutes later, Logan and Caitlyn dashed along the muddy trail. Thunder rumbled faintly in the distance. Logan's heart pounded with adrenaline. The aftermath of the thunderstorm left behind rain-soaked grass and broken tree branches. Thanks to the tennis shoes Olivia had loaned Caitlyn, she could maneuver the slippery terrain. Both were undeterred by the slick conditions.

"How far are we from the pond?" Caitlyn asked over his shoulder. Her feet splashed through the muddy puddles.

"Not far." Logan didn't want to give Caitlyn false hope, but over the next hill was a shed he'd built for his equipment. It was the closest structure to the pond. It would be the most logical spot Kyle would have taken Henry to ride out the storm.

As the two crested the hill, Caitlyn spotted the building. "What's that over there?" She pointed to the newly renovated wooden structure.

"It's one of my sheds. I built it a couple of years ago to store my equipment. I have a feeling that's where Kyle might have gone."

Before Logan finished the sentence, Caitlyn sprinted off at top speed. Her feet slipped and skidded on the muddy trail, causing her to nearly lose her balance a few times. Her legs pumped faster, propelling her forward as she neared the shed.

"Oh, no," Caitlyn shouted from the opposite side of the shed.

Logan rounded the corner to the front of the building. His heart sank when he spotted a large tree that had fallen in front of the double doors, blocking any access to the structure.

"Henry!" Caitlyn pounded on the side wall and gave it a couple of kicks.

"Mom! The door is stuck," Henry yelled.

Logan sent up a silent prayer, giving thanks the boys were safe. Now he had to get the tree out of the way. It was too large for him and Caitlyn to move.

"What about that window?" Caitlyn pointed to the left side of the shed.

Logan considered Caitlyn's suggestion. It would take time to get his tractor down here to pull the tree away from the door—maybe the window was the best option.

"Kyle, can you hear me?" Logan yelled. "Are you boys okay? Is anyone hurt?"

"No, we're fine, but we can't get out," he answered.

"A tree fell in front of the door. It's too big for us to move. Do you see the stepladder against the back wall?" Logan asked.

A few seconds passed. "Yeah, I see it."

"Do you think you and Henry can carry it to the window?" Logan prompted.

"Yeah, we can do it." Kyle spoke with confidence.

Caitlyn grabbed Logan's arm. "I don't know if I want Henry climbing the ladder. That's too dangerous."

"It's not much different from climbing a tree. We can bring Henry out first so Kyle can spot him from below. He'll be fine. It's not that high." Logan attempted to reassure Caitlyn. The look on her face told him he was wasting his breath.

Caitlyn weighed the options. She shot a look at the enormous tree and then back to the window and paused. "Okay, I guess that's the fastest way to get the boys out."

"It will be okay." Logan patted her arm.

After a few minutes, the boys had set the ladder up below the window. Logan was confident they wouldn't have a problem climbing to safety.

"Don't worry, Miss Caitlyn. Henry can reach the window without getting on the top step, but I'll break his fall if anything happens."

Kyle was a perceptive boy. He knew how worried Caitlyn was about Henry.

Logan stole a glance at Caitlyn. "He'll be fine." In less than five minutes, both boys had shimmied through the window. They were safely outside in front of the shed and eager to tell the adults about their big adventure.

From the moment Henry hit the ground, Caitlyn didn't want to let go.

"Mom, you're smothering me." Henry wiggled himself out of Caitlyn's arms. "I'm fine. I had the best time ever with Kyle! He knew just where to go. We ran through pouring rain and made it inside the shed just before big ice balls started bouncing on the roof. It was so cool!"

Logan held his chin high. Thanks to Kyle's quick thinking, the boys weren't seriously injured. He looked down at his nephew and nodded. "I'm proud of you."

Caitlyn moved closer to Kyle and wrapped her arms around him. "Thank you for taking care of Henry."

"You're welcome. I kept a close eye on him." Kyle looked up at Logan. "I'm sorry I let Callie off her leash. She got scared by the thunder and took off. Rocky ran after her. I tried to hold on to the leash, but he was too strong."

"The dogs! I was so worried about the boys, I forgot about them." Caitlyn turned to Logan.

"Don't worry. They run loose around this property all the time, so they know their way around. They'll find their way back home. I'm just glad these two fellas are okay." Logan ruffled the heads of each boy before turning his attention back to Kyle. "Let's get you home. Your mom's probably worrying herself sick."

"What about Donald?" Henry tugged on Logan's arm. "We need to make sure she didn't get hurt in the storm."

Logan tossed a quick glance at Caitlyn.

She nodded at Henry and then said to Kyle, "We can go down to the pond, but first your uncle needs to call your mother and let her know you're okay."

Five minutes later, Logan had shared the good news with Olivia. Jake had showed up at the house, so everyone was safe and accounted for.

Logan guided the group down the path to the pond. The closer they got to the water, the squawks of Canadian geese echoed in the air. "It sounds like the geese weathered the storm," Logan teased.

"I hope Donald is okay." Henry moved purposely ahead.

"I'm sure this isn't the first storm Donald has experienced, and it won't be her last. Animals have good instincts. They know how to protect themselves in bad weather. She's probably swimming around now, trying to get away from the pestering geese." Logan hoped that was the case. It would crush Henry if anything had happened to Donald.

The foursome crested the last hill overlooking the water. Henry ran, pumping his arms. He nearly stumbled several times. Kyle followed his friend.

"Wait! Don't get near the water!" Caitlyn shouted, but Henry ignored his mother's command.

Logan performed a quick assessment around the pond. Several trees a diligent beaver had been working on for the past few months had toppled over from the strong winds. The beaver would have plenty of timber to continue construction of the condo he was attempting to build from one edge of the pond to the other. For the past year, he'd worked hard to build his damn inside the pond. He exemplified the saying busy as a beaver.

Caitlyn and Logan caught up to the boys, who stood on the bank looking for Donald.

"I don't see her anywhere. Do you think the storm blew her away?" Henry kept his eyes focused on the water.

Logan moved closer to Henry. "My guess is Donald took shelter in a tree. She's got good eyes. If we hang out here for a minute, she might see us and come looking for some food."

In the distance, Rocky's familiar bark echoed

across the property. Logan turned his back to the water, placed his thumb and his index finger between his lips, and whistled. "Rocky! Come here, boy!"

Seconds later, the barking got louder when Callie joined Rocky.

Caitlyn turned and pointed to the ridge. "Look! Here they come!"

Rocky led the way, with Callie not far behind.

Logan watched as the animals plowed through the overgrown grass and fallen branches, soaked by the rain. Both needed a bath. With their tongues lolling and tails wagging, they appeared happy as ever.

Kyle and Henry broke out in smiles while Caitlyn stood nearby.

"Come here, girl!" Kyle called for Callie, but the dog had other plans.

The group watched as Callie splashed into the water. Rocky followed her lead.

"I guess I don't have to worry about giving them a bath now." Logan crossed his arms over his chest and laughed.

Caitlyn moved toward Henry and knelt in front of him. Obviously relieved to find Henry safe, now she tried to comfort him as he worried about Donald. What was the connection that Henry had with that duck?

Logan stepped closer, hoping to put Henry's mind at ease.

Henry looked up and squinted into the bright sun. "Where do you think Donald could have gone? The wind was so strong. What if she's somewhere in the woods hurt? We need to go look for her." He slowly walked away, his head down, and kicking his tennis shoe into the mud.

Caitlyn turned to Logan. "I've got to let him look for Donald, otherwise I know he'll worry that he didn't do enough to find her."

Logan nodded. "I agree. We can check the wooded area that surrounds the pond. Let's get the dogs."

After an exhaustive hour of combing every nook and cranny around the pond, it was time to call it quits for the day. Henry had remained silent during the entire search.

Logan stopped and gently touched Henry's arm before squatting in front of him. "I know you're worried about Donald. There's a chance the storm scared her so much she's afraid to come back while there's people around the pond. We should head back to my brother's house and give her a chance to come back on her own."

"Okay," Henry responded as the group retreated and headed to Jake's house.

CHAPTER TEN

WIRING ISSUE.

Check.

Early the following Saturday morning, Caitlyn sat hunched at Luke's kitchen table with her nose buried between the pages of her journal. Her shoulders relaxed. She could finally check off the wiring inspection.

Caitlyn picked up her coffee cup. Its contents sloshed over the rim, leaving two brown stains on the paper. That was the least of her worries.

As she scanned the remaining items on the to-do list, she dropped the pen and placed her fingertips against her temples. Worry had consumed her since three o'clock in the morning. Last weekend's hailstorm had caused damage to many residences in Bluebell while sparing others. Unfortunately, Last Dollar hadn't escaped the wrath of Mother Nature. It might take time, but Logan assured her there was no need to worry. The men who'd initially worked to replace her roof were busy helping the neighbors whose homes had a lot more damage than her farmhouse.

Besides the repairs, Henry had worried himself sick over Donald. Since the storm, the duck was still missing. With each day that passed, Henry complained more and more about an upset stomach. Caitlyn had done her best to keep his mind off Donald, but it was a losing battle.

Fortunately, the past week had delivered some good news. Lester returned and had worked on the wiring. Now everything was up to code.

Focus on the good. That was her mantra. Lately, the early morning hours were the time of day when Caitlyn had to guard her thoughts, especially with her financial situation. It was easy to become overwhelmed by the projects that still had to be addressed. She needed to keep her focus on the progress made with the help of the good people of Bluebell.

"Can we look for Donald today?" Henry entered the kitchen, rubbing his eyes. His hair stuck out in all directions and his face was fresh with pillow creases.

"Come sit next to me, sweetie." Caitlyn tapped her hand on the empty chair.

Henry took sluggish steps toward Caitlyn and flopped down into the seat. "You're going to say no because it's not on your list." He frowned and pointed to the open journal.

"Not exactly. If we have time today, we can stop by the pond. This morning I thought I'd take you out for breakfast at the Hummingbird Café. I know how much you love French toast and Miss Nellie said theirs is the best."

"So we can go to the pond after?" Henry sat a little straighter.

"After breakfast we're going over to the Garrisons' so I can help Miss Nellie cook for the church potluck supper tomorrow. I told you about it yesterday, remember?"

Henry's slumped posture returned. "Yeah, but you can't cook."

"It's not that I can't. I just don't really like it that much. But Miss Nellie is going to teach me how to make her special country-fried steak, and I'm going to bake brownies." Caitlyn snuggled up close to Henry. "Come on, it will be fun. Mr. Garrison said he'll take you out to their barn. You can help him feed his sheep. He even said he'd teach you how to milk their dairy cow, Betty."

No response. Normally, any mention of animals would perk Henry up and he'd be ready to go. But Donald consumed his thoughts. "After we're finished at the Garrisons', if there's still time, we'll make a stop at the pond. How does that sound?"

"Okay, I guess," Henry mumbled.

"Now go get dressed and brush your teeth. We'll head out for breakfast once you're finished."

Henry's chair screeched as he pushed away from the table. He stood but made no movement to get ready for the day.

"Sweetie, are you okay?" Henry's blank stare caused Caitlyn's heart rate to quicken. Was he having a seizure? This was often one of the first warning signs.

"Yeah. I just miss Donald. I'm afraid she's hurt." Henry turned and left the kitchen.

Caitlyn's heartbeat slowed, but her worries remained. That darn duck. If Donald didn't turn up soon, Caitlyn wasn't sure how she would convince Henry to stop worrying.

An hour later, Caitlyn and Henry stepped into the Hummingbird Café. Henry had barely spoken on the ride over. Caitlyn hoped it was because he was still sleepy. With the perfect weather, she took a seat at the bistro table outside.

"Good morning, welcome to the Hummingbird Café."

Caitlyn looked up at the older woman who'd offered the friendly welcome. "Thank you. This is our first time here." Caitlyn tilted her head toward the ball pit where Henry was laughing. Her shoulders relaxed.

"Is that your son?" the woman asked.

"Yes, that's Henry."

"I'm the owner—Sally Raphine." She extended her hand.

"Caitlyn Calloway," she said with a smile.

"Oh, yes, I've heard all about you. I'm sorry I haven't been able to come over to help with the renovations. The restaurant keeps me pretty busy."

Caitlyn waved her hand. "Please don't even think about that. I'm grateful to everyone in the town. They've gone above and beyond to help me get the house ready to sell." Caitlyn could never repay them for their kindness.

"So what I've heard is true? You're going to sell the property?" Sally's pleasantness seemed to fade. "I thought since it was your childhood home, you might change your mind."

Caitlyn considered the woman's remarks. If she stayed in Bluebell much longer, her decision to leave would only become more difficult. Henry's growing attachment to the town and its people caused her concern. "No, that's not an option. My life and my business are in Wyoming."

Sally pulled a stubby pencil with no eraser from behind her ear, along with the pad of paper from the pocket on her apron. "I understand. Now, what can I get you?"

"Henry will have an order of your famous French toast."

"And what would you like?"

The discussion about going home had soured Caitlyn's appetite. "I'll just have some black coffee, thank you."

Sally nodded. "Let me know if you change your mind. I'll be back with Henry's food shortly." Sally hurried off to the elderly couple who took a seat at the opposite end of the patio.

Caitlyn considered Sally's remarks. She realized Bluebell was the perfect place to raise Henry. But how could she uproot her business and move? If she didn't sell Last Dollar, how would she be able to pay off all the medical bills and past-due rent? She couldn't leave Wyoming without making things right with her landlord.

Considering such a move would only distract her from the plan to get the house ready to sell.

Caitlyn gazed over at the ball pit. Henry was playing with a little boy and girl who looked to be his age. Her heart squeezed, watching him frolic among the colorful balls. Even if it was for the moment, thoughts of Donald were far from his mind, and he was enjoying just being a little boy. With Henry's birthday coming up the last week of June, maybe she could bring him to the café to celebrate.

"Good morning. This is a pleasant surprise."

The familiar, deep masculine voice drew Caitlyn's attention from Henry. She looked up. Logan towered over her table, dressed in jeans and a T-shirt. He tipped the brim of his cowboy hat.

"Do you mind if I join you?" he asked.

Caitlyn's response to Logan's casual appearance was a little unnerving. Lately, the more she was around him equated to wanting more time with him. That couldn't be a good thing. "Of course, please, have a seat."

Logan slipped into the chair next to hers. His clean scent caught up in the breeze. He sure smelled good. She wished she'd taken the time to make herself a little more presentable. If she'd known she was going to see Logan, she might have even put on a touch of makeup.

Logan tilted his head toward the ball pit. "It looks like Henry's having a good time."

"Yes, he is now. I had to drag him here and bribe him with French toast."

"Well, you brought him to the right place. Sally has the best French toast in the state."

Caitlyn nodded. "That's what I hear."

"So why wasn't Henry interested in breakfast this morning?"

"I'll give you one guess." Caitlyn gave a forced smile.

"Donald."

Caitlyn nodded her head. "He can't get his mind off of her. I think part of the reason he didn't want to come for breakfast is because his stomach has been upset the last few days. At first I thought he had a stomach bug, but then I realized the poor little guy is worrying himself sick over Donald's disappearance. Do you think she'll come back to the pond?"

Logan shrugged his shoulders. "It's hard to say. It's been her home for quite a while, so unless she got injured during the storm, I can't see her not returning."

"I need to get his mind focused on something

other than that duck." She gave him a look with hopes of an answer.

"What's on your agenda for today?"

Caitlyn explained her plans to help Nellie with the church potluck supper. "I'd hoped Henry would be happy to spend some time with the Garrisons' farm animals today, but even that didn't get him excited."

Logan paused for a moment. "I'd like to run something by you, but think about it before you answer. Either way, you won't hurt my feelings."

Caitlyn couldn't imagine what Logan had in mind. She was desperate. "What is it?"

"How about after breakfast I take Henry over to my house? I planned to work with Sophie for a couple of hours this morning. Next week, she transitions to her new handler, so I have to make sure she's ready for the job. It might be good for Henry to learn what's involved with training a dog."

Caitlyn's first instinct was thanks but no thanks. After the hailstorm drama, she was uncomfortable letting Henry out of her sight. But she knew that was unrealistic, especially when they head home to Wyoming and he went back to school. The bigger reason for her hesitation was spending time with Logan. Henry longed for a father figure. In Henry's eyes, Logan was the perfect person to fill those shoes. Honestly, the more time with Logan, Caitlyn was feeling the same—another reason to say no.

Silence lingered at the table before Logan spoke again. "So? What do you think?"

Caitlyn twisted a strand of hair. "I don't know—with his stomach and all."

Logan laughed. "What if we make a deal?"

"What's that?" Caitlyn wasn't sure about making another deal with Logan.

"If Henry shows any signs of feeling sick, or not wanting to be with me and Sophie after fifteen minutes, I'll bring him back over to the Garrisons'? If he's having a good time and wants to stay, we can meet up at Mr. Pepperoni for lunch. Around one o'clock? Or you can text me when you're finished cooking with Nellie."

Caitlyn glanced in Henry's direction. He was still enjoying time with his new friends. For the past twenty minutes, Henry hadn't displayed signs of any stomach ailment. Instead, he was just having fun for a change. Caitlyn turned back to Logan.

"Come on, what do you say?"

A gorgeous smile parted his lips and she

caved. How could she say no to such a generous offer? The man obviously had a busy schedule, but he wanted to take the time out of his day to help Henry—to help her. Just like everyone else in Bluebell. With each day that passed, the love she felt from this town continued to tug at her heartstrings. "Okay, but first we have to ask Henry."

Logan nodded. "You're the boss."

Moments later, Sally brought Henry's breakfast to the table, along with her cup of coffee.

"Hi, Logan. It's good to see you this morning. Would you like some breakfast?"

"Hey, Sal. You know me. I will never say no to your French toast. I'll have that with a side order of hash browns and a large black coffee, please."

"You got it." Sally hurried back to the kitchen to put in the order.

Caitlyn motioned for Henry to come and eat. At first, he hesitated, but when he saw Logan at the table, he flashed a big grin and climbed out of the ball pit. He waved goodbye to his friends and raced over.

"Hi, Mr. Logan! I didn't know you were going to be here!" Henry pulled out a chair in front of his breakfast and flopped down. "Any sign of Donald?"

Caitlyn expelled a heavy breath. The ball pit had proved to only be a temporary distraction from Henry's fixation on Donald.

"No, not yet, but be patient. I think she'll come around."

"But it's been a long time since the storm," Henry said.

"Give her time, buddy. Did you have fun over there?"

"Yeah, but those kids had to go soon. Their mom and dad are taking them to the zoo in Denver."

Caitlyn's ears perked up. "That sounds like fun. Maybe we can do that before we go back to Wyoming." Caitlyn noticed Henry's expression sadden. He wasn't in a hurry to go back home. Especially if he couldn't see Donald before he left.

"Yeah, the zoo in the city is pretty cool, but your mom told me you're going to see some animals yourself today." Logan turned to Henry. "The Garrisons have quite a few critters. I think you'll enjoy your visit."

Henry shrugged his shoulders. "Yeah, I

guess it'll be okay, but I'd rather be out looking for Donald."

"Well, if you're not excited about going to the Garrisons', maybe you'd like to come with me." Logan paused when Henry bounced up and down in his chair.

"Yes! I'd rather go with you."

Caitlyn and Logan laughed at the same time.

"You don't even know where I'm going," Logan said.

"I don't care. Anywhere you go is fine with me as long as we're together."

Caitlyn's heart squeezed. She could feel Logan's eyes on her. Was she wrong in allowing this attachment Henry had for Logan to grow stronger? And if it was wrong, what did she plan to do about it? But she had an even bigger problem. What on earth did she plan to do about her own growing attachment to Logan?

HENRY TOOK A leap from the back seat of Logan's pickup. He turned with a giant smile. "Your truck is the coolest! Mom never drives with all the windows down. That was fun!"

Logan laughed and rested his hand on Henry's shoulder. "That's the best way to listen to country music—turned up, with the windows open, while driving down a country road. It's my favorite way to clear my mind."

"Clear your mind?" Henry looked up.

Logan would like nothing better than for Henry to live his life problem free. To have his biggest worry be a missing duck. But that wasn't how life worked. "You know how sometimes your head gets full of so many things you can't think straight?"

"Yeah, I know what you mean," Henry responded, sounding older than his years.

"How old are you again?" Logan joked.

"I'll be eight in three weeks," he announced proudly.

Logan made a mental note to ask Caitlyn if she had anything planned for Henry's birthday. If she gave the okay, there was nothing he'd like more than to throw him a surprise party. The kid needed some fun in his life. "So, what's on your mind these days, buddy?"

"Donald."

"What else?" Logan was curious what filled Henry's thoughts.

"Since Mom inherited the house, I keep thinking how cool it would be if we could move here. Every time I mention it to her, she tells me it's impossible. Do you think so?"

Logan didn't want to contradict anything Caitlyn had said to Henry. "Let me turn that question around to you." Logan challenged Henry, "Do you think it's impossible?"

Henry bit on his lower lip and crinkled his brow. "Before we came to Bluebell, I learned in Sunday school nothing is impossible with God. Would it be wrong for me to pray that Mom changes her mind and keeps the house so we can live here?"

Funny, after spending so much time with Caitlyn, Logan had prayed for the same thing last night. "If that's what's in your heart, it's not wrong. The more you can reveal your heart to God, the more he'll understand what's best for you."

"So I can keep praying that Mom will change her mind?"

Logan turned and reached for Henry's hand to head toward the paddock. "I think that would be okay."

Logan didn't share his heart with Henry, but he planned to continue praying for the same thing.

Once inside the gated area, Sophie ran straight to Henry.

"Sophie is such a cool dog. I'd love to have

one like her." Henry giggled as the dog covered his hands in sloppy kisses.

"Maybe one day you will, but you have to make sure you're ready to handle all the responsibilities that come with dog ownership."

"You mean like feeding it and walking it?"

Logan nodded. "Yes, but taking care of a dog involves more than that. If you're going to be a dog owner, you want to train the dog yourself or by a professional."

"Like you? Maybe if Mom lets me get a dog, I can let you train it," Henry suggested. "How long have you been training Sophie?"

The first day the volunteer puppy-raiser had brought Sophie to the ranch, Logan had fallen in love with her. He'd realized instantly she had the intelligence and temperament to be a great service dog. "I've been training Sophie formally for the last several months."

"Wow! She must know a lot by now."

"She's been a quick learner, haven't you, girl?"

Sophie barked and Logan reached to give her a good head rub.

"Aren't you training her to be somebody's eyes?"

"You're exactly right."

"What did you teach her first?" Henry fired off another question.

Logan liked Henry's curiosity. "First, I did the basic obedience training and taught her how to respond to verbal and physical cues. Once she learned those skills, I taught her how to navigate safely in different environments. Since the handler of Sophie won't be able to see what's around her, I had to train the dog how to stop at curbs, steps and other potential hazards."

Henry got down on the ground in front of Sophie. "You must be really smart." Sophie responded by covering Henry's face with wet kisses. Henry giggled. "When do you have to give her to that lady?"

Logan was confident Sophie was more than ready to take over the role of a professional service dog. "I take her to Denver next week."

Henry scratched Sophie underneath her chin. The dog flopped to the ground, rolled over onto her back, her legs up, and wiggled, waiting for a belly rub. Henry complied. "Isn't it hard to give the dogs away to strangers? I hardly know Sophie and I don't want her to leave. I can't imagine how you must feel."

Henry was an intuitive little boy. "You're right, it is difficult to let go of a dog after you've spent so much time with them. But it makes me happy to know all the good the dog will do for their new handler by enhancing their independence and safety. Keeping all of that in mind makes it a lot easier to say goodbye."

"That's cool you help people like that," Henry said.

Logan joined Henry on the ground and rubbed Sophie's stomach. She thanked him by wiggling faster and licking his hand. "Sophie is the one who does all the work and will continue to work hard. I only get her started off with the proper training."

"Boy, I sure wish I lived here. You could teach me everything you know and I could help you." A melancholy smile tugged at the corners of Henry's mouth.

If Logan could purchase the land from Caitlyn, he could use an enthusiastic helper like Henry to move forward with his dream. Logan plucked a blade of grass from the ground and stuck it between his teeth. "Can I let you in on a little secret?"

Henry's eyes widened. "Sure! I'm great at keeping secrets. As long as it's not anything against the law or anything that might hurt somebody, I guess it's okay not to tell my mom."

Logan laughed. "You're right. There are certain things you should never keep from your mother. This is a different secret. It's more of a dream." Once he'd shared his idea with his brothers, it was no longer a secret. Both Jake and Cody had been excited and supportive about Logan's potential business venture. They'd offered to help in any way they could.

"Like my dream to move here?"

Logan nodded. "Exactly like that."

Henry crossed his heart. "I promise I won't tell anybody."

"Okay, then. You know how I told you I rescued Sophie from an organization before I trained her?"

"Yeah, I remember. We had people like that come to our school one day. The lady told us they save dogs' lives. She said some people get a dog and then decide they don't want it anymore, so they just let it loose. The rescue place gets the dog adopted before something bad happens to them." Henry paused for a moment and crinkled his brow. He turned to Logan. "Did you know my mom adopted me?"

"Yes, your mother mentioned it," Logan answered.

"I don't know what would've happened to

me if she didn't, so I think adoption is a good thing for kids and for dogs." Henry smile was wistful.

Logan patted Henry on the leg. "You're right. It's a wonderful thing. That's where my dream comes in to play. I'd like to start a rescue organization to save and rehabilitate a larger number of dogs. By training these dogs to assist people with disabilities, or by improving their chances of finding suitable homes, I can make a positive impact. There's nothing like that available to residents in Bluebell or the surrounding communities. I'd like to educate the community about responsible dog ownership, animal welfare, and the importance of adopting rather than buying a dog. There are a lot of myths associated with shelter animals."

"Yeah, that's what the lady told our class. She said some people think no one wants the dogs because they're mean and stuff."

"She's right, but it doesn't mean the animal shouldn't have an opportunity at a second chance." Logan smiled. It was apparent Henry had listened to the representative who'd visited his class.

"Yeah, my mom gave me a second chance."

Logan admired Caitlyn for opening her

heart and her home to Henry. "Your mom is pretty amazing."

Henry mimicked Logan, pulling on a piece of grass and putting it between his teeth. "I think she likes you. Maybe you should ask her on a date."

The thought had crossed Logan's mind several times over the last couple of days. There'd been moments when they were together that he'd believed she might say yes if he asked her out to dinner, but Caitlyn had her mind set on leaving Bluebell. Why bother starting something that would ultimately end? "I like your mother, too, but we're just friends.

"Why don't we take Sophie for a walk down to the pond?" Logan needed to get his mind off the idea of going on a date with Caitlyn. As much as he'd love for that to happen, it wasn't in the cards.

Henry sprang to his feet. "Yeah, maybe Donald will be back."

After a short walk, they arrived at the water. Logan and Henry scanned the area, but there was no sign of Donald.

Henry's shoulders slumped. "She's not here. I don't think she's ever coming back."

For several minutes, they stood quietly.

"Are you okay, buddy?" Logan asked.

Henry's body trembled and his eyes widened as he staggered closer to the water's edge.

Logan's eyes narrowed. "Henry! Can you tell me what's wrong?"

The boy's breath became ragged and his face turned pale.

Sophie moved closer to Henry and whimpered.

Logan dropped to his knees beside Henry. He yanked his cell phone from his pocket to call Olivia. Logan quickly scrolled through his contacts and pressed her name. He prayed she wasn't with a patient.

She picked up.

"Olivia! It's Logan. I'm at the pond with Henry, Caitlyn's boy. He's having some sort of seizure. I'm not sure what to do. Can you come?" Logan paused and inhaled.

"Of course," Olivia responded, her tone urgent. "But check his body for any type of medical alert identification. A bracelet or necklace."

Logan scanned his arm and then pulled Henry's T-shirt away from his neck. "There's a necklace!" Logan pulled on the chain and read the silver medallion. "He has epilepsy!"

"Remove the necklace and get him safely on

the ground. Make sure there aren't any objects close by that he can grab and injure himself. Try to keep him on his side until I get there," Olivia instructed. "And, Logan, stay calm. The seizure should subside on its own."

The line went silent.

Logan followed his sister-in-law's directions. His heart pounded against his chest as Henry's symptoms continued. A mix of guilt and fear consumed Logan.

Why hadn't Caitlyn told him Henry had epilepsy?

CHAPTER ELEVEN

CAITLYN RAN UP the front steps to Logan's house. Her heart pounded against her chest. When she'd received Logan's frantic phone call while cooking with Nellie, it had taken her back to the first time she'd witnessed Henry having a seizure. Guilt settled in. She should have told Logan about Henry's medical background. But she'd wanted to protect her son. He didn't want people to treat him differently because of the epilepsy, especially Kyle and Kayla. Henry only wanted to be like other kids.

Caitlyn rushed through the front door without knocking. "Where is he?" she cried.

Logan stepped into the foyer. "You can relax. He's okay. Olivia is with him in the guest room. Remember, she's the town doctor, so he's in excellent hands."

"Please take me to him. I'd like to see him." As they neared the door to the guest room,

Olivia stepped out into the hall. She pulled the door behind her, leaving it slightly ajar. "He's sleeping like a baby now." Olivia looked at Caitlyn. "Don't worry. He was breathing fine and talking normally before he drifted off to sleep. I think Logan may be the one who needs medical attention. He was white as a sheet when I got to the pond." Olivia patted Logan on his arm.

Caitlyn moved to the door and peeked through the crack. Just as Olivia had said, Henry was sleeping soundly. She stepped toward Olivia and reached for her hands. "Thank you so much for taking care of him." Her eyes shifted on Logan. "Please accept my apology. I should have told you about the epilepsy before allowing you to be alone with Henry. I know how frightening it can be to witness a seizure when you don't know what's happening."

Silence hung in the air.

"I'm going to grab my bag and head on out. Logan has my number. Call if you need anything else," Olivia said.

"Thanks for coming, Liv," Logan said before Olivia headed back into the bedroom to retrieve her medical bag.

"Why don't we step out to the kitchen? I could use a cup of coffee," Logan suggested.

A few minutes later, Caitlyn and Logan sat at the kitchen table, each with a cup of coffee.

"I can make a fresh pot if you'd like," Caitlyn offered.

Logan took a quick sip. "No, this is fine. Thanks."

Outside, the car door slammed and the motor started as Olivia left the property.

"I can't tell you how thankful I am to Olivia." Caitlyn hesitated for a moment before reaching across the table and placing her hand on Logan's arm. "I'm thankful for you, too. Again, I apologize for not being up front with you. Henry has such a difficult time with kids bullying and excluding him."

"That's a shame. Kids can be so cruel," Logan said.

"Yes, they can. But if you don't know what's happening, witnessing someone having a seizure for the first time can be terrifying, as you experienced firsthand. Henry doesn't want to be different from other children, so he denies he has limitations. Earlier this year, before we got him on a new medication to help reduce the frequency and duration of the seizures, he had a lot of challenges at school. After having several seizures in the classroom, his classmates became frightened of being around him. The last thing I want is for Henry to be defined by his medical condition. I only want him to have a normal childhood."

"Have you ever considered getting Henry a seizure dog?" Logan asked.

"I don't know if that would benefit Henry." Last year, Caitlyn had done a little research, but once she'd seen the costs involved, she hadn't bothered to educate herself any further.

"I train seizure dogs to recognize the signs and symptoms of an impending seizure. The dog can often detect a change in the child's behavior and body language before a seizure occurs. By alerting the child or those around them, the dog can provide a warning which allows the child to take necessary precautions or to seek a safe environment."

"Interesting—could you tell me a little more?" Caitlyn asked.

"They serve a variety of purposes. For example, during a seizure, the dog can offer physical support and comfort. They can lie next to the child to prevent injury, provide a sense of security, and help reduce anxiety and fear. I can even train the animal to activate alarms or devices that can alert caregivers or emergency services for help."

"That's incredible." Training for a dog like Logan described would cost a fortune. Perhaps once she paid off her debt, she could afford to look into it.

"The dog can also be trained to go for help, like what happened today. If Henry was at the pond by himself, a seizure dog can find a trusted adult or caregiver and lead them back to the child. This can be especially helpful if the child is disoriented or unable to communicate their needs effectively."

"Well, that would never happen. I wouldn't allow Henry to go to the pond alone—or anywhere." Caitlyn knew many people saw her as overprotective, especially Henry, but she had good reason to be. Today was a perfect example.

"What about when Henry gets a little older? You can't follow him everywhere he goes. At some point, he'll need a chance to exercise his independence."

"I'm not sure Henry is ready for that." Caitlyn folded her arms against her chest.

"It's not my intention to push anything on you. I guess I'm surprised you wouldn't be more open to the idea, especially after mentioning being impressed by the news story about me."

Caitlyn remained silent.

"A seizure dog can offer Henry constant companionship and emotional support. You said it yourself. Henry doesn't feel like he has friends. The dog can provide comfort during times of stress or anxiety related to epilepsy. Having a loving and nonjudgmental companion can help reduce his feelings of isolation as well as promote a sense of security and well-being."

Caitlyn shook her head. "I'm sorry, Logan. It's not my intention to belittle what you do. I know you and your brothers help many people and your company does amazing things. It's just—" Caitlyn paused.

"You don't want to draw attention to Henry's limitations, right?" Logan said.

"Well, no, I don't. I think bringing a dog into the classroom or out in public places will only bring more attention to Henry. That's the last thing that he wants." Caitlyn ran her finger around the rim of her coffee cup.

Logan straightened his shoulders. "The last thing he wants or the last thing you want? Be honest."

Caitlyn's mouth fell open.

"I'm sorry. I was out of line. It's just a common initial reaction by both the handler and their family. No one wants to draw attention to their disability, but the reality is there should be more focus on individuals with special needs. The more educated, the better we can understand the need and perhaps exhibit more empathy. Kids might not be as frightened if they know what happens during a seizure. On the first day of school, if Henry had come into the classroom with a trained seizure dog, the teacher and Henry could have explained why the animal was there and the purpose it served. Then the children would have a better understanding when and if a seizure occurred in the classroom."

Caitlyn listened but didn't respond.

Logan cleared his throat and leaned forward. "I'll say one last thing and then I'll drop it. Introducing a seizure dog as part of Henry's therapy could enhance the quality of his life. It could encourage greater participation in activities he might otherwise avoid due to fear of seizures."

The sound of a door creaking echoed down the hallway.

Caitlyn looked at Logan. "Thank you for educating me on seizure dogs, but I don't think that is something Henry needs right now. Besides, he's too young to handle a dog."

Logan simply nodded.

Caitlyn was relieved Logan didn't push the issue. "Please don't mention this in front of Henry. As you know, he loves dogs. If he thought I was even considering bringing a dog into our home, he'd pester me to death."

"Of course, I won't say anything. But I still hope that you'll give it more consideration. It really could be life-changing for Henry."

Logan had a valid point. After listening to him explain the benefits of a seizure dog, it was clear to Caitlyn that a service animal would help Henry. But the reality of the situation stared her in the face. Owning a dog cost money, especially a trained service dog. Given her current circumstances, keeping a roof over their heads was her top priority.

"Hi." Henry entered the kitchen, rubbing his eyes. "I woke up and wasn't sure where I was."

"The doctor and Mr. Logan brought you to his house." Caitlyn jumped up out of the chair. "Are you feeling better, sweetie? Why don't you sit down with us? I can get you some water or juice if you'd like."

Logan stood. "I've got some orange soda—if it's okay with your mother."

"That would be fine." Caitlyn took Henry's hand and guided him to the kitchen table.

Henry stopped in front of Logan. "Hey, buddy. I'm glad to see you up."

Henry looked down at the floor before glancing up at Logan. "I'm sorry for what happened earlier. I didn't mean to scare you."

Logan placed a hand on Henry's shoulder. "I know you didn't. You're okay, and that's all that matters now. Have a seat and I'll get you some soda."

Henry remained standing. "I didn't want Kayla and Kyle to know I have epilepsy. That's why I didn't tell you. We've been having so much fun together. I'm afraid if they find out, they'll stop liking me."

Caitlyn's heart squeezed for her son. She would do anything to cure Henry. It wasn't fair that he had to deal with this kind of challenge.

"You don't have to worry about Kayla and Kyle. You can tell them you have epilepsy. They are your friends, no matter what."

Henry glanced at his mother before looking back at Logan. "I guess they can be my friends until we go back home. I don't like it there. No one wants to be my friend. Everybody is scared to be around me."

"Oh, sweetie. I know it feels like that, but once people get to know you and learn a little more about epilepsy, they're not afraid of you. Kids that don't want to be your friend just because you have a seizure now and then don't deserve your friendship. You're a special person. Never forget that."

"I don't want to be special." Henry sat down at the table and frowned. "I just want to be like everybody else."

Logan and Caitlyn exchanged glances. It wasn't uncommon for Henry to experience these meltdowns after a seizure. Caitlyn had learned to let it run its course and eventually Henry would bounce back.

Caitlyn checked her watch. "I did not know it was this late in the day. I'm sorry if we kept you from doing what you usually do on Saturday."

"No, you're fine. Like I told Henry earlier, Sophie's trained and ready to go to her handler, so the rest of my day is free." Logan rubbed his stomach. "I don't know about the two of you, but I'm starving."

Having only coffee for breakfast and skipping

lunch while helping at Nellie's house, Caitlyn's stomach grumbled at the mention of food. "I could definitely eat," she said.

"I'm hungry, too," Henry chirped.

"How about I drive us all into town for pizza?" Logan offered.

"Yum! I vote yes!" Henry jumped up and down.

"Pizza it is." Caitlyn glanced at Henry and laughed.

Logan leaned toward Caitlyn. "You'd never know he'd just experienced a seizure."

"That's how they are, sometimes, gone as quickly as they come."

They stepped outside and the gentle breeze stirred Caitlyn's thoughts. The idea of a service dog held the promise of transforming Henry's life. Deep down, Caitlyn knew Logan was right. Her heart sank with a mix of emotions as the truth gnawed at her conscience. A veil of secrecy covered the reality of her situation and prevented her from disclosing the real obstacle standing in the way. Waiting for her at home in Wyoming was a suffocating mountain of debt.

FRIDAY MORNING, THE first rays of sunlight painted the sky in pink and gold. Logan loved the tranquil stillness of the ranch in the early morning hours. It was a perfect morning for a horseback ride. The rhythmic sounds of hooves hitting the ground filled the air. Logan glanced at his younger brother, Cody, and tightened the reins on his chestnut quarter horse, Buck. The horse was a gift to Logan from Melody.

"Are you sure that's a good idea?" Cody asked. "Caitlyn told you she didn't think Henry was ready for a seizure service dog."

Late Wednesday night, Logan had texted Cody to invite him on an early morning trail ride. Since his conversation with Caitlyn last Saturday about the benefits of a seizure dog, Logan hadn't been able to get it off his mind. Why was Caitlyn so resistant?

"I know that's what she said, but I don't think she understands the true benefits. Henry's a great kid, but his self-esteem is low. He feels so isolated by the seizures, he's attached himself to a duck because it's different, like him."

"Donald?" Cody tilted his head.

"Yeah. From the first day Henry spotted Donald in the pond and noticed she differed from the other ducks, he's been obsessed. He's been worried sick about her because we haven't seen her since the hailstorm."

"The poor kid. So let me guess. The reason you brought me here this morning is to talk about Cooper. Am I right?" Cody shifted his Stetson as the sun climbed higher in the sky.

Over the last few months, Cody had been working with the two-year-old labradoodle. A friend working for a service dog organization in Denver had reached out for more specialized training. Cody was happy to oblige, since his friend had offered support and help over the years. "Has your friend found a partner for the dog?"

"Not yet. Initially, I was training Cooper for a woman in Colorado Springs, but she recently had to back out. She said it was for personal reasons, so I didn't want to pry. I'm going forward with Cooper's training. We agreed whoever needs a partner first, Cooper would go to that person," Cody explained.

God had a hand in all of this. Cooper was available and practically fully trained to work as a seizure dog, and Henry could benefit. The timing couldn't be more perfect. "If I finish up with Cooper's training, can I choose the partner?" Logan glanced at his brother.

Cody laughed and shook his head. "You don't give up, do you? Are you sure you want to do this?" Cody flashed his eyes on his brother. "Going against her wishes might not be the best way to get her to go on a date with you."

"Who said anything about me asking her on a date?" Logan was aware of his growing feelings for Caitlyn, but had they been that obvious to his brother? Maybe so. Even little Henry had mentioned a date.

Cody flashed a mischievous grin. "Come on, buddy. Let's be honest. It's like you've got a giant neon sign hanging above your head. 'I'm head over heels for Caitlyn Calloway!'" he exclaimed, unable to suppress his laughter. "Jake and I were just talking about it on Sunday. We were watching the two of you at the potluck supper. Even Nellie can see it."

Nellie? Logan's stomach knotted. How would she know? Of course, Logan was well aware of the fact that Nellie knew everything that happened in Bluebell. "You all are imagining things. Caitlyn and I have a business relationship, that's all."

"It's obvious to me and probably everyone else within a ten-mile radius that you've fallen hard for Caitlyn. It's about time you opened up that big heart of yours. You've got a lot of love to give. Melody would want you to move on and to be happy."

Falling for Caitlyn once again was the last thing Logan had expected. Of course, the first time it had merely been a secret crush, but now, as much as he tried to fight it, Caitlyn had found her way back into his heart. He couldn't deny it—but he had to. Her plan was to return to Wyoming. As far as Logan could tell, when Caitlyn had a plan, she stuck to it. "Maybe so, but Caitlyn will leave as soon as she sells the house." Logan's heart sank at the thought. "Now, can we get back to the reason I brought you out here?"

"Right—Cooper. So, you really want to do this?"

Logan couldn't shake the lingering suspicion. Did Caitlyn's hesitation to get a service dog for Henry stem from her financial situation? Several instances flashed through his mind. Caitlyn hunched over her journal while she meticulously calculated repair costs and wrestled with the financial burden of readying the farmhouse to put on the market. "The other day, Henry mentioned he had a birthday coming up at the end of the month. I can't think of a more perfect gift."

Cody laughed. "Well, it's your call. If that's what you want to do, Cooper won't require much additional training. He's been a fast learner."

"Since I took Sophie up to Denver on Tuesday, the timing couldn't be more perfect."

"So, how do you plan to handle this gift? Are you just going to spring it on her?" Cody asked.

"I've thought about it, and I have an idea. I'm going to call her today and ask her if she has plans for Henry's birthday. It's coming up two weeks from Saturday. I'd like to host a surprise party for him at my house. I'm going to talk to Olivia today about having Kayla and Kyle invite some children from town. From what I gather, he doesn't have a lot of friends back home in Wyoming."

"A party sounds like a great idea. I can't imagine Caitlyn would say no. I can help you out with anything you need."

"Thanks. I'll probably take you up on that." Logan could always count on Cody.

"Still, I have my doubts about springing Cooper on Caitlyn at the party. What if she says no and Henry has already met the dog? He'll be heartbroken."

Logan agreed with Cody. The last thing he'd

ever do was cause Henry any pain. "Look, I haven't figured out all the logistics of it, but one thing I can guarantee is I will discuss it with Caitlyn before Henry ever sees Cooper."

Logan and Cody rode in silence as they made their way back to the stable. With only the horses' hooves echoing across the tranquil countryside, Logan was at peace with his decision to go forward with his plan. Logan hoped to ease any financial concerns for Caitlyn. He wanted to help her recognize the positive impact Cooper could have on Henry's well-being. Logan was more determined than ever to help Caitlyn, the woman who'd captured his heart for the second time in his life.

CHAPTER TWELVE

EARLY SATURDAY MORNING, Caitlyn was up before daylight with a glimmer of hope and an extra pep in her step. The past week had been a whirlwind filled with good news. Repairs on Last Dollar were moving along. Caitlyn finally saw a promise of light at the end of the tunnel. Thanks to Logan's determination and the help of a few volunteers, the roof repair was on the schedule for next week. If everything went well, Caitlyn hoped to have the house on the market after the Fourth of July. According to the real estate agent, it was a perfect time to sell since potential homebuyers like to be settled before the start of a new school year.

Besides the good news on the repairs, there'd been a heartwarming surprise. One that created a feeling of weightlessness each time it graced her mind.

Last week, a call from Logan that wasn't

about the repairs on Last Dollar had caught Caitlyn off guard. He had offered to throw a surprise party for Henry. Logan had explained how after Henry had mentioned in passing that he had a birthday coming up, he couldn't get it off his mind. Henry deserved to have a surprise party thrown in his honor with all of his new friends from Bluebell in attendance. Logan's thoughtfulness overwhelmed Caitlyn. The only problem was how would she be able to keep it a secret for the next two weeks? Henry was a curious little boy, and he always seemed to have his eyes and ears open to catch items.

Footsteps pitter-pattered in the hall, heading toward the kitchen. Caitlyn glanced up from her cup of black coffee and journal. She pushed her chair away from the table and stood, placing her hand to her chest. Henry came toward her, already dressed for the day.

"Well, isn't this a nice surprise? I thought I'd have to drag you out of bed this morning since you stayed up past your bedtime last night."

Henry smiled. "It was fun. Thanks for letting me stay up later to watch the movie. The popcorn was good, too. I liked the cinnamon you sprinkled on it."

Caitlyn's heart warmed. Last evening had

meant so much to her. It was a special night and one that was long overdue. Lately, all Caitlyn thought about were repairs in need of attention, a depleting bank account, past-due rent and getting out of Bluebell as fast as she could. Last night proved that she'd lost sight of what was truly important. Creating special moments with her son was what mattered most. "I'm happy you had a good time. I think we need to do that more often, don't you?"

Henry ran across the room and wrapped his arms around her waist. The day she'd signed the adoption papers flashed in her mind. The opportunity to be Henry's mother had been an extraordinary gift from God. Each passing day brought Caitlyn a sense of joy beyond measure. Providing Henry with love and a stable future was a priority. It was the reason she got out of bed each morning.

"Maybe we can do it every Friday night?" Henry looked up with a grin that revealed another missing tooth.

"That sounds like a great idea." Caitlyn cupped Henry's chin with her left hand and touched his lower lip with her right index finger. "Hey, what's this?"

Henry giggled. "I almost forgot to tell you. My front tooth fell out this morning."

"I see that." Caitlyn tickled his stomach. "You'll have to be sure and put it under your pillow tonight."

"I will." Henry flopped down on the chair. "Maybe it was all of that popcorn that shook it loose."

Caitlyn laughed. "Maybe so, but I think it's because you're getting older." A part of Caitlyn would like to keep Henry at this age so he'd never grow up and leave her to have a life of his own, but that was silly. "Speaking of—I know someone who has a birthday coming up." She slid into the chair beside Henry's.

The room grew silent except for the faint hum of the refrigerator.

"Well, aren't you excited?" Henry's lack of interest in his upcoming birthday concerned Caitlyn.

Henry shrugged his shoulders. "Not really. It's just another day."

Caitlyn's heart sank. "Not to me, it's not. It's your special day. Last year you started dropping hints about birthday presents a month before. What's different this year?"

Henry squirmed in the chair. "I only want

two things, but I don't think I'll get either."
He put his elbows up on the kitchen table and
placed his hands to his cheeks.

Caitlyn was afraid to ask why he wasn't excited about his upcoming birthday. What if she
couldn't fulfill Henry's birthday wishes? Whatever it was, she'd do everything in her power
to make this year his best. She drew in a breath
and released. "Do you want to give me a hint?"

"The only thing I want for my birthday is
to see Donald before we leave. I miss her so
much." Henry looked to the bay window, as
though hoping to see Donald waddle up onto
the back patio.

Caitlyn had had a feeling Donald would be
one of the two wishes. Unfortunately, she didn't
know how to bring the duck back. Logan had
assured her that eventually Donald would return to the pond. But how could he be so sure?
What if by the time the duck came back she and
Henry are long gone? Maybe she could fulfill
his second wish. "What's the other, sweetie?"
She held her breath.

Henry paused. "To never leave Bluebell," he
blurted. "I wish we could move into Last Dollar
and make it our home, like it was yours when
you were little. Please. Why can't we?"

"I've explained why that's not possible, sweetie." The joy she and Henry had experienced the night before was now a distant memory, replaced by the challenges of life. Caitlyn wanted nothing more than to give Henry everything his little heart desired. "Would you like pancakes for your breakfast? We have time before I take you over to the Garrisons'." Caitlyn needed something to keep her mind busy.

The plan was to speak with Nellie in private about Henry's epilepsy before dropping him off to help her with the store inventory. She and Logan would then meet in secret about Henry's birthday party. That's what she kept telling herself, but her heart tried to convince her that this meeting was something more.

Henry looked up. His hair nearly covered one eye. "Can I have chocolate chips?"

Caitlyn made a mental note to add "get Henry's hair cut before the party" to her to-do list tucked inside her journal. "Of course you can."

"Do you think after I finish helping Mrs. Garrison in the store, Mr. Garrison will let me play with some of their animals? He told me the other day they were getting a couple more baby goats." He stared off into the air. "I sure wish we could get a goat."

"I'm sure you'll be able to play with the animals. Just promise me you'll be on your best behavior." Her gentle reminder wasn't necessary. People often complimented her on Henry's good manners.

Caitlyn got up from the table and kissed the top of Henry's head. "I'll get those pancakes going."

Over the next twenty minutes, she kept busy cooking Henry's breakfast, but her thoughts were on her date with Logan. Wait a minute— this wasn't a date. It was simply planning her son's surprise birthday party. Nothing more. She bit her lower lip and twisted a strand of hair. But if it was only a planning session, why was she so worried about choosing the right outfit to wear?

An hour later, Caitlyn's stomach twisted when she stepped inside the Hummingbird Café. Before leaving Luke's house, she'd spent ten minutes staring at her outfits hanging in the closet. She finally decided on her pink sundress paired with white wedged-sole sandals. Caitlyn wasn't sure why, but she wanted to look especially nice for her meeting with Logan. Who was she kidding? She knew why.

Caitlyn ignored her rapid pulse and panned

her eyes around the crowd enjoying an early lunch. The aroma of sweet onions and steak teased her senses. Having skipped breakfast with Henry, her stomach protested in rumbling response.

The sound of a chair screeching across the walnut wood-plank flooring drew Caitlyn's attention to the far corner of the restaurant. She spotted Logan standing. Her palms moistened when she noticed he was holding a cluster of white and pink forget-me-nots. Feeling as though her feet weren't touching the floor, she floated closer to his table.

With his head slightly tilted, Logan offered her the flowers.

"These are gorgeous. I rarely see them in other colors besides blue." Caitlyn accepted the gift. "Thank you." Her voice shook as their eyes connected.

Logan nodded, his lips parted. "They match your dress." He did a quick once-over of her outfit and his cheeks blushed with color. "You look beautiful."

"Thank you," Caitlyn stuttered. "I can't remember the last time I got dressed for a da—"

Logan stared down into her eyes. "It's okay. You can call it a date." Logan smiled and pulled out the chair directly across from where he'd sat earlier.

Caitlyn's face felt hot as bacon grease in a sizzling skillet. How could she have called it exactly what it wasn't? But if it wasn't a date, why couldn't she stop thinking about what it would be like if Logan kissed her? Caitlyn settled into her chair before her legs gave in from under her. Logan followed her lead. "I'm sorry. I shouldn't have said that."

Logan leaned in. "You didn't. I did. And to be completely honest, it felt great to say it." His eyes twinkled.

What was happening? So Logan thought it was a date, too? Had they both concluded this was indeed a date? She paused and recalled her earlier actions. Preparing for her meeting with Logan, she'd carefully applied her makeup and had taken extra time picking out the outfit she would wear. Her body temperature rose at the realization that she was on her first date since the breakup with Jeffrey. Logan was right. Calling it a date felt great.

AN HOUR AFTER Logan first pulled out the chair for Caitlyn and the two admitted they were on a date, the atmosphere turned playful. Over lunch and copious amounts of sweet tea, they each shared stories about their pasts.

Time was like a horse out of the starting gate. Logan wanted the afternoon to go on forever. He wanted to learn everything possible about Caitlyn Calloway. What were her dreams? Did she want more children? But the guise of their so-called meeting had to be addressed. Henry's party. Truth be told, Logan already had everything under control—almost everything. The one thing that did matter was discussing his gift to Henry. He had to find the perfect segue. Logan agreed with Cody. Springing the dog on Caitlyn at the party was definitely a way to backfire his entire plan.

"I suppose we should do a little party planning." Caitlyn dabbed her lips with the cloth napkin.

How did she do that? It was as though she'd read his mind. Had Caitlyn also read the part where he wondered what it would be like to kiss her? "You're right." Logan watched Caitlyn remove the ubiquitous journal from her bag. "I wondered when that would make an appearance," Logan laughed.

"I couldn't sleep last night, so I made a list of things I need to pick up at Garrison's. If they don't have some items, I'll make a trip to Denver since I need to do a little clothes shopping."

Logan's ears perked up at the mention of Caitlyn traveling to Denver. "Maybe we could go together."

"You're already doing enough. Henry and I can go."

Logan took in a couple of deep breaths. "Really, it's not a problem at all." It was a problem if he couldn't take her. The idea of Caitlyn and Henry going alone to Denver didn't sit well with him. But if he told her the reason, she might think he was acting irrational. Denver was a safe city, but after what had happened to Melody, Logan doubted whether any city was safe. As silly as it sounded, if Logan had his way, everyone he loved would stay in the safe little town of Bluebell and never leave.

"Why don't we go over the list I made first and go from there?" Caitlyn suggested.

Caitlyn opened the journal. They both leaned in at the same time and their heads bumped.

"Sorry," they said in unison, laughing.

Logan enjoyed the proximity to Caitlyn. He could smell her shampoo. It reminded him of the honeysuckle back in Virginia.

"The good news is I've already taken care of

most of what you covered on your list." Logan continued to scan the numerical listing, running his finger down the page.

Caitlyn took a pen from her bag and double-checked the list. "So you have already sent out the invitations and ordered the cake?"

Logan nodded. "Yes, ma'am, that's all done. I didn't think it would be fair for me to offer to throw a party for Henry at my house and then dump all the preparations on you."

"Maybe not, but he is my son. I can't expect you to do all the work." Caitlyn pulled away, creating a little distance between them.

"I'll be honest. I sent a few text messages, but once I told Nellie to spread the word, the entire town was aware of the party in under an hour." Logan grinned. "Besides, I've left you with the most important job that didn't make your list."

Caitlyn gazed down at the page before looking back up at Logan. She tapped her finger against her lower lip. "I'm afraid to ask what that might be."

"While preparing for the party, it's imperative you keep it a secret from Henry. You've probably already realized that Bluebell is a town where everyone seems to know what's going on. Of course, some, who shall remain nameless, make a point of knowing more about their neighbor's private life than others." Logan smirked.

Caitlyn chuckled. "I'll do my best to keep Henry in the dark. It won't be easy, though. He doesn't seem to miss a thing. I've made a point of not leaving my journal lying around, even though he's never showed much interest in what I write."

"I think as long as we do our communications about the party through text messages, we should be okay. Since I'm taking care of purchasing all the party supplies, you don't have to worry about Henry finding anything around Luke's house."

"I wanted to discuss that with you." Caitlyn leaned back in her chair. "Can you keep a tally of all of your expenses for the party so I can reimburse you?"

Logan had expected some pushback from Caitlyn. "No way. This party was my idea, so I am paying for everything. Henry is a great kid, and he deserves a special day."

Tears sprung from Caitlyn's eyes. She quickly grabbed her napkin.

"What's wrong? Why are you crying?" Logan placed his hand on Caitlyn's arm.

"I'm sorry. This is embarrassing." She wiped her face with the napkin. "It's just—I can't tell you what this means to me. Henry has so many challenges in his life. It's nice to know someone else cares."

"There are many people in this town who care for Henry—and for you. Maybe you don't realize it, but it's true," Logan told her.

Caitlyn nodded her head slowly. "I'm starting to see that, but my concern is Henry's growing attachment to you and this community. It's going to be difficult for him when it's time to leave."

"What about you?" Logan kept his eyes focused on Caitlyn. "Do you have any feelings about leaving?"

Caitlyn slowly shook her head. "I don't have any other option."

"Can I get you both some more sweet tea?" The young waitress holding a pitcher of tea slipped up to the edge of the table, catching them off guard.

Logan watched as Caitlyn's shoulders relax in relief at the opportunity to change the subject.

"I'd love a refill." She pushed her glass toward the pitcher.

"Same here," Logan responded.

The waitress refilled the glasses and moved to another table.

Logan glanced at his watch. He was running out of time. There was no easy way to bring up the subject of Cooper, other than to just say it. "There's something else that's not on your list that I need to talk with you about."

Caitlyn took a sip of her tea. "Let me start a new page." She placed her finger on the paper, but Logan touched her hand so she couldn't turn the page.

"No, this doesn't need to be written. It's about my gift to Henry."

Caitlyn's eyebrow squished together. "But the party is your present. It's the most special gift he'll receive."

"Not necessarily. There's something I can give to Henry and to you that's far greater than any party I can host. I know you said no when I mentioned it before, but I hope once you hear me out, you'll change your mind."

Caitlyn picked at the corner of her journal. "I assume you're referring to the seizure dog?"

Logan nodded. "Yes, but there's something I need to ask you. I hope the question won't offend you, but I have to know. Is the only reason you said no to Henry having a service dog because of financial reasons?"

Caitlyn's expression went blank, and she turned away.

Logan had his answer. He had assumed that was why. The subject of money was never easy to discuss, but he had to try. Logan reached and took her hand. "You can talk to me. There's nothing to be ashamed of. I'm your friend and I'd like to help you."

Caitlyn faced him again. She hesitated for a moment before straightening her shoulders. "I'm broke." She picked up her glass and drained the last of the tea. "That's the reason I have to sell Last Dollar, because I'm down to my last dollar." She half laughed. "That's a bit of an exaggeration, but I'm pretty close. Despite the health coverage I have for Henry, since his diagnosis, the medical bills have nearly sent me into bankruptcy. I'm behind on my rent. Our landlord has been patient with me, but if I don't catch up soon, Henry and I are going to lose our home."

Logan's stomach turned. It was worse than he'd imagined. "I can help you."

Caitlyn wiped her eyes. "You've done so much already. You and everyone in this town have helped me get the house ready to put on the market. But the financial situation is my problem and I have to fix it."

Logan understood Caitlyn's determination to maintain her independence. "I admire you for everything you're doing to give Henry the best life, but you don't have to do it on your own. A service dog could benefit him and possibly help to reduce some of your unexpected medical bills, particularly with the emergency room visits."

"I'll be honest with you. I've researched those benefits, so I know what you say is true. But I've also researched the cost involved in training a dog to help someone like Henry. There's just no way I could afford that right now."

"But that's where you're wrong." Logan leaned closer to Caitlyn. "With God, all things are possible."

For the next fifteen minutes, Logan provided Caitlyn with the backstory on Cooper, and how the dog had become available. He had to give her credit. Caitlyn listened intently and even scribbled down a few notes in her journal.

"So, Cooper has had the training to work as a seizure dog?" Caitlyn asked.

Logan nodded. "Yes, pretty much. I've been working with him, but he's as ready as he's going to be to transition to his handler."

Caitlyn sat quietly for a moment.

Logan was aware Caitlyn didn't want to be anyone's charity case. She had a lot of pride, so it was important for him to make things clear. "The organization who initially trained Cooper operates on donations from individuals and corporations. It's their business to train and gift the dogs to people in need of a service dog. So, if you don't take Cooper, someone else will. And that person won't pay anything either."

Caitlyn stared straight ahead, processing the information Logan had provided. Countless emotions moved across Caitlyn's face, but he couldn't get a feel for which direction she was leaning, so he waited patiently for a response.

"When can I meet Cooper?" Caitlyn smiled.

Hope flamed like a lighthouse keeper's oil lamp. Having Caitlyn agree to meet Cooper was the first step in his plan to keep Caitlyn and her son in Bluebell. Of course, having her say yes to his offer to buy Last Dollar was a big jump from saying yes to meeting a service dog. But Logan had faith and a plan. Caitlyn wasn't the only one keeping a to-do list. At the top of Logan's list was convincing Caitlyn to stay in Bluebell.

CHAPTER THIRTEEN

"WHY ARE WE walking to Mr. Logan's house? Wouldn't it be a lot faster just to drive over there?" Henry inquired.

Caitlyn lost her footing as they climbed the grassy path that connected Luke's home to Logan's property. Following two weeks of party planning, the big day had arrived. She could hardly contain her excitement. When her foot slipped a second time, she clenched her teeth. She should have worn her flat sandals or maybe even tennis shoes, but she'd decided on the wedge-heeled sandals because they looked better with her outfit. She'd wanted to look good for Logan. "It's such a nice day today I thought you'd enjoy a walk. Plus, it's your birthday. I want to spend as much time as possible with you." Caitlyn reached for Henry's hand.

Henry looked up at her. "I guess walking isn't so bad, but since we're doing so much of it, can we go by the pond and check to see if Donald has come back?"

Caitlyn glanced at her watch. The party would start at noon, so most of the guests were probably at Logan's house by now. That was the reason she and Henry were walking instead of driving. Last night, Logan had sent a text suggesting they walk so they could come inside around the back of the property to avoid seeing all the cars parked in the driveway. She knew Henry would be full of questions. "We don't have time to stop at the pond, maybe later. Mr. Logan is expecting us for lunch. We don't want to keep him waiting."

While they continued the hike, Caitlyn's excitement for Henry's big day grew. Last week, after meeting Cooper, the sweet labradoodle, she could hardly wait for today. The party would surprise Henry, but Logan's gift would be the highlight of the day. Henry had dreamed of having a dog and now, thanks to Logan, that dream would come true.

Several minutes later, Caitlyn crested the top of the hill. The early afternoon sun was warm against her face as she peeled off her yellow cardigan and tossed it over her right arm. The three-quarter-length striped top and jean capris provided more than enough warmth for Caitlyn.

"So where do you think Mr. Logan is going to take me for my birthday lunch?" Henry asked.

"He didn't tell me, so I suppose he wants it to be a surprise."

"I like surprises." Henry skipped down the path.

Caitlyn looked down at the bottom of the hill and spotted Logan stepping out onto the patio. He looked up as though he sensed her presence. Or maybe that was a dream. Her heartbeat quickened. Caitlyn couldn't deny feeling just as excited at the thought of spending more time with Logan as she was for Henry's big day.

Thoughts of Logan had lingered in her heart since their date at the Hummingbird Café. The repairs on Last Dollar were wrapping up, limiting her time with Logan, and leaving an ache in her chest. Only cleaning and detailing remained, which she and Henry could do on their own. How had six weeks passed so quickly?

During their time apart, Logan's words weighed heavy on her heart. *With God, all things are possible.* Upon her arrival in Bluebell, her one goal was a better life for Henry. Selling the property was the only way to provide her with a stable foundation for Henry's future. But time spent with Logan and experiencing small-town living had made her realize what was truly important. The love of family and friends mattered most. Selling Last Dollar wasn't what was best for Henry. Could she somehow keep the house? Maybe sell the land? Would that leave her with enough money to pay her landlord and Henry's medical bills? What would happen to her barrel racing school?

Logan threw up a hand and waved.

Henry ran to Logan and wrapped his arms around Logan's waist. The hug lingered.

Caitlyn closed her eyes. Warmth filled her body while her heart demanded answers. Was there a way she could give Henry his birthday wish to remain in Bluebell?

"Happy birthday, kiddo." Logan was the first to pull away from Henry as Caitlyn stepped onto the patio.

"Thanks! I feel like we've been walking for days," Henry laughed.

"Oh, come on. My house isn't that far." Logan turned to Caitlyn. "What about you?"

Caitlyn looked down at her feet. "I would have been a lot better off if I'd worn tennis shoes."

"But they wouldn't have gone as well with

your outfit, right?" Logan smiled. "By the way, you look great."

Logan moved closer and gave Caitlyn a quick hug. She yearned for his touch to linger.

"Let's go inside and get you some water before we head out for lunch." Logan placed his hand on Henry's shoulder and tossed a wink in Caitlyn's direction.

Caitlyn could hardly contain her excitement. Thanks to Logan, this would be a day her son would never forget. She watched as Henry pushed open the French doors and stepped inside.

"Surprise!" The crowd of partygoers, now like family, cheered. Their hoots and hollers echoed throughout the home.

Henry turned around to face Caitlyn and Logan. "Is this all for me?" His eyes widened in surprise and confusion.

Overwhelmed with emotion, Caitlyn couldn't speak. She followed Logan into the house.

The open space encompassing the family room and kitchen was overflowing with children and adults clapping and cheering. Their faces ignited with affection. A spark of anticipation danced in her chest, knowing that the man she was falling for had orchestrated this party for Henry. "It's all for you, sweetie." Caitlyn moved closer and gave Henry a hug.

Henry's eyes darted from one person to another. "How did they know it was my birthday?" he asked, his voice a mix of confusion and awe.

Caitlyn knelt in front of Henry. She wiped the tears from her eyes. "Mr. Logan arranged this surprise party to celebrate you," she explained, her voice shaking. "They're here to let you know they think you're pretty special."

Henry's face lit with radiance, overcome by all the attention. A large group of children raced to his side, bearing gifts and shouting birthday wishes.

Caitlyn watched with overwhelming gratitude for the love and acceptance that surrounded Henry. The townspeople had welcomed her and Henry with open arms and embraced them as if they were long-lost family. As she watched Henry's face beam with joy, a sense of peace overpowered Caitlyn. Bluebell was where they belonged.

"Doesn't he look like a lovesick puppy dog?" Jake side-eyed Cody and then reached out and squeezed Logan's shoulder. Since Logan had first spotted Caitlyn coming down the hill, he hadn't taken his eyes off her. His mind swirled with thoughts of hosting future birthday parties for Henry—together, maybe with a couple of their own kids. Earlier, when they'd hugged, he'd sensed something different about her, but he hadn't been able to quite put his finger on it until now. He watched as Caitlyn moved effortlessly through the crowd. She laughed and connected with everyone around her as though this was their home and they were hosting the party together—as husband and wife. Could that be what she wanted, too? Oh, man. His brothers were right. He was falling in love with her. "Come on, guys, someone is going to hear you."

"It's not like everyone in town doesn't already know. Well, everyone but you," Jake said.

Jake was usually right, but this time, he couldn't be more wrong. Logan knew exactly how he felt about Caitlyn. He wanted to build a life with her and Henry. But with her plans still in place to leave Bluebell, he needed to let her know his feelings without threatening her desire to remain self-reliant.

"You can't let her get away. This is your second chance. But you're running out of time," Cody added.

Cody's words rang true. This was exactly what had kept Logan awake at night for the past week. "It's not that easy. She has her reasons for selling the farmhouse and returning to Wyoming." Logan never kept secrets from his brothers. But sharing Caitlyn's financial situation wouldn't be the right thing to do.

"You need to let her know how you feel before it's too late," Jake said. "There's nothing more I want for you than to have what Olivia and I share."

"Thanks, buddy. I appreciate it."

Logan had witnessed the change in Jake's life when he and Olivia had married. After Jake had lost his first wife, Logan had questioned whether his brother would ever find happiness again. But God had brought Olivia into his life and everything had changed for the better. And now God had done the same for him by orchestrating this reunion between him and Caitlyn.

Logan inhaled a deep breath and expelled it. "I've decided I'm going to put an offer on Caitlyn's childhood home. Maybe if she stays and rents the property from me for a while, it can give us a chance at a future together. I plan to speak with Larry at the bank about getting a loan."

"Oh, man, this is huge." Grinning, Cody slapped Logan on the back.

"You think?" Logan gazed around the room to make sure nobody could overhear their conversation. "Can we keep it down?"

"So when are you going to propose?" Jake asked.

"Hold on a second. I just said I need more time." Logan rubbed the back of his neck. "We haven't even had a first date."

Jake shook his head. "That's not what I heard. Nellie told me that Sally Raphine told her you two were on a date at the Hummingbird Café."

"Yeah, Nellie told me you even gave her forget-me-nots," Cody added.

"Boy, nothing gets past that woman, does it?" Even though Logan and Caitlyn had both thought their planning session at the café was a date, it hadn't been official. Logan wanted to take Caitlyn on a legitimate date. One where he picked her up at the door and presented her with the biggest bouquet of forget-me-nots he could hold in his hands.

"Dating is so overrated," Cody stated.

Jake and Logan laughed.

"I guess that's why you're still single with no prospects." Jake nudged his younger brother. "So, have you told Caitlyn about your plan to buy the property?"

"It's kind of complicated."

"What's complicated? You love her and she loves you," Cody said.

Logan put up a hand. "Whoa, I don't know if she loves me."

"That's not what Nellie says, but whatever. You want her to stay in Bluebell, don't you?" Cody asked.

"Of course I do." But is that what Caitlyn wanted? Was she open to the possibility of a future with him?

"Any idea on when the house goes on the market?" Cody asked.

"Since addressing all the major repairs, she will list it after the Fourth of July."

"The Fourth is a week from today." Cody's eyes widened.

"You don't say." Logan was aware of the ticking clock.

"What about her barrel racing school? Do you think she would give that up?" Jake asked.

"I could never ask her to do that. It means the world to her, but I believe there's a demand here in Bluebell. There's only one facility like hers in Denver, but I recently heard the instructor Mitchell McCain is getting ready to retire."

"That sounds like perfect timing to me," Jake said. "Maybe you should contact him to find out more details on the class sizes and enrollment numbers."

Logan was one step ahead of Jake. "I left him a voice mail yesterday. His greeting said he's out of the office and would return calls on Monday. I'm sure I'll be able to talk with him early next week."

"Caitlyn is sitting on a desirable piece of property. Last year, the Bakers' property had a bidding war the first day it went on the market. Are you prepared for that?" Jake asked.

"The market isn't as hot as it was last year, so I'm not too concerned." Logan was more worried about his loan being denied. He couldn't risk losing Caitlyn and Henry. They both had become an important part of his life. He wasn't ready to let them go.

Jake moved a little closer and spoke softer. "I don't want to be pessimistic, but what if Caitlyn says no to your idea?"

"Believe me. I've had plenty of sleepless nights thinking about that. Caitlyn and I both carry some relationship baggage. It's taken me a long time to get over losing Melody, but I'm ready to take a chance on love again. Caitlyn's last relationship left her pretty jaded. If she has reservations, I'll give her all the time she needs. But I'll do everything in my power to prove how much I love her and Henry."

Cody playfully nudged Logan's arm. "Come on, man. You've got this. Caitlyn is crazy about you."

Jake patted Logan on the back. "Opening your heart to someone is always risky, but it's worth it." He tipped his head and whispered, "You better get over there before some other cowboy tries to swoop in on her."

Logan glanced across the room at Caitlyn. She offered a sweet smile, providing him with the confidence he needed. "I'm not about to let that happen."

Cody grabbed Logan's arm as he took Jake's advice. "One more question. When are you going to give Cooper to Henry?"

"Caitlyn and I thought it was best to do it after the party, once everyone else has gone home." Logan hoped he and Caitlyn could have a little alone time after Henry went to bed. That was another reason Logan had asked Caitlyn and Henry to walk over to the party, so he could walk them home.

"Make sure you take some photos or a video. I want to see Henry's reaction," Jake said.

"Will do. Thanks for listening. And don't forget to take some food home with you, otherwise I'm going to have leftovers for the next month." Logan turned and headed to Caitlyn, who stood alone, sipping a cup of punch, staring out the French doors that went to the patio.

Logan slipped up behind her and whispered, "It's a million-dollar view, isn't it?"

Caitlyn smoothed her hair. "I was hoping you'd come over and enjoy it with me," she sighed.

Logan's insides vibrated. He wanted nothing more than to enjoy the breathtaking scenery and every other precious moment with Caitlyn for the rest of his life.

"You and your brothers all have fantastic views. I've been spending as much time as I can on Luke's wraparound porch. Hanging out on the swing makes me forget about all of my troubles—at least for a while." She smiled.

Was she spending any of that time thinking about him? Or possibly reconsidering her plan for leaving Bluebell? Logan wasn't sure how much longer he could keep his feelings for her contained. The atmosphere swirled with a sense of possibilities.

"Thank you for today, Logan." Caitlyn turned and touched his arm. "I can't tell you how much this day means to Henry. How much it means to me. You've made Henry the happiest little boy in the state of Colorado."

"He deserves all the happiness in the world." Logan paused for a moment, his gaze unwavering. "You both do."

Caitlyn stood quietly. A tear ran down her cheek.

Logan lifted his thumb to her face and gently wiped away the tear. "This is a day for smiles, not for tears."

"I know." Caitlyn shook her head. "I'm sorry, but I'm just so happy."

"So am I," Logan confided. "I promise you, the best is yet to come."

Caitlyn nodded quickly. "You're right. I can hardly wait to see Henry's face when he meets Cooper."

Logan took Caitlyn's hand. "Let's go somewhere private." He led her outside to the empty patio area. A cool breeze brushed his face as he gently intertwined his fingers with hers. "I'm excited for Henry to meet Cooper, too, but that wasn't exactly what I was referring to when I said the best is yet to come," Logan clarified while his heart pounded in his chest.

Caitlyn looked up. Her eyes shimmered with emotion. "I can't imagine things ever getting any better than they are at this moment."

Logan stepped closer. He tenderly cupped her chin with his hand. His heart pounded with nervous anticipation.

Caitlyn's eyes met his and she leaned in.

Logan softly pressed his mouth against hers. There was no resistance as she fell into his arms. He savored the delicate softness of her lips and the warmth of her breath with the hope the feeling would last forever.

Ever so slightly, the kiss grew in intensity until Caitlyn slowly pulled away and looked up. Her eyes sparkled with a newfound understanding. "I was wrong. This is better."

CHAPTER FOURTEEN

Two hours later, after the last guests had said their goodbyes, Logan's house was finally empty. While Henry played outside on the patio, Caitlyn was enjoying the lingering effects of Logan's lips against her own. She stood at the kitchen sink and mindlessly washed the dishes, reliving how safe she felt in his arms. The kiss was something she'd hoped for, yet it had caught her totally by surprise. But that was Logan—a man full of surprises.

"What are you doing over there?" Logan approached, his earlier smile replaced with a frown. "I won't have the mother of the guest of honor washing dishes." He tugged the dishtowel from Caitlyn's hand.

"It's the least I can do after the spectacular party you threw for Henry. You shouldn't have to clean up by yourself." Caitlyn scanned her surroundings. "Look at the place. It's a mess."

"If I was concerned about it, I would have taken Nellie up on her offer to clean up with some ladies from church. Don't worry about any of that now. I can take care of it later. It's time to introduce Henry to Cooper." Logan took Caitlyn's hand and guided her to the patio doors. "You go ahead outside and hang with Henry while I get Cooper from the kennel and bring him around."

Caitlyn jumped up and down, clapping her hands.

"Shh…you don't want to spoil the surprise," Logan laughed.

Caitlyn dropped her hands to her sides. "I'm sorry. I can't wait to see his reaction. It means the world to me you've done this for Henry."

"Be patient. You won't have to wait much longer. Go ahead outside with him, but don't say anything about the dog."

Caitlyn watched Logan head to the front door. She did as he instructed and stepped out onto the patio. Logan's selflessness and kindness overwhelmed her. Cooper would change Henry's life. She took a deep breath to steady her emotions.

Henry wasn't aware Caitlyn had joined him on the patio, so she remained quiet, watching him play. Her eyes watered in anticipation. This would be a moment that belonged to Henry.

Seconds later, the sounds of a barking dog caused Henry to jerk his attention away from the toy car. Henry's eyes popped wide open. He dropped to the ground when he spotted Cooper running toward him. The dog covered Henry's face with sloppy licks. "Where did you come from?" Henry giggled as Cooper rolled over onto his back with his legs up in the air.

Caitlyn walked closer, but stopped when Logan stepped onto the patio.

"Is this one of the new dogs you're training?" Henry asked. "I think he likes me."

Logan knelt in front of Henry and the dog. "You might be right. I've never seen him this excited to meet someone."

"What's his name?" Henry rubbed Cooper's belly while the dog licked his hand.

"His name is Cooper."

"That's a cool name. Is he going to help be somebody's eyes like Sophie?"

"Actually, he's trained to work as a seizure dog."

Caitlyn watched for Henry's reaction.

Henry pulled his hand from Cooper and looked up at Logan. "Like my seizures?"

Logan nodded. "Exactly like yours."

Henry bit on his lower lip. "That's good. I hope the dog helps the person."

Caitlyn fought back her tears.

"Well, I guess you can let me know." Logan looked over at Caitlyn and motioned her to come over.

Caitlyn's legs wobbled as she moved closer. The reality of what was about to happen settled in. Henry was about to receive a gift that could change his life forever, all thanks to Logan.

"What do you mean?" Henry asked.

"Do you want to tell him?" Logan asked Caitlyn.

She forced down the lump that had formed in her throat. "No, I think you should be the one."

Logan nodded. "Cooper is your dog."

Henry's face squished. "I don't understand."

Logan sat beside Henry on the concrete. "Cooper belongs to you now. He's going to help you manage your seizures."

"How can he do that?" Henry asked.

"Cooper can detect the signs of an oncoming seizure," Logan explained. "He has a remarkable ability to sense changes in your body, even before you realize something is happening."

Henry's brow furrowed. "How can he do that before I know?"

"It's hard to understand, but dogs have an incredible sense of smell. Cooper can detect the unique scent your body releases when a seizure is about to happen. When he recognizes the scent, he'll do everything in his power to alert you and those around you to make sure you're safe."

Henry's eyes widened with realization. "For real?"

"Yes, indeed. Cooper will be right by your side. When he senses a seizure, he might bark, paw at you, or even run to get help. He'll do whatever he can to make sure you're protected and taken care of."

"That's so cool." Henry turned to Caitlyn. "Did you hear that, Mom?"

Caitlyn shook her head. "I did. That's pretty amazing." Caitlyn took notice of the sense of relief that washed over Henry's face as he absorbed the information. The fear of seizures had always lingered in the back of his mind, but now, with Cooper by his side, he felt a new-found sense of security.

"But Cooper is more than just your seizure dog. He'll be your loyal companion. He's here to provide you with unconditional love and support. When you're feeling down or lonely, he'll be there to snuggle with you, play with you, and make you smile. He's your best friend, always ready to listen and comfort you."

Henry's eyes glistened with tears of joy. "I love him already." He leaned over, wrapped his arms around Cooper's neck, and buried his face into the dog's coat. "He even smells good!"

Logan pulled the leather leash from his back pocket and secured it to Cooper's collar. He passed the leash to Henry's hand.

Henry turned his attention from Logan to Caitlyn. "So, I can really keep him?"

"Yes, sweetie. Cooper belongs to you."

"But you said I couldn't have a dog."

Logan looked at Caitlyn and winked. Her pulse quickened.

"Mr. Logan changed my mind."

Henry jumped to his feet and threw his arms around Logan's neck. "Thank you! You've made this birthday the best one ever. I can't believe I have a dog of my own!"

Tears streamed down Caitlyn's cheeks as she watched the love her son had for Logan. She couldn't deny the positive impact Logan had made on Henry's life by giving him a trained seizure dog. Yet, beneath the surface of her gratitude, there was a pang of worry. She'd ignored calls from the landlord. To buy some time, she'd sent him a text message that she'd have his money soon. But would that mean leaving Bluebell? Thoughts of separating Henry from Logan weighed heavily on her heart. But an even greater weight was the thought of leaving the man she loved.

"I DIDN'T KNOW you were such a talented cupcake baker." Logan playfully nudged Cody while placing the first tray of patriotic cupcakes decorated with red, white and blue frosting on the table.

Cody slipped his hands into the back pockets of his jeans, pleased with himself. "They look pretty good, don't they? I saw them in a magazine."

"Wait until you try some of my homemade lemonade," Jake chimed in. "I was up past midnight squeezing the lemons."

Logan laughed at his brothers and took in his surroundings. The prediction of a July Fourth washout had never materialized. The afternoon sky was void of clouds, allowing the warm summer sun to fill the town square, now a bustling scene of activity.

Everything had come together, not only with the holiday celebration, but with Logan's plan. He'd invited Caitlyn and Henry to a picnic lunch with him today, since burgers and hot-dogs weren't being served until later in the day. Caitlyn had said yes and even offered to bring the food. When the time was right, he wanted to share his intentions with Caitlyn about her property. Once he heard from the bank, he planned to put in an offer on the farmhouse and the land, to give them time to explore a future together.

The kiss they had shared the day of Henry's birthday party had transformed their friendship into something more. Logan felt it, yet Caitlyn still planned to return to Wyoming.

"So have you convinced Caitlyn to stay in Bluebell?" Cody asked, draping a red-, white- and blue-checked tablecloth over a third table.

The bank had called him on Wednesday, requesting more documentation for the loan. He'd also received an update from his attorney that the home would go into the multiple listing database. "I'm going to tell her today I plan to put in an offer after I receive the loan approval. She'll list the property on Monday."

"We better change the subject. Here comes Nellie and her posse," Jake warned, and busied himself setting out liters of soda and paper cups.

The cheerful chatter of the ladies from the church grew. They approached the tables, carrying trays covered with tinfoil.

Nellie made a beeline for Logan. "You and your brothers have done a wonderful job setting everything up. Hank will be here with the flags and several banners any minute."

"We'll be ready," Logan assured Nellie.

"Has Caitlyn arrived?" Nellie scanned the grassy area where the band was setting up for the concert later this afternoon.

Jake cleared his throat and threw an eye roll in Logan's direction.

"I haven't seen her, but I'm sure she and Henry will come," Logan said.

Nellie waved her hand in the air. "Of course they will. Did you know her house goes on the market on Monday?"

"Yes, I heard something about that."

"I stopped by the farmhouse yesterday to see if Caitlyn needed any help cleaning." Nellie pinched the skin on her throat. "You better hurry and propose or that girl will be long gone back to Wyoming. Today would be the perfect day. You know, Nelson proposed to Thelma during the town's July Fourth celebration. I also have a couple of friends whose grandchildren got engaged here. Proposing marriage during the fireworks is quite romantic, don't you think?"

Jiminy crickets. Nellie's mind never stopped working.

"You know she's in love with you, don't you?"

What? Wait. Had Caitlyn said something to Nellie or was the woman simply sharing her opinion? Either way, Logan was desperate and running out of time, so he couldn't ignore her comment. "Did she tell you that?"

Nellie quickly covered her mouth. "Oh, mercy. I wasn't supposed to say anything." She glanced over her shoulder and stepped closer. "Promise you won't let her know I said something."

Logan put up his hand. "I promise." He rolled his shoulders, waiting for an answer.

"The poor girl is smitten with you. She told me she'd like to stay in Bluebell, but she has some financial reasons that make it impossible.

That's why she needs to sell the house." Nellie turned to the sound of a dog's bark. "Oh, goodness, here comes Caitlyn and Henry now. Please don't mention our conversation."

Nellie scurried off in the opposite direction of Caitlyn. Her face flushed in red.

Caitlyn wants to stay in Bluebell. Why hadn't she told him?

"Hi, Mr. Logan! Happy Fourth of July!" Cooper pulled Henry to Logan's side.

"Same to you, buddy. Hey, Coop. Are you behaving?" Logan reached down and patted the dog's head.

"Cooper has been great. Even Mom said she's never seen a dog that acts this behaved," Henry huffed, trying to catch his breath. "There's Kyle and Kayla! I'm going to introduce Cooper to them." Henry took off running toward the cotton candy kiosk.

"Don't go off too far, Henry!" Caitlyn called out.

Logan spun on his heal when he heard Caitlyn. Smiling, he struggled with the emotions swirling inside him. Nellie's news had caught him off guard. He'd sensed Caitlyn might have feelings for him, but he hadn't known she'd changed her mind about leaving Bluebell. His heart raced and his mind couldn't keep up with his thoughts. There was a part of him that wanted to drop on one knee and propose this second, but he needed to stick with his plan.

"Good afternoon." Caitlyn approach, smiling and carrying a large basket.

He caught a whiff of her honeysuckle shampoo It sparked a memory of their first kiss. Dressed in faded jeans and a red-and-white peasant blouse, Caitlyn had pinned her hair up, revealing the slim arc of her neck. Her appearance wasn't helping to calm Logan's pulse. She looked more gorgeous than ever.

Logan took a quick peek inside the basket.

Caitlyn snapped it closed and playfully tapped his hand. "That's our lunch for later."

Logan jerked his hand away. "Yum…it sure smells a lot like my mother's crispy-fried chicken."

"That's because it's her recipe. Nellie gave it to me when she stopped by yesterday. Henry and I enjoyed it so much when you made it for us, I thought I'd return your generosity," she confided, her eyes shining.

Logan wondered if Nellie had passed along the fried chicken recipe before or after Caitlyn had confessed her love for Logan. A soft chuckle escaped his lips.

"What's so funny?" Caitlyn asked.

"It's nothing. I'm just hungry, that's all." Logan glanced at his watch. "If you two are ready to eat, I can finish up here and meet you and Henry at one of the picnic tables at the park in a few minutes."

"It's a date." Caitlyn winked. "I'll get Henry and we'll grab a table." She turned on her heel and went to tell Henry.

"CAN COOPER AND I go play cornhole with Kyle, Kayla and Mr. Jake until the fireworks start?" Henry downed the last of his soda and jumped up from the picnic table.

"Okay, but make sure you stay with them until I come to get you," Caitlyn instructed.

Logan was happy to see that Cooper had helped to ease Caitlyn's mind, allowing Henry to have more freedom to be a kid. He took the last bite of the crispy-fried chicken. The flavors mingled on his tongue. "Don't worry about Henry. Jake and Olivia can keep an eye on him. We can go watch the fireworks with them later."

Caitlyn nodded and watched Henry run off with Cooper.

"Your chicken turned out perfect. My mother would be proud." Logan got up from his place across from Caitlyn and rounded the table to sit beside her.

"I'm happy you enjoyed it." She smiled.

"If you cooked a brown paper bag, I'd probably enjoy it." Logan's shoulder bumped hers as he sidled closer to her.

Caitlyn laughed.

Logan took a deep breath and turned to face Caitlyn. "I have something important I'd like to talk with you about."

Caitlyn's expression turned solemn. "What's wrong? This sounds serious."

After days of rehearsing what he wanted to say, Logan decided not to beat around the bush. He took Caitlyn's hand. "I've been thinking. I want you and Henry to stay in Colorado, so we can build a future together."

A mix of surprise and confusion flickered in Caitlyn's eyes. "But I need to sell the property to pay off my debt. I thought you understood."

"I understand. That's why I want to purchase the house so you and Henry can remain in Bluebell. You can rent back from me. It can give us time to see where this is headed." Logan looked down when Caitlyn pulled her hand away.

"I can't expect you to take care of my financial problems. You and the rest of the town have already done more than enough to help me get in a position to sell the house."

Logan brought his hand back to hers, and their eyes connected. "You would still have your independence and be in the position to pay off your debt. It's no different from you selling to a stranger, except if I buy the house, you can rent from me."

"You want to be my landlord? Even knowing what a risk I am?"

"What can I say? I like to take risks." He shrugged. "Besides, we both benefit. I get rental income and you can stay in Bluebell like you want."

"How did you know I changed my mind?"

"Take a guess."

"Nellie. That woman couldn't keep a secret if her life depended on it." Caitlyn shook her head.

"You got that right."

Caitlyn's eyes softened. "But my barrel racing school and all of my students are in Wyoming. How could I possibly move everything to Bluebell?"

"I've been doing research. We can not only move your school to the Last Dollar property, but we can expand it because there is a need. The only school like yours is in Denver and it's closing because the owner, Mitchell McCain, plans to retire. I've already been in contact with him. He's offered to work with us." Logan placed his hand under Caitlyn's chin. "We'll make it work together. We only need more time."

A glimmer of hope filled Caitlyn's eyes. "Are you sure this is what you want?"

Logan nodded slowly. "I want you and Henry here in Bluebell. If given the opportunity, I want us to have a chance at happiness."

"You've already made me happy, Logan," Caitlyn whispered. "More than you'll ever know."

Logan placed his hands on Caitlyn's cheeks, leaned in, and kissed her. But this time, Caitlyn didn't pull away. Instead, they remained in each other's arms until the first fireworks of the evening ignited the sky.

CHAPTER FIFTEEN

"I COULD GET used to this." Caitlyn sipped on a glass of iced tea and settled back on the cushioned lounge chair. A chorus of crickets filled the property while an aroma of steak sizzling on the grill filled the air. She leaned her head against the soft cushion. The children were inside munching on hamburgers and hotdogs with Nellie, who had volunteered to babysit for the evening.

"Once you and Henry are permanent residents, we can do this all the time." Logan turned to Jake, who stood flipping the meat to ensure it cooked evenly. "Jake and Olivia love to host cookouts in Jake's overly expensive outdoor kitchen. Isn't that right, big brother?" Logan smirked at Jake.

Since Logan had shared his plans to purchase Last Dollar, her feet hadn't hit the ground. Moments like this evening reminded Caitlyn of the potential for a beautiful future with Logan. The warmth and acceptance she and Henry found within Logan's family and the entire community of Bluebell had left her heart full.

Olivia sat down in the empty chair beside Caitlyn's. A sense of excitement filled her eyes. "It's true. Jake and I were just saying once you're settled in Bluebell, we can do this more often. Not only is it great for us to hang out with other couples, but the kids love to have their cousins—" Olivia flushed.

Logan laughed at Olivia. "It's okay to call Henry a cousin, Liv. Right now, he might not be legally in the family, but if I have my way and this beautiful woman agrees to be my wife one day, Henry will be a legit cousin." Logan winked at Caitlyn.

"Yeah, Luke and his family don't make it back to Colorado as much as we'd like. And, of course, we're still waiting for Cody to settle down and start having a family. But by that time, Kayla, Kyle and Maddie might be off to college," Jake joked. "Okay, let's eat."

Olivia was the perfect hostess, directing Caitlyn and Logan to the outdoor table with citron candles and a large vase of forget-me-nots in the middle. Jake ferried the steaks from the grill on a platter and served everyone before taking one himself.

Logan cut into his meat and took a bite. "The steak is perfect."

"I agree," Caitlyn said after trying a taste.

"Well done, hon." Olivia patted Jake on the back.

"Thanks. I'm glad you like it." Jake placed his napkin on his lap and turned to Caitlyn. "How's everything going with the offers on your property? Any updates from the agent?"

Caitlyn had prayed Logan's loan approval would happen sooner rather than later. "There's been one offer so far, but it was way below my asking price."

"Don't worry, it will all work out." Logan spoke with a reassuring smile. "Speaking of, I forgot to tell you, Mitchell McCain sent over a list of his students who are interested in signing up for your school."

Caitlyn's stomach squeezed. "Isn't that a little premature? I haven't officially moved the school to Colorado. What if something happens?"

Logan leaned over and kissed Caitlyn's cheek. "Nothing is going to happen. Mitchell has explained the situation to everyone, so they understand. Promise me you'll quit worrying about every little thing."

"What will happen to your existing students in Wyoming?" Olivia asked.

"Fortunately, before I came to Bluebell, my class of six graduated. We had the ceremony a week before I left town. My next class doesn't start until the fall. So far only two students have registered. I've contacted the parents and explained my circumstances. They were very understanding especially after I gave them the name of another instructor close to my school."

"See, everything will work out fine. So you don't need to go home and start scribbling in that journal of yours." Logan shrugged and took a bite of his corn on the cob.

After everyone had finished their meal, Olivia and Nellie rounded up the children to come outside for ice cream. Giggles and laughter, along with the occasional bark of a dog, filled the air. The kids gathered around the picnic table with dripping cones in their hands, their eyes wide with excitement.

Caitlyn watched Henry interacting with the kids and her heart warmed. If everything went as planned, this could be Henry's forever home, thanks to Logan.

Moments later, Caitlyn heard an odd sound overhead. She looked up and blinked in disbelief as she watched a familiar figure swoop into the backyard. It was Donald. She couldn't believe her eyes.

"Mom! Look!"

Henry was the first of the children to spot the duck. His eyes widened with surprise and joy. "It's Donald! She came back because she knows I'm not leaving Bluebell!"

A wave of relief washed over Caitlyn. Even with Cooper in the picture, Henry had worried incessantly about Donald since she had gone missing. He'd believed the duck had left because she'd known he and Caitlyn would leave Bluebell and return to Wyoming.

Henry raced to the duck, but Cooper got there first. With all the commotion, Donald got spooked and flew away. Henry turned in tears. "She's gone again."

Logan jogged over to Henry and knelt in front of him. "Don't worry. Donald just got scared by all the excitement. I think she popped in to let you know she's back. I'm sure she's flown back to the pond."

"Really? You think so?" Henry wiped his eyes.

"Positive." Logan took Henry's hand. "If it's

okay with your mom, we can walk over there and look. It won't be dark for a while."

Henry spun around to Caitlyn. "Can we?"

"Of course you can. I'll stay here and help Olivia clean up."

"We want to go, too!" Kayla and Kyle chimed in.

"Jake, you take the kids. They need to walk some of that sugar out of their system." Olivia picked up Maddie. "I'll get this sleepyhead ready for bed."

Nellie moved across the patio and opened her arms. "Let me take care of this little one. I'll get her bathed and into her jammies."

"Thanks, Nellie."

"Okay, kids. Are you ready to go find Donald?" Logan asked.

"Yes!" The children cheered and Cooper responded with a bark.

Caitlyn watched Henry take Logan's hand, and they headed out. Logan seemed sure Donald would be at the pond. For Henry's sake, she hoped he was right.

As Caitlyn grabbed a couple of plates from the table, her cell phone vibrated in the back pocket of her jeans. She set the dishware back down, removed the device, and tapped the screen.

Urgent. Check your email. These letters came in the mail today. Susan

Before leaving for Colorado, she'd asked her neighbor, Susan, to collect the mail. She'd given her permission to open anything that didn't appear to be junk. "I've got a work-related email I have to take care of. I'll be inside in a minute to help you with the dishes," Caitlyn called out to Olivia.

"Take your time," Olivia responded and stepped inside.

Caitlyn opened the email and her legs grew weak. She dropped into the nearby chair. Susan had forwarded a scanned letter from the hospital. They'd threatened legal action if Caitlyn didn't pay the past-due bills in full. Susan had also sent a scanned letter from an attorney representing her landlord. He demanded all back rent to be paid or the eviction process would begin.

THE FOLLOWING MORNING as Henry slept, Caitlyn paced Luke's kitchen floor drinking her third cup of coffee. Unable to sleep, Caitlyn had left her bed at dawn. For the next hour, she'd sat on the front porch and prayed for guidance. Later, she'd returned to the kitchen table, opened her laptop and composed a response to Susan's email.

Yesterday, after Logan, Jake and the kids had returned from the pond, and confirmed Donald was back on the water, Caitlyn and Henry had abruptly left Jake and Olivia's house. She'd blamed the onset of a headache, which had actually hit her after reading the unexpected email from her neighbor. Logan had sensed she was upset and questioned her, but she'd insisted it was just the headache. Caitlyn had decided not to bring up the impeding legal action against her. This was her problem to deal with.

Caitlyn settled back in front of her laptop to clean out her mailbox. Apart from the email Susan had sent yesterday, Caitlyn had neglected to check her emails since last Thursday. Most people texted these days, anyway. She scrolled through the messages, deleting one week of junk mail that had somehow made it into her box. Her finger moved from the delete key when she spotted an email from her real estate agent. He explained he'd had to leave town unexpectedly for a family emergency, but wanted to share the written offer he'd received on Last Dollar.

Logan still hadn't heard from the bank. Why

was it taking so long? Maybe that's the way things operated in a small town. Until they approved him, Caitlyn had to consider all offers, so she opened the correspondence from her agent.

Caitlyn's heart pounded in her chest. If she hadn't already consumed a pot of coffee this morning, she would have thought she was dreaming when she read the size of the offer. Her agent explained that a developer wanted the house and all the property to open a dude ranch resort.

Was this the answer to her prayers? With all the money on the table, she could pay everyone in full and have a substantial nest egg in savings. She'd have to walk away from everything—everybody. An opportunity to be debt free was something she'd never dreamed could happen. At what expense? To fulfill Henry's desire to grow up in Bluebell? A future with Logan? What about the land Logan needed to move forward with his rescue organization?

Caitlyn closed her laptop without responding to her agent. She wrapped her arms around her stomach and leaned forward. She'd wait until Logan got his loan approved and made his offer before she declined the developer's offer.

EARLY SATURDAY EVENING, laughter and lively chatter filled the church social hall. The annual pancake supper was in full swing. The aroma of sweet syrup and coffee filled the air along with the sounds of utensils clicking against plates.

Logan leaned back in his chair and scanned the long table of smiling faces. A sense of contentment filled him. Being here with Caitlyn by his side, Henry, and his family gave him a glimpse into his future.

"Any word on your loan?" Jake leaned across the table.

Logan shook his head. "Nothing yet."

"You'll hear something soon." Jake stood. "I'm going back for seconds."

Logan couldn't shake the feeling that maybe the delay in hearing about his loan troubled Caitlyn. Since the cookout at Jake and Olivia's house when she'd developed the sudden headache, Caitlyn hadn't been herself. He couldn't quite put his finger on it, but she seemed preoccupied. Had she changed her mind?

Suddenly, a million scenarios played through his mind. He needed to know. "Let's go outside for some fresh air," Logan suggested.

Outside the church, Logan took Caitlyn's

hand and headed toward the gazebo. They took a seat on the wood bench.

"This is nice, isn't it?" Logan broke the silence. "There should be a brilliant sunset this evening."

"It's beautiful." Caitlyn shivered.

"Are you cold?" Logan extended his arm over Caitlyn's shoulder and pulled her close.

"No, just a chill. I'm fine."

The worry he saw in Caitlyn's eyes told him otherwise. Anticipation built in his chest. He needed to know what was bothering her. "Have you changed your mind about staying in Bluebell?"

"Of course not." Caitlyn squirmed in the seat. "Why would you think that?"

"You've seemed distant the last several days. I thought maybe you'd reconsidered." Logan bit his lower lip.

Caitlyn's hands trembled in her lap. "The last thing I want to do is to get you involved in my financial issues, but I can't keep this to myself any longer."

Logan rubbed her back. "Sweetie, you can tell me. No matter what's bothering you, I'm here for you."

"The hospital is suing me for the medical

bills I owe for Henry's treatment." Caitlyn's voice quivered. "They want their payment—like, yesterday."

"I know this is upsetting for you, but everything will work out," Logan said, trying to shut the door on the doubt attempting to creep into his mind.

"It's not only that…my landlord is suing me for the past-due rental income. I'm being overwhelmed by these lawsuits. I don't know how to handle it all."

Caitlyn's phone chirped. She fumbled with her crossover bag. "I'm sorry. I need to make sure that text isn't from my landlord."

"No, go right ahead." Logan looked away while Caitlyn read her message. He focused his eyes on a pair of male and female cardinals perched on the nearby ornamental pear tree bursting with white blooms.

Caitlyn slid her phone inside her bag and released a heavy sigh.

"Is everything all right?" Logan leaned closer.

"That was a message from my real estate agent."

"And?" Logan assumed there had been another offer made on her property.

"This is all so confusing. I wanted to mention

it to you, but I needed to pray about it first," Caitlyn said.

"If you don't want to talk about it, that's fine. I understand."

Caitlyn fingered the gold chain around her neck. "I've received another offer." She turned with tears in her eyes. "It's from a developer and it's more than I could have ever imagined."

Logan's chest tightened. Was she going to accept the offer? He swallowed the lump in his throat and reached for her hand. "I want what's best for you and Henry. Whatever you decide, I will support you."

"Thank you for saying that. Of course, it's tempting, but your offer is so much better." Caitlyn squeezed Logan's hand. "I told him I'd have to think about it and get back to him."

Logan's shoulders relaxed. Caitlyn wanted to stay. She wanted a chance at a future together. "Let's go back inside. I could use another stack of pancakes." Logan stood and held her hand tight. He never wanted to let go.

Later that evening, Logan had the windows down on his truck heading up the driveway. The radio played a country song about a love-sick cowboy. He smiled as the singer sang about being head over heels in love. It was a song he could have written himself.

His cell phone rang as he walked inside the kitchen. Logan pulled the device from his pocket. It was Larry from the bank. He'd sent Larry a text message that morning to check on his loan status. An unsettled feeling took hold when he answered the call.

Following a brief conversation, Logan said goodbye. At first, he didn't move or breathe. When his arm dropped to his side, still holding the phone, his first thought was Caitlyn. How would he tell her the bank had declined his loan?

CHAPTER SIXTEEN

A WEEK HAD passed since Caitlyn had reluctantly signed the papers accepting the offer from the real estate developer. After Logan broke the news the bank had declined his loan, she'd had to face the harsh reality. She and Henry had no choice but to return to Wyoming. She tried to explain the situation to Henry, but he didn't fully grasp the implications.

"Sweetie, go put on a clean shirt. We'll be leaving for Kyle and Kayla's house in a few minutes," Caitlyn gently told Henry, hoping to find some way to cheer him up.

Caitlyn had appreciated Olivia's thoughtfulness when she'd called to invite her and Henry to a farewell cookout. Saying goodbye to Logan, his family and Bluebell weighed heavily on her heart.

Henry flopped into the kitchen chair and pouted. Cooper curled up on the floor at his feet, thumping his tail. "I don't really want to go."

Caitlyn's heart ached for Henry. It would be hard for him to leave behind everything he loved in Bluebell. "Don't be silly," she said, trying to sound upbeat. "You always enjoy seeing Kyle and Kayla. We'll have fun. I promise."

"But we're leaving in a couple of days," Henry replied. "I'll probably never see them again, just like I won't ever see Mr. Logan or Donald."

Caitlyn slipped her hands into the back pockets of her jeans and knelt beside Henry, staring into his eyes. "That's not true." She spoke with confidence. "We can come back and visit. Plus, Mr. Logan said he would come to visit us in Wyoming."

Henry's eyes brightened, reflecting a glimmer of hope. "Really?"

"He promised, and you know Mr. Logan doesn't break his promises."

Caitlyn wasn't entirely sure if Logan had made the promise to placate Henry or if he intended to make a trip to Wyoming. But Logan had never given her any reason to doubt his word. He wouldn't make such a promise and not follow through, especially if it would disappoint Henry.

"Now, run along and change your shirt." Caitlyn stood.

"Okay." Henry sprang from the chair and hugged Caitlyn. "Thanks!" He ran from the kitchen. Cooper followed behind on Henry's heels.

Caitlyn's shoulders relaxed. Keeping Henry encouraged the past several days was a challenge. She had a hard enough time keeping her own feelings in check since she wasn't ready to leave Bluebell, and especially Logan.

Her cell alerted her to a new text message from her agent, pulling her from thoughts of a future with Logan. Caitlyn walked to the island, picked up the device and read the text.

Problem with inspection. Call me when you can.

Caitlyn rubbed the back of her neck. With so much going on, the inspection report had slipped her mind. The past few days had been a whirlwind of mixed emotions as she and Henry prepared to head to Wyoming. It had been more difficult for Caitlyn to believe selling the farmhouse and using the proceeds to pay off her debt was the best thing to do for Henry.

And was leaving Logan the best for her? But what other choice was there given the pending lawsuits? She stared at the text. With the repairs completed, why did her heart skip a beat when she dialed the agent's number?

Fifteen minutes later, Caitlyn sat at the kitchen table and gazed outside the bay window, watching two rabbits nibble on grass in Luke's backyard. Her mind replayed the conversation with her agent, which had left her reeling. The home inspection had come back yesterday. It revealed termite damage underneath the house. The real estate developer had withdrawn his offer. She placed her hands over her face. Relief and disappointment battled in her mind. Was this part of God's plan? *All things work together for good.* The sickness she felt in the pit of her stomach sure didn't feel so good.

The sound of footsteps entering the kitchen extinguished the loop replaying in her mind.

"What's wrong, Mom? Why are you just sitting there? Don't you need to get ready, too?" Henry's head tilted to one side.

Caitlyn took a deep breath, holding back tears. Henry stood there, wearing a freshly changed polo shirt and looking so grown up.

She smiled and opened her arms. "You're right. I do have to get ready, but I need a hug first."

LOGAN WALKED UP the hill to Jake and Olivia's house and took a deep breath. The late-afternoon sun illuminated a warm glow over the property. After Caitlyn had accepted the investor's offer, a constant ache had gnawed at his chest, knowing this day would come.

Earlier, Logan had prepared himself to say goodbye to Caitlyn and Henry, but only until he could figure out a way for them to be together again. Deep in his heart, he believed God had brought them together a second time for a reason. Knowing this had given him the strength to put a smile on his face and enjoy the cookout with his family and friends.

"Uncle Logan!" Kayla raced across the grass and flung her arms around his waist. "We've been waiting for you to get here so we can play horseshoes. It'll be me and you against Kyle and Uncle Cody."

Logan scooped Kayla up into his arms. "They don't have a chance."

"Hey, brother." Jake approached with a bottle of water in his hand.

"Let me talk to your dad for a minute." Logan put Kayla back on the ground.

"Okay, but don't forget to come to the horseshoe pit." Kayla skipped to the patio.

Jake eyed Logan. "I have to say, you don't look like a man who is about to say goodbye to the woman he loves. I figured you'd be trudging up the hill like you had concrete in your boots."

Logan scanned the patio but didn't see any sign of Caitlyn. "Come on. Isn't there some song about how goodbye doesn't have to mean forever?" Logan reached for his brother's water and took a long pull before passing it back. "You know me. I never give up."

"Yeah, I know. She and Henry aren't here yet, but I guess Caitlyn must have told you already."

Logan scratched his cheek. "Told me what? I haven't talked to her since the day before yesterday."

"That's strange. I thought you would have been the first to know—forget I said anything." Jake waved his hand.

"Forget what? What are you talking about?"

Jake stepped closer. "The investor withdrew his offer on Caitlyn's property."

Logan drew his head back. *Are you kidding me?* Wouldn't he have been the first person Caitlyn would have told? "Are you sure?"

Jake nodded. "Larry told me yesterday while I was at the bank. Apparently, the inspection report showed termites, so the guy walked. He had his eye on another property, so he pulled his offer on Caitlyn's land and jumped on the other."

"Is Larry here? I'd like to talk with him," Logan asked.

"No, he's at the bank working on some big deal, but he said he'd be by later."

"Hi, Henry!" Kyle shouted from the patio.

Logan spun on his heel and spotted Caitlyn and Henry walking down the hill. "I need to find out what's going on. Can you take Henry with you and cover for me at the horseshoe pit?"

"Absolutely." Jake patted Logan on the back.

"Hi!" Henry and Cooper ran ahead of Caitlyn.

"Hey, buddy." Logan winked at Henry and reached down to give Cooper's head a scratch.

Caitlyn avoided eye contact with Logan, but smiled as she approached. "Hey, guys."

Jake stepped forward and gave Caitlyn a quick hug. "It's good to see you. If it's okay, I'd like to take Henry down to the horseshoe pit. The kids have a friendly little match going."

"Cool! Can I?" Henry looked up at his mom.

Caitlyn nodded. "Sure. Have fun."

Logan and Caitlyn stood in silence while Jake led Henry and Cooper down to the games.

"So anything new with you?" Logan hadn't meant to tone irony in his voice, but wasn't he entitled to a little sarcasm?

Caitlyn tucked a strand of hair behind her ear. "I guess you've heard."

"About the termites? Yeah." Logan reached for her hand. "Do you want to take a walk?"

She accepted his hand. "Sure."

They strolled in silence for the first couple of minutes, listening to the children's laughter in the distance. A hawk cried out overhead.

Caitlyn spoke first. "You're right about news spreading like wildfire in a small town. I only found out about the inspection an hour ago. My agent called me. How did you hear?"

"Jake was at the bank yesterday morning. Larry told him." Logan slowed his pace and looked at Caitlyn. "So what now?"

"The place is back on the market. Henry and I will leave as planned."

Logan felt a twinge of regret. If only he'd

gotten the loan, Caitlyn and Henry could stay like they'd planned before the developer had come to town. He stopped walking and placed his hands on Caitlyn's face. "Don't worry. Everything will work out." Logan gently kissed her lips and held her close.

Caitlyn pulled back and looked up into his eyes. "Do you promise you'll come visit us in Wyoming?"

Logan ran his hands through her hair and nodded. "I've already been checking flights."

She smiled. "I guess we'd better head back."

"Yeah, Nellie might spread rumors we've run off to elope or something," Logan said, laughing, but he would elope in a heartbeat if Caitlyn agreed.

An hour before sunset, the flames on the grill still flickered while Jake and Olivia made sure there was plenty of food for their guests. Logan found solace, since most of the town had gathered to say goodbye to Caitlyn and Henry. Everyone loved them. The townspeople's somber expressions of the reason for the party mirrored his own. With Jake and Olivia's help, Logan set up a circular bistro table with a candle and an arrangement of forget-me-nots.

"I hope Jake and Olivia are okay with us

commandeering their special spot. It's so beautiful here."

"Full confession—it was their idea," Logan said.

Caitlyn's cell phone rang. "I'm sorry. I should have turned the ringer off, but with the house being back on the market, I don't want to miss a call."

"No, by all means, go ahead."

Caitlyn picked up the phone and stepped away from the table.

Logan watched Caitlyn's expression fluctuate between confusion and half smiles. By the time she ended the conversation and returned to the table, she had tears rolling down her cheeks.

Logan jumped from his chair and hurried to her side. "What is it? What's wrong?" He rubbed his hand along her arm.

"That was my agent. An offer came in on my property." Caitlyn wiped her eyes.

"It must be a good one."

Caitlyn studied Logan's face. "It's for the full asking price."

Logan's feelings were mixed. Even though Caitlyn seemed to have made peace with selling her home, a part of him still wanted her to keep it in her family. "That's good—I guess."

"You guess? Is that all you're going to say?" Caitlyn leaned forward and folded her arms across her stomach. "Logan, my agent told me you made the offer."

Logan coughed and took a drink from his glass of water. "He what? He's mistaken. They denied my loan, remember?"

"I don't understand. Maybe I better call him back." Caitlyn grabbed her phone and hit Re-dial. "It's gone to voice mail, but the box is full."

Thoughts swirled through Logan's head. Was this some sort of prank? Maybe someone had stolen his identity. There had to be a logical ex-planation. "Let's go up to the house. Larry is supposed to stop by this evening. Maybe he'll have some answers."

Logan and Caitlyn walked at a steady pace in silence, holding hands. As they crossed the property, Logan noticed the house normally lit up was dark. The crowd that had gathered out-side earlier was gone. "Okay, I feel like we're in the twilight zone. What's going on?"

Caitlyn's grip tightened on his hand. "Where is everyone? Where's Henry?" Her pace quickened while she pulled Logan along the grassy path.

Once they reached the patio, Logan flung the French doors open.

"Surprise!" Light filled the area, revealing the entire town packed inside Jake and Olivia's family room and kitchen.

Henry ran to Caitlyn. "Mom, did you hear? We get to stay in Bluebell! Mr. Logan bought our house."

Logan and Caitlyn stood frozen. The room filled with silence as Jake, Cody and Larry approached from across the room.

"What in the world is going on here?" Logan's voice raised as his eyebrows squished together.

Larry laughed. "I guess you guys better tell him." His glances shifted between Jake and Cody.

"We pooled our money and put down the forty percent cash deposit the underwriter required for your loan to be approved," Cody explained. "We started the process after the bank denied your loan, but once the investor came along with his big offer, we figured we couldn't come up with that much cash. It was all Luke's idea. He wished he could be here, but the triplets have the chicken pox."

Larry extended his hand. "Congratulations, son. You're the new owner of Last Dollar."

Cheers and applause broke out as the town stood side by side.

Logan's heart swelled with pride and humility as he realized the impact of his brothers' selfless act of generosity.

Caitlyn looked at Logan's family. Tears pooled in her eyes. "I don't know what to say." She turned. "Logan, I never expected…"

Logan gently took both of her hands into his own. A grin spread from ear to ear. "Nothing is ever impossible when you have God, family and friends by your side. Welcome home."

EPILOGUE

One year later

"I CAN'T BELIEVE our first summer camp starts in less than a week." Caitlyn closed her journal and placed it on the checkered picnic blanket.

"And you're already fully booked for next summer." Logan snuggled up to Caitlyn and kissed her neck. "Didn't I tell you, Mrs. Beckett, the best is yet to come?"

A tear trickled down her cheek. She looked up at the cloudless blue sky, unable to respond. How quickly kisses with Logan became second nature. Of course, for her and Logan, everything seemed to happen quickly.

Following their brief engagement and wedding, there'd been no time for a honeymoon. As soon as she and Henry had moved into Logan's house, Caitlyn had gone to work on her to-do list. Turning Last Dollar into an all-inclusive barrel racing camp had been Logan's brilliant idea. The camp would offer week-long stays hosting girls from all over the country during June, July and August. The rest of the year, the home would provide overnight accommodations to people interested in rescuing a dog from Logan's organization. In addition, lodging was available to Beckett's Canine Training.

"Hey, no tears allowed on Henry's birthday."

The entire family, along with many friends from town, gathered to celebrate Henry's big day. The sound of his laughter while skipping stones across the pond with his cousins brought warmth to her heart. Since the day Logan had officially adopted Henry, her son had worn an unrelenting smile. She loved seeing him this way.

"Mom! Dad! Look!" Henry pointed to the water.

Caitlyn looked up at Henry, but the sun's glare prevented her from seeing what had caught his attention in the pond.

Cooper barked at the commotion.

"Let's go see." Logan jumped up and extended his hand to help Caitlyn to her feet.

Standing at the water's edge, alongside Logan, Jake, Olivia, Cody and the children, Caitlyn placed her palm to her heart. It was Donald. She was gliding across the glistening water with eight fuzzy ducklings trailing behind.

Logan placed his arm around Caitlyn and pulled her close. "The best is yet to come," he whispered into her ear.

"This is the best birthday ever!" Henry whooped. "Donald isn't alone anymore. She has a family now—just like me."

Caitlyn smiled. She'd never kept a secret from Logan, but she wanted to share the news with him privately, at home later. Earlier in the week, during her doctor's appointment with Olivia, she'd shared some symptoms she'd been experiencing. Olivia had done a few tests, and before Henry's party had started, had texted with the results. Caitlyn was six weeks pregnant. Logan was right. Sometimes the unexpected events in life made the greatest memories.

Caitlyn whispered back into Logan's ear, "I think you're right. The best is yet to come."

★ ★ ★ ★ ★

Sunflower Farms
Redemption
Stacie Strong

MILLS & BOON

Debut author **Stacie Strong** was born and raised in Jacksonville, Florida. She and her husband raised two children, and as empty nesters, now have a soft spot for rescue cats. Stacie worked in corporate America for fifteen years before moving on to education. Currently, she is an academic adviser at Jacksonville University, where her students surprised her with the Wind Beneath My Wings award, honoring her for her dedication to students.

Visit the Author Profile page
at millsandboon.com.au

But they that wait upon the Lord shall renew their strength; they shall mount up with wings as eagles; they shall run, and not be weary; and they shall walk, and not faint.

—*Isaiah* 40:31

DEDICATION

This book is dedicated to my parents,
who supported me in every way.
Thank you, Mom and Dad.

CHAPTER ONE

"ARE THERE ANY volunteers to milk old Betsy here?" Rose McFarland asked the small crowd gathered in the barn for her talk on farm animals. Weekends at Sunflower Farms in sunny Florida were busy, and this Saturday was no different. A number of hands flew up, mostly kids, as the adults stood by and watched. She scanned the room for someone old enough to follow instructions. Her eyes landed on a familiar face in the back. One she hadn't seen in a long time.

Jesse.

His dark eyes held hers for a heartbeat. She was the first to break the contact and glance away.

Rose sucked in her breath as she calmed herself. Everyone was waiting for her to pick a volunteer, not turn to a pile of mush...

Ex-boyfriends had a way of doing that to a girl.

Rose cleared her throat and quickly selected a young boy for the task. She led him to a stool next to Betsy, then explained to the group how to milk a cow. The whole time she spoke, she was aware that Jesse watched her every move. It was hard to concentrate, but somehow, she managed to get through her speech. Whether she rushed through it or spoke clearly, she had no clue. All she could think about was her unexpected guest.

Betsy lowed at the boy's clumsy attempt to milk her. Rose reached down and helped him with his hand placement, giving him more direction until finally he was successful. Milk streamed into the bucket. With a snaggletooth smile, the boy grinned up at Rose.

"You did it. Great job. Just a few more squirts, and we'll let someone else try," Rose said absently. She pushed her long ponytail off her shoulder. Even though she was dressed in a short-sleeved gingham top and shorts, she suddenly felt hot.

When she ushered the boy off the stool, the small audience gave him a round of applause.

"We have time for another volunteer," Rose offered.

Again, many hands went up and a chorus of "Me! Me! Me!" filled the barn.

Rose shot a sugarcoated smile Jesse's way. It only took him a second or two to catch on that he'd just been volunteered. He slowly shook his head.

Rose ignored him, marched through the audience and pulled him up to the front of the group. He wore blue jeans and a polo shirt, and his black hair was shorter than he used to wear it. Somehow, he was more handsome than she remembered. How could that be?

"Hello, sir. What's your name?" Rose asked as she pulled him toward the stool.

"You know my name," he countered. His voice was deeper, more mature. He'd always been more than a head taller than her petite height. That hadn't changed. He stared down at her, his dark eyes sparkling with amusement.

She lifted her chin. "I think I've forgotten it. It's been so long since I've seen you. Something like ten years, you know." She said it loud enough for the crowd to hear, as if it were all part of the show.

Jesse played along and sat on the stool. "My name is Jesse."

"Ah…that's right. It's Jesse. Well, Jesse, go ahead and try milking Betsy. Or do you need me to show you how first?" she challenged.

"Nah," he drawled. "I think I have it." Jesse expertly milked Betsy, as if he'd milked a thousand cows before. The rhythmic sound of milk hitting the stainless steel bucket filled the room. Jesse glanced up at Rose. "There. How'd I do?"

"Great job. It's like…like you're an old pro," Rose stammered.

Come on, Rose, spit it out, she thought. Maybe it wasn't such a good idea to call Jesse out. Now that he was next to her, it was harder to think.

"I've done my share of milking cows, if you'll recall," he said under his breath, loud enough for only Rose to hear.

Nearby, a little girl begged to try. Rose realized she needed to get on with the talk and send Jesse away. When was the last time a guy had made her this nervous? Reluctantly, Rose said, "Th-thank you so much, Jesse. We'll give the next person a turn."

The crowd clapped when Jesse stood, and he gave a good-natured bow. Rose rolled her eyes. Really? Why did people always love him?

Jesse waggled his brows at Rose and treated her to a lopsided grin, then took his place in the back once again. Rose's traitorous stomach did a little flip-flop, which was completely irritating. This was the same guy who'd broken her heart once. She shouldn't give him a second thought.

Rose rushed through the rest of her lecture about cows, skipped the chickens and goats portion, and dismissed her small audience early. She had to admit, Jesse's unexpected appearance had rattled her.

A minute to collect herself was necessary. This was the same guy that had left her ten years ago. They'd been young and in love…and he'd just left. How could he do that to her? And now he shows up after all this time and expects her to be excited to see him?

Out of the corner of her eye, she saw Jesse head toward her. She ignored him and abruptly turned to lead Betsy out of the back barn door, toward the corral. Rose wasn't ready to talk to him.

"Wait up," Jesse called. He pushed his way through the crowd and followed her out.

Rose heard him but didn't stop until she reached the corral gate. She swung the door open with a shaky hand, then closed Betsy in. When Rose turned to leave, Jesse was in her path. His broad chest blocked her way.

He smelled clean like fresh soap. She hated that she liked it. Rose tipped her head back to look him in the face. "What are you doing?" she asked, exasperated.

"I'm getting your attention, since you're determined to ignore me."

"I'm not ignoring you. I'd like to point out I let you help milk Betsy. Now, if you will excuse me, I have work to do," she countered, even though he was right; she was totally ignoring him.

"I need to talk to you."

"Now's not a good time. Weekends are our busiest days, and Justin called in sick, so I'm short-staffed." Rose stepped around him and headed back to the barn with a determined step. She let the door close in his face.

Jesse was nothing if not persistent. He opened the door and walked in behind her. "I'm here. Let me help?"

Rose came to an abrupt stop, turned and glared at him. "Now you're offering to help? Where have you been the past year, since your father passed away? And may I ask, where were you when he was sick? You've been gone for ten years."

"I came back for the funeral," he protested.

"Whoopee. You deserve a medal," she said, annoyance obvious in her voice.

"I know you're angry, but you of all people know my history with him."

She knew Jesse had left to get away from his father, but Rose was the casualty of that decision. His leaving broke her heart. Then after his father passed away, he should have come back to help with the farm that he inherited. But he still chose to stay away. She couldn't help that it was a sore subject for her.

Rose shook her head. "I'm not having this conversation right now. I have work to do."

The crowd had mostly dispersed from inside the barn, but there were still a few patrons nearby who openly gaped at them. Jesse pulled Rose to a corner and lowered his voice. "If you're that busy, let me help today."

She really did need the help if she wanted the day to run smoothly. She'd be a fool to let him go. But deep down, she knew she'd be a fool to let him stay.

Finally, she gave in. Putting her hands on her hips, she stared up at him. "Against my better judgment, I will take you up on the offer. That is, if you think you can find your way around. We've made some changes over the years."

"I think I can handle it," he said dryly.

"Fine. You can help. Do you remember how to drive the tractor?"

He let out a low chuckle. "I spent more hours than I'd like to remember on a tractor. I'm sure it will come back to me. Kind of like riding a bike...or milking a cow. Right?"

Rose ignored the joke. "Great," she said. The word came out a little shrill. She cleared her throat. "Justin was supposed to run the hay-rides today. It's one of our most popular activities. You can take over for him. Let's get you a schedule, then I'll take you to the tractor."

Again, she left him in her dust as she walked out the front of the barn and threaded her way through the crowd. The gift shop was located on the first floor of the garage, and Jesse followed Rose inside. She noticed him scanning the room. They'd recently redecorated. A large counter with the cash register took up one wall, and the other three were loaded with shelves and souvenirs. The room was painted a cheerful yellow and the black Sunflower Farms sign, that Rose had designed, hung behind the counter.

"This is new," Jesse commented. "I like it. It's very nicely done."

Rose smiled. She hated to admit it, but his praise meant a lot. Even though she hadn't inherited the place like Jesse, she'd put her blood, sweat and tears into it. It was her baby. "Thanks. I'm glad you like it. The visitors park their cars out front and have to walk through the gift shop to pay for their entrance into the farm. Most end up walking back through at the end of the day to purchase something."

"Clever."

"Yes, I thought so." Rose led him to the counter. "Let me introduce you to Lolly. She works in the gift shop."

Lolly's blond head was tilted down as she counted out change for a customer. When the guest left, Lolly smiled at Rose and Jesse. "Hi!" She was always in a good mood, making her the perfect person to greet arriving guests.

"Lolly, this is Jesse. He's Mr. Cooper's son. He owns Sunflower Farms now."

"Nice to meet you." Lolly reached across the counter and shook Jesse's hand. She seemed a little starry-eyed as she gazed up into his handsome face.

"Nice to meet you, as well," Jesse said. He'd always been oblivious to the attention he attracted from the opposite sex.

"I am so sorry about your dad," Lolly offered.

"We all miss him terribly. He was a wonderful person."

Jesse shuffled uncomfortably, but to his credit, he didn't get into his difficult relationship with his father. He politely answered, "Thank you."

Rose jumped in. "Jesse has offered to fill in for Justin today with the hayrides. Can you hand him a schedule?"

Lolly pulled out one of the brochures. "Here you go. The first hayride starts in a few minutes, so you may want to head out there."

Jesse perused the brochure. "This is impressive. The farm has come a long way. Are you open to the public every day?"

"Just the weekends. People come out to see the sunflowers and for a glimpse of life on a farm," Rose said.

"I see there are a few other classes this afternoon. Rose, do you give those classes, too?"

"I do, and speaking of which, the gardening class starts soon. We need to get a move on. Let me show you to the tractor you'll be using."

Rose directed Jesse down an out-of-the-way dirt path that led to the warehouse. Her nerves were starting to calm, so she didn't rush ahead but walked next to him.

"You've been gone for a long time," she said finally. "Why did you come home?"

"That's something I want to talk to you about," he said.

She glanced up at him. Even in the bright afternoon light, his eyes were nearly black. She'd always envied him for his long lashes. Rose caught herself and looked away.

"Well, you came at the worst time," she said. "Saturdays are our busiest day."

"Yeah, I see that now. Sorry. I thought it'd be a good time to catch you." He kept his hands tucked in his pockets as they walked.

"You should have called ahead."

"I didn't think about it."

"Well, think about it next time," she chastised. Then immediately berated herself. What was she thinking? The guy owned the place. He was her boss.

But he was also her ex-boyfriend. Didn't that give her the right to call him out?

What was the real reason he'd shown up today? She'd been running everything for years. Even when Mr. Cooper was healthy, she'd taken over management of the farm. As he grew more ill, he'd put her name on the bank accounts and she'd started paying the bills and the salaries. It was almost like the place was hers.

At the warehouse, she checked her watch. They were running behind. "We'll have to talk later. For now, we need to get the hayride going."

The tractor was hooked up to a flatbed trailer covered with fresh hay. Jesse circled the tractor and trailer, examining them. He kicked a tire or two in the process. He picked up a piece of hay, twirled it between two fingers, then stuck the end in his mouth.

It reminded Rose of his dad. She'd seen James Cooper do the same thing countless times. She kept the observation to herself. No doubt Jesse wouldn't appreciate being compared to him.

"I can't remember. Did you guys ever offer hayrides when you lived here as a kid?" Rose asked.

"No, and I'm surprised that you do now. Maybe it's the firefighter in me, but this doesn't look all that safe." He tugged at the trailer's tailgate to check its security.

"Firefighter, huh?" she asked.

He looked over at her, "Yeah. Why?"

Rose shrugged. "No reason. Just didn't know that's what you'd ended up doing since you never stayed in touch with me or your dad. Anyway, the hayride is safe enough," she said. "We don't let the kids get on without an adult, and you'll need to drive as slow as the tractor will go."

She entered a security code on the warehouse keypad, reached inside and grabbed the tractor keys. She gave Jesse the code in case he needed to get back in, then instructed him about the hayride route.

As Rose handed Jesse the keys, their hands brushed momentarily. She ignored the goose bumps that went up her arm. Jesse seemed un-fazed.

"Thank you. It'll be in good hands, I prom-ise," he said as he jumped up into the seat.

"Better be."

He waggled those eyebrows at her again. "Trust me, you won't be sorry."

She had the uncomfortable feeling she would be *very* sorry. What did his unexpected appear-ance mean?

He cranked the noisy tractor. "You want a ride?" he offered over the hum of the engine.

"No, thanks. I'll walk back." She watched the tractor and trailer disappear down the dirt path, kicking up a trail of dust.

Time for her gardening class to start. Inhaling deeply and blowing out a steadying breath, she set out on her trek to the main house and garden. It was a long walk back, but her thoughts were consumed by Jesse.

Back when they dated, he was a good guy, and now he was probably quite the catch if he was still single, but Rose had her heart broken by the man once. It had devastated her. So, whatever this visit was about, she'd have to keep her distance. She was sure he'd leave again... maybe for another ten years.

THE TRACTOR RUMBLED ALONG, causing Jesse to bump and sway with each dip of the trail. From the high seat, he stole a parting glimpse of Rose and was reminded of the day he'd left her long ago.

She'd been a skinny eighteen-year-old girl, standing outside her house with tears in her eyes. He'd ended things between them and left, breaking both their hearts.

He hadn't allowed himself to think about that in years. But being back on the farm had created a tidal wave of memories. He'd stayed away from Sunflower Farms because of the bad memories of his mom's death and how his dad treated him after that. Now that he was here, it wasn't his mother or father he was thinking of.

Memories of Rose flooded back. He'd loved her, even if it was only puppy love. He'd always felt guilty for breaking up with her the way he did, so suddenly. One day they were high school sweethearts, the next he was on his way to the University of Kentucky, with no plans to look back. She'd stayed in the small town of Eagletin, Florida, to get her degree in agriculture sciences at the local university, while he had wanted nothing more than to escape from home.

Jesse shook his head to clear it. He needed to pay attention and figure out where he was going. The dirt trail ended, and he found himself in a field behind the main house and barn. The grass was short and dry, as if it hadn't rained in forever.

He followed the signs to the hayride pickup area, passing several picnic tables with families sitting in the cozy October sunshine, eating their lunches. As he passed the garden entrance, he noticed a small crowd was gathered inside. Were they waiting for Rose to give her class on gardening? Since she was on foot, they'd be waiting awhile.

Jesse rolled up to the hayride staging area. A line of people waited behind two brightly colored orange cones. He greeted them and started helping the first group aboard. The flatbed filled up quickly, and he set off on the well-worn path.

They rode through acres and acres of sunflowers, an impressive display of God's beauty in the fall, with its sea of yellow against a powder-blue sky. The blossoms had faces as large as plates and stems as tall as a man.

As Jesse drove them to the citrus grove at the back of the property, he recalled how his parents had planted seedlings when he was a small boy. Now the trees were tall and full of oranges, lemons and limes that would be ready to pick in the next few months.

The last leg of the ride had them going through the strawberry fields, finally ending in a full circle back at the hayride staging area.

By the end of the day, he'd made several trips around the property, and he'd barely seen Rose. When he did spot her, she was busy helping guests or giving classes. After only one day of observing her, he could tell she was the glue that kept the place together. But was it too much to manage by herself with his dad gone?

He'd been surprised to see her lead the talk on the farm animals. The Rose he'd known in high school had always been smart and outgoing, but now she was a self-assured, confident woman.

Later, the last of the guests drove off as the afternoon sun moved lower in the sky. Long shadows ran across the yard, and the warmth of the day was replaced with the cooler air of autumn. Jesse put away the tractor and went in search of Rose. As he walked, the scent of the land brought back vivid memories of his childhood on the farm, both good and bad.

He passed Lolly emptying trash cans near the picnic tables. "Have you seen Rose?" he asked her.

Lolly greeted him with a friendly smile, "You can try the barn. She's probably putting the animals away and feeding them."

"Thanks." Then Jesse thought to add, "Do you need help with the trash?"

Lolly seemed surprised by his offer. "No, I've got this. You go on. Thanks, though."

Nodding, Jesse strolled over to the barn. Two horses had already been put away in their stalls. They hung their elegant necks over the doors, and Jesse paused long enough to pet one of them, a brown horse with a white blaze. It nuzzled Jesse's hand, but nickered when it saw Rose round the corner with a bucket of feed.

"I know what you want, buddy," Jesse said to the horse eyeing the food.

"Try again." Rose pulled up next to him. "She's not a buddy."

Jesse chuckled. "Whoops. Sorry, old girl." He scratched her neck. "What's her name?"

"That's Missy, and over there—" she nodded toward a black horse "—that's Moe."

"They're pretty friendly."

"Yeah, well, like the rest of us, they've gotten used to entertaining the crowds."

Rose opened Moe's stall door, went in and dumped feed in his trough. Missy was next. Jesse stepped back and stayed out of the way. When she came out with the empty bucket, she stopped beside him. "I'm surprised you're still here. I would have thought the hayride would have scared you away for another ten years."

"I guess I deserve that." Seemed like she was still angry at him for leaving.

"I'd say you deserve more than that."

"I need to talk to you. It's important," Jesse said.

Rose stood with her shoulders squared and

her head held high, like a woman in charge. She tossed her ponytail over a shoulder. Little wisps escaped and fell loosely around her face. Back in high school, she'd always kept her hair highlighted blond. Now it was her natural shade of light brown. She was prettier than he remembered. In his time away from Eagletin, she'd grown up. He was sorry he wouldn't be here long enough to get to know the woman she'd become.

"It's been a long day, and I need to clean up and get some rest. We have to do it all over again tomorrow," Rose said.

"I know you're busy. Let me help you put things away, then we can talk."

Rose bit her lip as she studied him. "Fine. Did you put the tractor in the warehouse?"

"Of course."

"That's a start. Come on, you can help me with the rest of the animals."

They moved the cow—Betsy, he remembered—into a stall and fed her. Then Jesse followed Rose outside, and together they fed and watered the rest of the animals.

"What do you think of the farm now? Is it different from what you remember?" she asked him.

"It's something else. I'm dumbfounded by the changes. I had no idea I'd find it this way."

She grinned at him. "I know. It's come a long way."

"I can't get over how many visitors were on the grounds today. When I lived here as a kid, we only had the strawberry picking open to the public. We sold the sunflowers to florists, but they were never the main business for the farm," he mused aloud. "A busy Saturday back then meant a dozen or so families would come out to pick strawberries just during the season. Today, I'm sure I saw several hundred people come through. It felt more like an amusement park attraction than a farm at times."

"I can't tell if you think that's good or bad." Rose handed Jesse an armful of hay and led him to the goat pen. He scattered the fresh hay for the goats while she refilled their water troughs. The four goats followed her around bleating until she stopped long enough to pet them.

Jesse watched her give each of them attention. "It's just different from what I remember."

She straightened up and led Jesse out of the pen. "We had to do something. Your dad was going to lose the farm if we didn't figure out another revenue stream. We still sell the sunflowers and citrus, and we have the strawberry picking, too, but there's a market for the farm experience. Petting the animals, learning about agriculture, and most of all, people want to see and pick the sunflowers when they're in season. You have to admit, it's one of the most beautiful things you've ever seen."

"It is. And you've been strategic planting flower fields near the front of the farm where the guests are. Back in the day, we never had this many fields."

"It was a learning process. We've definitely adapted over the years. Next weekend is the fifth annual Sunflower Festival. Now talk about impressive, we'll have twice as many people here for that."

"It's hard to believe this place could be more crowded. I'm surprised my dad lct you make changes or have a festival. He was always so set in his ways."

They were headed toward the chicken pen, but Rose stopped and turned to study him. "I know you had a strained relationship with him, and he was the reason you left. But you have to know, he changed."

Jesse shook his head. "It's hard for me to

imagine that. You have no idea how awful he was to be around after my mom died."

"I remember. I know you tried to hide it from me when we were dating, but there were times I caught glimpses of it. Especially when I worked weekends here. And then after you left, he needed my help even more. I agree, he was a difficult man to be around back then, but I'm telling you, he changed."

Jesse held up a hand to stop her. "Don't. I didn't come here to talk about him. He doesn't get off that easy."

"Fine. Not today, but one day, you need to hear it. Come on, we're losing sunlight."

They checked on the chickens and filled their water dish. With the coming evening, they had moved to their coop for the night. She shut them in.

Jesse followed Rose back to the gift shop. "Where are you living now?" he asked.

"I'm living on the farm. I moved into the second floor over the gift shop, what used to be the garage years ago. Turned it into a small apartment."

"I'm surprised you didn't move into the main house after my dad passed."

"It never felt right. Truthfully, it belongs to

you. It wasn't my place to take over. Besides, my apartment is comfortable."

Lolly walked out of the gift shop and stopped when she saw them approach. "Hey Rose, everything's clean, the day's sales are in the safe, and I restocked the shelves. I'm heading out now. Will I see you at church tomorrow morning?"

"I'll be there. Save me a seat."

"Will do. It was nice meeting you, Jesse. You're welcome to come, too," she offered.

"I thought you all had the farm open to the public tomorrow."

"We do, but it doesn't open until one. So, there's time for church in the morning. Really, you should come. Everyone would love to see you again," Rose said.

"I think I'll pass this time."

"Okay, maybe next time, then. Good night, you two," Lolly said.

They watched her get into her car and drive away, then Rose turned to Jesse. The sun had set, leaving them in the evening twilight. A nearby floodlight sensed their movement and switched on. Fingers of light wrapped around them in the darkness.

"Thank you for helping today," she said. "I'm

sorry I couldn't make time for you earlier, but you took me by surprise. So, what was it you wanted to talk about?"

Jesse stuck his hands into his pockets as he picked his words. Perhaps blunt was best.

"I want to sell the farm."

CHAPTER TWO

ROSE HAD TO pick her jaw up off the ground.

"Did you say you want to sell the farm? But why?" she asked, in shock. When Jesse had said he needed to talk to her, she hadn't imagined it was to tell her this.

Jesse ran a hand through his hair. It struck her that his face appeared haunted in the shadows from the floodlight. "I can't live here after what I went through. Not after everything."

"But you don't have to come back," she said, trying to keep calm. The man was threatening her livelihood. "I can run this place. I've been doing fine this whole time." She didn't mention all the problems she dealt with daily; that was the nature of the business. "The place makes a profit, so technically that's your money. We can keep everything the way it is. You don't have to step foot on this property again if you don't want to."

"You're not hearing me. I've been thinking about it since my father passed last year, and I just don't see a scenario where I would want to keep this place."

She felt like she'd been punched in the gut. "But how could you do this? It's my home and my job. Plus we have seven employees who would be out of jobs, too, if you sold it."

Jesse shifted uncomfortably. "I'm sorry for that, but I can't keep something I don't want."

"Sure, you can. You've done a fine job of keeping it this past year and staying absent. We can keep everything status quo."

Jesse shook his head, "I hear you, but you should know I'm seriously considering selling it. I don't want you to get your hopes up that I'll change my mind."

"Wow. Message received." Rose felt all the old painful feelings rush back; the heartache and sadness she'd lived with after he'd left her. Eventually, she'd picked herself up and moved on with her life. But now he was back and threatening to sell the place, and a new kind of hurt moved in. Not just the fear that she'd lose her home and job, but that she'd lose the life she loved, as well.

Jesse's news settled like a dark cloud over

them. They grew awkwardly silent. He cleared his throat. "I think I better head out." Jesse fished around in his pocket and pulled out his car keys.

It was probably a good idea. Rose worried she was on the verge of saying something she might regret. Instead, she said, "You know, the house is full of your dad's stuff. Your mom's, too, for that matter."

Jesse paused. "Yeah, I kind of thought that might be the case. Something else I've put off. Would you mind if I came back on Monday and start cleaning it out?"

Inwardly she had to laugh. How ironic that he was asking her permission when a minute ago he was threatening to sell the place.

"It's your place. You can do whatever you want," she said through gritted teeth.

"I know that, but I still want to be respectful of you."

"Sure you do." With her fists clenched by her sides, back ramrod straight, Rose stared him down.

Jesse wasn't stupid. He undoubtedly knew he'd said enough for one day. Thanking her politely, he stepped out of the halo of light they'd been standing in and made his way to the last car in the parking lot.

Rose watched his twin taillights drive away. Funny, it wasn't the shock of his reappearance or even the anger that he might sell her beloved farm that she felt at his departure. It was unease. As though her life was about to be changed forever, whether she liked it or not.

Monday morning, Jesse returned to the farm. As he drove up to his childhood home, the sunrise painted the scene in glorious light. The farmhouse and barn sat amid acres and acres of sunflowers that glowed a brilliant yellow in the morning sun. As a kid, he'd never noticed the beauty, but he'd been gone for so long. It was different to see it through the eyes of an adult.

Or maybe he'd never noticed its beauty because when he was fifteen, after his mom died, he'd walked around with his head down, hoping not to be noticed.

Jesse cleared his mind. He'd learned a long time ago to push back the bad memories. Usually that wasn't a problem, but being back at the farm brought them to the surface.

He focused instead on the sunflower fields. Many of the sunflowers were wilted and their leaves were turning brown. He'd noticed it on Saturday but hadn't given it much thought. He'd been so preoccupied with seeing crowds of people around his childhood home and distracted by seeing Rose after all this time.

Jesse scanned the rest of the farm. It wasn't just the flowers suffering. The grass was dry, too, like it hadn't seen rain in forever. It made sense. The last few months had been unusually dry for northern Florida. Summers generally consisted of daily afternoon showers that kept vegetation lush and green. This year, any rain showers had been few and far between. He'd never seen anything like it. As a result, the fire station had been getting more calls for brushfires. He hoped the drought would end soon.

The car came to a stop in front of the gift shop. His mind was heavy now that he realized how the farm was struggling. How had Rose been coping with this? Maybe it would be a relief to her if he sold the place.

Jesse climbed out of his car and looked around, expecting to see Rose or at least someone. The place was like a ghost town, the opposite of Saturday when visitors covered every nook and cranny of the farm. Jesse checked his watch and sighed. Seven o'clock in the morning was a little early, he supposed.

The gift shop was locked, so he went around the building. Rose said she lived above the shop—maybe he'd find her there? He took the steps two at a time and knocked on her door.

After a few minutes, the door flew open. "What are you doing here so early?" Rose snapped.

Jesse tried not to notice how adorable she looked standing there in an oversize T-shirt, cotton shorts and her hair loose around her shoulders. "I couldn't sleep, so I thought I would come over."

She narrowed her eyes. "You couldn't sleep? Did it ever occur to you that maybe I could sleep?" She sounded put out. He couldn't blame her.

"Sorry. I figured you got started early, seeing how you live on the farm. Guess I was wrong."

Rose held her door partially open, shaking her head in annoyance. "Yes, normally we are up early, but Mondays are the one day I allow myself to sleep in just a bit. After the busy weekend, it's my recovery day."

"I'm sorry. Please go back to bed. I'll wait in

my car until you get up, and then we can try again," he said, smiling.

"You think you're funny, don't you?"

He shrugged. "Sometimes. Though I prefer to call it charming."

"I've got news for you, that's not charm."

"Wow, somebody needs coffee."

She studied him. "You're not going away unless I let you in, are you?"

He flashed her another smile. Judging by the grumpy look on her face, she wasn't dazzled.

"Fine. I'm up now. Come on in." She opened the door wide.

Jesse stepped into her apartment. It was a small studio, with a bed, couch and kitchen crammed into one room. Not at all the dusty, unfinished space he remembered as a kid.

He shoved his hands into his pocket, unsure whether he should sit. Instead, he followed Rose to the kitchen and leaned a hip against a counter.

Ignoring him, she grabbed a coffee tin from a shelf. On bare feet, she padded back and forth over the hardwood floors and grabbed a mug, cream and sugar. Jesse watched her, appreciating this side of her that he'd never seen when they were young and dating. All this time he had dreaded coming back, but now that he was here, she was a surprise. Even if she was a little angry about his absence…and a little mad that he wanted to sell the farm.

When the coffee was ready, Rose fixed herself a cup. She didn't offer any to Jesse.

"If you give me a minute to get dressed, I'll walk you over to the house and unlock it for you. I couldn't find a spare key, but I can get one made for you."

"Thanks, I appreciate it."

Rose grabbed some clothes out of a dresser and went into the bathroom to change.

Jessie decided to help himself to some coffee while he waited. Sipping the hot drink, he glanced at the pictures on her refrigerator and recognized her parents in one. Another photo showed Rose with his dad, Lolly and other staff, all wearing matching yellow Sunflower Farms T-shirts. His dad looked older than he remembered, but he also looked happy. Why did it sting to think he may have been happy?

Jesse took his mug over to the sofa and made himself comfortable. A few minutes later, Rose joined him wearing jeans and a clean T-shirt. She'd brushed her hair and pulled it up into a high ponytail. She was fresh-faced and too pretty. He forced himself to look away.

Rose pulled on a pair of worn-out boots, then set her empty mug in the sink and turned off the coffeepot. Jesse gulped down the last few drops from his mug and set it down next to hers.

Rose watched him, her hands on her hips. "I see you helped yourself to my coffee."

"I didn't think you'd mind. There was plenty," he challenged.

Rose clucked to herself, then headed for the door with her back stiff and head held high.

It was going to be a long day.

Jesse knew better than to comment further. Following Rose down the stairs from her apartment, he tried to change the subject. "How's the sunflower crop this year? I couldn't help but notice everything looks dry."

Rose hit the bottom step and turned back at his question.

Jesse hadn't expected her to stop so abruptly and plowed right into her. Instantly, he reached out and steadied her. Hands lingering at her waist, he stared down into her blue eyes.

Rose stood with her hands at her sides like she was paralyzed. She didn't try to break away.

Why had he broken up with her when he left for college? He knew why, but for the millionth time he doubted his decisions when it came to Rose. It was something he had to live with, but standing next to her like this, he had his doubts.

A woman's voice broke through his thoughts, "Well, this is awkward."

Jesse and Rose both turned toward the interruption. A small elderly woman with short silver hair stood below the stairs, carrying a large paper bag in her arms.

"Grammy! What are you doing here so early?" Rose asked. She immediately stepped away from Jesse like she'd been caught doing something wrong.

"What am I doing here so early? What's he doing here so early?" the woman asked, nodding toward Jesse.

"Grammy," Rose admonished. "He just got here. Do you remember Jesse Cooper? We dated in high school. His dad owned this farm." She gave her grandma a peck on the cheek, then pulled the bag out of her arms.

Recognition lit her grandmother's face. "You were the football star Rose dated."

Jesse nodded. He hadn't thought of his football days in quite a while.

"You're the one who broke my Rose's heart."

Rose rolled her eyes. "Grammy, please…"

Jesse took the last step down and held out his hand. "Yes, ma'am. I suppose that's me. Nice to see you again, Mrs. McFarland."

"Oh please. You make me sound like I'm eighty years old." She shook his hand. "You can call me Grammy like Rose does."

"I didn't know you were stopping by today. What did you bring?" Rose asked as she peeked in the bag.

"I was cleaning off a bookshelf and thought I'd bring you some of my favorites."

Rose pulled out a cookbook and a hardback about crocheting. Her brow wrinkled in confusion. "Thanks, Grammy, but I'm not sure I need these…"

"Go on and take them. I taught you to crochet when you were little. And cookbooks are always handy. There's a few more in there you'll like."

Rose put the books back in the bag and smiled at her grandmother. "Do you have time for coffee?"

"No, honey. I have to get going. I'm meeting Sally at the YMCA for water aerobics."

"That sounds fun. I'm glad you're trying new things," Rose said.

"We'll see. I just hope it's not full of old people."

Jesse glanced at Grammy to see if she was serious. Her face was completely straight.

"Okay," Rose said. "Next time, let me know you're coming, and maybe you can stay awhile."

As soon as Grammy left, Rose sighed and shook her head at the bag of books.

"What's wrong?" Jesse asked.

"She does this all the time. She cleans out a closet, and I end up with the junk she doesn't want to throw away."

"Maybe she just thinks you need to learn how to cook," Jesse joked.

Rose gave him a dirty look. "Not funny, Jesse Cooper. Come on, I have stuff to do."

"Now you have stuff to do? I thought it was your sleep-in day," he teased.

"I'm going to ignore that." She started toward the main house. For someone so much shorter than him, she sure could walk fast.

"What are your plans today?" Rose asked him over her shoulder.

"I thought I would go through the stuff in the house and start packing it up."

"There's extra boxes in the gift shop if you need them." Rose let him into the house, then left to do chores.

As Jesse walked from room to room, memories of his past swept through his mind. An electric hospital bed sat in the middle of his parents' room. A wheelchair and a walker stood in another corner. It was all a stark reminder that his dad had been ill before passing away from cancer.

Had Rose been his only caretaker? Jesse realized he'd never asked.

He walked over to the closet and saw that it was full of clothes. His dad never cleared out his mom's stuff. He'd never let her go.

And he'd blamed Jesse for her death.

Jesse blamed himself, too. He'd been fifteen and learning to drive. He and his mother were coming home from church when another car had swerved and hit them. The collision had sent their car off the road, and it'd flipped several times, killing his mother. If he hadn't insisted on driving, she would have lived. It truly was all his fault.

Jesse backed out of the closet. Before he could stop himself, his legs carried him through the house and out the front door. He couldn't do it. The memories were too hard. His chest hurt.

In the distance, he heard the rumble of a motor. Rose was coming up the drive on a utility terrain vehicle, all windblown and beautiful. When she saw him standing on the porch, she pulled up and cut the engine. Her light blue eyes shone like diamonds in the morning sun.

"What are you doing out here? Already packing your bags and running away?" she asked.

"I'm not running away. I just need some air. It's harder than I expected being in that house."

"I was just about to go water the sunflower fields. Why don't you come help?"

"Are you looking for free labor?" he challenged.

She smiled at him. "Always."

"I can help water the fields. How hard can it be?" he said.

"That's right, you're a firefighter," she teased. "You should know your way around a water hose." She patted the seat next to her. "Come on, let's go. The fields aren't going to water themselves."

"Can I drive?" he asked.

Rose laughed. "Now you're just pushing your luck."

ROSE WATCHED JESSE walk around the UTV and hop on. The years had been kind to him. The lean teenager she'd known had filled out. What was already a good-looking face had matured into an incredibly handsome man.

She was angry with him, but if she were completely honest with herself, a tiny piece of her was actually thrilled to see him again.

Starting the engine again, she took off with a lurch. Jesse heaved forward.

"Hang on," Rose said automatically.

"Now you tell me," Jesse said over the noisy engine.

"Don't be a baby."

"You should have let me drive."

"You don't know where you're going," she said.

"I drove the hayride all day Saturday. I think I know the layout of the farm like the back of my hand."

"That's just one big circle. You don't know the shortcuts anymore."

Rose took a less-used path through the sunflower fields. The big blossoms and long stems whipped past them in a blur of yellow, green and brown. When they reached the outskirts of the farm, she rolled to a stop next to a large crop sprinkler, jumped out and dragged it down the row of flowers. Jesse followed her out of the UTV and waited as she positioned and started the sprinkler. When she finished, she gave him a pointed look. "What are you waiting for? Make yourself useful."

He shook his head. "Why are you doing this by hand?"

"You're here for ten seconds, and you already know better?"

"It's a simple question. I just don't recall ever having to water the sunflowers by hand when I was a kid. That's what the irrigation system was for."

"We've had some problems with the irrigation system this past year."

"Really, what kind of problems?"

She thought about evading the question, but there was no way to dance around the truth. "The irrigation system doesn't work."

"Have you had anybody out here to look at it?"

"Gee, I never would have thought of that. Now did you come out here to question me or to help?" Rose hated being questioned. She didn't know if it was the fact that she was a woman, young or short, but she always felt like men didn't give her enough credit. Like she couldn't manage a large successful farm or deal with the problems that came with it.

"All right, I told you I would help. I'll help."

Rose swallowed the retort on the tip of her tongue. They had work to do. "The sprinklers run every three rows. Go ahead and set up the next sprinkler, and we can alternate until we get to the end," she said.

"I can do that."

"Great, let's get to it."

Jesse gave her a funny look, then said, "You know, I don't remember you being this bossy when we dated."

Rose lifted her chin up a notch. "I'm sorry if I come across as bossy. You have to understand I'm not the same girl you dated all those years ago. I'm all grown up, and I have a farm to run. I'm used to giving orders. Everyone and everything around here depends on me and the decisions I make. I don't have time for people to question me at every turn."

With that, she pivoted briskly, her long ponytail flying over one shoulder as she stomped off.

For the next thirty minutes, they set up sprinklers and successfully avoided conversation until they headed back to the UTV. Jesse didn't ask to drive this time but sat silently next to her in the passenger seat.

Rose glanced at him as he pushed a hand through his damp hair. His clothes were drenched from moving the sprinklers, which was rather comical. She suppressed a smile. She'd moved those sprinklers enough that she had it down to a science, leaving her dry as a bone, but he looked like a drowned rat.

Jesse stared straight ahead.

Rose giggled, then started laughing so hard her eyes watered.

Slowly, Jesse turned his head, and with a stoic face asked, "What's so funny?"

Rose wiped her eyes when she could talk again. "I thought firefighters knew how to handle a water hose."

"I don't know what you're talking about," Jesse said stiffly. "I handled the sprinklers just fine."

Rose couldn't help but grin at the man. "Sure you did." She started the UTV, but this time he was ready and grabbed the side to brace himself.

Rose couldn't resist. "Hey, if you stick your head out the side, maybe the wind will dry you off."

"My luck, you'd drive past a tree and nail me in the head."

"I would never," she said, all innocence.

Rose took a dirt path to the edge of the property, where the land bordered a lake. She came to a stop near the water. The morning light reflected off the surface in a million sparkles.

Jesse's dark eyes passed over the area. "I'd forgotten about this place," he said quietly. "Man, it looks just the same as when we used to come out here."

Rose's earlier irritation was forgotten. Laughter had a way of making a person feel better. "Nothing much has changed. Though the water level is lower because of the drought the last few months," she said.

Jesse surveyed the water. "You're right, it is lower."

"We had some good times out here swimming, sunbathing and hanging out," she said.

"Yeah, good times. I thought I was all grown up because I could invite a few friends over to the lake, listen to music, and stay out late." He laughed.

Rose cut off the engine to the UTV. "You want to go walk out on the dock?"

"As long as we're here…"

They strolled down the dock side by side, Rose keenly aware of his closeness. The wood boards were faded from years of Florida sunshine and creaked under their weight.

"Do you ever come out here anymore?" Jesse asked.

"Not really. We're always busy, and I just don't have the time. I wish I did, though. Now that I'm here, I realize I've missed it."

They reached the end, and Rose sat down with her legs crisscrossed, feet tucked under her thighs. Jesse sat next to her, dangling his long legs over the dock edge. Casually he leaned back on his palms and faced the water. The sun had started to heat up the day, but occasionally a soft breeze stirred the air. For a few minutes they sat in silence.

"What are you thinking?" Rose asked.

"I guess mostly that it's a different way of life out here at the farm. I'd forgotten that part. I've become so accustomed to living in Jacksonville, within walking distance to restaurants and stores. I've gotten used to the noise. You know, cars, people, stuff like that. Out here, it's peace and quiet."

"Mostly peace and quiet, unless you're here on

the weekend, and then it's busy. But you're right. It is a different way of life. Do you miss it?"

"I don't know. I didn't think so, but now that I'm here and see how beautiful everything is this time of year, it's eye-opening. But there's more to life than beauty. I had a tough time after my mom died. My dad made things real hard for me. That has a way of overshadowing everything else when I'm here."

"I can understand that. You went through a lot. Still, this place is a rare gem. Before we made Sunflower Farms more visitor-friendly, I traveled around the state to some other public farms for ideas. I came back here and slowly started making changes, with your dad's blessing. It was hard for him to let go of the reins at first, but he trusted me. We grew even more sunflowers and really started promoting them, then added our own touches like the classes and hayrides. It wasn't just picking strawberries anymore, but all the other stuff you see. Nobody else's farm is like ours. It's one of a kind. I want you to know that before you decide to sell it."

"I'm starting to see that."

"And you'll have to make sure to come back next weekend for the Sunflower Festival."

"You mentioned that the other day. What all goes into it?"

"We work with the church to put it together, and the proceeds go to families in need in the community. We've been doing it for about five years now. This year it's for a young family who was displaced from their home because of a fire. You may know them. Johnny Taylor's family? He graduated a couple of years ahead of us in high school."

Jesse sat up straighter. "Yeah, I do remember him. We played football together. You're not going to believe this, but that fire was in my district. It was in the middle of the night, and the place completely burned down. Fortunately, his family escaped along with all their pets."

Rose couldn't believe it. "What a small world. His mom goes to my church. She told us about the fire. Johnny and his family have been staying with her. They could use the money to help start over while they wait for the insurance to come through."

"I'd like to do something for them. Maybe I can help in some way with the festival."

"That'd be great. It never seems like we have enough volunteers, it's always so busy." Rose gasped at a sudden thought. "Oh…is there any chance you could bring out a fire engine for a day?"

"Yeah, I don't see why not. I'll check to make sure there isn't anything we're already committed to that weekend, but I'm sure we could do it at least one day. And I might be able to find a couple of volunteers to help man it."

Rose clapped her hands and beamed at him. "The kids will love it. Can they go inside the cab and crawl around the truck?"

Jesse grinned at her, clearly amused. "I think that could be arranged. And we can bring some of the gear and let them try it on."

"That'll be a huge hit. Thank you." For the first time since he'd arrived, Rose felt herself soften a little toward Jesse.

"Don't thank me yet. Let me make sure we're available first."

"I have confidence in you. I'll pencil you in," she teased.

"Well, in that case, I guess we have to be there," Jesse said with a chuckle.

They grew quiet again. Across the lake a white egret stood gracefully in the water close to shore. Every now and then he pecked at the water. Some crows cawed from the nearby treetops. The sun hid behind fluffy white clouds

that kept the heat at bay. Jesse watched his surroundings in silence.

"I still can't believe you would consider giving this place up. This farm. It's my whole life.
Please don't sell it," she said.

Jesse's eyes went from the lake to hers as he
grew serious. "I understand that but I don't
know if I can do what you're asking."

"If you sell it, you'll break my heart all over
again. This time you'll take away my home
and my job."

"You make it sound like it's such an easy decision. But it's not."

"Please consider all the people working here.
There's seven employees, plus the seasonal help
that depend on the extra money."

"I'll consider all of that in my decision," Jesse
said. He shifted his attention back to the lake.

Probably better to let him think on that for
a while. Rose checked her watch. "It's getting
late. We better head back. I have some things
I need to do."

"What, more watering?"

"Actually, I do have to move the sprinklers
in an hour, so if you dry out by then, maybe
you can help."

Jesse laughed. He looked down at his clothes.

He was already dry from the warm sunshine. "I'll help if you need it."

"I'm kidding. I'm sure you need to get back to clearing out the house."

They both got up and walked back to the UTV in silence. Jesse took his place in the passenger seat. On the way back to the house, they chatted about the different sides of the business and what crops did well on the farm and which didn't. Jesse had grown up around it and had a wealth of knowledge. He asked the right questions and understood the highs and lows of farming more than anyone. It really was a shame that he didn't seem to want to take over the farm after his father.

"Have you completely given up on fixing the irrigation system?" he asked her at one point.

Rose felt her shoulders drop. "Trust me, we've looked at it. We've repaired it many times, but it's old and it needs to be replaced. No more Band-Aids are going to work. And that's going to be expensive."

"Maybe it's a sign that it's time to sell."

"That's not a sign. It's just life. Things break, and you have to replace them."

"In this case, it should have already been replaced. Everything's so dry. The farm can't go without an irrigation system."

"It's autumn. Leaves turn colors, the grass dies. It's normal. You're making more out of it than it is." But she knew he was right. Normally northern Florida was still lush green in October.

She hated that Jesse had noticed the dry crops. The staff had been killing themselves watering the fields by hand for months, and honestly it could have been so much worse. She knew they could have lost it all.

It made her look bad, like she was incompetent at running the farm. Rose hated that the most.

"Selling this place wouldn't be the worst thing in the world," Jesse insisted. "You have an agriculture degree and a ton of experience. There's so much you could do. You could own your own farm."

She frowned at him. "I don't want another farm. This is my home."

They drove the rest of the way in silence. When Rose parked at the main house, Jesse said, "Thank you for taking me to the lake." His short black hair had dried and was now windblown in the front. It made him look younger. Rose had a flashback of the teenager she'd been in love with.

She shook off the memory. "You're welcome," she said coolly.

"Don't be mad, Rose. We should be able to talk about selling the farm like two adults."

"I don't know what you mean. I'm talking, and I'm listening…just like an adult."

Jesse climbed out of the vehicle and squinted down at her in the bright sunshine. "I can see that. I just want you to consider all sides. It could be a relief to let this place go. Especially in light of the irrigation system needing to be replaced." With that, he double tapped the roof of the UTV and backed away as if to signal her to go. At the last second, he added, "Oh, hey, would you mind if I come back tomorrow with some of my things? I have the week off and could probably get more done if I just stayed."

"It's your house. Do what you want," she said.

"I know. But I didn't want to step on your toes."

"I have pretty tough toes. I think I'll be okay." She dug in her pocket, pulled out the house key and threw it at him.

He was quick and caught it next to his head then gave her a stunned look.

"Keep the key so you don't have to wake me up tomorrow," she said.

Rose drove away before he could say anything else. It stung that she had to admit the irrigation system didn't work. She should have found a way to pay for a new one. She was also mad he'd been gone for so long and that he was thinking about selling the place. She hadn't worked all these years to turn this place around, only to have him thoughtlessly sell it. If that happened, she would be devastated.

CHAPTER THREE

THE ALARM WENT off before the sun came up. Rose hit the clock to end the torture and rolled over with a groan. Unbidden, thoughts of Jesse sprang to mind. Sitting next to him at the lake yesterday brought back more memories than she'd been prepared for. Maybe it hadn't been such a good idea to take him there.

Rose got dressed, then left her apartment to be greeted by the sunrise lighting the sky. Glorious shades of pink and peach hung over the vast fields of colorful sunflowers. As dry as the conditions were, somehow they'd managed to keep the farm alive. Rose knew that had been an answer to prayer.

She also prayed for a solution to the irrigation system, and she prayed for rain. She was still waiting for those prayers to be answered.

Everything was quiet on the farm. The employees weren't due for another hour, and she had the place to herself. There was an autumn chill in the air this morning, but by afternoon, the day would be warm and sunny.

Rose started her morning with the usual chores. She fed the animals, led the horses out to pasture, milked Betsy, then let her join the horses. Once the barn was empty, she cleaned out the stalls, took fresh hay to the goats and spent a few minutes petting them. Lastly, she let the chickens out of their coop. The friendly hens walked in a line down the coop ramp, clucking loudly, as if greeting her.

"Good morning, ladies," Rose said to the hens, then added "and you too, Rocky," when the rooster pranced by. She was rather fond of the chickens, having raised each one by hand. When the coop was empty, she collected a basket of eggs.

Back at her apartment, Rose made scrambled eggs and toast, then set the rest of the eggs aside for Grammy.

After breakfast, Rose left her apartment and went downstairs to her office in the gift shop. The room was small, with her desk and cabinets taking up most the space. One window had a view of the parking lot, and on the other wall the window faced the sunflower fields. Rose sat down at her desk, grabbed a pencil and her Sunflower Festival binder, and went through her to-do list. She had everything planned, practically down to the minute, to get ready for the festival starting on Friday. There were only three days left for preparations. That made her a little nervous, but she knew they would pull through. The past four years, the festival has been a success. This year would be no different.

Absently, Rose chewed the pencil eraser as she reviewed her notes, then checked off some completed items. She sent reminder texts to the church members who had volunteered to do setup and to work at the festival. Then she called the pastor to confirm the plan to recognize the Taylor family in church on Sunday, and to announce the Sunflower Festival was raising money for them.

When Rose was finished, she put away the notebook and spent half an hour paying bills for the farm. She wondered if Jesse would be the least bit interested in looking over the books, seeing how much money was coming into the farm and how much was going out.

Rose said a silent prayer to God to continue to provide and to allow them to stay open.

Suddenly, her phone buzzed with a text. One

of her employees, Justin, was calling in sick again. Rose sighed. She liked Justin. He was a good kid, but now there was more work for the rest of them and with the worst possible timing. With the festival coming up, everyone already had extra duties, and she really needed his help clearing a fallen tree from the garden. She shook her head in frustration.

Just then, a car drove up. Rose glanced out the window to see Jesse parking his car. Grabbing a bag from the car, he went around the gift shop and headed to the farmhouse.

He'd only brought a small duffel bag? What about food? Had he thought that far ahead? And was he really planning to sleep in his old dusty room?

Rose finished up with her office work and went back upstairs to her apartment to grab some clean linens for Jesse. Before heading out the door again, Rose stopped in front of a mirror to check her appearance. Out of habit, her hand smoothed over her hair, even though it was still neat. Why did she care what she looked like? Just because Jesse Cooper was back, didn't mean she needed to look perfect.

Rose left the apartment, headed over to the main house, and stopped at the front door.

When James Cooper lived there, she'd always knocked before entering. At some point in James's last year, she'd stopped knocking. He'd become so ill from cancer, she'd found herself over at his house all the time to help him. The formality of knocking had long been forgotten.

Never would she have imagined she'd be back on that same doorstep, knocking once again. This time with Jesse on the other side. Rose rapped on the door, waited a few minutes and when Jesse didn't answer, walked in.

JESSE SET HIS bag down on the bed and turned to take in his surroundings. His bedroom was exactly as he'd left it as a teenager. How many hours had he spent here, staring up at the ceiling? Sadness and guilt would consume him as he'd replay the accident in his mind, over and over. Even though the police had told Jesse it hadn't been his fault, he'd always felt it was. Even worse, his dad had blamed him.

Jesse heard footsteps and turned toward the door. He half expected it to be his father. Dread washed over him like he was fifteen again. When Rose appeared in the doorway, Jesse sighed in relief.

"Hey there," she said. She seemed to be holding a stack of sheets in her arms.

Jesse quickly pushed aside his dark thoughts. "Good morning."

"I see you're here early again," Rose said. She was dressed casually, with her hair up in the same tight ponytail that showed off her perfect oval face. Her big blue eyes studied him. Even in faded jeans and a T-shirt, she was a knockout.

"Yeah, but I came straight to the house this time. You can't blame me for waking you up." He smiled.

"No, I can't blame you. Instead, I can blame the million and one things I need to get done today," she said. "I've been up since before dawn."

"I got up early, too. I couldn't sleep again last night. After being here yesterday and with everything I need to do this week, there's so much spinning around in my head. I've also been thinking about the irrigation system. I want to look at it. Maybe see if there's anything I can do."

Rose's hackles seemed to go up. "Don't you believe me when I say it's beyond fixing?" she asked.

"Of course I believe you, but if there's any way I can help, I want to. I grew up around it, and more than once I was forced to help my dad work on it."

"Fine, but it's a waste of time. We've done everything."

Jesse shrugged. "Okay, then it's a waste of time. But at least let me try. I really don't mind."

Rose narrowed her eyes. "I hate it when you're nice. After the way I left things with you yesterday, you're making me look bad."

Jesse chuckled. "Come on, Rose, you could never look bad."

She grew silent and put a hand up to her hair as if to smooth it down. Was that a blush on her cheeks? Finally, she shoved the stack of linens at him. "Here. This is for you if you're sleeping here tonight. Clean sheets and a quilt."

"I hadn't even thought that far ahead, to be honest. I appreciate it."

"You're welcome. I saw you only had one bag with you. Not sure what you plan to eat, but hey, that's not my problem." She chuckled.

Jesse shrugged, then laughed. "I'll figure it out. Thank you for the clean sheets." He realized he wasn't sure what else to say. It had been easy to be around each other when they dated, but now it felt a little awkward.

"I'm heading out, now. Come find me if you

need me," she said. Maybe she felt the awk-
wardness, too.

Jesse watched her leave, then glanced down at
the stack of sheets she'd handed him. He lifted
the sheets to his nose and the freshly laundered
scent made him smile.

He made the bed, then opened his duffel bag
and hung a couple of shirts on empty hangers
he'd found in the closet. Then he moved on to
his parents' room with a box full of heavy-duty
garbage bags.

Jesse bagged his mom's clothes first. When
he had about ten large bags, he decided to ask
Rose if he could borrow her truck to take the
clothes to the closest Goodwill, about twenty
minutes away.

On his way out of the bedroom, he noticed
a Bible on the nightstand. He didn't remember
his dad ever reading the Bible. Jesse picked up
the book and flipped through it, surprised by
the handwritten notes in the margins of several
pages. They were all in his dad's messy scrawl.

Rose had told him that his father had
changed. Maybe he'd finally found some solace in faith. Jesse found that hard to believe. He
set the Bible back down. It hurt to think about.

Why couldn't he have changed when Jesse still lived with him?

He left the room, along with his troubling thoughts.

On his way to find Rose, he passed the two horses in the pasture. At the sight of Jesse, Missy trotted over to the fence. She nickered as if calling to him. Jesse stopped and petted her head and her soft, glossy neck. The horse seemed to enjoy the attention, nuzzling his hand.

Jesse had to admit, his spirits were lifting. Just being outside in the sunshine had a way of clearing his head.

"I'm sorry I don't have a treat, sweetheart. I'll try to scrounge up a carrot or apple later, I promise. What do you say about that?"

The other horse, Moe, was fifty feet away and ignored him. If he had an apple, no doubt Moe would be his best friend, too.

Jesse continued his search for Rose. Taking a chance, he headed toward the garden. It was easy to spot. The area was surrounded by a short, white picket fence, and an arbor stood at the entrance, covered in fragrant, blooming jasmine. Colorful flower beds lined the inside of the fence, and garden boxes grew a variety of vegetables and herbs in the middle of the garden. Toward the back, roses grew, resembling a proper English garden, meant to be strolled through and admired. Sprinklers watered the perimeter. Everything was lush and green, like the drought hadn't affected it at all.

The garden took up at least an acre. Jesse followed the stone pathway toward the roses. He passed through a tunnel covered in thick green vines and pink roses and emerged into a garden maze with rose petals littering the path.

How had he not known all of this was back here? In his time away, he'd missed so much. Who had created this? His father or Rose? He chose to believe the latter. For some reason, he didn't want to believe it was his father.

At last, Jesse found Rose in a back corner of the garden, where a large oak tree had fallen and crushed part of the picket fence. She was kneeling next to it, clearing out some of the small branches. Nearby, Grammy sat in the shade on a bench, chatting while Rose worked. Sunglasses sat on top of Grammy's head, holding her short hair back.

She gave Jesse a broad smile when she saw him. "You're still here?" Grammy asked in surprise.

"Yes, ma'am, I'm still here," Jesse said.

Rose paused in her work and looked up. A smudge of dirt stretched across one cheek.

Instinctually, he wanted to wipe it off. But he kept his hands to himself. Grammy might have a thing or two to say about that.

"I finally found you." Jesse said to Rose.

"I didn't know I was lost," she replied. She wiped the back of her gloved hand across her cheek and made the smudge worse.

Amused, Jesse smiled. She was adorable.

"This garden is amazing," he said. "I had no idea you had this many flowers back here."

Rose sat back on her heels. "Well, things change when you're gone for so long."

Rather than react to her tone, Jesse simply said, "This place is stunning."

She tilted her head, as if trying to decide whether he was being sincere. "Thanks. It's a lot of work." She sighed and gestured toward the fallen tree. "Sorry, I'm aggravated because Justin called in sick today, and he was supposed to help me clean up this mess. Plus, there's so much work to do before the festival this weekend. Grammy said she would help, but you can see her version of helping."

"I'm right here, darling. I can hear you,"

Grammy said from where she sat in the shade. "Besides, you know I'm only here for moral support."

Jesse scratched his chin as he surveyed the huge fallen tree. "I can help you for a bit. Do you have a chainsaw?"

"Really? You'd help me?" Rose asked, surprised.

"Yeah. Of course."

At once, Rose grabbed a chainsaw from the ground on the other side of the tree and handed it to Jesse. "Here you go."

It wasn't his first time using one. He studied it for a few seconds, then cranked it up and sliced through a thick branch like it was butter. He shut the chainsaw off and set the branch down to cut it up in smaller pieces.

"Impressive. They teach you that in firefighter school?" Rose teased,

"You forget I grew up here," Jesse said with a laugh. "I've cleared a few trees in my time."

For the next hour, he cut up the tree and Rose loaded the pieces into a wheelbarrow to haul to a stack of firewood nearby. They talked as they worked, while Grammy supervised from the bench.

"Did you create this garden by yourself?" Jesse asked, pausing the chainsaw to wipe sweat from his brow.

Rose threw another log into the wheelbarrow. "Most of it, yes."

"Where do you even start with something like this?"

"I've always loved gardening. Grammy and my parents gave me rosebushes for every special occasion. You know, because of my name and all."

"Very sweet," he said.

"Then when we decided to open up the farm and make it public, my brain got creative. I wanted to make an area people could walk through. Someplace nice to take pictures besides the sunflowers. I kept adding to it over time, until it grew into all this."

"It's magnificent. You've created something truly wonderful here. I can't imagine the amount of work it takes to keep this maintained."

"Yeah, it's a lot of work. The staff helps, but I end up out here every day. There's always something that needs to be weeded, picked or pruned. And with the drought, I've had to keep up with the watering."

"No wonder you need so much staff. This place has really grown."

Jesse threw the last of the wood into the

wheelbarrow and hauled it away. When he returned to the garden, Rose was slowly pulling a large flowerpot across the ground.

"Need help with that?" he asked.

"That would be great," she said, panting.

Jesse helped move the pot. "There you go," he said as he brushed his hands off. "You know, I wanted to ask if I could borrow your truck to haul a load of clothes up to the donation center. Is that okay?"

"Sure, you're welcome to use it. I guess that means you're making progress in the house?"

"A little. I managed to clear out my mom's clothes, but that's about as far as I got." He didn't mention that he was dreading touching his father's things.

"I can't believe your dad left your mom's stuff there all these years," she said.

"I know. He never could deal with her death, but you already knew that." Jesse took a deep breath and let it out in a sigh.

Rose offered him a crooked smile. "I do. I'm sorry."

"Don't be. I knew this would be tough. It just stirs up all those old memories I've worked so hard to forget."

"I know he was tough on you, but doesn't it

count for something that he changed eventually? He did become a better person."

Jesse frowned.

"He wasn't always a bad guy, like you remember. He turned his life around," Rose said.

"Too little, too late."

"Is it really too late?" she challenged.

"As far as I am concerned. The man I lived with was a bad guy. You were his employee. He treated his employees decently, but he saved the meanness for me."

"I know how he treated you wasn't fair for a teenage boy who just lost his mother. And you have every right to those feelings. But you've carried this hurt and anger around for too long. When you left, it affected him. He may not have told you he loved you, but I promise you he did. Eventually he found his way to church, and that led him to God, and it changed everything about him. His attitude, his work, his view on life in general. He became a better person. It truly was wonderful."

"Forgive me if I find that hard to believe. He never went to church when I was growing up. It always was just my mom and me going. He'd stay behind to work the farm." But Jesse recalled the Bible he found in his parents' room.

He kept that information to himself. He wasn't ready to admit that his father could change, much less forgive him.

Not today.

Desperate to change the subject, Jesse asked, "So, how about that truck? Can I borrow it now?"

"I'll have to run and get the keys for you. But before you go, could I ask one more favor? Could you help me move some more flower-pots?"

"She can use your big strong muscles," Grammy chimed in with a sparkle in her eye and a wink for Jesse.

Jesse pretended to look around. "Who me? Big strong muscles? You must be joking."

"Don't let it go to your head," Rose said with a laugh. "Come on, now help me. The pots probably weigh eighty pounds each with soil in them. I'm sure you could lift them without a hitch."

Jesse moved four pots, one by one. They were in fact heavy, but he pretended they weren't. Was he trying to impress her? That question he decided not to explore.

As Jesse set the last pot down, his cell phone vibrated in his pocket. He wiped his hands and reached for his phone. It was his realtor. Jesse walked a few steps away for privacy.

"Hey, Jesse, it's Ray," the voice said on the phone.

"Hey, man. What's up?" Jesse peered over at Rose. She was fiddling with the pots, too far away to hear anything.

"I've made some calls like you asked, to see if anyone was interested in buying the farm you inherited. I found an investor who's very interested. He even made an offer of $1.4 million."

When Ray told him how much the investor was offering for the farm, Jesse was pleased. It was a bit more than he'd originally expected he'd get. "That's not bad," Jesse said.

"Do you want me to accept and draw up a contract?"

"I—I had no idea there would be interest so soon. I mean, I just got here. There's a ton to do before the house will be cleared out and ready for a new owner."

"I don't think that'll matter. This is a well-known commercial builder. He's not buying it to live there. If I had to guess, they're planning to bulldoze it and build a strip mall or a housing development."

Jesse's eyes went back to Rose, who was watering the flowers he'd just moved. Could he really sell the farm out from under her? She'd lose her home and everything she'd worked so hard to create.

It was a good offer, though. If he passed it up, another one might not come. The housing market was in a slump. This could be his only chance.

Ray went on, "They'll need an answer soon."

"I have to think about it. This is a huge decision, and it impacts other people, not just me. When do I need to decide?"

"As soon as possible, but if you need to think about it, I'm sure you can tell them next week at the latest."

"Okay. I'll give you a decision by then." Could he really sell the farm? What would that mean to Rose?

Jesse got off the phone and walked back over to Rose and her grandmother.

"Everything okay?" Rose asked as she turned off the hose. She knelt to pull up a couple of rogue weeds that dared to grow near a rosebush.

"Just some business. Nothing major." Jesse knew he would need to tell her about the offer, but it could wait. He needed to think about it first. Besides, every time he brought up selling the farm, it only made her angry. If he sold it, would she ever forgive him?

ROSE STOOD UP from her weeding and took off her gloves. She surveyed the garden and realized she wouldn't be able to get everything done. It was a good thing Jesse had agreed to help, otherwise it would have taken her the entire day to clean up the fallen tree. She'd still have to find time to fix the fence. There was never enough time in the day to do everything.

"I'm at a good stopping point," she said to Jesse. "Let's go get those truck keys for you." She turned to Grammy. "Are you ready to head back?"

"I guess I am. Never mind I was enjoying spending time with my granddaughter."

"We can still spend time together. You can come up to my apartment for some lemonade," Rose offered.

Grammy rose from the bench and straightened her shirt, then pulled her sunglasses down over her eyes. "No, I think I'll leave now and drive back to my house. I have things to do."

Rose shook her head. She'd just said she wanted to spend time together. Her grandmother was a contradiction sometimes. Maybe that was where Rose got it from. With Jesse back in town, her emotions were all over the place…angry, excited, happy to see him, unhappy to see him.

Rose and Jesse said goodbye to Grammy at her car, then dropped off the wheelbarrow and tools in the barn and headed to her apartment.

Rose tried to center herself. She was stronger and smarter than ever, and she could take care of the farm on her own. Never mind the endless problems that always seemed to be popping up. With a little bit of sweat, hard work and prayer, she'd get by. She always had. She didn't need a man to help her.

She didn't need Jesse Cooper.

The thing was, she had appreciated his help with the downed tree in her garden. But she needed to remember that his visit was only temporary. At the end of the week, he'd pack up and be gone once again.

When they reached her apartment, Rose ran upstairs to grab the keys, leaving Jesse outside in front of the gift shop. Glancing in a mirror on the wall, she came to an abrupt halt. There was a streak of dirt on her cheek. How long had that been there? Surely Jesse had seen it.

He must think she was some country bumpkin who was dirty and sweaty half the time.

Running into the bathroom, she washed her face and hands. Her face rosy from a good scrubbing, she checked her hair quickly, satisfied to see her ponytail still in place. Grabbing the truck keys on the way out, she closed the door behind her and came to a stop.

At the bottom of the stairs, Jesse leaned against the wooden rail, his long legs crossed at the ankle and his elbows on the rail. He looked carefree and at peace as he watched her descend the stairs. You would never know he was struggling with his past. The man was a pro at hiding his feelings.

The Jesse she knew in high school had seemed like a normal teenage boy who loved sports and made decent grades. He'd been one of the most popular boys in school, fun and happy—until the accident happened. He'd lost his mother and childhood in one fell swoop.

Rose reached the bottom of the stairs and tossed him the keys. It was the same old truck that Jesse's dad had used on the farm for as long as she could remember.

"Here you go. It's parked out front. I trust you know how to drive a stick?"

Jesse gave her a look. "If I recall, I was the one that taught you how to drive that truck."

Rose laughed. "You're right. Now I'm the one wincing when some new hire grinds the gears." She tucked a loose strand of hair behind an ear. "I suppose the truck is yours now. I hadn't realized until now."

Jesse raised his brows as if it had not occurred to him, either. "I suppose you're right. But just so we're clear, I would never take the truck from you if you don't have another of your own."

"Don't worry, I have a car," she assured him.

"Okay then." He looked relieved.

"Hey, thanks again for helping with that tree. Could I bother you with one more thing? When you get back, could you help me pull some boxes out of the warehouse? I need to start decorating for the Sunflower Festival, or it'll never all get done by the weekend. I was going to ask one of the staff to help with some of the bigger boxes, but since you're here, would you?" She smiled sweetly, hoping that would help convince him.

"Yeah, of course. Do you want to do it now, before I go?"

"I would love to get started if that doesn't mess up your schedule."

He rubbed his chin. "It'll delay me from cleaning out my dad's things… So in that case, I'll definitely help you. Anything to avoid that haunted house."

Rose chuckled. "You're incorrigible."

He waggled his brows. "No, I just really don't want to clean out that room."

"Well, I know better than to pass up free help if you're willing. Let's take the truck to the warehouse. You can drive."

"Sure, you let me drive the old beat-up truck but not the UTV yesterday," he kidded.

She laughed.

At the warehouse, Rose entered a code in the keypad, opened the door and flipped on the light. The boxes were stacked in the back, and Jesse's eyes took in the large pyramid before him. The top row brushed the warehouse's twenty-foot ceiling. "We're moving all those?"

Rose rolled her eyes. "Come on. It's not that bad."

"I pictured two or three boxes, like what we'd put Christmas decorations in. There have to be thirty or forty boxes here," he complained.

"Yep, we take our Sunflower Festival very seriously," she joked.

Ignoring her attempt at humor, he said, "Well, let's get to it. Do you have a lift to get to the top boxes?"

"We have a ladder."

"A ladder? That's it? Seems dangerous."

"You'll be fine. You're a firefighter, I bet you're used to climbing ladders."

"I am, but that's not the point."

"What is the point? I'm not asking you to climb the Empire State Building." Rose straightened her back, as if that would make up the difference in their height. Jesse was still taller, but she was used to being the boss, and he did not intimidate her.

"I know that. It's just this is how accidents happen. Whoever stacked this did not plan well. I would have done it completely different."

"Well, if you stick around, you can help me put it all away next week, and we can do it your way. But for now, let's get to it."

Jesse gave up and followed Rose to help her set up the ladder. Together, they pulled down all the boxes marked Sunflower Festival and loaded them on the truck. It took them two trips to haul everything from the warehouse to the barn, where the boxes would stay during setup for the festival.

Finally, Jesse left Rose to her unpacking while he ran his clothing donation errand. Even though she could have had some of the farm employees set up the lights, she chose to do it. She didn't mind the extra work because it was a good cause, plus she was picky when it came to decorating.

Rose started with the boxes of hanging lights and poles. They always hung thousands of lights for the festival's barn dance. Tediously, Rose tested each strand to make sure their bulbs worked, placing the faulty ones in a small pile to be worked on later. One of the Sunflower Farms employees, an older man named Tony, swung by to help. He put the poles together and began to set them up in the barnyard.

Before Rose knew it, Jesse was back. He walked into the barn with a takeout bag in one hand and a couple of drinks on a cardboard tray in the other. His eyes roamed the mess in surprise. "Wow. What's up with all the lights?"

"We're hanging them today for the festival."

"We?"

"Yes. *We*. Thanks for volunteering." She gave him a sly smile, daring him to protest.

"Funny, I don't recall volunteering."

"Don't worry. It won't take too long."

"Well, that changes everything," he said dryly. "Of course, I'll help if it won't take too long."

She eyed him. Had she gone too far? He'd already helped her out most of the morning.

Jesse continued, "Anyway, are you hungry? I picked up some lunch."

Rose put down the lights she'd been holding. "I'm starving." She stepped around a couple boxes and led Jesse outside to a picnic table. "What did you bring?" she asked as her stomach growled.

"I picked up some burgers from the new place next to the Goodwill. Thought we could try it out." They sat across from one another at the table, and Jesse handed her a soda. "Diet for you, if I recall."

"You recall correctly. Thanks." Rose took a big sip as she watched him open the bag and start pulling out their food. The smell of fresh fries hit her nose, and her mouth watered. "I can't remember the last time I ate fast food," she said as she popped a fry in her mouth.

"You're kidding, right?" He handed her a burger and a few napkins.

"No. I'm on the farm most of the time. Last time I checked, there are no fast-food joints here."

"You're probably better off. This stuff's not good for you," he said as he took a huge bite of his burger.

Rose shook her head. "Yeah, I can tell you're really worried about your cholesterol."

Jesse took another bite. His dark eyes watched her, dancing with humor.

Rose had to glance away.

She unwrapped her burger and took a smaller bite than Jesse. *Delicious.* They ate in silence, scarfing down their lunch, then lingering over the last of the fries.

"I was wondering," Jesse said at last, "how your parents are doing."

"They're good. Both fully retired now and enjoying it entirely too much. They bought an RV last year and have been traveling all over the country," Rose said. "I barely see them anymore, but it was their dream, so I'm happy for them."

A small smile touched Jesse's lips, "Good for them. They were always so nice to me, even before you and I started dating. When I would see them at church, they'd always ask how I was doing. They were good friends with my mom before…you know."

"They always were so fond of you and your mom," Rose agreed, not sure what else to say.

"Did they keep their house when they bought the RV?"

"They sold their house and bought a smaller place. They didn't need a big house and yard anymore for just the two of them. Their new place isn't far from here, which makes me happy because I like having them nearby. Even if they are gone half the time," she said.

"Are they traveling right now?" Jesse asked as he grabbed another fry.

"Yeah, they're finishing up a road trip out west. Mom keeps texting me photos. I'm so jealous. I don't know why they never took any of these trips when I was growing up." Rose took out her phone and showed Jesse a few of the recent ones of the Grand Canyon.

"Wow, looks amazing. It's so dry and different from Florida and our tropical climate here. It's like a whole other world."

"I know but if we don't get some rain soon, it'll be like the Grand Canyon here, too," Rose griped as she swiped through a few more pictures. "They should be home soon. They promised to be here in time for the festival this weekend."

"I'm sure you'll be glad to have them back."

"It does make me happy. I can't wait to see them."

"You were always lucky to have such great parents and the perfect childhood. You have no idea."

To Jesse's credit, he didn't sound bitter. His childhood had been good until the accident. Still…it was time to change the subject.

"So, seriously, you want to help me hang the lights?" she asked as she put her phone away.

"Sure thing."

She balled up her burger wrapper, tucked it into the white bag and then stood from the picnic table. Jesse shoved the last two fries in his mouth, threw his trash in the bag, too, and tossed it into a garbage can by the barn door. Then he followed Rose around the barnyard with a small stepladder, looping the lights in graceful swags between each pole.

Every now and then, Rose stepped back, eyed the swags critically, and if they didn't match perfectly, she made him adjust them.

"Nothing has changed," he said. "You're still the same perfectionist you were in high school."

"Who, me?" she asked. But deep down she knew he was right.

"Remember when we decorated for prom? It took twice as long as it should have because everything had to be perfect."

"You're exaggerating. It took twice as long because everyone was goofing off. Including you, mister."

He didn't bother to deny it, but simply moved the ladder to the next pole.

"That's perfect," Rose said when he had adjusted another long string of lights.

"I remember how pretty you looked," Jesse said casually.

Rose didn't know where that came from. Was he talking to her? She looked around and only saw Tony on the other side of the yard working on the poles. She was sure he wasn't calling Tony pretty.

Rose felt her face turn pink. "What?"

He glanced down at her. "Prom night. I remember how pretty you were. I felt like the luckiest guy to be with you."

Rose didn't know what to say. She just stared up at him, thinking about that night ten years ago. He remembered? And he thought she was pretty?

Jesse continued, "You wore a teal-colored gown and your hair was all fancy."

That broke the moment, and she laughed. "You thought my hair was fancy? That's what you remember?"

"Yeah. You fixed it different. It was up in some kind of updo, with soft curls all around your face."

"You're right. My mom took me to the hair salon to get it fixed all fancy, as you would say. And that dress, oh my, I loved that dress. I saved up all year, so I could buy it."

Jesse moved the ladder to keep stringing lights. "Do you remember that night? It was so much fun. And man, I liked you so much back then…" His words trailed off, as if he suddenly realized what he'd said.

Rose stood there speechless. That was what she remembered, too, including how much she'd liked him. But she didn't dare say it out loud.

Jesse looked down at her. Their eyes met and held. "I'm sorry about leaving you the way I did."

They weren't talking about the prom anymore.

"Are you?" she whispered, even though Tony wasn't within earshot of their private conversation.

Jesse stepped down from the ladder to face

her, a string of lights held between them. It wasn't lost on Rose that she'd been telling him to forgive his dad, but she wasn't sure she could forgive Jesse.

"Just stop. Don't say anymore," she said.

"Stop? You want me to stop apologizing? For ten years, it's eaten away at me, the way I left you. Believe it or not, I loved you back then. But I had to go, and you couldn't come with me. I didn't want you to give up your dreams. I am sincerely sorry for what I did to you."

She saw the emotions on his face, the sincerity in his eyes. Rose took a deep breath. "Why are you saying this now?"

"Because now that I'm back home, I realize how badly I hurt you. I handled everything all wrong. I was young and dumb and selfish, and if it makes you feel any better, I missed you so much after I left."

"But not enough to come back," she said simply.

She saw the pain in his eyes, but she refused to feel sorry for him.

"It was complicated," was all he said. He stood still, looking at her a moment more, then went back to the ladder. Rose followed with the lights.

She didn't know how to respond. It had been complicated for her, too, but she hadn't left him. She wouldn't have done that to him.

IT TOOK AN hour for them to put up all the lights. Jesse watched as Rose made sure every detail was perfect. Tony had placed a few of the poles in the wrong place, so she had Jesse pull them up and move them to make an exact square in the barnyard.

Jesse glanced over Rose's head at Tony, who rolled his eyes good-naturedly. Apparently, the man knew what to expect when working with Rose.

As they mounted lights around the barn doors and along the barn walls, Jesse listened to Rose and Tony joke around like old friends. Jesse guessed Tony to be about his dad's age. He actually liked him quite a lot after just knowing him a short time.

Finally, when Rose was satisfied, Tony went on his way to take care of chores and Jesse followed Rose back into the barn.

"Can you throw those in a box and carry them up to my apartment?" she asked, pointing at about ten strands of faulty lights on the floor.

"I'll see if I can get them working later. Here are some extra bulbs, put those in the box, too."

"Sure thing." Jesse packed up the lights, walked them over to her apartment, and set them down at her door. He glanced at his watch and saw that it was already after four. It was too early to call it a day, but he had no desire to go back to cleaning out the house again.

When he got back to the barn, Rose had unpacked several more boxes. It looked like a party store had exploded in the barn. Red, gold and orange decorations were strewn everywhere. How had that happened in the five minutes he'd been gone?

Rose was examining a large wreath made of straw and colorful autumn leaves when she spotted him. "There's so much more to do," she said.

"I can see that. You want some more help?" Jesse offered, though he had a feeling she'd already designated some jobs for him.

"I would love more help. I'll even throw in dinner later. That is, if you still like spaghetti."

Jesse grinned. "You remembered that's my favorite."

She grinned back. "Of course."

"I think I can be bought with food." He

would have done it for nothing, but he kept that thought to himself.

"I thought so. You've more than earned it today." She handed him the wreath, then pulled an exact replica of it out of the box. "These go on the front of the barn doors. You'll see hooks already there to hang them."

Jesse took both wreaths and hung them on the barn doors. He stood back to make sure they would be straight enough for Rose, tipped one a little more to the right, then nodded in approval. By the time he returned to Rose, she'd laid out six more identical wreaths.

"They're multiplying," Jesse said. "What are we doing with those?"

"Those go on the walls outside the barn, you'll see more hooks. You hang, I'll keep unpacking stuff."

Rose pulled out colorful autumn garlands to wrap around the poles holding up the twinkle lights.

"I see you have this down to a science," Jesse noted as he tied off the top portion. She wrapped the garland gracefully around the pole and secured it at the bottom. It was exactly the right length.

"Yep, we're careful taking them down and

packing them each year, so we can reuse them. I have a system."

"Do you usually do all this by yourself?"

"No. Tony helps, but as you saw, he was more than happy to let you take over as decorating assistant this year."

Jesse laughed. "I can't blame him."

Rose pouted playfully. "Come on. This isn't so bad."

"No, it's not. He's the one missing out on the spaghetti."

"I don't usually make him spaghetti, so you should feel special," she teased.

"I do feel special."

"Besides, I saw the overnight bag but no groceries. I figured you didn't think as far ahead as dinner."

"It's embarrassing how easy it is for you to read me." They walked to the next pole and added garland. "What did my dad think of all this hoopla?" Jesse asked, glancing down at Rose.

She carried the box of garland to the next pole. "Hoopla pretty much describes what he thought. He didn't understand why we should go through all the trouble. He didn't mind us having the festival for a good cause, but he didn't see the need for the decorations, the dance, all the extra stuff. In his mind, it was extra work."

"I hate to say it, but I kind of agree with him."

"All the extra work, that's what makes it special. It can't be just another busy Saturday, with the same old classes and hayrides. We get this place all dolled up, like a church on Easter Sunday. We want people to remember it and come back next year. Our festival has gotten us noticed nationally. Every year, it gets bigger and we get more coverage. It's something special."

Rose's passion impressed Jesse. She was the backbone of Sunflower Farms and probably the reason for its success in recent years. He could see why his dad had put all his trust in her.

"I'm starting to think this place is lucky to have you," he said.

"No, I'm lucky to be here," she countered.

Later that afternoon, Rose released Jesse from his decorating duties. He watched her head off to take care of the animals, and when he was sure she was gone, he went back over to the tool cabinet in the corner of the barn.

He'd spied a new white picket fence panel leaning against the wall, waiting to replace the garden fence crushed by the old oak tree. Jesse grabbed the fencing and some tools and carried everything to the garden.

He wanted to do something nice for Rose. That morning, she'd been stressed over her employee calling in sick and having to clear that tree by herself. If he fixed the fence, it would be one less thing for her to worry about. He still wanted to check the irrigation system, but that would have to wait. The day was almost over.

Why was he doing all this? He hadn't planned on helping around the farm. He acknowledged there was something about rolling up your sleeves and getting your hands dirty, that spoke to him. He'd forgotten what it was like to be around nature, have the sun on your back, and to break a sweat through manual labor. What would it be like to be around this all the time as an adult? Jesse couldn't imagine. It was something he couldn't wait to get away from at eighteen but being here now, it made him wonder. He could see why Rose loved it but this was her world now, not his. He would never move back. As he worked on the fence, his mind went back to the conversation with his realtor. He wanted Jesse to make a quick decision about selling the farm.

Should he tell Rose about the offer he received? He didn't want to upset her more but he knew the right thing to do would be to tell her.

CHAPTER FOUR

ROSE ADDED THE spaghetti to the boiling water on the stove, then stirred the tomato sauce bubbling in another saucepan. Anxiously she checked the time again. Why was she so nervous? This wasn't a date. It was just two old friends sharing a meal.

Two old friends with a history...

A few minutes later, she heard his knock. Quickly checking herself in the mirror, she tossed her loose hair over her shoulder and smiled. She walked over to the door to let him in. Butterflies fluttered in her stomach when he smiled at her from across the threshold.

"Hey there, come on in," she said as she opened the door all the way.

"Thanks. It smells delicious."

He walked past and Rose couldn't help but notice the scent of fresh soap. His hair was combed back and still damp. Like he'd just showered.

Rose inwardly shook herself. This was not a date.

"Don't get too excited," she said. "The sauce isn't homemade or anything."

"That works for me." He shoved his hands into his jean pockets. "I'm just glad you invited me, otherwise, I'd be hightailing it to town right about now to pick up some fast food."

Rose laughed. "Have a seat. I just put the spaghetti in, so it'll be about ten minutes." She went back to the kitchen and checked the sauce one more time.

Jesse sat on the couch, stretched his long legs out and made himself comfortable. The studio was small enough for them to carry on a conversation with him in the living room and her in the kitchen.

"Thanks again for your help today," she said. "I'm not sure how busy you'll be the rest of the week, but there's plenty more to do if you have the time."

"I'll keep that in mind. I promised myself I wouldn't procrastinate tomorrow, so I plan on attacking my dad's bedroom. Maybe later this week I can help again."

"Honestly, I think it would be good for you to see what all goes into the festival, since this is your farm now. Maybe you'll want to come back here one day on a more permanent basis."

Jesse's face changed suddenly, like he wanted to say something but was holding back. Instead, all he said was, "Maybe."

They chitchatted some more while she drained the pasta, and they made their plates. Sitting at the kitchen island, Jesse ate heartily, helping himself to seconds before Rose had even eaten half her plate.

After a while, her nerves settled, and she felt that old comfortable feeling sitting next to Jesse. He had an easygoing personality and had always been fun to be around.

Quite the opposite of herself. The older she got, the more uptight she'd become. Being in charge was a big responsibility. She had a lot on her shoulders with the farm, and making sure it was profitable was no small feat. It had been tougher when Jesse's dad was diagnosed with cancer. She'd watched him deteriorate for months until he couldn't care for himself anymore. That was when she stepped up, doing as much as she could to help him around the house. She began taking him to doctor appointments, pharmacy runs, and shopping for him. When it became too much for Rose to care for him and manage the farm, her dear friends, Mr. and Mrs. Dawkins from church, started making daily trips to the farm to help. The Dawkins would give Rose a break and would sit with James, while she worked on the farm. In his last two weeks of life, a local hospice caregiver came to the farm and helped as well. Finally too weak to get out of bed, James Cooper faded away. It had broken her heart to go through it with him, and it still hurt to remember it. Jesse had no idea how bad it had been.

A low whistle caught her attention. "Earth to Rose," Jesse said, waving his hand in front of her face.

Rose pulled herself out of the dark memory and glanced over at him.

"You okay?" he asked.

"Yeah. Just thinking."

"About what?"

"I'm not sure you want to know."

"Sure I do."

"I was thinking about your father and how sick he was at the end. How hard it was to take care of him and this place. By myself."

Jesse studied her. "You're right, I don't want to know."

"Do you think you'll *ever* want to know?" she asked patiently.

"I hope so. I'm just not there yet. Coming back to the farm was a big step. I'm still adjusting to the shock of being here again. I'll let you know when I'm ready to talk about him, and then I'll hear what you have to say," he said softly.

Rose nodded and went back to her spaghetti. It would do no good to push him. He might never be ready to talk about it. She, more than anyone, knew what Jesse had gone through with the man. But he never got a chance to see what a good man of faith his father had become. She wanted Jesse to know that. She wanted his dad to be remembered as a good person. Was that even possible? And why was it so important to her?

Because she knew he needed to forgive his father in order to heal his own wounded heart.

They finished eating in silence. At last, Rose picked up her dishes to carry to the sink, then gestured at Jesse's empty plate. "Are you ready for me to take that or are you planning on thirds?"

"I can have thirds?" he teased.

"With the way you eat, I'm sure you could make room for fourths."

He laughed lightly. "You think you know me so well. No, I'll pass on having more. I'm stuffed." He patted his stomach, then stood. "You made dinner, let me do the dishes."

Rose was surprised. "Who? You?"

"Sure. You forget I'm a bachelor. I've had to learn how to do my own dishes."

"Have at it then. I'll put the leftovers away, you wash."

Together, they made quick work of the cleanup. Rose packed the extra spaghetti and sauce into some plastic containers while Jesse washed the plates and pots. As he was finishing up, she pulled a towel out of a drawer and stood next to him to dry the dishes.

"I see the hens have been working overtime," Jesse said with a nod toward a basket of eggs on the counter.

Rose laughed. "Eggs are plentiful around here. I set those aside for Grammy today, and she forgot to grab them before she left. I'll take them to her tomorrow. She lives just down the road, like ten minutes away."

"One of the perks of living on a farm. Lots of eggs," Jesse said.

"One of the many perks," Rose added. "Help yourself to some if you want."

"Thanks. Maybe later." Jesse rinsed the last pot and set it on the counter for Rose to dry. "We make a pretty good team."

"Yeah, well, that was never the problem with us, if I recall," she said matter-of-factly.

"I suppose you're right. What we had was special." Jesse pulled the stopper and let the soapy water go down the drain. Drying his hands, he leaned his hip against the counter.

"Do you think you'll ever get married?" she asked. Personally, she didn't think she'd ever find anyone like Jesse again. That was the reason she'd barely dated since he'd left. No one ever could measure up to him.

"I don't know. I've dated, but it's never been quite right with anyone. Maybe one day, though. How about you? I'm sure there will be somebody out there for you. Someone better than me, that's for sure. I was nothing but a disappointment, I realize that now."

Rose put the last pot away in the bottom cabinet, then stood up and rubbed her forehead with a free hand. "Seems we're getting serious again. I guess it's inevitable when you have unfinished business like we do." She searched for a way to express what she felt. "Disappointment isn't the word I would use. You were everything to me. I loved you. When you left, I wasn't disappointed. I was shocked and heartbroken. That's what I was. Not disappointed."

"I'm sorry. I really am."

Rose stared at him. She could see his regret for his actions written all over his face—the way his jaw was set, how sad his eyes were, and the tight line of his lips. In a way, she hoped he felt bad. At the time, she'd felt worse.

Changing the subject, she asked, "Did you save room for dessert? I have some rocky road ice cream." Without waiting for an answer, she pushed away from the sink and grabbed the ice cream from the freezer. The brief rush of cold air felt good on her hot face.

When she turned back, she bumped into Jesse's chest.

Confused, Rose tilted her head up and searched his eyes. He took the ice cream from her hands and set it on the counter. Then he put his arms around her in a hug. Leaning down, he rested his cheek on the top of her head and just held her.

Rose was too surprised to say or do anything. Then slowly her arms circled his waist. Jesse sighed softly.

A long-forgotten sensation came flooding back...that feeling of contentment in his arms. She felt seventeen again, young and innocent. All the hurt she'd been carrying temporarily slipped away, as she gave in to her memories of the young man she'd once loved.

JESSE KNEW THE minute Rose let her guard down. She went from stiff and unsure in his arms to soft and sweet. She was petite and even felt delicate in his arms, but he knew she wasn't weak. Quite the opposite. She had a backbone of steel. He wanted to protect her and keep her safe. He also wanted her to know how sorry he was for everything.

Leaving her had been the worst thing he'd ever done. And the stupidest.

Holding her in his arms brought back so many memories. He didn't move or say anything for a long time, too afraid he'd break the spell, and she'd push him away. He knew this would be short-lived. There was no doubt about that.

This could get awkward. He let her go.

She stepped back out of his arms, her eyes cast down.

He realized he wasn't ready to let go. He remembered the connection they'd once shared.

Before he changed his mind, Jesse reached out, lifted her chin and kissed her.

Hesitantly, Rose kissed him in return.

When he pulled back, she studied him. He wondered what she was thinking.

"I really am sorry for everything," he said.

"I know," she said simply.

Jesse was kind of hoping for more, like maybe she forgave him. Did he really expect one hug and a short kiss to change everything between them?

Rose picked up the ice cream again, grabbed some bowls and spoons and started scooping. Her movements were shaky as if he'd flustered her. Soon they were both sitting at the island with their bowls of ice cream.

When Jesse finished his, he stood up. "I better get going. I'm sure you've had enough of me for one day," he kidded.

She shook her head. "No. I hate to say it, but it's been nice having you around. When do you go back to work?"

"I'm off the rest of the week," he reminded her. "I'll go back Monday."

He thought he saw something flicker across her face. A touch of sadness, maybe.

"By the way, I confirmed the fire truck for the Sunflower Festival," he said. "They can come each day, and I've got a volunteer to help with the truck."

With the change of subject, she shifted back into business mode. "That's great," she said. "Do you think they could give some safety talks, too?"

Jesse gave her a peculiar look. "I thought people were coming here to have fun," Jesse said. "Being lectured on checking the batteries in your smoke alarms doesn't sound all that fun to me."

"When you put it that way, I guess not. I was just trying to think of how to make the most of it."

"Don't worry, we do this all the time. The guys will bring the gear and let the kids try it on. My buddy Mike might be willing to tell some stories if he finds the right time for it. Either way, the truck is always a big hit."

"All right. I'll take your word for it. Thank you."

"Well, I better get going. Thanks again for

dinner." He took his bowl to the sink and rinsed it out.

As Rose walked him to the door, he realized that he hadn't mentioned the offer on the farm. Things had been going so well… He hated to spoil the evening by bringing it up. But she needed to know.

"Rose, there's something else I wanted to tell you."

"It's been quite the night, I don't know if I can handle anything else," she said dryly.

"No, I'm being serious," he said, tension suddenly filling him.

"From the look on your face, I'm guessing it's not good."

"It can be good. It just depends on how you look at it." Uncomfortable, he shoved his hands in his pockets. "I've received an offer to buy the farm. You should know that I'm seriously considering it."

Rose looked crushed. "You would really sell this place?"

"Why would I keep it?"

"Because I'll run it. You won't have to lift a finger. It doesn't get much better than that."

"I don't want the farm."

"How can you say that? This is your legacy. It's been in your family for three generations.

And your mother loved this place. You had fifteen good years here growing up when your mom was still alive. Doesn't that mean anything to you? All you ever focus on are the three years after her death!"

"Before she died we were actually a happy family. I could tell how in love my parents were. But then I ruined everything when I killed her," he said crudely.

Rose grabbed his arm. "You *didn't* kill her," she said firmly. "You were in a car accident. You were only fifteen and just learning to drive. Even an experienced driver couldn't have prevented that other car from slamming into you. It was an accident. Give yourself a break. It wasn't your fault."

"He blamed me."

"Your dad was wrong. He couldn't see past his own loss to act like the father he should have been. He shouldn't have blamed you. And you shouldn't blame yourself."

"All that doesn't matter now. He's gone, and I don't live here anymore. I live in Jacksonville, I'm a firefighter, not a farmer. And I think you should know, I've been offered a decent amount to sell the farm."

"You'll regret giving up your family legacy," she reiterated.

"No, I won't," he said, more out of stubbornness than anything. He didn't know if he would regret it or not. He still planned to think about it thoroughly before he decided what to do. The problem was, he had to decide by next week.

"Do you mind me asking, how much did they offer?"

"$1.4 million."

Rose didn't flinch. "I'll admit, that's a lot of money. But if you sell this place, you'll put seven people plus me out of work, and I'll lose my home and everything I love. For what? Money. I knew you could be foolish, but I never thought you were greedy, too."

"I'm sorry, Rose, but I'm not doing it to hurt you."

"Well, you would hurt me. Again."

"I can only say I'm sorry so many times. I've made no decision yet, so don't be mad at me. I'll let you know either way, when I decide."

"I'll be praying that you make the right decision this time," Rose said.

"Don't you get tired of all the problems that go along with running this farm? Fallen trees, droughts, broken irrigation systems, employees calling in sick. And those are only the problems I've seen in the few days I've been back. I can only imagine what else there is that you haven't told me about. If I sell this place, you wouldn't have to worry about any of it anymore. And just so you know, I would give you some of the money, so you could start over."

"You mean you'd give me a severance package," she said bitterly.

"Well… I—I…" Jesse tripped on his words. "That's not what I meant." But now that she said it, he supposed she was right. "I don't want you to worry about being kicked out on the street. You would have enough money to live on until you figured out what to do."

Rose's face turned red with anger. "You know, one minute you act like this great guy, helping me out today, even being charming. You apologized… We shared a kiss. Then you tell me you're still considering selling the farm, and it reminds me that I don't know you anymore."

"Come on, Rose. I'm the same guy you've always known."

"Yes, you are. You're the same guy that left me."

Rose opened her front door.

That was her cue for him to leave. Who could blame her for being upset with him?

"Thank you for dinner. I really appreciate it. I feel bad for leaving on a sour note like this," he said.

Rose closed the door on him.

CHAPTER FIVE

CARRYING TWO MUGS of hot coffee, Rose crossed the dry front yard and walked up the porch to the main house. She'd been up since dawn, feeding the animals and doing her morning chores. Out at the rose garden, she'd been surprised by the repaired fence where the fallen tree had been. She had a strong suspicion Jesse was the one who'd fixed it. The coffee was a thank-you for fixing it.

With time to cool off, Rose could see why he'd consider selling the farm. But it didn't mean she liked it. He thought this place was a lot of work, and it was, but it was worth it. Yes, things broke, and issues came up, but she dealt with them. And sometimes she worried about making payroll or paying the bills. Currently, they couldn't afford a new irrigation system, and because of the drought, it was the worst timing. But she couldn't let Jesse see her worries or he'd be even more convinced she couldn't manage the farm.

She needed to help him fall in love with the place so he would want to keep it.

Rose knocked on the front door.

After a minute, Jesse appeared at the door. Surprise lit his handsome face. "Hey. I wasn't expecting you."

"I come bearing coffee." She shoved a mug toward him.

"Thanks. You read my mind. I've been dying for coffee all morning. I can say with certainty, I did not plan well when I came out here from Jacksonville."

"Told you so."

"Yes, you did." Jesse took a big sip.

"You could have come to my place for some coffee," she said.

"Yeah, right. After the way we ended things last night? I figured if I asked you for a cup of coffee this morning, you'd throw it at my head."

She tried not to smile. A corner of her mouth lifted anyway. "Aren't you being a little dramatic?"

He lifted his brows. "You think?"

Rose laughed. "Okay, maybe not. Sorry about

that. You just took me by surprise with the offer on the farm."

"I can understand that." He took another sip.

"But we're adults now, so I decided to put on my big girl pants and play nice. Maybe I can even talk you out of selling the place."

"You're welcome to try, but I'll have to do what I feel is best."

"I understand. And thank you, by the way."

"For what?"

"Fixing the garden fence. I know it was you." She shook her head. "I don't know where you found the time."

"No worries. It's not a big deal."

Rose looked past Jesse into the house. "It looks the same in there. I thought you planned to clear this place out?"

Jesse glanced over his shoulder. "It's a slow process. Don't forget I spent half the day yesterday helping you. Do you want to come in for a few minutes?" He held open the door for her.

Rose hadn't planned on staying, but she found herself nodding, nonetheless. She ignored the way it felt to brush his arm with hers as she passed him.

"I've been thinking about keeping the table," he said, following her into the kitchen. "I have a little one in my apartment, but this piece is much nicer."

"Then keep it. Though I will say, it is perfect for this space." Standing with one hand on her hip and the other holding her coffee, she surveyed the large kitchen. The solid farmhouse table had probably been in Jesse's family for a couple generations, made back when furniture was built to last.

"It does look like it was made for this room, doesn't it?" he said.

"Couldn't you just see yourself living here? Sitting at the same table you sat at as a kid… raising your own family?" she asked.

Rose could see the sadness wash over Jesse's face. "I've never thought about it. I mean, I want a family one day, but I never envisioned myself living here. I guess I always felt like my dad would live forever, which meant I would never come back here."

"I think we may have our lives planned out. But often God has something else for us. Nothing we can imagine, and often much better."

"That sounds like something my mom would have said. She always had words of wisdom for me like that."

"She was a smart woman."

"Wonderful, too." He ran a hand through his short hair and walked up to the window. He stared absently at all the lights and decorations they'd put up around the barn, but she wondered if he was actually seeing them. "Something about being back makes me think of her," he said at last. "You know, I dreaded coming here for fear I would be overwhelmed with the memories of him, but I never considered I'd be blessed with memories of her, too."

He glanced back at Rose. This big strong man in front of her suddenly looked vulnerable, and her heart went out to him.

"I think you're going to be okay," she said. "What you're going through, it's what a lot of people go through when they lose their parents. It's part of the grieving process."

"But I'm not grieving him."

"Aren't you? I think in your own way, you're coming to terms with losing him again."

Jesse just shoved a hand in his pocket and turned back toward the window.

It was clear he was finished talking. Rose strolled around the kitchen, quietly opening cabinets and the pantry door to see what else he might need for the week. She stopped short at the coffee maker on the counter.

"Ah, look here. I thought you couldn't make coffee. You had a coffee maker hiding in plain sight," she said.

He smiled over his shoulder, "Yeah, I found that, too, but there's no coffee. I need to make a grocery run today, so I don't have to keep bothering you."

She shook her head. "You're not bothering me. I told you last night, it's been nice having you around." She was glad to see him sort of back to his happy-go-lucky self. "Show me what you've done so far in the house."

"Sure, come on back." Jesse led her to the main bedroom.

Rose felt a lump in her throat, and her eyes watered as she looked around. Unlike Jesse, she missed James Cooper. After he'd found God, a kind of peace and healing had settled over him. The difference in him had been like night and day. Everyone around the farm noticed.

"I have some time this morning. Would you like help?" she asked.

"If you're offering, I'll take it. I feel like I'm up to my eyeballs in clothes."

"I wonder if the Taylor family could use any furniture, since they lost everything in the fire. I mean, they're going to get the proceeds from the festival this weekend, but I'm sure they could use furniture too."

"That's a good question. A lot of it is pretty old, but maybe they'd like some of it."

Rose stepped outside for a moment to call Lizzie, Johnny Taylor's wife. Within ten minutes, Rose had found a home for most of the furniture. She went back inside to tell Jesse the good news.

"I'm glad I thought of the Taylors before you gave everything away," Rose said. "I'm hoping that and the money we make with the festival will get them on their feet again." She shoved her phone back in her pocket. "Now, where were we?"

Jesse handed her some garbage bags. "You were about to help me, otherwise I'll be here for the next month sorting this all out."

"I wouldn't mind that. It's nice having you here."

His dark eyes caught hers, and Rose resisted the urge to glance away.

"I can't stay," he said seriously. "You know that, right? Whether I sell this place or keep it, I would never live here."

Disappointment settled in. She'd known all along he was only here temporarily, but deep inside she realized she wanted him to stay. She'd missed him. She knew better than to let old feelings resurface, but some things just couldn't be helped. And it was a contradiction to everything she'd been telling herself…that she couldn't trust him again.

She played it off like it was no big deal. "Oh, I know. Honestly, I don't know why I said that. You've been clear you want nothing to do with this place." For good measure, she added, "Besides, I still hadn't forgiven you for leaving." She gave him a tight smile and went to work.

They took loads of trash to the farm's dumpster and loaded the medical equipment in the back of the truck with the last of the clothes.

Jesse closed the truck's tailgate with finality. "I think that about does it for now. I'll run these to town and bring back the truck." He wiped his brow on his forearm.

"Actually, I need to pick up the dunking booth for the festival. Do you mind if I come along, and you can help me grab it on the way back?"

"I don't mind at all. Are you ready to go now?"

"Let me go to my apartment and fill up a water bottle to take. You want one?"

"That'd be perfect. Holler when you're ready. I'll be inside."

Rose watched Jesse for a moment as he went up the steps and back into the house. He'd always been on the thin side, but he had filled out over the years.

She forced herself to get moving. She ran up to her apartment and grabbed her things, plus the basket of eggs for Grammy. She texted Jesse on her way back down the stairs and met him at the truck.

"Why don't you drive?" she asked, walking around to the passenger side.

"Sounds good to me," he said.

"I thought we could drop off these eggs at Grammy's house too. It's on the way."

When they were settled in the truck, she handed him his water bottle, then put the basket of eggs in her lap. She'd ridden in this truck thousands of times, but it felt completely different with Jesse by her side. She flashbacked to them as young teens on a date. They truly hadn't had a clue about life back then. They'd been busy navigating the treacherous waters of high school, and then the anguish of Jesse losing his mom. They'd been through a lot, but she preferred to remember the happier times.

Now if she could only get Jesse to think like that.

Nervously, she tucked a loose strand of hair behind one ear, then made herself relax against the worn-out leather seat.

After they pulled out on the main road, Rose showed Jesse how to get to Grammy's house a few miles away. When he parked, Jesse made no move to get out.

"Come in with me for a minute. Unlike me, I promise Grammy won't bite," Rose said.

Jesse laughed. "You said it, not me."

She smiled at him. "I know I can be a little difficult at times."

Jesse climbed out of the truck and stayed silent as he followed her up to the door. As they waited for Grammy to answer the doorbell, he asked, "Hey, do you think your grandma would want any of the medical equipment we're donating? Like the walker or the shower chair?"

Rose cut her eyes toward him. "If you value your life, do not mention it to her."

"Why? She might need them one day."

She shook her head. "Grammy doesn't consider herself old, and if you even suggest that she is, she'll give you an earful. Trust me, she's corrected me more than once."

"I think you're overreacting."

Just then, the door opened. "Rose," Grammy exclaimed like she hadn't seen her all year. She looked at Jesse. "And you. You're still here?" she asked, sounding surprised.

Rose glanced up at Jesse. This time, she was the one waggling her brows at him.

"Yes, ma'am," he said politely. "I'm still here."

"Hmm." Grammy studied him, then seemed to remember her manners. "Come on in, you two."

Rose and Jesse followed her through a hallway to the kitchen. "We can't stay long. I just wanted to bring you the fresh eggs I promised you." Rose handed her the basket.

"Thank you, sweetheart." Grammy took the basket and gestured toward the table. "Sit, have some iced tea with me."

"We really can't…" Rose started to say.

Jesse cut her off. "Iced tea sounds great," he said, taking a seat at the table.

Rose glared at him. This was supposed to be a quick stop. However, she went along with it and moved to a cabinet and started pulling out glasses while Grammy grabbed a pitcher of iced tea from the refrigerator.

"What are you up to today?" Grammy asked as she poured tea for the three of them.

"We're running errands, but later we have to keep setting up for the festival," Rose said. "What about you?"

"I've been cleaning, but later I have a date," she said with a grin.

"Really? With who?" Rose asked.

"His name is Bob. I met him the other day at water aerobics."

"So, it wasn't all old people after all," Jesse said.

"What?" Rose asked.

"That's what Grammy said the other day before she left for water aerobics. She hoped everyone there wasn't old."

"Well, they were all a bunch of old-timers, but Bob went out of his way to make me laugh, so I agreed to one date," Grammy said.

This wasn't too surprising. Grammy had a busy social life and went on dates every so often. The irony wasn't lost on Rose that her grandmother's dating life was more active than her own.

"If he makes the cut, why don't you bring him to the Sunflower Festival?" Rose said.

"We'll see," Grammy said idly.

Rose felt her phone vibrate in her pocket. It was a text from her mom that read, Saying goodbye to the canyon today. Here are a few pics for the road.

Rose scrolled through four pictures of her mom and dad at an overlook of the Grand Canyon. They looked tanned, healthy and happy. That made her smile.

"More pictures from my parents' road trip." Rose turned the phone so Grammy and Jesse could see.

"Beautiful view," Grammy said.

"Looks like they're having a great time," Jesse added.

"They're on their way back now." Rose shoved her phone back in her pocket. "We better get going. We have a lot of errands to run this afternoon."

They said goodbye to Grammy, but not before she gave Rose another bag of random things she didn't want anymore. Rose took the bag obediently. She'd learned long ago not to resist. Grammy always won.

Once back in the truck, Rose went through the bag. Brand-new pink slippers that were not Rose's size; a matching fuzzy robe that Rose would never wear; and a pair of generic sneakers with Velcro instead of shoelaces. Rose shoved everything back in the bag.

"I told you, she always does this. Don't tell Grammy, but we'll drop this bag off at Goodwill, too."

Jesse laughed. "Come on, that pink robe looks just like you."

Rose tossed him a dirty look. "Careful. If you're here long enough, she'll start giving bags to you, too. Just ask Tony."

"Anything is better than 'are you still here?'" he mimicked Grammy's frequent question.

"That's what you get for leaving."

"I get an old lady's attitude?" he asked.

"Yep."

"Now I know where you get it from."

"Hey!" Rose playfully slapped his shoulder.

"While we're in town, can we drive past the old high school?" Jesse asked. "I haven't been back since I left."

"I haven't been back, either. I heard they put in a pool and built a new gym. While we're there, let's stop at the Sunlight Café and have lunch, then it'll really feel like old times."

"Is that place still around?" His voice held a hint of nostalgia. "Oh man, I loved their wings back in the day."

"It's still there. I go every now and then. Always loved their fries. They have that special seasoning sprinkled all over them."

"I remember."

"Do you do much cooking?" Rose asked suddenly. "You said you make spaghetti. Anything else?"

"I know my way around the kitchen."

"Really? What's your specialty?" she asked, glancing over at him.

"I guess my favorite thing is grilling. Does that count?" His dark eyes studied the road ahead.

"Grilling? I thought you said you lived in an apartment."

"I do. I'm on the second floor, and I have a private balcony. The grill's out there."

"That's the one thing we don't have on the farm. A grill. I wouldn't even know how to use one if I had it."

"It's pretty simple. You just turn on the gas, let it heat up for a few minutes and you're set. Occasionally you need to replace the gas, but that's easy enough."

"I'm sure you are oversimplifying it. What kind of things do you make?"

"Steak."

Rose chuckled. "Somehow I knew you would say that. What else?"

"Burgers, chicken, chops, fish... Pretty much anything you get from the meat or seafood counter. Sometimes I'll smoke pork butts and take them to the firehouse. The guys love that."

"Maybe we shouldn't be talking about food when I'm starving."

"No doubt. Now I'm in the mood for barbecue."

"Me, too. We can go to the Sunlight Café another time."

Ten minutes later, they dropped off their load at Goodwill, then with stomachs rumbling, they went in search of barbecue.

"You live around here, you should know where to go," Jesse said.

"I don't get out much. Maybe we don't have any barbecue places in town."

"It's the South, of course there's barbecue. Why don't you look it up on your phone?" Jesse asked as he drove down a random street.

"Oh, right." Rose pulled out her phone and asked Siri. Soon, they had two places to choose from.

They found the closest place a few streets over. Jesse pulled into the parking lot for a hole-in-the-wall barbecue joint. The overhead sign had a large cartoon pig wearing an apron and a chef's hat. Porky's Grill House flashed in bright red letters. The parking lot was packed for the lunch rush, a good sign. Jesse circled around looking for a spot, then gave up and parked across the street.

Jesse held the restaurant's door for Rose, and she stepped into a small dining room humming with chatter and clinking dishes. To their left was the kitchen, where a man stood at the edge of a massive oven, rotating large slabs of meat over a roaring fire. The delicious aroma of cooking meat assaulted her senses, and Rose found her mouth watering in anticipation.

A hostess led them to the last open booth. Jesse waited for Rose to sit, then sat down opposite her. The menu was a typical meat-and-two-sides affair. Everything looked delicious.

Jesse tilted his menu out of the way, saying, "Lunch is on me."

Rose glanced at him. "What? You don't have to, you know."

A sparkle entered his eyes, and his mouth curled up in an endearing little half smile that Rose knew was useless to resist. "I know," he said, "but you made me spaghetti last night.

Plus, you helped me clean out the bedroom all morning. I owe you."

"I'm sure I'll need more help with the Sunflower Festival coming up."

"Then I'll gladly help you."

"We'll see about that. I was going to ask you to muck the stalls in the barn when we get back," she said.

"Were you? I suppose I might be able to help with that," he parried.

"Oh, and did I tell you, I need someone to help me try out the dunking booth?"

"I can do that, too. I've got a good arm." He held up an arm and flexed his biceps.

She gave him a devious little smile. "That's not what I mean, and you know it. I need someone to get in it and give it a whirl."

"I bet you do. I'm not promising anything."

Rose laughed. "You are easy to tease."

The waitress came over and set two glasses of water on the table. "Are you ready to order?"

"Sure. Rose, you want to go first?" Jesse asked.

"I'll take the pulled pork with slaw and beans and a glass of sweet tea," she said.

The waitress scribbled down the order, then turned to Jesse. "And you?"

"I'll take the ribs and beef brisket with the slaw and beans, as well. Sweet tea for me, too." When the waitress scurried away with their orders, Jesse leaned toward Rose. "Out of curiosity, who normally sits in the dunking booth?"

"This is the first year we've had it. I got it specifically for you." She smiled at him.

His eyes narrowed as if he was trying to figure out whether she was still teasing him.

Finally, she burst into laughter. "I'm joking. We have the dunking booth every year. Mostly folks from church volunteer to sit in it. The preacher is usually willing, and there are a few others I can count on. But by the end of the day, the kids take it over. It's a lot of fun."

Jesse playfully wiped his brow like he'd just escaped with his life. "And here I thought I would be stuck in it for the whole day."

"Don't worry, I'll need volunteers for the pie-throwing contest, too."

"When you say 'volunteers,' you actually mean someone who gets hit in the face with the pies?"

She gave him a big grin. "Now you're catching on. I always knew you had a brain in that pretty head of yours."

"Oh, I'm catching on, all right... Catching on to the fact you think you're funny."

"Or I'm getting even with you," she said lightly.

Jesse waggled his brows at her. "So you think I'm handsome, do you?"

"You're shameless."

"What do you mean?" he asked innocently.

"You know what I mean… You're a shameless flirt. You always have been."

"That's why you love me."

"I loved you once. Who says I still do?" she asked.

Jesse didn't have a quick rebuttal but sighed instead.

With his silence, Rose took the opportunity to ask something she'd been wondering. "So, you didn't tell me if you were dating anyone," she said, growing serious.

Jesse's brown eyes studied her. "Nobody right now."

"Right now? Does that mean you *were* dating someone?"

"There was someone for a few years. We were engaged and everything, but we broke up recently."

"If you don't mind me asking, why did you break it off?"

"It was mutual. We'd outgrown our relationship. We did more disagreeing than agreeing.

We finally both realized we had gotten engaged because it'd seemed to be the next step, but we actually didn't make each other happy anymore. Being with somebody shouldn't be that hard. Neither one of us wanted a miserable marriage. Marriage is hard enough without starting off on the wrong foot."

"I'm sorry to hear that. Do you miss her?"

"This is terrible, but no, I don't miss her. Is that awful or what?"

"No, it sounds to me like you two did the right thing by calling it off."

"Yeah, we did. How about you? Are you dating anybody?"

Rose shifted uncomfortably now that she was in the hot seat. How could she answer this without sounding pathetic? "No. I don't have time for dating. Besides, there hasn't been anybody in a while that I've wanted to date."

"I find that hard to believe. I'm honestly surprised you aren't already happily married with a couple of kids."

"Maybe I would have been, if you'd stayed." She hadn't meant for that to slip out.

His brow lifted; she could tell she'd surprised him.

"I don't know what to say to that," he said.

"Sorry, but it's true. Don't you ever wonder where we'd be if you'd stayed in Eagletin?"

"You wouldn't have wanted me to stay. I wasn't the guy you needed me to be. I couldn't be around my father anymore."

"So, you've said. But haven't you ever wondered?"

"Yeah, sure I did. I also regretted leaving you, but I did what I had to."

"You could have done it differently. I would have gone with you if you'd asked." She hadn't planned to bring the past up again, but it'd been unavoidable.

"That wasn't an option. If you'd gone with me, you would have given up your dream school here. I couldn't let you give up your dream."

"It should have been my choice."

"Maybe you're right, but there is nothing I can do to change it now," Jesse said.

What could she say to that? He was right in that they couldn't turn back time and change things. Rose felt like they'd hit a stalemate. At that moment, the waitress dropped off their sweet tea and a basket of hot garlic bread. "Your lunch will be out in a couple of minutes," she said, then dashed off.

Rose grabbed a piece of garlic bread. "This smells yummy," she said as she tore the bread in two. They grew silent as they nibbled.

"Hey, you know what we should do?" Jesse asked, popping the last piece of bread in his mouth.

"What?" Rose asked.

"We should go for a dip in the lake for old times' sake."

Rose didn't know how to respond. It was probably the last thing she should do if she didn't want to get any more attached than she already was. But what if showing him how much fun it was to be back on the farm would convince him not to sell? Maybe he would have a change of heart. There were good memories there, too, and he could make new ones. With her.

"What?" Jesse said. "You have something against swimming on a hot day?"

"I don't know. I have a lot to do before the festival. And it's October, you know."

"It's also Florida, and it's ninety degrees outside. I think you can sneak away for an hour."

She shrugged, "I guess I could take a short break. Wait... Did you bring a suit?"

"I did."

"So, you planned this?"

"Maybe." He had the nerve to look sheepish.

He hadn't changed a bit. "Fine. We'll go swimming. But we are putting up the dunking booth first."

"Fine."

"And if you're going to get wet anyway, you can try it out."

"I'll pass," he said.

"Come on," she wheedled.

"Only if you try it out, too."

"We'll see."

The waitress brought their lunches, and Rose immediately dug into her pulled pork. Everything was delicious. She ate as much as she could, then pushed the plate away. "I'm stuffed."

"You're not going to finish that?" Jesse asked as he polished off the last of his beans, leaving an empty plate.

"There was too much. You can have the rest of mine."

"If you don't want it, sure, I'll take it." He pulled the plate over and finished it off. "Mmm, the pulled pork is good."

Rose remembered how they used to share food. It was like déjà vu all over again.

JESSE PAID THE BILL, left a tip and headed out of Porky's with Rose. Lunch had been more fun than he anticipated. Rose was more fun than he anticipated, now that her temper had finally cooled off.

They walked back to the truck and Jesse started the engine. "Okay, where to?"

"The high school's not far from here. Let's go there."

"Sounds good." Jesse pulled out onto the street.

"Do you know where you're going?"

"Sure," he responded, though in truth he felt turned around. He used to know the streets of Eagletin, but he'd been gone so long that things had changed. His memory of the area had faded, too.

Rose was silent for a moment, then chimed in, "Um…we're going the wrong way. Unless you're taking the long way."

"The long way, of course." He shot her a quick smile, then changed direction.

Rose didn't say a thing.

Fifteen minutes later, they drove past the high school slowly. "It looks smaller, doesn't it?" Jesse asked.

"Yeah, it does. But it also looks the same."

"Do you want to get out and walk around?"

Rose looked out the window. "School's in session, so we better not. I'm pretty sure they don't want random people walking around campus."

"You're probably right."

Jesse drove around the block to view the other side of the school. In the large new pool, students with brightly colored caps and goggles swam while the PE teacher yelled from the sideline. The water rippled and sloshed over the sides.

Jesse rounded the corner and drove up the other side of the school. They came up to the new gym. Twice as big as the previous gym, and gleaming in the sun, it was hard to miss.

"Nice. The students here probably don't have a clue how good they have it."

"Nope. Not a clue," she said.

Jesse slowed the truck and pulled over in the grass to give them a good view of the school. "Man, we had so many good times here."

"I know."

"It makes you wonder what the old gang is up to," he said.

"Some of them are still around, others like you have moved on. You know, if you're still around Sunday, you should come to church. You can see some of the old gang there. Richie, Shea, Tyler, they all still go there. Richie and Shea are married now and have a baby."

"Really? I never knew they were an item."

"They weren't a couple in high school, but in the last five years, they started dating and got married. They're good for each other."

"Well, I'm glad they got their happy ending." Both Richie and Shea were good people; they deserved to be happy.

Someone should be happy, even if it wasn't him.

Oh, he was quite satisfied with his life. Being a firefighter was fulfilling, though lately he had started to wonder if it was something he wanted to do for the rest of his life. He had plenty of friends at work and dated some, even if he had struck out when it came to long-term relationships. Sometimes he just felt a little lost, like he was searching for something but couldn't figure out what.

He forced himself back to reality and glanced at Rose to see if she was ready to drive on. But the words didn't come. He was struck by how beautiful she was. Her eyes were ice blue in the bright afternoon light. She wore little makeup but didn't really need any. Her face and arms were tan from working outside, and her usual ponytail suited her. Though she was small in stature, she had a big personality and could hold her own with the best of them.

When she caught him staring at her, she asked, "What's wrong? You're looking at me funny."

"It's nothing." Jesse turned away in embarrassment, as if she could read his mind. He cleared his throat, then started the truck.

Rose gave him directions to the party rental store where she'd rented the dunking booth. The thing was huge and took four people to load it. Luckily it fit in the bed of the truck and they could close the tail gate. When they got back to the farm, Tony and Justin helped Rose and Jesse get the booth out of the truck and set it up.

Jesse walked around the booth, inspecting it. Gently, he tugged the bull's-eye. It was attached to an arm that released the seat. The whole thing looked sturdy, but that didn't mean he wanted to be the one sitting in it. "So, are you adding the water now?" Jesse asked as he glanced around for the nearest hose.

"Nah. We'll wait till Thursday or Friday for that," Rose said.

"Then what was all that talk about me testing it for you?"

"Simple. I just wanted to scare you. You know, keep you on your toes." She gave him a sugary-sweet smile and walked away.

Jesse watched her as she headed back to the barn, her sass radiating in each jaunty step. She'd sure had him going. He'd been ready to jump in the booth if she'd asked him nicely enough. How could he say no to her?

He thought about the ultimate decision he would have to make about the farm. Could he really sell it? Could he do that to Rose?

Did he want to keep the farm for himself? For the first time, it wasn't an outright no for Jesse.

He took a moment to survey his surroundings. The distant golden sunflower fields swayed in the afternoon breeze, their beauty truly stunning. Beyond the sunflowers were the citrus grove and the strawberry fields. He turned toward the barn and was reminded of all the animals that lived there. Betsy the cow, the horses, chickens and goats. What would become of them if he sold the farm? Would the new owners want them? Where would they go? Would Rose take them with her? How could she, when she had no place to go?

Guilt washed over Jesse. He didn't think he could do that to Rose or the other farm employees. Would it be right to let someone turn this one-of-a-kind farm into a housing or commercial development?

Rather than go back to the house and start cleaning out the next room, Jesse wanted to go after Rose. By the time he followed her into the barn, she had already started to unpack more decorations.

Rose glanced up at his footsteps. "So, you're here to help?" she asked.

"I'm here to steal you away for an hour."

One brow went up. "To do what?"

"Swimming at the lake. Let's cool off."

"If you're that hot, I can fill up the dunking booth after all," she said with a laugh.

"Very funny," he said dryly. "Come on. You can get away for a little while. I'm pretty sure there won't be a decoration emergency in the next hour."

"How do you know? This is the first year you've been around for the festival preparations.

We have decoration emergencies all the time," she said, matter-of-factly.

Jesse walked over to Rose, took the armful of baskets she held and put them back in the box. She watched him silently, like she didn't know what to say.

He took her hand and gently pulled her toward the doors. "Come on. It won't kill you to have a few minutes of fun. If it puts you behind, I promise I'll help with the decorating."

"You promise?"

"Promise." He saw tension leave her face, and she smiled, flashing her even white teeth.

"Okay. But only for an hour, and then we come back."

"Got it. Now go change, and I'll meet you in five minutes. We can take the truck this time," he said.

She paused, then added, "Do you think we should invite the staff, too? I think they'd like the break."

Jesse hadn't planned on making it a party, but how could he say no to her? "Sure. The more the merrier."

"Great! I'll send them a text."

ROSE SENT OFF a text to the employees who were on the farm. There were only five of them on Wednesdays, three guys and two women. They were all going to think she'd lost her mind, or that it was a gag. They never took a break like this—a swim in the middle of the afternoon? With a big weekend coming up?

But wasn't that the best reason of all? They could all use a carefree hour to take a swim.

Rose ran up to her apartment to change. The thought of Jesse waiting on her made her feel like a nervous teen about to go on her first date. She rushed around, dropping everything she picked up.

What was wrong with her? She was a grown woman, not a lovesick teenager. She should stay and work on setting up the Sunflower Festival, not run off for a swim. But since she'd invited everyone else, that made it okay, didn't it? Too late to cancel now anyway.

Honestly, when was the last time she did something spontaneous? The sad truth was never. Jesse was always the fun one, and she'd always been serious. If he was only going to be here for a few days, what was the harm in enjoying his company?

She knew how to be careful. She could guard her heart. At least, that was what she told herself.

Rose changed into a one-piece swimsuit,

pulled on some shorts and a tank top, slipped on flip-flops and grabbed two towels. She ran down the stairs before she did something stupid, like change her mind and go back to work. She was doing this, and she would have fun, she told herself. She deserved a break from all her work and her worries about this place.

Jesse waited in the cab of the truck with the engine running. She opened the door, and music poured out. It was a song from high school that she used to love, and all kinds of memories came flooding back.

Jesse saw her and turned down the volume. "Great song," he said, as if that explained why he'd turned it up so loud. "Did you text everyone?"

"Yep." Rose felt her pulse quicken as she climbed in next to him. She tried to ignore it.

"Are they coming?"

"I don't know." Which was the truth. No one had responded to her text.

Jesse took a shortcut to the lake. A cloud of dust followed the truck down the narrow path.

"You know, I used to go out to the lake all the time as a teenager just to get away from my dad," he said. "I haven't thought about this place in years. I think I've blocked it out, like everything else that had to do with the farm and my childhood."

He'd blocked her out, too, Rose thought.

The truck emerged into the clearing next to the lake. A couple of the farm guys were already doing cannonballs off the dock.

"Guess they saw your text," Jesse said dryly as he parked.

"I guess so," she said with a chuckle. "Why do I have a feeling this isn't the first time they've been out here?"

"Because it probably isn't."

"And why do I feel like there's not much more getting done today?"

Jesse smiled. "I can't imagine why you would say that."

They got out of the truck and strolled down the dock. Rose tossed a towel to Jesse, and he caught it easily with one hand. "Thanks," he drawled as he set it down at the end of the dock, then pulled off his shirt and slipped out of his shoes.

The two farmhands, Ricardo and Justin, were swimming around in deep water. Jesse had already met Justin, so Rose quickly introduced Jesse to Ricardo.

The guys immediately hooted and hollered for Jesse to throw Rose into the lake.

She shot them an indignant look. "Hey! Where's your loyalty?" She turned to Jesse, backing away. "Don't you dare, mister."

Jesse had the good sense to leave it alone. He held his hands up in surrender. "I would never," he said innocently.

Rose stiffened and waited until he'd moved past her on the dock. Not to be outdone by the other guys, Jesse took a running leap, pulled his knees to his chest and cannonballed into the lake. The splash covered everything within fifteen feet, just missing Rose.

Seconds later, Jesse surfaced in a rush, shook his wet head, and wiped his eyes. "Come on Rose, get in! The water's refreshing." His smile was infectious.

Unable to stop a grin, Rose pulled off her shorts but decided to leave her tank top on over the swimsuit. She put her hair up into a messy bun; there would be no cannonballs for her. Like a mature adult, she padded over to the ladder and slowly stepped down into the water. Her feet hit the bottom of the lake, and she bounced around on tiptoes until she faced Jesse.

"Ooh, this is colder than I expected," she said, biting her lip as she grew used to the temperature. The water reached her chest.

"It feels wonderful," Jesse said. He spread out his long arms and floated on his back next to her.

"I used to love swimming here in the summer," she said, squinting under the bright sun. "The lake used to feel like bath water, it was so warm."

"I can remember coming here and then getting in trouble because I wasn't doing my chores." Jesse sighed. "But it was worth every minute."

"You didn't always get in trouble. I think that's just what you've chosen to remember."

Jesse seemed thoughtful. The rumble of a UTV broke the peace of the lake. Tony drove up with the two other farm employees, Alexa and Susie. They all walked down to the end of the dock, various stages of amusement and disbelief on their faces.

"What is happening here?" Alexa called. "I told these guys there's no way Rose is giving us an afternoon off to swim. I had to come down here to see it for myself."

Rose laughed. "Not the whole afternoon. Just for an hour." She wondered if she would regret going along with Jesse's plans.

"We'll see," countered Jesse at her side.

Tony wasn't shy and jumped in the water.

"We don't have swimsuits," Susie said.

"Jump in anyway," Jesse said.

The two girls seemed to notice him for the first time, and interest showed on their faces. "And who are you?" asked Alexa.

Rose rolled her eyes. Jesse wasn't her boyfriend or anything, but that didn't mean she wanted to share him with Alexa or Susie. Trying hard to keep her voice indifferent, Rose answered. "That's right, you all haven't met. This is Jesse Cooper, Mr. Cooper's son. He owns the farm now."

That bit of news caught their attention. Their eyes went wide.

"Jesse, this is Alexa Johnson," Rose continued. "She's been with us for about two years now. She's my citrus expert and takes care of the citrus grove. And to her right is Susie Allen. She's been with us for almost a year. She helps me with a little bit of everything around the farm."

"Nice to meet you," the girls each said, almost in unison.

They decided not to go swimming but were happy to take off their shoes and dangle their feet over the edge of the dock. They chatted with Jesse for a few minutes while they watched everyone else swim.

"So, are you moving back to the farm?" Alexa asked. She'd never been shy. Susie, always the quieter one, was content to listen.

"No. I'm just here to clean out the house. I'll leave Monday after the festival."

"You're not going to live there? Seems like a perfectly good house going to waste."

Rose watched Jesse field the questions, all good ones. She knew him well enough to know when he started to feel uncomfortable. He set his mouth in a straight line and the answers became shorter.

"Ah...no. No plans for anyone to live there," he said.

"Oh, that's a shame. Seems to me you should let Rose live there or rent it out. I'm sure people would pay big money to come live on a farm for a week."

Jesse immediately shot that down. "I won't do that. It's fine that the farm is open to the public, but we aren't going to have strangers staying overnight like a hotel." He politely excused himself to go swim a few laps.

Rose hated that she was aware of where he was the whole time as he swam. To distract herself, she swam over to Justin and Ricardo but left as soon as they started threatening to dunk her. She ended up going back to where the girls sat at the dock and chatted with them.

After a while, she got out of the water, grabbed her towel and sat on the brittle grass near the shore. It was just as dry near the lake as it was up at the farm. A soft breeze blew, and she was content to sit in the warm autumn sun while she dried off. Lazily, Rose laid back on the towel and closed her eyes, resting an arm across her face to block the sun. She heard her coworkers splashing in the distance, but other than that, all was quiet.

On the verge of falling asleep, Rose was startled when cold water dripped on her warm skin. Before she even opened her eyes, she knew it was Jesse because nobody else would dare. A deep chuckle confirmed it.

She sat straight up with a squeal. "What are you doing?" Narrowing her eyes, she wiped the drops off her face. "I was half asleep," She scolded.

Jesse laughed it off as he threw his towel next to hers and plopped down on it. He shoved a hand in his wet hair and pushed it back, then gave her a lopsided smile. "Sorry." Teasingly, he leaned to one side and gently bumped shoulders with her. "You're about as prickly as a porcupine sometimes."

"You're right, maybe I am."

They were quiet for a minute, watching the others enjoy the lake. Eventually, Justin and Ricardo swam to the dock ladder and climbed out of the water. Alexa and Susie pulled their feet up, put their shoes back on and headed toward the UTV.

"This was fun! Thanks for inviting us," Tony called to Jesse and Rose as the girls loaded into the UTV. "We're heading back now."

Justin and Ricardo soon followed. They waved goodbye to Rose, then left on foot back to the farm.

With everyone gone, a hush settled over the lake. The afternoon sun was moving further west, a sign they'd been there for some time.

Rose realized she was reluctant to leave. "I wish we could stay right here forever. Don't you?" She stared out at the lake, but out of the corner of her eye she could see Jesse look at her. She felt herself blush but tried to act cool. She would not give him the satisfaction of knowing how much he affected her.

"I do, too."

She faced him. "You know, you're welcome

to stay here permanently." She kept her tone light, but she was dead serious.

"I know. Trust me, I know. And it's getting harder by the minute to leave. I never expected to have these feelings."

Was he talking about feelings for the farm or for her? She wasn't at all certain.

Keeping a level head, she reminded herself to treat him like a friend. "It's normal to have them. You grew up here. And if they're good feelings, maybe you can start visiting more often. Take an interest in the farm. If you don't want to live here, fine, but you can still be part of it."

"I know. I'm starting to see that now." He paused, like he was searching for words. Finally, he said, "Thank you for being so understanding."

"Well, sometimes I want to kick your butt if I'm being completely honest. But I also don't like kicking someone when they're already down. I know more than anyone what you've been through. You should be proud of yourself that you came out a stronger man for it."

"Thank you."

Rose stood and grabbed her towel. "You ready to head back? I can think of about a dozen things I need to do before I call it a day."

"Of course. If you're ready, then I'm ready," he said good-naturedly.

Rose offered a hand to help him up. Jesse smiled and let her pull him to his feet. When their fingers touched, it felt as intimate to Rose as if they'd kissed. She dropped his hand as soon as he was standing and headed toward the truck with him close behind.

How was she going to get through the rest of the week with him always around?

The more serious question: How would she handle it when he was gone again?

CHAPTER SIX

Jesse steered the truck down the shady trail as he and Rose headed back. The afternoon sun tipped further west and beams of light shot through the tree canopy. Though his swimsuit was mostly dry, he sat on the thick towel anyway to protect the old leather seats. Rose had her towel snuggly wrapped around her waist. She sat next to him with her seat belt stretched over her lap, a contented look on her face. She seemed much more relaxed now, like the swim did her some good.

"I was thinking about running back into town to get some groceries for the house," he said. "Why don't I make you dinner tonight? If you don't have other plans, that is?" His eyes darted back and forth from the road to Rose. Her cheeks were sun-kissed, and her hair was still pulled up on top of her head in a messy bun, with little tendrils of hair escaping everywhere.

"My only plans consist of unpacking decorations and putting up what I can before it's time to feed the animals and call it a night. Dinner sounds fabulous."

"Do you need anything from the store while I'm out?"

"Not the grocery store, but…" Rose checked her watch. "It's almost four. Could you pick up the rest of the games and booths I rented from the party store? They're open until six. There are four more games I planned to get. They didn't fit in the truck with the dunking booth but you should be able to get them in one trip, it's nothing too heavy. It'll save me from having to go back to town tomorrow to get them."

"Sure, I can swing by and pick them up. Do you have any special requests for dinner?"

"Maybe something healthy, since we splurged for lunch."

"That's not quite what I meant." Jesse pulled up to the stairs to Rose's apartment, put the truck in Park and cut the engine.

Rose made no move to get out. Instead, she looked at him as if puzzled. "What did you mean?"

"Oh, I don't know. Like if you wanted steak, seafood or chicken. I don't think I'm in the mood for salad. I worked up an appetite with all that swimming."

Rose laughed. "A salad isn't the only healthy option. Have you ever heard of vegetables or lean meat? That kind of stuff. You know, be creative."

"Ah, got it. I'll figure something out and surprise you." He absently tapped his fingers on the steering wheel.

Rose climbed out of the truck, then turned back to face him in the cab. "You know, I don't have a grill. You'll be forced to use a stove," she teased.

"I think I can handle a stove."

"In that case, do you want to cook at my place?"

Jesse rubbed his jaw as he thought about it. For some reason, he had the urge to make dinner at the farmhouse. "I think I want to make dinner in my old house. I haven't emptied out the kitchen yet, so I should be able to find what I need."

"Suit yourself. Don't forget to rinse off the layer of dust from everything."

He laughed out loud. "Come on, it adds flavor."

"I'll catch you later, smarty-pants. Don't forget to pick up my booths. Just text me when dinner's ready." She shut the passenger door before he could say anything, then ran up the stairs and disappeared into her apartment.

Jesse caught himself smiling after her. Rose had a way of bringing out the best in him. He'd missed that. It made him happy just being around her.

The women he'd dated over the years had never lived up to the high bar she'd set. There'd been times when he'd even wondered if his memories of her were accurate. Had he placed Rose on some pedestal, like she was the perfect girl? But being here with her again, he realized she was simply wonderful. They were good together.

The problem was, they weren't a couple. And that was all his fault, wasn't it? He could kick his younger self. But what good would that do? He'd done what he had to do to survive.

Jesse changed clothes back at the house, then headed to town, thoughts of Rose on his mind the whole time. He would need to make a decision about the property sale very soon, yet he was no closer to knowing what he wanted to do. Maybe he should just pass on the offer for now. But what if he didn't get another offer like it? Was he willing to let this chance pass by? What good was it to hang on to the farm if he had no intentions of ever working on it or living here?

Jesse had enjoyed his day with Rose, meeting the staff and the afternoon swim at the lake. What if every day could be like that?

After the house was cleaned out, maybe he could start fresh. His father was truly gone and couldn't hurt him anymore. Maybe it was time to let go of the pain and remember the better times, when his mother was alive and the three of them were a happy family. What if he could live here and start over with his own family?

When Jesse returned to the farm, he brought the groceries into the kitchen. In addition to ingredients for dinner, he'd bought a bag of apples to share with the horses. He took out two small ones and shoved them in the pockets of his khaki shorts. After the groceries were put away, he drove the truck to the barn and unloaded the games and booths that he'd picked up. Rose had been right; they were much more manageable than the dunking booth. One was a colorful fishing booth, another a ring toss, and the third was a mini golf green complete with balls and putters. The fourth was a painted wooden pumpkin and scarecrow stand where people could pose for pictures. He set everything inside the barn next to the remaining boxes of decorations.

Jesse half expected to see Rose in the barn and was disappointed when she wasn't there. He left the barn in search of her.

The sun sat low in the western sky, casting long shadows over the empty corral. His gaze darted across the distant fields in search of Rose's familiar form. The horses nibbled on grass in a nearby pasture, so he took the five-minute stroll out to them to share the apples. It didn't take Missy any coaxing. She trotted over and greeted Jesse like they were old friends. She was already his favorite.

"Here you go, old girl. A special treat for you, just like I promised." He pulled out one of the apples and held it out to her on a flat hand. In a couple horse-size chomps, the apple disappeared.

When Moe saw him feeding Missy, he walked up and gently nudged Jesse's shoulder.

"Don't worry, I'm not leaving you out." Pulling out the second apple, Jesse offered it to Moe. He stroked the gelding's neck as he gobbled up the apple.

From there, Jesse walked over to the goat pen. Amused at their bleats of welcome, he slipped through the gate and took a few minutes to pet the friendly goats.

"I'm sorry I didn't bring you anything, but Rose will be here soon with your supper."

A little white goat bleated as if in complaint.

"You talking to goats now?" Rose asked from behind, startling Jesse. A little thrill shot through him.

He stood and turned toward her. "I rather like talking to goats, they don't talk back."

Rose had changed back into jeans and a T-shirt and she held a bin full of hay for the goats. "I don't know if I should take your answer personally or not."

"Just teasing. You want some help?"

"That would be nice. Thanks."

Jesse opened the gate for her and helped her pass out the hay to the goats.

"So, did you just get back?" she asked.

"A few minutes ago. I put the games and booths inside the barn. Will those be enough for the festival?"

"We have more coming on Thursday from the church."

"That's good." Jesse threw down some

hay, then grabbed another handful. "Dinner shouldn't take long."

"I'm almost finished with my chores. I just need to get the horses in and then clean up a little."

"How about you come over in an hour? Would that work?"

"Perfect. Should I bring anything?"

"I don't think so. I've got everything covered. But thanks."

When they finished feeding the goats, Jesse went back to the main house and started dinner. He didn't know if Rose would think a rice pilaf was healthy, but he figured he'd get a gold star for the salmon and asparagus at least.

Right on time, Rose rang the doorbell. When Jesse answered the door, he wasn't prepared for what he saw. Yes, Rose was always beautiful, but tonight she took his breath away. She wore her hair down and straight. It was a shiny, golden honey-brown color. She wore jeans with a blue blouse that brought out her light blue eyes. Her cheeks were pinker than usual thanks to her sunburn.

Jesse had to mentally shake himself. "Hey there. Good timing. Come on in." He tried to be smooth but feared she knew him well enough to know he was the same goofball he'd always been.

"Thanks. Is dinner ready?" She walked past him with a covered plate in her hand.

"Just about. I was waiting for you to get here before I threw on the fish."

She turned back to face him. "Fish? That sounds healthy."

"I hope you like salmon."

"I love it." She handed him the plate. "Here, this is for dessert."

Jesse lifted the aluminum foil and inhaled the smell of fresh chocolate chip cookies. "You didn't have to bring anything, but I'm so glad you did."

"I couldn't come empty-handed," she said, grinning.

"When did you have time to make these?"

"It's nothing. They were slice-and-bake. Cookie dough is like milk and eggs. I always have some on hand."

"Well, thank you. Come in, make yourself at home." Jesse led Rose into the kitchen and set the cookies down on the table. On the stove, a hot skillet waited. Jesse started the salmon. "These only take a few minutes. Go ahead and grab yourself something to drink out of the fridge."

Rose pulled out a pitcher of lemonade, grabbed a glass from the dish rack on the counter and poured herself a drink. "I'm impressed. You already have the table set and everything," she said, putting the pitcher back in the refrigerator.

"Oh ye of little faith. I told you I would make dinner," he said.

"Is there anything I can do?"

"Nope, I have it handled. Just relax. I know it's been a long day."

She scratched her head and looked around the kitchen as if she wasn't sure what to do with herself. "I'm not used to relaxing. I normally go nonstop until I conk out at night. There are always so many chores that need to get done."

Jesse flipped the salmon, then glanced at her. "Do you need more help around here?"

"If you mean, should I hire more people, the answer is no. But if you're asking whether I could use your help around here, the answer is yes."

She looked hopeful, and it broke his heart in a way he had not expected. Even though he was starting to not hate the farm anymore, he didn't want to commit to anything. All of this was new for him and unexpected.

"I can't promise to help any more after this week," he said slowly. "I've been clear about not staying. This is about closure for me."

"I know. But a girl can dream, can't she?" She went over to the table and sat down.

Jesse plated the warm rice and asparagus, then added the salmon at the last second. He carried the two plates to the table.

Rose rewarded him with an appreciative smile. "This looks delicious. Thank you."

"You're welcome. Anytime." Jesse took a seat across from her, where he'd always sat growing up. Old habits were hard to break. It didn't feel right sitting in his mom's or dad's spot at either end of the table.

Rose paused with her fork in midair. "This is really good. It definitely exceeded my expectations."

Jesse laughed. "Thanks. I'm glad you're not disappointed."

"Now that I know you can cook, I won't be feeling sorry for you anymore or imagining you over here hungry."

"I guess I just ruined my chance for more sympathy spaghetti, didn't I?"

Rose ate some of the asparagus, then asked, "So, is this your smooth move for the ladies? Cooking for them?"

Jesse shook his head at the question. "What? Why would you say that?"

"I'm just wondering if this is the meal you make for all your dates."

"You think this is a date?"

"No, that's not what I meant," Rose said in a rush. Her pink cheeks turned pinker.

She was adorable.

But he realized she wasn't wrong about dinner. "Okay, I may have to confess something to you. I have made this dinner for a date or two. But I promise you, this is not some elaborate plan to make a move. It just happens to be in the rotation of about a handful of things I can make that turn out good."

Through narrowed eyes, Rose studied him. Finally, she laughed. "Okay, I believe you. And I can't wait to try what else is in the rotation."

"Good, because it's in the fridge all ready for tomorrow night."

She raised her brows. "And what is that?"

"Don't you want to be surprised?"

"Not at all. Spill it."

"Well, I make the best homemade chicken Marsala."

"Ooh, that sounds yummy." She took a sip

of her lemonade, then turned thoughtful. "Can I tell you something?"

Jesse set his fork down and sat up straighter, ready for whatever it was she had to say. "Of course. You can say anything to me."

"It's been weird having you around the farm. When I first saw you Saturday, I recognized you, but you were more like a stranger to me. Do you know what I mean? You'd been gone for so long, I realized that I didn't know you anymore. But after spending the last couple of days with you, I realize you're still the same guy I knew back when we were kids. I feel like I blinked, and you're here again. That fun-loving, sweet guy I knew is here again. Teasing me, flirting with me, finishing my plate at lunch, just like old times."

"I know what you mean. I have to say, I dreaded coming back home. I could only think about how hard it would be to face my dad's memory. But that's only been a small part of this homecoming. Having you here and remember-ing how good we were together has been un-expected. It's been good for me, too."

"But yet, you don't want to stay?"

Jesse didn't know how to answer that. If he did sell, it would ruin everything with Rose.

"Give me time. I'm figuring it out as I go. Can we enjoy tonight, though?"

"Sure," she said. However, her whole body stiffened as she went back to her dinner.

Jesse took a bite of salmon. "You know, I was thinking about your rose garden. Do you advertise it like you do the sunflowers?"

"No. Folks usually stumble on it when they finish with the gardening classes on Saturdays. It's nice and all, but the sunflowers are our bread-and-butter."

"I don't think you give yourself enough credit. That rose garden is stunning. We should be advertising it along with the other things like the classes, the sunflowers, the strawberry picking. It can all be part of the experience."

She looked at him funny.

"What?" he asked. Did he have food on his chin or something? He wiped his mouth with a napkin.

"You said 'we.' *We* should be advertising it."

"Oh, well…you know what I meant. *You* should be advertising it."

"I'll have to think about it," she said. "We already have thousands of brochures printed up, and it'd cost money to make any big changes to the website. I would have to think of an angle and figure out what would attract people the most."

"The way I see it, you've already done all the hard work by creating the garden. Now you just have to promote it. The next time you print the brochures, think about adding it."

"I guess so." She didn't seem too convinced.

How could she not see how amazing it was? Jesse decided to change the subject to something she was more comfortable with. "I've been thinking about joining you at church this Sunday. It'll be good to see everyone again. I can't remember the last time I attended services."

"Before college?"

"Pretty much." He started in on the rice.

"I think that's great. It'll give you a chance to see some old friends. So, you go back to work Monday?"

"Yeah. I kind of dread it."

"Why?" she asked, leaning back as if to study him.

Jesse shrugged. "It's nice to be on vacation, even though this isn't a real vacation."

"Ah. You're going to miss me. I knew it."

Jesse laughed. "That, too."

"Seriously, though, you don't like your job?"

Rose asked. She took a final bite of salmon, then pushed her plate away.

"I like being a firefighter," Jesse said thoughtfully. "The first couple of years I loved it. It was my dream job. Every boy wants to be a firefighter when they grow up, right? I've made some great friends, and I've learned a lot, but lately I've been thinking about moving on. It's hard to explain, but sometimes I feel like there should be more in my life than just work."

"Maybe your soul's secretly yearning to be a farmer," she said with a grin.

Jesse laughed. "Yearning? I don't think I'm yearning to do anything."

"I think it's a sign from God that it's time to come home," Rose said lightly as she reached for the cookies.

"And this is my home?"

"Of course, this is home. Don't you see, this farm is wonderful. I love this place."

"My dad should have left it to you then."

"I wish he had. Then I wouldn't be worried about you selling it."

Jesse looked away, suddenly uncomfortable.

She grew serious. "If you have any affection for me, I am begging you to hang on to this place. Let me run it. You won't have to do a thing. Please don't sell the farm."

"As much as I would love to make you happy, I can't keep this place just for you. I originally had no plans to keep it, and yes, I've been wavering over this decision. But if I keep it, it has to be my decision."

He thought he saw her eyes water, but she was so stubborn she didn't let any tears slide down her cheeks. Instead she blinked a few times. He knew she would refuse to cry in front of him.

"I think I better go now," she said.

"Please don't go away mad."

"I'm not," she snapped. "It's just time to go home and get some sleep. I'm exhausted. Dawn comes real fast when you live on a farm. But you wouldn't know anything about that, would you?"

He widened his eyes at her tone. "I think I can remember what it's like to get up at dawn to work in the fields. To come home from school and have a list of chores a mile long. I grew up here, remember?"

"I thought you'd forgotten all that. It's why you ran away at eighteen, isn't it? To forget?"

"I ran away to escape my father. Not the farm itself."

"Well, he's gone now. Maybe it's time you came home for good."

Jesse didn't want to argue with her. Rose had been the best part of his week. He didn't want to make her mad or hurt her. He hated to admit it, but she might be right. Could the farm be part of his life?

Rose pushed her chair back and stood up. The mood had been ruined, and she was clearly set on leaving. Jesse stood as well.

"I'll leave the rest of the cookies here for you," she offered.

"Thanks," he said awkwardly. He followed her to the front door.

"Thank you again for dinner. It was really good."

Jesse held the door open, not quite ready to let her go. There was a time he would have been comfortable enough to lean in for a kiss, but that was long ago. If he were to try something like that right now, she'd reject him after the tension of the last ten minutes. They needed to keep things friendly anyway. His visit was just that. A visit. He'd be leaving Monday morning.

"Good night," he said at last.

"Good night." Rose gave him a tight smile. He could see the resignation on her face as she left.

Jesse watched her walk away into the night, the short trip back to her apartment. The evening had been kind of strange. He and Rose had this push and pull when they were around one another. One minute they were keeping each other at arm's length and the next they were drawn to one another. He had the impression she felt the same way. It was confusing and he wasn't quite sure what to do about it.

Jesse was starting to wonder what it would be like to be on the farm more. Not necessarily move back but visit more. Of course, that would mean keeping it.

Jesse shook his head. He wasn't sure what he wanted.

CHAPTER SEVEN

THE NEXT MORNING, Jesse rose early. It was already Thursday, and he needed to get as much done as possible before the Sunflower Festival started on Friday. First, he wanted to check the irrigation system because watering the sunflower fields by hand was a lot of work. How did Rose keep up with it?

Jesse grabbed a toolbox and shovel on his way out. After a couple hours of troubleshooting, he thought he knew what the problem was; it was something his dad had shown him long ago. Jesse headed to town for the hardware store, bought the supplies he needed and went back to make the repairs. As he tested the irrigation system, he said a little prayer that it would work. When the old system roared to life, Jesse practically danced with joy. He couldn't wait to surprise Rose with the news.

For the time being, he went back to the

house to continue Operation Cleanout. Jesse went through each room in the house, emptying drawers and clearing off surfaces. He ended up throwing a lot of stuff away, but did come across a small jewelry box hidden in the dresser. Lifting the lid, he found his parents wedding rings along with his mom's diamond engagement ring. He recalled his mother saying the engagement ring was passed down from his grandmother. There was other jewelry in the box, but Jesse felt like the rings were the real treasure. He closed the lid and moved the box to his room for safe keeping.

Jesse finished his parents' bedroom and moved on to his father's office. Emptying his father's desk, he stumbled on some old news clippings from his high school football days. Surprised, Jesse sat back in the office chair and skimmed through the articles. Why would his dad save these? He'd never cared about Jesse's games or anything else he did after his mother was gone. At least that was what he'd always thought.

Jesse pushed away from the desk, leaving the clippings behind, and walked out. He had to get away from the house and everything it represented. He needed time to absorb...to think.

Automatically he went in search of Rose, the one person who would understand what it all meant. She'd been back in his life for less than a week, and she was already the most important person he knew. He needed to share with her what he'd found.

His long legs carried him to the barnyard. The booths and games he'd picked up the day before had been set up that morning, and the place looked festive with the lights and decorations. He found Rose in the garden, on her hands and knees pulling weeds. She jumped when he reached her.

"Jesse! You startled me," Rose said. She straightened and wiped her brow with the back of her hand.

"I'm sorry. I just had to talk to somebody." Jesse stood over her with his hands on his hips.

She squinted up at him against the bright sun. "Why? What's wrong?"

"Everything's okay," he promised. "It's just I found something today, and I'm not sure what to think about it."

"Come on, let's go sit in the shade. Tell me what you found." Rose led him to a bench under a row of arches covered in rose vines. The space was shady and the scent of roses hung thick in the air. "What's going on?" she asked, her voice filled with concern as she waited for his answer.

Jesse propped his elbows on his knees and clasped his hands. "Today, when I cleaned out my dad's desk, I ran across some newspaper clippings that he saved from when I was in high school. They were articles from the local paper about the football team. They had my name and picture in them."

"You always were one of the best players on the team, and you made it to the playoffs. It's not surprising you were in the paper."

"It's not that. It's the fact that he saved them. To my face, he barely acknowledged I was even on the football team. He never asked me how it was going, and he never went to any games. I honestly thought he didn't care about it at all. So why would he save the articles?"

"Because he did care about you."

"He didn't act like it. He barely talked to me. It was like two strangers living together, coexisting. Not a parent and their only child. When he did talk to me, he was mean and angry. I never could do anything right in his eyes, and he made sure I knew it."

Rose shook her head. "I'm sorry. I know it was hard." She rubbed his back in comfort.

"He was really angry with me after the car accident. He blamed me for my mother's death. I blamed myself." Jesse squeezed his eyes shut. "You know, I lived with him for almost three years after my mom was gone, and it never got better. Why didn't he ever tell me he was following my games? It would have meant the world to me."

"I don't know for sure, but maybe he didn't know how to express himself. Some people are no good at saying the right thing. Add in the fact he was still grieving for your mom."

Jesse scrubbed his hand across his face in frustration. This went against everything he'd believed. He'd always thought of his father as the villain.

Rose continued, "After you were gone, I got to know him. I think he hit rock bottom, being left alone. He lost your mother, and then you left him. After a while, he started to go to church. We were all a little shocked to see him there. I really think it took him finding God for him to change. He became a better man, like he found an inner peace."

"I haven't told you this," Jesse said slowly,

"but he left me a phone message once. It was just a few years after I left home. He said he was sorry and asked me to call him or come see him. I was still so angry with him that I never did. I deleted the message and forgot all about it."

"You have to believe he loved you. I know he had an awful way of showing it when you were a teenage boy, but he loved you." Rose reached over and squeezed his hand.

Just then, Alexa walked up to them. "Hey, Rose," she said. "Pastor Ronnie is here along with a bunch of other folks. They're looking for you."

"Thanks. They're here to help me finish setting up for the festival. I'll be right there."

Alexa nodded. "I'll let them know you're coming." She left them alone once again in the garden.

Rose glanced at Jesse. "Are you going to be okay?"

"Yeah, I'll be fine. I was just shocked and had to tell somebody or explode."

"Why don't you come with me to say hello to Pastor Ronnie? I know he would love to see you after all these years."

Jesse followed Rose out of the garden, then

remembered the good news. "Oh, I looked at the irrigation system and figured out the problem. I was able to get it going."

Rose stopped in her tracks, "You were able to get it working? How? I was told by the company I called that we needed to replace it. They said they couldn't fix it."

Jesse scratched his chin. "Hmm. Sounds to me like they were trying to sell you an irrigation system."

Annoyance flashed across her face. "Maybe you're right. They'd make more money installing a new one over repairing the old one. I told you it was pricey. I feel like such a sucker."

"Don't blame yourself. How would you know otherwise?"

Rose started walking again, her arms across her chest and her eyes studying the ground. She was either deep in thought or upset.

"Hey, the important thing is that the irrigation system works, right?" he pointed out. "No more hand watering."

She squinted up at him. "You're right, but it's frustrating. We've worked our fingers to the bone watering this place for months. I wish you'd come back sooner."

Jesse didn't respond to that, but inside, he was starting to feel the same way.

When they reached the barnyard, the volunteers milled around as they waited for Rose. Two trucks in the parking lot held more games and booths.

Jesse recognized his old pastor immediately. Salt-and-pepper hair had been replaced with a head full of white hair, and there seemed to be more wrinkles than before. A large grin split Pastor Ronnie's face when he saw Jesse, and he thrust a hand out to greet him. "Jesse Cooper. Welcome back. You have been missed, son." His deep voice was full of emotion, like he meant it.

Jesse shook his hand, genuinely happy to see him. "Thank you, sir. I've missed you all, too."

An older couple next to Pastor Ronnie turned toward Jesse, and he recognized the Dawkinses instantly. Their smiles were huge as Mr. Dawkins shook Jesse's hand and Mrs. Dawkins gave him a hug.

She stepped back and gave him a once-over. "Jesse Cooper, you are all grown up and handsome as can be."

Jesse shook off the compliment. "Good to see you, Mrs. Dawkins. It's been ages."

Two young men walked over, and Jesse recognized one of them as his old friend Tyler from high school. Back then, they'd gone to the same church and were pretty tight. After Jesse left for college, they'd lost touch.

Tyler smiled when he recognized Jesse. "Hey, man. I can't believe it's you."

"Yeah, good to see you."

They gave each other a brief brotherly hug.

Remembering his manners, Tyler introduced a friend standing next to him as Robert. A young woman joined them, and Tyler threw his arm over her shoulder. "This is my fiancée, Kim. I don't know if you two remember each other. She went to our high school, but she was a couple years behind us."

"Nice to meet you. I've heard lots of stories about you," Kim said.

"Nothing too awful, I hope." Jesse was only half joking.

"No, no. All good," she reassured him. "Thank you for letting us have the festival on the farm. This year it's for a cause that hits close to home. Our friends Johnny and Lizzie Taylor."

"I'm glad we can help them. Though this is all Rose's doing."

"Isn't she so great?" Kim added. "We just love Rose."

Jesse hid a proud smile.

Just then, Rose called for all the volunteers to gather so she could assign them their duties. Everyone joined except for Pastor Ronnie and Jesse, who hung back to keep catching up.

"How long has it been since you've visited?" Pastor Ronnie asked. They were the same height, but the pastor was a large man and probably had a hundred pounds on Jesse.

"Ten years. I left right after high school."

"Seems like only yesterday you were a little boy hanging onto your sweet mama's skirt."

Jesse's heart warmed. "I think I remember that."

"You know, we've missed your mother and your father."

Jesse didn't want to be rude and held his tongue about his father. He still found it hard to have anything good to say. He managed to croak out a thank-you.

If Ronnie noticed he was uncomfortable, he did not let on. "Are you here to help with the Sunflower Festival this year?"

"I actually came back to clean out my parents' house. It just so happens the festival is at the same time, so I've kind of been recruited to help."

"Good timing. The festival is a lot of fun every year. We all look forward to it. I'm sure Rose is happy to have you back."

"Let's just say she was a little surprised to see me, but after getting over her initial shock, she's been great."

"Isn't there some history between you two?" Pastor Ronnie asked, his arms folded over his chest.

Jesse's eyes landed on Rose, organizing volunteers across the barnyard. "You have a good memory. We dated in high school, but that was a long time ago."

"That's what I thought. She's a good girl. I've watched her grow up and take over this farm. When your dad grew too sick to take care of himself, she took care of him, too. Any man would be lucky to have her as his wife."

Jesse wasn't much in the mood to talk about his dating life with his old pastor. "You're right," he agreed politely. "Any man would be lucky to have her."

As if she'd heard him, Rose caught his eye and smiled at Jesse. He nodded in her direction. A minute later, she walked up to them. "I have a job for you two, if you're up to it, Pastor," she said. "I need you to take our Sunflower Festival sign and hang it at the entrance. You'll need the ladder. And you can carry it down there on the truck."

As Jesse and the pastor drove down to the farm's entrance and hung the twenty-foot sign, Jesse told him about college and becoming a firefighter.

"None of us have seen you in so long. Did you stay away because of your father?" the pastor asked as they drove back to the barnyard.

Jesse parked the truck but left it running as they talked. "I did. We weren't close... He didn't make things easy for me after my mom passed away. I left as soon as I could and never wanted to come back while he was still here." That was way more information than he'd planned to share, but the pastor had a way about him that made a person want to tell him everything.

Pastor Ronnie looked at him with understanding in his eyes. "I am sorry, son, for what you've been through. Life is not always fair. To lose a loving parent at such a young age, it couldn't have been easy for you."

"When my mom died, I pretty much lost

two parents. My dad was so heartbroken over her loss that he barely spoke to me, and he was so angry when he did. You see, he blamed me for the accident."

"What if I told you he regretted how he treated you? After you left, he started attending church. It took you leaving for him to realize how alone he was. One day he came to visit me. I tell you what, all I saw was a broken man." The pastor shook his head. "He had so much regret and guilt when it came to you. How he treated you, how he wasn't there for you. He regretted it all."

Jesse studied the pastor. Rose had tried to tell him his dad had changed, but he hadn't been ready to accept it. Was he finally open to hearing about his father's regret?

The pastor continued, "I told him that if he was truly sorry, God would forgive him, but he had to forgive himself, too." Pastor Ronnie paused and looked Jesse straight in the eye. "Today, I want to say something to you. I think that you're carrying around those old hurt feelings toward your father. Don't you think it's time that you forgive him? Let go of that pain?"

Jesse didn't know what to say. They sat in the truck in silence, the AC humming. He stared down at his hands gripping the steering wheel. Pastor Ronnie had hit the nail on the head. How could he have known?

The pastor patted Jesse's shoulder. "That's all I'm going to say for now. You come find me if you have any questions or if you want to talk some more."

Jesse nodded. "Thank you, Pastor. It's a lot for me to think about. I appreciate you taking the time to tell me, though."

"If you're going to be around for a while, why don't you come to church on Sunday? Everybody would love to see you again."

Jesse smiled. "Rose is already twisting my arm to come. I plan on visiting this Sunday."

The pastor gave him a warm look. "Don't you know, it's not visiting when it's the church you grew up in... It's coming home."

CHAPTER EIGHT

TOWARD THE END of the afternoon, the last of the church volunteers left. Rose meandered through the rows of games and booths lined up in an open grassy field, a short distance from the picnic tables and where the food trucks were going to be. Everything had been hung, decorated and staged for the long festival weekend. Jesse had helped with the setup all afternoon. Rose had noticed that he recognized a couple of the church volunteers and met a few new ones, as well. Everyone was so friendly and willing to help, she hoped it made him miss the sense of community of a small town. Would it make him miss the farm enough not to sell it? Perhaps make him want to return on a more permanent basis?

Rose hadn't had a chance to talk to him anymore about his dad, and maybe that was for the best. He needed time to think.

She hated that the week with Jesse was almost over. It had flown by. She'd grown attached to him again, practically over night, but was the feeling mutual? She had a feeling that it was, but she couldn't be sure. He'd made it clear he didn't want anything to do with the farm, and there was still a good chance he would sell it.

Deep down, Rose knew she should be careful with her heart. Jesse had left her once to get away from his father and the farm. If history had taught her anything, he could leave again. She needed to be prepared. Could she really trust him?

Jesse stood at the dunking booth with a hose, filling it with water. Rose walked over to him.

"Hey there. Is the tank almost full?" She stopped next to him and peeked in. The water was close to the fill line.

"Yeah, I'm about to shut it off." Jesse rested his arms on the edge of the tank as he watched the water slowly rise.

"I was about to take a ride to the sunflower fields and pick some fresh blossoms for tomorrow," she said. "A lot of folks pick their own, but others will wait and buy them as they're leaving. Do you mind helping me? It'll go faster with two people."

"Sure. Let me just shut off the water, and I'll join you."

"I'll swing by and get you." Rose grabbed the UTV from the barn and picked Jesse up near the hose spigot. "Hold on," she said, then hit the gas pedal.

Jesse grabbed hold of the vehicle's frame just in time. "A little more warning next time, would ya?"

"Come on. How long have we known each other? I think by now you'd know how I drive."

Jesse laughed. Rose picked up speed, the wind whipping past them as the motor roared. It felt good to sit down after being on her feet all day, but it was also a preview of the long weekend to come. Rose reached the front of the sunflower fields but kept going toward the back pastures.

"Where are you going?" Jesse asked over the noise of the engine. "I thought we were picking sunflowers."

"We are. But the fields closest to the barn and parking lot will get the most foot traffic this weekend. We're going to pick flowers at the opposite end, where visitors won't go."

"Smart. I never would have thought of that."

"Sure you would. Hang around here long enough, you'll figure it all out again."

"I don't know about that. A lot has changed since I left."

"Yes, but there's a lot that's the same."

Jesse was quiet for a minute, then said, "It was nice to see Pastor Ronnie and Tyler today. I've missed them."

"Don't forget the Dawkins, too. They're such a sweet couple. They helped me care for your dad toward the end. They would take turns and come over to sit with him during the day while I was busy dealing with the farm. Then at night, I'd stay with him."

Rose expected him to change the subject, but instead he seemed to absorb the information.

He scrubbed his face with one hand, then sighed heavily. "You did so much for him. How long was it like that, someone having to care for him twenty-four hours a day?"

"Two months."

Rose reached the back of the sunflower field and drove through two long rows of blossoms as golden as miniature suns. Eventually, she stopped in the middle of the field with nothing but sunflowers around them, radiant with the sunset light. The irrigation system had only been running a day, and already the flowers seemed perkier.

Rose said a silent thank-you to God because she knew it was an answer to prayer. She cut the engine, and nature's silence surrounded them. She stared out at the ocean of sunflowers, not really seeing them. Was Jesse finally ready to hear about his dad?

"Your dad fought lung cancer for a year. He went to chemo treatments on his own and took care of himself as long as he could. I checked in on him periodically and helped with things like shopping, picking up his meds, cooking, housework, bills and taking care of the farm. He managed on his own for a while like that, and I thought things would get better. But then he went downhill practically overnight. The last two months, he was too sick to take care of himself. Mr. and Mrs. Dawkins started helping me during the day while I worked the farm, and then I took care of him at night. In his final two weeks we had hospice coming out. The hospice nurses would visit regularly to check on him and make sure he was comfortable, but they didn't stay. It was up to us to care for him." She turned to face Jesse.

He met her stare with sad eyes. "I'm sorry I put you in that situation."

"You didn't put me in that situation, I did. I was your dad's friend. He needed help, and I helped him. I'd do it again. I'm not telling you all this to make you feel bad, Jesse. I'm telling you so you know what your dad's last year was like. Whether you hate him or not, he was still your father. You should know what happened."

"You're right."

"Of course I'm right. I'm always right. When are you going to learn this?" she joked, attempting to ease the tension.

Jesse laughed. "You're impossible." He reached over and pretend to ruffle her hair.

Rose ducked away. "Be nice, because this impossible girl is your ride back. Now, come on, let's cut some flowers before we lose what's left of daylight."

She'd brought a couple pairs of shears and several large bins to fill with flowers. "When you cut the flowers, leave the stems a couple of feet long."

"Yes, ma'am. I've cut sunflowers before. I remember," Jesse said, matter-of-factly.

Rose smiled at him as she handed over a pair of shears. "Forgive me. I'm used to bossing everyone around, or nothing would get done right around here."

"No apologies needed. You've done a great job with everything. No complaints from me."

"Thank you. Now, come on," she said.

Working side by side, they quickly filled the bins with big sunflower heads on long stalks, their large brown centers full of seeds.

"I remember picking sunflowers with my mom," Jesse said. He placed another flower in an already full bin, its petals glittering with drops of water from a recent soaking. "We sold most of them to florists, but we did keep the imperfect ones. We'd let them mature so we could harvest the seeds. My mom would give away goody bags full of seeds to her friends and family. She was known for it, and people would always ask us for them. I think she liked blessing others."

Rose paused to join him in the memory. "I remember her handing out the bags at church. She gave one to my mom and dad. I was just a kid, and I thought it was the best thing in the world."

"What do you do with extra seeds now?"

She laughed. "What do you think? We sell

them in the store. I told you, we had to get creative to make money any way we could."

"Smart. I think you did the right thing."

"We sell all sorts of stuff besides the seeds. Did you meet Lolly last weekend?"

Jesse nodded.

"Lolly is a rock star when it comes to canning and jarring what we grow. I give her free rein, and she makes whatever's in season that she's in the mood for. Everything from strawberry jam to pickles to orange marmalade to jalapeño jelly."

Jesse made a face at the last menu item.

Rose laughed. "Don't knock it until you try it. Jalapeño jelly is better than it sounds. Add a little cream cheese and put it on a cracker…" She paused to rub her belly. "Yummy."

"I'll take your word for it." Jesse looked doubtful as he snipped another stem. "What else have you changed around here to make money?"

Rose thought for a minute. "We tried breeding the goats and chickens to sell, but I never had the heart to let any of them go. I probably doomed myself when I started naming the babies. I just got too attached."

"You always were a softy."

"That's what your dad said, too."

Jesse noticeably stiffened.

"I'm sorry. I wasn't trying to bring him up again."

"It's okay. I need to stop being sensitive."

Rose liked having Jesse working at her side. He'd been a downright hero, first helping clear that tree, then fixing the fence, then repairing the irrigation system. She really could get used to having him around. But she knew he'd be leaving in a few days. Who knew if he would come back?

Or if he would sell the farm?

The dark cloud of the unknown future hung over her. He'd seemed to embrace the farm life the last few days. How could he turn his back on all of this? How could he turn his back on her again?

"Penny for your thoughts," Jesse said next to her.

Rose threw a blossom into her bin, carried it to the UTV and switched it out for the last empty bin. "I was just thinking to myself it's nice to have you back." She omitted the part where she worried that he'd leave for good and sell the farm.

"It's been nice catching up with you and

spending time together," he agreed, following her to a fresh row with dozens of blossoms waiting to be cut.

It was that time of day when dusk settled over the land, right before night fell. In the twilight, Rose could just make out Jesse's dark eyes. It made her heart ache just a little. The man had no idea the turmoil he could put her through with just one look.

"I know you're still deciding whether to keep the farm or not," she heard herself say. "Regardless of what you choose, do you think we can stay in touch this time?"

Jesse sighed heavily. "I would love nothing more. But I think if I sell the farm, I'll probably be the last person you want to talk to."

She gave him a crooked smile. "You have a point. So, I guess you can't sell the farm."

Though Jesse laughed, she could tell she'd touched a nerve when he said, "I wish it were that easy."

CHAPTER NINE

ON FRIDAY MORNING, the first day of the Sunflower Festival, the farm came alive with activity. A stream of vendors and at least fifty volunteers arrived at the farm first thing. The festival was always a little crazy on the first day, but the rest of the weekend, it usually ran smoothly.

An hour before the noon opening, Rose gathered everyone around the barnyard to go over the schedule of events and answer any questions. Afterward, she noticed Jesse casually leaning against the barn door, watching her with an amused smirk on his face. He was devastatingly handsome in his navy blue firefighter uniform. She knew he was volunteering today but hadn't thought twice about what he would wear.

"Hey there. You clean up nice," she said, walking up to him. She wanted to ask if all

firefighters looked half as good in their uni-
forms as him.

"Thanks. I figured I better look the part."

"You definitely do. So, what's up? Were you
waiting on me?" Rose wore her yellow Sunflower Farms T-shirt like the rest of the staff,
distinguishing them from the festival volunteers. She held a clipboard with the schedule
in one hand, the other on her hip.

"Yeah. We have the fire truck in the field.
I think it's where you wanted it. I was hoping
you'd run out there and check it's in the right
place before we pull everything out."

"I actually was heading that way. Come on,
we'll walk out together."

On the way to the fire truck, they were
stopped several times by volunteers, mostly old
friends from church and high school who recognized Jesse. Many handshakes and hugs later,
Rose and Jesse finally reached the fire truck.

His gaze roamed the area. "I see you put us
next to the lineup of food trucks. I hope the
festival visitors see us, too."

"It's strategy. People will wander by as they're
checking out the food. Trust me, you'll get lots
of foot traffic today."

"That makes sense. I can't believe how many people I've already run into today."

"I bet you'll see lots more before the day is over."

"I forgot how friendly everyone is here."

"Eagletin is a good place to live and to raise a family."

"I'm starting to see that."

Rose hoped he appreciated it enough not to sell it, but decided against mentioning it at that moment. He had to figure it out on his own. And if he didn't, she'd somehow deal with the loss—and her broken heart.

Just then, they were joined by another firefighter, also in a navy blue uniform. Jesse introduced them. "Rose, I would like you to meet my good buddy, Mike. Mike, meet Rose."

She shook his hand. "Thank you so much for volunteering today. I can't tell you how much we appreciate you donating your time."

"I am happy to be here for a good cause," Mike said with a wink. "If there's anything I can do for you, just let me know." He held Rose's hand a little longer than necessary.

Jesse gave his friend a dirty look, and inwardly Rose smiled, wondering if Jesse was a little jealous. When was the last time she had two men interested in her romantically?

"I'm sure Rose is busy and needs to get going," Jesse said to Mike, who at last let go of her hand.

"I won't keep you then, but I hope you'll stop by later," Mike said to her.

"Definitely," Rose answered. She gave Jesse a big grin as she walked away. It wouldn't hurt Jesse to think there was a little competition, and if she were being honest with herself, it was nice being noticed for once.

By THE AFTERNOON, the temperature crept up to the eighties. The crowd was thick, and visitors kept coming. Other than a few hiccups, the festival had got off to a good start. Grammy stopped by to chat with Rose at the festival information booth.

"There you are," Grammy said. A tall older gentleman, with gray hair and glasses, was at her side.

"Grammy! I was wondering when I'd see you," Rose said as she set down her clipboard. Her eyes went to Grammy's guest.

"Let me introduce you to my new friend

Bob," Grammy said. "Bob, this is my beautiful granddaughter, Rose."

Rose shook Bob's hand, laughing. "I don't know about beautiful. More like sweaty and exhausted. But it's nice to meet you."

"You're beautiful all the same. The outdoors and sunshine give you a healthy glow," Bob said.

Rose already liked the man. "Thank you. Welcome to our farm. Are you two having fun at the festival?"

"It's been nice catching up with folks," Grammy said. "I ran into Jesse by the fire truck. I'm surprised he's still here."

"Grammy, please give it a rest. Jesse promised to help with the festival, and the firefighters have been a big hit."

She raised her brows. "Yeah, a hit with all the single ladies," she said with a chuckle.

Rose rolled her eyes, then felt her phone buzz in her pocket. She pulled out the phone and answered, "Hello?"

"Rose, it's Lolly. The guy running the kissing booth had to leave early. Do you have someone else who can work it?"

"I'll figure something out. Don't worry, I'll take care of it." Rose hung up and blew out an exasperated breath. The kissing booth was a big moneymaker, and she hated to lose out on what it could make in the next four hours. Yeah, the booth was a little silly, maybe cheesy, and definitely old-fashioned, but it had become part of the fun that folks expected.

She suddenly had a brilliant idea. She knew a certain handsome fireman who didn't have a shy bone in his body.

Rose said goodbye to Grammy and Bob, then headed for the fire truck. When she approached, Mike had a crowd of little kids sitting in the grass listening to him talk about fighting fires like it was career day at school. The kids were mesmerized.

Jesse stood off to the side, leaning against the truck.

Rose sidled up next to him. "Hey there. Mike is so good with them."

"Tell me about it. I think he missed his calling." Jesse pushed away from the truck and straightened. "How are things going?"

"Good. But..." Rose gave him a sheepish look. "I have a favor to ask."

"Sure, anything," Jesse said.

"I need someone to take over the kissing booth."

His face fell. "Anything but that."

"Why not? Please. I'll owe you."

"Why don't you do it?" he asked.

"Because I'm running the festival. I can't be tied down to one booth."

He shifted his weight from one foot to the other. "Is there any chance you'll take no for an answer?"

"Nope," Rose said.

"Fine. Show me what you want me to do."

They left the fire truck in Mike's capable hands, and Rose led Jesse to the kissing booth.

Jesse hesitated in the front of it and read the sign they had added. "Sunflower Farms Sweetheart… Oh man. You're kidding, right?"

"Come on. You can do it. Jump on back there." Gently, Rose pushed him along.

He stepped inside the booth. "What do I have to do?"

Rose pointed to a second smaller sign and read it off, "Five dollars a kiss from the Sunflower Farms Sweetheart. All proceeds go to the Taylor Family Fire Fund."

Jesse crossed his arms over his chest, "I don't know about this. And I don't know how I feel about kissing strangers."

Rose really couldn't blame him for balking. "Relax. It's for a good cause. You're a nice-looking guy. People will pay you five dollars a kiss."

He narrowed his eyes at her. "What kind of kiss are we talking about?"

She laughed. "Don't worry. I promise nothing more than a kiss on the cheek."

Resigned, Jesse agreed. "Fine. I guess I can do that. But don't tell Mike or the rest of the guys where I went, or I'll never hear the end of it."

"Agreed. Hey, look, you have your first customer."

Mrs. Dawkins handed a five-dollar bill to Rose, who put it in the cashbox. Jesse leaned down and planted a quick peck on her cheek.

"Thank you, Jesse." She giggled and made a big deal out of the kiss, all in good fun.

Jesse laughed along, until he spotted more ladies coming over. Rose's grandmother was next in line, with Bob good-naturedly waiting with her.

"You're still here?" Grammy asked Jesse.

"Yes, ma'am, but at the moment, I wish I were anywhere but here," Jesse answered in good humor.

"Grammy, you're not allowed to tease him," Rose said. "He's doing me a favor by working the booth."

"Honey, he's doing us all a favor. I do love a man in uniform." Grammy held up a five-dollar bill and waited for her kiss.

Jesse squeezed his eyes shut and mumbled, "What have I gotten myself into?"

Rose patted him on the arm. "I have a feeling you're going to be very popular." She walked away, chuckling as she saw the line getting longer and longer...

THE NEXT DAY of the festival, Saturday, was just as busy. Jesse purposefully stayed clear of the kissing booth. He made a mental note never to let Rose talk him into doing that again. The afternoon had been awkward and uncomfortable, but he'd managed it okay. Though, he had to admit, she'd been right. He'd raised a lot of money for the Taylors, and he'd only had to sacrifice his pride to do it.

Mike brought the fire engine back out, and he and Jesse stood under the warm October sunshine and greeted folks as they wandered by. Kids were in awe of the truck and enjoyed climbing on it, then took turns trying on the gear. Elementary school boys and girls stared up at them with a bit of hero worship, like they were as great as superheroes.

Jesse remembered being the same way when he was a kid. He also noticed some of the moms staring a little too much as they waited for their kids. Mike enjoyed the attention and flirted shamelessly while Jesse kept everything professional.

Like yesterday, Mike gave talks whenever a crowd gathered. Jesse leaned on the truck and listened as Mike recounted a tale of the worst fire he'd ever seen and how he saved the day. Yeah, Mike liked to embellish some, but it was a good story.

An older couple stopped next to Jesse. "Is that you, Jesse Cooper?" the woman asked.

Jesse recognized the man and woman instantly. They were Rose's parents. They were a little bit grayer and older than he remembered, but it was definitely them. He'd know their warm smiles anywhere. "Anne, John, it's good to see you. How are you?"

Rose's mom pulled Jesse into a big hug, and he leaned down to embrace the petite woman. When he straightened, John greeted him with a pat on the shoulder, saying, "We're good! Rose told us you were here. She said to follow the trail to the fire truck, and we'd find you. Although she never said anything about the crowd."

Jesse chuckled. "The crowd isn't for me. It's for the master entertainer over there." He pointed toward Mike. "Stick around long enough, and you can hear how he single-handedly saved the world from the largest fire ever… or something like that."

"As interesting as that sounds, we actually want to hear about you. How are you? We were surprised to hear you were back in Eagletin," John said.

Jesse inhaled deeply as he tried to think of how to put it into words. How was he? Confused. Unsure what to do with the farm. Unsure about what was happening between him and their daughter.

Instead of saying all that, he said what they wanted to hear. "I'm doing great. As you can see—" he gestured toward his uniform "—I'm a firefighter, and it's a great career. I've also been out here at the farm all week, cleaning out my folks' home. Thought I would stay to help with the festival."

"Does this mean you plan to be at the farm more often?" Anne asked. She stared up at him with the same intelligent blue eyes as her daughter. She reminded him of Rose in every way: small stature, big personality.

Jesse shrugged. "I haven't decided. As you know, there's a lot of history for me here, some good and some bad. I'm not sure how involved I want to be."

"That's understandable, though I'm sure Rose loves having you back," Anne said.

John interjected, "Whatever you decide, the farm will be in good hands with Rose."

"I agree," Jesse said at once. "Rose is amazing, and what she's done with this place is something else." He would hazard a guess she hadn't had a chance to tell them that he might sell the property. But he wasn't going to bring it up now.

"Yeah, this whole sunflower business brought the farm back from the brink of bankruptcy. It was all her idea to open it up to the public," John said.

It only made Jesse admire Rose even more. "It was a great idea. Who knew this would go over so well?"

"So, are you married now?" Anne asked, just as blunt as her daughter. John subtly elbowed her.

Jesse tried to hold in a chuckle. "No, ma'am.

I'm not married and currently not dating any-one." He knew what was coming before she could even get it out.

"You know, our Rosie is still single," Anne said.

"Oh? You don't say." Jesse played along.

John laid an arm over his wife's shoulder to usher her away. "Come on, Anne. Let Jesse be. He's been back five minutes, and you're already playing matchmaker. Let's go find something to eat. We can catch up later." He waved goodbye as they walked on.

Jesse waved back, relieved that John had intervened. He'd always liked her parents. If only he could have had the same kind of happy childhood she'd had.

The day flew by until it was nearly time for the barn dance that evening. As the sun set, Jesse went back to the house to clean up and change out of his uniform into jeans and a long-sleeved Western-style shirt appropriate for the theme. By the time he stepped back outside, night had fallen.

Under a half-moon, the thousands of white lights they'd hung lit the barnyard. Couples danced underneath them while other folks hung out on the perimeter socializing. Jesse made his way through the throngs of people, stopping repeatedly to greet old friends as he passed by. It made him miss small-town life like he never had before. This would be what he gave up if he sold the farm.

He'd have to give up Rose, too, because she would never forgive him.

The countdown had begun. Jesse had one more full day to spend at the farm, then he would return to work in Jacksonville. And he'd have to get back to the investor with a decision on whether to sell. A week ago, Jesse had made up his mind that he wanted nothing to do with the farm. He hadn't counted on the good memories that flooded back or hearing the stories of how his dad had changed.

He also hadn't planned on how much he still felt for Rose. It was hard to make a clearheaded decision with her around, when all he wanted to do was please her. Perhaps it was for the best he was leaving. But that didn't mean he couldn't enjoy tonight.

Jesse searched for Rose in the crowd. When he found her, she was on the dance floor in another man's arms, moving to a slow song. She wore a red dress and cowboy boots, her honey-brown hair falling over her shoulders in glossy waves. She was beautiful, and Jesse couldn't take his eyes off her.

A hint of jealousy sprang up that it wasn't him holding her. He tamped down the feeling. She wasn't his girlfriend, and even if she was, she could dance with whomever she wanted.

The song came to an end, and the guy let go of Rose. Springing into action, Jesse weaved through the crowded dance floor to get to her before someone else snatched her up. A couple people recognized him as he worked his way through. Jesse nodded in acknowledgment but kept on his pursuit.

Rose saw him headed her way, and from across the dance floor, their eyes locked. A wide smile spread across her face.

Jesse liked it when she was happy. He liked it too much.

Finally he reached her and held his hand out in invitation. "May I have this dance?" he asked as the next song started.

"Yes," she said, placing her hand in his.

Jesse pulled her into his arms. It felt like home.

They swayed in time to the music. The two of them together like this was like a dream. He'd be content to stay this way forever.

Rose tilted her head up. "I barely saw you today. How did things go?" she asked.

"Great, especially since I wasn't stuck in the kissing booth again," he said with a grin.

Rose laughed. "You survived, as I knew you would."

"With no help from you. You dropped me off and left me to fend off the wolves."

"I wouldn't call little old ladies wolves."

"Ha, that's what you think."

Her eyes sparkled under the lights. "It was the uniform. Women love to see a guy in uniform."

"Are you saying you like me in uniform?"

"Maybe," she conceded. "Now shut up and dance with me." Her arms tightened around him, and she laid her head against his chest.

Inwardly Jesse smiled. Why did it make him happy to know that Rose liked him in his firefighter uniform? All he knew was that he didn't care one bit about all those single moms at the kissing booth. It was Rose he longed to impress.

ROSE HELD ON to Jesse as they floated around the dance floor. With her arms wrapped around him, she leaned into his warmth. Her cheek rested against his chest, and she inhaled his fresh clean scent. Content, she sighed.

She was happy. She had thoroughly enjoyed spending the week with him, but he would leave soon. She had to be prepared, but deep down, she knew it would still hurt.

Jesse interrupted her thoughts. "You look pretty tonight, Rose. But then again, you always look pretty."

Her face flushed at his praise, and she was thankful for the low lighting. "Thank you. You look nice, too."

Jesse laughed. "You're just saying that because you have to be nice back."

"Yeah, you're right," she teased, and they both laughed.

"So, what do you think of the dance?" she asked.

"I'm impressed by how many people came out for it and what a success it is. And the string lights look spectacular. Whoever helped you with them should be given an award."

Rose rolled her eyes. "Give me a break, if I'd left it up to you, they'd all be crooked."

Jesse laughed.

Rose added, "Seriously, now you can see why I've been running around all week like a chicken with its head cut off. But it was worth it. We're going to raise a lot of money this weekend for the Taylors."

"I forgot to tell you, Mike and I have been collecting money from the guys at the firehouse. We've raised $3,500 to add to the fund."

Rose gasped. "Wow! That's wonderful. Make sure you tell the guys how much we appreciate their help."

"I will, but they were happy to chip in. A lot of them were there the night the Taylors' house burned down. It was heartbreaking."

She shook her head. "I can only imagine."

Jesse and Rose moved in sync across the dance floor. She'd forgotten what a good dancer he was, so light on his feet. And he knew how to lead. She'd be content to dance with him the rest of the night, but too soon the song came to an end. She reluctantly stepped out of his arms, though he didn't seem to want it to be over, either.

A popular line dance started, and the floor quickly became packed. Jesse grabbed Rose's hand and led her through the crowd to the refreshment stand. He released her hand once they were in the clear. Rose was disappointed he let go.

"Would you like a drink?" he asked, smiling at her.

Rose felt her stomach do a little flip-flop. She tucked her hair behind one ear. "I'd love to try the hot apple cider. It's Lolly's recipe."

Turning to the lady serving drinks, he ordered two. Together they took their steaming cups and walked away from the crowd and loud music. Rose took a careful sip. The combination of cinnamon and apple was delicious.

"Let's find somewhere to sit," she suggested. "My feet are killing me. If I've learned anything today, these boots are not for dancing."

Jesse laughed. "I guess they aren't the boots you use to muck the stalls."

"They are not."

They left the dance behind and strolled into the darkness beyond the barnyard. With the music fading and all the visitors forgotten, they reached the empty picnic tables and sat down next to each other under the moonlight.

Rose let out a big sigh and pulled one boot off, then the other. She closed her eyes and savored being side by side with Jesse. "I have a new appreciation for what you do," Jesse said into the silence.

Rose opened her eyes and sat up a little straighter. "Why do you say that?"

"I've watched you manage this farm all week, juggle the many problems that come with it, work from dawn to dusk, and still, you manage to give yourself wholly to this festival all for the purpose of raising money for the Taylor family. And you do it with a smile on your face…" Jesse hesitated, then leaned to the side and gently bumped shoulders with her, adding, "I mean, most of the time you have a smile on your face," he teased.

"Most of the time," she agreed. "I think you know by now, this farm is my life. It comes from my heart."

"I can see that."

The moon lit the area enough that in the distance Rose could see the sunflower fields. Soon the flowers would die for the winter, and they would have to start the cycle all over again and plant a new crop in the spring. Would Jesse be around to help?

A slow song started in the distance. The light melody carried across the fields.

"Come on. You owe me another dance," Jesse said.

"Please don't make me walk back." Rose slipped her boots back on as she said it.

Jesse pulled her up, and they stood facing one another. "Dance with me here, then," he suggested with a serious expression.

The romance of it all wasn't lost on Rose…a dance in the moonlight with her old love. Never in a million years had she imagined he'd come back home or that they would reunite. And here they were. Together again. But for how long?

She looped her arms around his neck and stared into his eyes. They slowly danced to the distant music, both quiet as they studied one another. She would forever remember the way he looked under the moonlight, and how she imagined there was love in his eyes when he looked at her, whether it was true or not.

When the song ended, Jesse leaned down and kissed her, soft and sweet.

She had worked so hard to keep her emotions for him in check all this time. But she was worn out from it and just wanted to love him. Even if only for a few days.

Jesse ended the kiss. Then like a gentleman, he walked her back to the dance.

What did this mean for them? For her? For the farm? Rose had more questions than answers.

CHAPTER TEN

JESSE TURNED INTO the church parking lot early Sunday morning and shut off the engine. The lot was already almost full, which was impressive. Half the church members had been at the barn dance until late last night.

"Glad to see the festival didn't hurt turnout this morning," Rose said as she glanced around the parking lot. Dressed in a simple yellow sundress, she somehow looked fresh and rested after the busy weekend.

"I was thinking the same thing," Jesse said. "It would have been too easy to sleep in today."

"Nah, the festival's not over. Sunday church is just a much-needed break in the middle. Also, the Taylors will be at the service, and the pastor will be bringing them onstage to talk about the festival. Anybody who hasn't come out yet will be gently reminded to show their support."

Jesse laughed. "You mean guilted into coming to the festival."

Rose laughed. "Your words, not mine."

Inside the church, Jesse was stopped over and over, shaking hands with old friends and being introduced to new ones. Once they were settled in the pew, he glanced over at Rose, and she grinned back.

"What are you smiling about?" he asked.

She shrugged, then admitted, "I just like having you here with me. It's nice."

He reached over and squeezed her hand affectionately. "Yeah, it is."

Just before the service started, Lolly slipped in next to Rose. They exchanged a few words and giggled a little before Lolly said hi to Jesse.

A minute later, Rose's parents and her grandmother walked down the aisle and filed into the empty seats on the other side of Lolly. Anne set her purse on the floor, leaned over and gave quick hugs to Rose, Lolly and Jesse. "I've missed you all so much," she said as she sat down.

"Good morning," Rose's dad greeted everyone as her grandmother waved at them.

The service began, and Jesse sat up in his seat,

a little nervous. It had been so long since he'd attended church.

Pastor Ronnie's sermon was on forgiveness, and it felt like everything he said had been meant for Jesse. He'd come to church to please Rose, but never once had he considered how it might affect him. Like everything else lately, he'd misjudged it. In the end, the service gave him more to think about when it came to his dad and the forgiveness Jesse withheld.

The hour passed by quickly, and soon Jesse was dropping Rose off at her apartment.

"Thanks for driving," she said as she slid out of the car. "I'm heading up to change and eat lunch real quick before the festival starts. You want to come up for a sandwich?"

"Thanks, but no. I feel like driving around a little before this place gets busy again."

Rose narrowed her eyes at him. "Are you okay? You've been awfully quiet."

Jesse smiled reassuringly. "I'm fine. I just need a few minutes alone."

"Okay, but you know where to find me if you want to talk or if you change your mind about the sandwich."

Jesse nodded back. With a heavy heart, he drove over to the sunflower fields. He parked on the edge where he and Rose had picked flowers. Some folks had a view of the mountains or a beach, but how many had a breathtaking view of a majestic sunflower field? He took his time and appreciated the sea of yellow and green underneath the vast blue sky.

This was all his.

And this had been his father's. The same man who had shunned Jesse and made life unbearable after his mother died.

He got out of the car and strolled down a row. The sunflowers were as tall as him, and it felt like he walked through a floral tunnel that had no end in sight. He shoved his hands in his pockets as he kicked up the ground in front of him. His pace was leisurely while his mind wandered.

Who was he kidding? He wasn't punishing his father by staying mad at him. The man was dead. He was only hurting himself.

Maybe it was time he saw everything from his dad's point of view. The man had been crushed when his beloved wife died, and it was that unbearable pain that caused him to treat Jesse so poorly. His dad hadn't acted that way because he didn't love Jesse. He acted that way because he'd lost his true love and he couldn't cope with it.

Those three years after her death, he had loved Jesse. He'd just been too torn up to show it properly. His actions were overshadowed by tragic loss.

Did that make it okay the way his old man acted? No. But now Jesse could see it through the eyes of an adult. And along with that realization, he also knew it was time to forgive him.

Apparently, his dad's outlook on life changed when he found God. He must have finally accepted the loss of his wife and he must have regretted the way he'd treated Jesse. In the end, he became a better person.

Jesse sadly wished he had been around for that. He wished he'd called him back when his dad left that message. He wished he'd been there for him when he was sick. He wished he had returned in time for that...but he knew that wishing would get him nowhere.

What he could do was forgive him and finally let it all go—his father's failures and his own.

And that was exactly what he did.

In the middle of the sunflower field, Jesse closed his eyes, lifted his head toward the sky and sucked in a breath. As he let out the air, peace settled over him.

Jesse forgave his father, and he forgave himself.

Turnout on the last day of the Sunflower Festival was great, but Rose was happy to see the huge event come to an end. The remaining volunteers finished cleanup just before sunset. With the busy afternoon, Rose hadn't had a chance to speak to Jesse again.

The lights were on in the main house, so she headed over. Like a moth to the flame, she was drawn to him, carrying two glasses of iced tea to share.

Jesse answered the door. "Hey there," he said, sounding genuinely happy to see her.

"Hi… I brought refreshments. I thought we could sit down and celebrate the success of the festival." Rose lifted one glass and offered it to him.

Jesse took it and opened the door all the way. "Thanks. Come on in."

"I thought we could sit on the porch, like the old days."

He looked surprised. "Oh…sounds good."

They walked over to the old-fashioned porch

swing and sat down. It creaked as they pushed off. Rose made a face. "I hope this thing doesn't break. I guess it's pretty old."

Jesse shrugged. "Nah, it's fine. I gave it a test drive the other day."

Rose lifted her glass, "I'd like to make a toast. Here's to another successful year of the Sunflower Festival and to your first festival ever."

"To the Sunflower Festival," Jesse repeated, then clinked her glass with his.

Rose sipped her tea, then set her glass on the floor. "We raised over $43,000," she announced, "and it's all going to the Taylors."

Jesse seemed astonished by the amount. "Wow. I never dreamed you'd raise that much. That's something else."

Rose grinned at him. "I know. It was so much work but well worth it."

"I had no idea the farm could make that much money."

"Keep in mind it was a charity event, so we charged more than normal for admission. Plus, we had a couple thousand people attending this weekend. That's a lot of people paying admission. We don't make as much on our normal weekends, or have that many visitors, but we still do pretty well."

"That's unbelievable. My turn now," Jesse said as he raised his glass. "Here's to you, Rose. You are the backbone to this place. You are an incredible woman."

"Thank you," she said, touched by his words. They clinked glasses again, then sipped their tea as the swing rocked back and forth.

"Did you catch Pastor Ronnie in the dunking booth? I heard it took a while before someone finally dunked him," Rose said.

"Yeah, I did," he said innocently. "Who do you think nailed him?"

"Was it you?" Rose laughed out loud. "I wish I'd seen that."

Jesse chuckled. "I'm pretty sure some kids recorded it on their phones."

"I'll have to get my hands on that footage. I'll bet Pastor Ronnie wasn't too happy, especially after he welcomed you back with open arms."

"Trust me, there's no hard feelings," Jesse said.

"Like you're one to talk about hard feelings. You're still angry at your dad."

He didn't make the quick comeback she was expecting. He shifted uncomfortably next to her and cleared his throat.

Rose could kick herself. "I'm sorry. I shouldn't have said that. That was insensitive."

"It's okay. Actually, I had a breakthrough today. I've been wrestling with this all week. Today I finally made peace with my dad. I forgave him."

It was Rose's turn to be shocked. "Really?"

"Yeah, really," Jesse said lightly. He leaned back and rested an arm over the back of the swing.

Her heart melted just a little. "I'm proud of you. I know it wasn't easy, but it was the right thing to do."

"It was. With what you said about him changing and then finding the newspaper clippings and add in the pastor's sermon this morning… I knew it was time to let the past go. I feel like a burden's been lifted. I didn't realize how unhealthy it was, carrying around all that baggage. All that pain and hate, eating away at me for so many years. I also finally have a clearer picture of why he acted that way. I think it really comes down to how much he loved my mom and the fact he couldn't deal with her loss. He still loved me, he just couldn't show it because of the pain he was in."

"I think you're right. I wish you could have

been around after he found God. He was a different man."

"I wish I had, too. I'm also sorry I wasn't here for him when he was sick."

"It's okay. He was in good hands, and we gave him lots of love until the end."

"Thank you for that."

"You're welcome. Now, maybe you can put all this to rest and finally be happy."

Jesse looked thoughtful as he stared out into the yard. The sun had disappeared over the horizon, and they swung quietly in the glow of the porch light. The night air was chilly, and Rose wrapped her arms across her chest for warmth. A comfortable silence stretched between them.

"Are you really leaving tomorrow?" she asked at last.

Jesse looked at her, then rested his outstretched arm on her shoulder. He pulled her into his side and ran a hand down her chilled arm. "Yeah, I am," he said with a touch of resignation.

"Are you coming back?"

"I don't know."

"You don't know?" Rose asked. "I thought for sure if you forgave your dad, you would want to keep the farm."

"That's just it, I don't know. I need to go back home and do some soul-searching. You have to understand, the farm was never my dream."

"I know," Rose said quietly. "It was mine."

Rose finished up her tea, made her excuses, and left. She'd wanted to celebrate their successful weekend together, but their conversation only put a damper on everything.

Rose didn't understand Jesse. He acted like he enjoyed her company, yet he planned to leave and not come back. What about her? Why wouldn't he come back for her?

She should have listened to her own instincts and protected her heart. Now it was too late.

He would break her heart all over again.

CHAPTER ELEVEN

JUST LIKE HE said he would, early Monday morning, Jesse gave Rose a quick hug goodbye, then left. There were no promises made or any assurances about their relationship. Just a simple goodbye. Rose shouldn't be disappointed. She'd known all along this was coming. Yet here she was, upset and frustrated all the same.

Church volunteers helped take down the festival decorations and return the games and booths. Then life went on like before the festival, and more important, before Jesse's appearance.

Regardless of what happened or didn't happen with Rose's love life, she had a farm to run. She buried herself in work in an attempt to keep herself busy and her mind off Jesse. He'd been gone a few days…but who was counting?

She led Missy and Moe to a pasture to graze, then went to the barn to milk Betsy.

She grabbed a pail and stool and sat next to the cow. She patted her side, and Betsy flicked her tail and mooed in greeting. Rose efficiently milked her, all the while her mind on Jesse.

Those old feelings for Jesse had definitely come back. There was no denying she still loved him. And either he was the best actor that ever lived or he felt something for her, too. She tried to stay positive and believe he would return to the farm, but the longer she went without hearing from him, the more doubt filled her mind. What if she'd been wrong to trust him again? What if he left for another ten years?

She had to remind herself that she was a strong woman. She didn't need a man in her life to be fulfilled.

When Rose walked Betsy out to join the horses in the pasture, she heard the irrigation system turn on in the sunflower field. A cloud of mist surrounded the blooms, raining down much needed moisture. Another reminder of how much it meant to have Jesse's help last week. He'd saved the day when it came to the drought.

Rose felt her phone buzz in her pocket. She pulled it out, unable to suppress the hope that it was finally him. *Come on, Rose*, she silently reprimanded herself.

The text was from her mom. Do you want to come over for dinner tonight?

No, she wanted to have dinner with Jesse.

It was aggravating how disappointed Rose was that it wasn't him.

Jesse or no Jesse, Rose had to eat. She fired back a quick text. Sure, what time?

How about six? I can't wait to see you.

Sounds good!

Her mom sent back a kissy-face emoji with some hearts.

Rose smiled, shoved her phone back in her pocket and headed toward her apartment. A nice black sedan coming down the long driveway caught her eye. It rolled to a stop in front of the gift shop.

Tony saw the car, too, as he was walking back from the sunflower fields. Rose waved him off, letting him know that she would take care of it. When she approached the car, a man in a business suit rolled down his window.

"I'm sorry, we're closed today," Rose said.

"I was actually looking for Jesse Cooper," he said, looking up at her through dark sunglasses.

"He's not here, he lives in Jacksonville. Is there something I can help you with?"

"Would you mind if I drove around the farm? I'm the investor buying this place."

Her stomach lurched, and suddenly she felt like she would throw up. Coolly, she said, "Now's not a good time. Please call to make an appointment." Abruptly, she stormed off before the man could say anything else.

She flew upstairs to her apartment, fumbling with the door. Her shaky hands would not cooperate, but finally she got the door open, stepped in and slammed it shut.

"Stupid, stupid, stupid," she said angrily in the silence of the room. She paced around the studio furiously. She didn't know whether to scream or cry.

So that was why Jesse hadn't called her. He'd decided to sell the farm and couldn't face her. Coward.

She'd been a fool to fall for him again. The man had destroyed her once. What had she expected this time? She should never have let her guard down and trusted him.

Rose did a couple more laps around the

apartment. Finally she came to a halt, pulled out her phone and called Jesse. It rang several times, but there was no answer.

She hung up when the voice mail came on. She needed to speak with him. She needed to know how he could do this to her. If he wasn't answering her calls, then she would go down to the firehouse to talk to him.

Grabbing her purse, she ran downstairs. As she was getting in the car, she had an idea. She would need to stop at her parents' house on the way.

JESSE SAT ON his bunk, exhausted. It was the first time he'd had a chance to rest in days. They'd been fighting an uncontained forest fire, another result of the nasty drought. He'd taken a couple of extra shifts to help out—and to keep his mind off Rose. The problem was, he still hadn't decided what to do about the farm.

One of his coworkers called out, "Cooper, you have a visitor."

"Okay. Coming." Jesse sighed, then got up to see who his visitor was. He wasn't expecting anyone.

In the firehouse lobby, he found Rose peering out the window, her back to him. His heart filled with warmth. Exhausted or not, he was glad to see her. "Rose. I can't believe these guys left you standing out here and didn't invite you inside."

She turned. Immediately, Jesse knew she was mad. Her mouth was set in a hard line, and her eyes shot daggers at him. She balled her hands next to her sides and stood ramrod straight.

His smile dropped. "I'm happy to see you but what's wrong?"

"Don't try to be charming with me, it's not going to work. Why didn't you tell me first?" Her words were loud and angry, and some of the guys came to the doorway to see what was going on.

Jesse shooed them away and shut the door for privacy. He turned back to Rose and said calmly, "Come on, let's take a walk outside." He took a step toward her and she shrugged him off. He had never seen her so angry.

"I don't want to take a walk," she barked.

"Okay, fine, we don't have to walk. But I don't know why you're mad."

"Really? You can't figure it out? Let me say it then… I know you went through with the deal to sell the farm," she snapped.

"What?" Jesse felt like he was in an alternate

universe. What was happening? "I don't know what you're talking about."

"Don't play dumb. The buyer came out to the farm to look around. How could you do that? You should have warned me."

Jesse shook his head, "Again, I don't know what you're talking about. I haven't made any deal. I haven't even made a decision on whether to keep it or not, for that matter."

He could tell Rose wasn't listening. She was too fired up to talk rationally. She paced back and forth in the small lobby. She was dressed in T-shirt, jeans and work boots like she'd come straight from the farm. Her hair was pulled back into her usual ponytail.

When she started talking again, it was more to herself. "I knew you were going to be trouble when you came back. But did I listen to my instincts? No, I played right into your hands, like I was some teenager with a crush… Waiting for you to call me, waiting for your texts, like I didn't have a lick of sense." She was agitated, clearly not her normal self.

Abruptly, she came to a halt. "Let me buy the farm. My parents said they would help me with the money. Together, we can buy you out. Please don't sell it to a stranger."

Jesse rubbed his jaw. This was not what he'd expected. "I don't know what's going on, but you're misinformed."

That only made her angrier. "You're right, I was misinformed the minute I started trusting you again."

He held up his hands. "Can I interrupt for a minute?"

She grew silent and crossed her arms defensively as she waited for him to finish.

"I haven't sold anything. I've been so busy in the last few days with the forest fire along I-95 that I've barely had time to eat or sleep, much less sell my family farm. But trust me, you will be the first person I inform if I decide to sell. I promise I'll give you the first chance to bid on it, if that's what you want. I won't do anything behind your back."

Rose stared at him blankly. He could see the wheels turning in her head, but she was still spitting mad. "Well, I would hope so," she said curtly, then pivoted and left in a huff.

What just happened? Jesse's heart raced from the encounter, but he felt like he'd handled it as well as he could have.

Mike cracked the door open and leaned in. "I couldn't help but notice Rose was here. She didn't look so happy with you. What's going on? Are you okay, man?"

Jesse blew out a big breath. "That woman is going to be the end of me."

Mike laughed. "Aren't they all?"

"She thought I sold the farm." Jesse ran a hand through his hair as he followed Mike back toward the firehouse kitchen.

"Well, are you going to sell it?"

"I haven't decided." Jesse grabbed a cold bottle of water out of the refrigerator and took a swig.

"What's been stopping you from deciding?"

"Originally, I didn't want the farm because it reminded me too much of my dad and what I went through with him. But I finally made my peace with that. Now it's more about what kind of career I want. I can't decide if I want to be a firefighter or a farmer. I've built a life here, I've got a good career, but I'm not sure I want to do this for the rest of my life. Meanwhile, being back on the farm last week felt good. It felt right, living the country life and being home again. The biggest surprise of all was reconnecting with Rose. She's an amazing person."

Mike shrugged. "I don't understand what the

problem is. Why can't you own the farm *and* be a firefighter? Do both."

Jesse stared at him. Now that he'd forgiven his father, there really wasn't anything holding him back. Why hadn't he realized that? And there was a reason Rose was a distraction. Because he had genuine feelings for her. But did she feel the same way? She'd repeatedly told him she loved the farm, but did she love him, too?

AFTER ROSE LEFT the firehouse, she drove back to the farm still fuming mad, but also embarrassed by her rash behavior.

If Jesse had ever thought about getting back together with her, surely she'd just blown it. She had assumed the worst, gone to the firehouse ready to tear into him, and he'd been the levelheaded one. Not her.

Slowly, her mind cleared. This whole thing was a wakeup call to the very real possibility that he could still sell the farm. Just because he spent one week with her and she'd imagined the old feelings between them were still strong, it didn't mean he felt the same way. He had a whole other life now. Maybe he didn't want to give it all up for an old girlfriend. Maybe he was happy with the way things were.

The one positive thing that came out of this fiasco was that he promised he would give her the first crack at buying the farm, and that was a relief. Though that would mean he wasn't returning, and deep down inside that hurt.

At six, Rose arrived at her parents' house for dinner. By then, she was over the anger and completely regretting her behavior. She gave a quick knock at the door, then walked in.

Her dad was in the recliner in the living room watching the news. "Rose, come in," he said when he saw her. He stood up and wrapped her in a warm hug. "How's my girl?"

"I'm okay." *Not good.*

Her mom and grandmother came out from the kitchen to greet her with a hug apiece.

"You're right on time, and everything's ready if you want to eat," her mom said.

The four of them went to the kitchen where the table was already set. Her mom set down a roast next to some side dishes. The aroma wafted over to Rose, but it did nothing for her. She had been so upset all day that she barely had an appetite. She fixed a plate anyway. Her mom had gone to a lot of trouble making a nice meal, and she didn't want to be rude.

Rose had barely swallowed her first bite

when her mom asked, "How did it go with Jesse? Is he going to let you buy the farm?"

Grammy's brow lifted questioningly.

"Jesse may sell the farm," Rose explained to her, "so Mom and Dad have agreed to help me buy it."

"That sounds like a wonderful idea. You've done so much for that place, you should be the one to buy it," Grammy said.

"I know. Anyway, I went up to the firehouse where he works and asked if he would give us the first chance to make a bid for the house, and he agreed he would." Suddenly Rose crumbled. She put her head in her hand and closed her eyes.

Rose's mom rubbed her shoulder comfortingly. "Honey, what's wrong? That's good news, isn't it?"

Rose dropped her hand from her face and took a ragged breath. "It is good news, I just hate the way I behaved. I was so upset that I went in there yelling at him like some lunatic. I made such a scene. I should never have done that. I could just die of embarrassment."

Rose's mom smiled with understanding. "It's not the end of the world. I'm sure if you apologized, he would accept it."

"I know. You're right."

They talked more about the farm, and Rose realized her parents were genuinely excited about going into a partnership with her to own the farm. Grammy even said she'd pitch in and give Rose an early inheritance gift if she needed more financial help.

She really had the most supportive family ever.

Somehow Rose made it through dinner, but she didn't hang around like she usually would. Instead, she wanted to go back to the farm, to be alone and lick her wounds.

When she turned down the driveway toward the farm, her headlights lit the familiar path. Her home. She parked next to the gift shop and got out.

Instead of going upstairs to her apartment, Rose walked over to the main house. Once again, it was empty and dark, like it had been for the past year before Jesse decided to show up. She sat down on the porch swing with a heavy sigh and looked up at the sky. The moon and stars peeked out between the clouds. It was so beautiful and peaceful out there. Why would anyone want to give this up?

Each creak and moan of the old swing reminded her of the night she and Jesse sat on the porch after the festival. She'd felt so close to him. Had it been an act? If it wasn't, she'd probably scared him away after today.

Regret and heartache filled her.

He'd broken her trust ten years ago when he left her, and it was still affecting her. She had believed the worst of him today instead of giving him a chance to explain. She should have trusted him.

Rose pulled out her phone for the umpteenth time and willed him to call. But she knew it wasn't happening tonight. Maybe never.

She tapped the screen and started a new text message.

I hope you will accept my sincere apology for barging into your work and being outright ugly to you. You didn't deserve that. You were right, I was misinformed. I am sorry I jumped to conclusions. I hope you will forgive me.

With her finger hovering above the screen, Rose hesitated a heartbeat. At last she gathered her courage and hit Send. She knew she should shove the phone back in her pocket and forget about it, but instead she sat there and pathetically stared at the text, hoping for a reply.

The message note went from Delivered to Read.

Three little dots danced up and down on the screen. Jesse was typing something on the other end.

Rose held her breath, hoping it was the same levelheaded guy from before.

The reply came through: Who is this?

What? Rose sat up straighter.

The three dots started dancing again, then a new message popped up.

Just kidding. There's nothing to forgive. I've already forgotten about it. You should, too.

Rose smiled, then texted back.

Thank you...and you're not funny!

His simple reply was YW.

You're welcome.

Rose would take it.

She leaned back on the swing and gently pushed off again. In the distance, the wind picked up, and dry leaves skittered across the yard. Cool air moved in and sent a chill up her bare arms. Soon the patter of rain surrounded her, slow at first, and then crushing. Lightning streaked across the sky, followed by thunder seconds later.

Rose smiled to herself. The rain had finally come.

SUNDAY MORNING, ROSE followed Lolly into church and found their usual seats on the third row. Soon after, her parents and grandmother joined them. In the few minutes before the service started, everyone was talking about the storm that hit earlier in the week and how much they'd needed the rain.

Rose set her purse on her lap, then leaned back in the pew. She glanced down at the empty seat next to her and couldn't help but think of Jesse. It was hard to believe only a week ago he'd come to church with her. She'd secretly hoped he would show up today. But after the way she treated him, he'd probably stay clear of her. Who could blame him? She really messed things up. Not her finest hour. But she couldn't change it, so now she had to live with her actions.

At least he'd agreed he wouldn't sell the farm without offering it to her first. She might not end up with the guy, but it should be a consolation that she could keep her job and her home.

Thoughts of Jesse were interrupted as a large body stepped over Rose on their way to the empty seat. Her line of sight hit the back of a gray dress shirt while she shifted her knees out of the way. The man sat down just as the service started. She glanced over to give her new neighbor a friendly smile, only to be stunned to see Jesse.

The worship leader took the microphone and began welcoming the congregation.

With wide eyes, Rose stared dumbly at Jesse.

He smiled at her, wearing that crooked grin of his that she loved.

Slowly, she smiled back.

The congregation stood and started to sing. Together, Jesse and Rose joined in.

Rose couldn't stop smiling.

When the service ended, she nervously grabbed her purse and made small talk as the congregation shuffled outside. In the parking lot, Rose said a quick goodbye to Lolly and her parents.

Grammy hugged Rose, then pulled Jesse into a warm embrace. "I see you're still here," she said with a sparkle in her eyes. It wasn't a question this time, as though she expected him to leave any moment. Rather, she sounded happy to see him.

"Yes, ma'am," Jesse said, grinning.

"I'm no fool. I can see what's going on. All I have to say is, don't you hurt my Rose again."

"No, ma'am. I won't."

Rose couldn't believe her grandmother just said that. She bit her lip and looked away, pretending she hadn't witnessed the exchange.

Grammy left, and finally they were alone. There was so much Rose wanted to say, but she didn't know how to start.

"I'm surprised you came today," she said at last.

"Are you? Good. I wanted to surprise you."

"You did? Even after the way I behaved the other day at the firehouse?"

"What? That? It was nothing. I told you to forget about it."

They reached her car, and Rose turned to face him. "It was something, and I'm mortified I behaved that way. I'm sorry. I hope you'll forgive me."

"I guess you're not letting it go. Believe it or not, I understand why you were upset. I'm sure I looked pretty guilty when the investor stopped by the farm. Let's forget it ever happened."

"I'd like that." Relief filled her after agonizing over her blunder all week. Even though his text said he'd forgiven her, it was different talking to someone in person.

"And I have a confession," Jesse added. "I have a real surprise for you,"

He seemed like he was bursting to tell her something. His eyes sparkled with amusement, and he rubbed his hands together like he couldn't wait. He suddenly looked ten years younger, like the playful teenager he once was.

"What's the surprise?" Rose's heart fluttered as her own inner teen went giddy.

"It's waiting back at the farm. I have to show it to you for you to understand."

She cocked her head to the side as she tried to think of what in the world it could be. "Okay, I'll play along. This better be good."

"It is. Trust me," he said as he started backing away toward his car. "Meet you back at the farm." He ran across the church parking lot to where he parked.

The fifteen-minute drive to the farm felt like an eternity. Rose couldn't remember the last time she'd had a surprise. Perhaps it was that first day Jesse showed up at the farm. She'd been shocked to look across the barn and meet the laughing eyes of his handsome face while she gave her farm animal class. At the time it wasn't a wanted surprise, but life, it seemed, had a way of doing that.

They turned into the Sunflower Farms drive, and Rose followed Jesse's car up to the gift shop. It was early, and the place was still closed to visitors. Jesse walked over to her as she climbed out of her car and took her hand.

"Where are we going?"

"To your surprise."

He pulled her along, every now and then glancing back at her.

"I think you're taking me to the garden. Am I right?" she asked.

"I don't know. Guess you'll have to wait and see," he teased.

The suspense was killing her. At last he stopped in front of the garden. A new large wooden sign hung in the archway. It was beautifully painted with rose vines and read Rose's Garden.

Rose gasped. "It… It's lovely… When did you have time to put this up?"

A wide grin broke across his face. "Why do you think I was late for church?"

She shook her head. "But I don't understand. Why did you put it up?"

He turned toward her and gently squeezed both her hands. "This is a gesture to show my gratitude to you for everything you've done. This is in honor of your amazing rose garden, but more importantly it's in honor of you, Rose. You are the best part of Sunflower Farms. You've been running it for years, and it's better than ever. Forget me selling the farm. I've decided to keep it, and I want you to be my partner. It will be ours together."

"Jesse... I... I...don't know what to say," she stuttered, heart racing.

"Wait, I'm not done. It's more than the farm. I've been searching for something that I couldn't put my finger on. I thought it was my job, but now I have figured it out. My life isn't complete without you. Rose, I want you to be my partner in life. I loved you when I was eighteen, and after all this time, I've come to realize that has not changed. I still love you... If you'll forgive me for leaving and have me back, you'd make me the happiest man in the world."

Rose felt her eyes water as she absorbed every word. "I'm so happy you came back. I've never stopped loving you, either." She squeezed his hands for emphasis. "I understand now, you did what you did for me. It hurt, I won't lie. But like you knew it was time to forgive your dad, I realize it's time to forgive you for leaving me and to trust you again."

Jesse leaned down and kissed her, then pulled back. "We've wasted so many years, when we could have been happy together."

"I think that was part of the journey in order for us to appreciate what we have now. And to appreciate what we'll have for years to come."

Jesse kissed her again, then pulled her tightly into his arms. Butterflies flew in her stomach. She would remember this moment forever. It was funny how life was like that—when least expected, a person could be blessed with something greater than they ever imagined. Rose felt those blessings profoundly. She had everything she'd ever wanted: friends, family, this amazing farm, and now Jesse, an incredible man that she loved. He was the last piece of the puzzle to make her life complete. In that moment, Rose's heart felt like it could explode with happiness, and she said a silent thank you to God.

EPILOGUE

Two months later…

JESSE HELD THE small box open. In it lay his grandmother's engagement ring, passed down to his mother, and now it belonged to him. He'd found it while cleaning out his parents' room that first week back on the farm. It was one of the few things he chose to keep because it was a family heirloom. Nervously, Jesse snapped the box closed and shoved it into the pocket of his pants.

Leaving his apartment in Jacksonville, Jesse made the one-hour drive to Sunflower Farms to pick up Rose for their date. One thing was for sure, he would not miss the long commute to the farm once they were married. He would move back to his childhood home…provided she said yes.

Jesse rubbed his sweaty palms on his pants

as he drove. Why was he nervous? They loved each other. Why wouldn't she say *yes*? Still, he couldn't relax. It was such a big moment, and nothing was ever guaranteed.

Jesse drove down the farm's long driveway and parked below Rose's apartment. Anxious to see her, he took the stairs up two at a time, then knocked. He'd told her to dress up, that he wanted to take her somewhere nice for the evening. When she answered the door, she flashed him a brilliant smile. She looked radiant in a pink dress, with her hair falling in soft waves around her shoulders. She wore lip gloss, and her cheeks were flushed with excitement.

Her eyes grew wide when she saw him. "Wow. You look so handsome," she said. "You should wear a suit and tie more often."

"Thank you. And you look amazing," he complimented back.

Rose glanced down at her dress, "Oh, this old thing," she joked. Then daintily she lifted one foot, as if to model her shoe. "I even wore my new high heels."

"Very nice. Ready to go?"

"Yep. Let me grab my purse."

Jesse was keenly aware of the ring hidden in his pocket as they walked down the stairs holding hands. Did she notice his sweaty palm? If she did, she was polite enough not to say anything. He held the car door open for her.

"Thank you," she said, sliding gracefully into the car. Jesse rushed around to the other side and got in.

"Where are we going?" she asked as he started the engine.

"A nice little restaurant I found between here and Jacksonville."

"I'm surprised you wanted to dress up. I don't know what's gotten into you, Jesse Cooper, but I like it. I always knew you were a romantic at heart."

"Don't tell anybody," he teased, turning onto the country road.

After driving for five miles, he turned onto the highway. The evening sun was starting to set. They easily chatted as the miles slipped past them.

Finally, they reached their destination, a historic Victorian house that had been turned into a charming bistro. Jesse parked across the street in a small, crowded lot and they got out.

"This place is beautiful. How did you ever find it?" Rose asked.

"I heard a couple of the guys talking about it at the station and thought we could try it."

Jesse patted his pocket, to reassure himself the small ring box was still there. A zing of nervousness went through him.

They crossed the road and reached the front of the restaurant. "I can't wait to see their menu," Rose said. "I'm in the mood for..." Abruptly her words were cut off as she slipped on the first step and fell.

"Whoa!" Rose said, hitting the ground. It happened too fast for Jesse to catch her. Rose laughed it off as she collected herself and sat down on the bottom step. "I'm okay... Ooh, maybe not," she said, grabbing her ankle. "I should never have worn these heels."

Jesse crouched down and examined the injured ankle; it was already swelling. "I better take you to the emergency room. You may have broken it."

The nearest hospital was twenty-five minutes away in Jacksonville. They checked into the busy ER and waited hours to be seen. It was after ten o'clock when Rose was finally discharged with a badly sprained ankle. Jesse pushed her in a wheelchair toward the hospital exit.

"You think the restaurant is still open?" she asked, sounding hopeful.

"I called and they've already closed. Why? That pack of crackers we shared from the vending machine didn't fill you up?" he teased.

"Maybe as an appetizer, but that was hours ago. I'm starving."

"Yeah, me too."

After they left the hospital, Jesse spotted a fast-food joint from the highway and they stopped for burgers. Once they'd eaten, they had a good laugh at how the evening had turned out.

Finally turning in to Sunflower Farms, on impulse, he drove past Rose's apartment. The headlights lit a path through the grass ahead of them.

"Where are we going?" Rose asked.

"You'll see."

"Jesse Cooper, it's been a long night. Please don't play games with me."

"Rose McFarland, it's been a long night for me too. Just trust me."

Jesse took them to the field with the picnic tables. Stopping next to the table they had sat at the night of the barn dance, he helped Rose out of the car. She hobbled over, sat down on the wooden bench, and looked up at the dark sky. "It's such a clear night. There's millions of stars out tonight," she said in awe.

Jesse sat next to her and took a deep breath. He was too nervous to stargaze. His heart raced in his chest, thinking about this important moment.

"This is nice. Thank you for bringing me out here." Rose said. "At least we can end the night on a good note."

Jesse stood up, reached in his pocket, and pulled out the little box he'd kept hidden all evening. When he knelt on one knee, in front of Rose, she gasped, covering her mouth with both hands.

"Jesse… What are you doing?" she asked breathlessly.

He flipped open the box so she could see the diamond ring.

"Rose, you are the love of my life. You bring me so much joy and I want to spend the rest of my life with you. Will you marry me?"

In the moonlight, Rose's eyes sparkled with unshed tears. "Yes. I'll marry you."

Jesse carefully took the ring out of the box and slipped it on Rose's finger. Then he stood, and pulled her up into his arms.

Now he was truly home.

★ ★ ★ ★ ★

WESTERN

Rugged men looking for love...

Available Next Month

A Lullaby For The Maverick Melissa Senate
The Rancher's Reunion Lisa Childs

....

Fortune's Convenient Cinderella Makenna Lee
The Cowgirl Nanny Jen Gilroy

....

 LOVE INSPIRED

Training The K-9 Companion Jill Kemerer
The Cowboys Marriage Bargain Deborah Clack

Keep reading for an excerpt of a new title
from the Special Edition series,
TAMING A HEARTBREAKER by Brenda Jackson

Prologue

Sloan and Leslie Outlaw's wedding...

"Sloan definitely likes kissing you, girlfriend."

Leslie Outlaw couldn't help but smile at her best friend's whispered words. "And I love kissing him."

She'd married the man she loved, and she'd had her best friend Carmen Golan at her side. Leslie followed her friend's gaze now and saw just where it had landed—right on Redford St. James, who was being corralled by the photographer as Sloan took pictures with his best man and groomsmen.

Unease stirred Leslie's insides at her friend's obvious interest.

Leslie had known Redford for as long as she'd known Sloan, since she'd met both guys the same day on the university's campus over ten years ago. Redford had been known then as a heartbreaker. According to Sloan, Redford hadn't changed. If anything, he'd gotten worse.

"Carmen, I need to warn you about Redford," Leslie said, hoping it wasn't too late. She'd noted last night at the rehearsal how taken her best friend had been with Redford. She'd hoped she was mistaken.

"I know all about him, Leslie, so you don't need to warn me. However, you might want to put a bug in Sloan's ear to warn Redford about me."

Leslie lifted a brow. "Why?"

A wide smile covered Carmen's face. "Because Redford

St. James is the man I intend to marry. Your hubby is on his way over here. I will see you at the reception."

Leslie watched Carmen walk toward Redford. Marry? Redford? She had a feeling her best friend was biting off more than she could chew. Redford was not the marrying kind. He'd made that clear when he'd said no woman would ever tame him.

Chapter One

Two years later...

Redford St. James froze, with his wineglass midway to his lips, when he saw the woman walk into the wedding reception for Jaxon and Nadia Ravnell. Frowning, he immediately turned to the man by his side, Sloan Outlaw. During their college days at the University of Alaska at Anchorage, Sloan, Redford, and another close friend, Tyler Underwood, had been thick as thieves, and still were.

Redford had been known as the "king of quickies." He would make out with women any place or any time. Storage rooms, empty classrooms or closets, beneath the stairs, dressing rooms ...he'd used them all. He had the uncanny ability to scope out a room and figure out just where a couple could spend time for pleasure. He still had that skill and used it every chance he got.

Although he, Sloan and Tyler now lived in different cities in Alaska, they still found the time to get together a couple of times a year. Doing so wasn't as easy as it used to be since both Tyler and Sloan were married with a child each. Tyler had a son and Sloan a daughter.

"Why didn't you tell me Carmen Golan was invited to this wedding?"

Sloan glanced over at Redford and rolled his eyes. "Just

like you didn't tell me Leslie had been invited to Tyler and Keosha's wedding three years ago?"

Redford frowned. "Don't play with me, Sloan. You should have known Leslie would be invited, since she and Keosha were friends in college. In this case, I wasn't aware Carmen knew Jaxon or Nadia."

Sloan took a sip of his wine before saying, "The Outlaws and Westmorelands consider themselves one big happy family, and that includes outside cousins, in-laws and close friends. Since Carmen is Leslie's best friend, of course she would know them." Sloan then studied his friend closely. "Why does Carmen being here bother you, Redford? If I recall, when I put that bug in your ear after my wedding, that she'd said she intended to one day become your wife, you laughed it off. Has that changed?"

"Of course, that hasn't changed."

"You're sure?" Sloan asked. "It seems to me that over the past two years, whenever the two of you cross paths, you try like hell to avoid her. Most recently, at Cassidy's christening a few months ago." Cassidy was Sloan and Leslie's daughter. Redford was one of her godfathers, and Carmen was her godmother.

"No woman can change my ways. I don't ever intend to marry. Who does she think she is, anyway? She doesn't even know me like that. If she did, then she would know my only interest in her at your wedding was getting her to the nearest empty coat closet. The nerve of her, thinking she can change me."

"And since you know she can't change you, why worry about it?"

"I'm not worrying."

"If you say so," Sloan countered.

Redford's frown deepened. "I do say so. You of all people should know that I'll never fall in love again."

Before Sloan could respond, his sister Charm walked up and said the photographer wanted to take a photo of Jaxon with his Outlaw cousins.

When Sloan walked off, leaving Redford alone, he took a sip of his wine as he looked across the room at Carmen again. Sloan's words had hit a nerve. He *wasn't* worried. Then why had he been avoiding her for the past two years? Doing so hadn't been easy since he was one of Sloan's best friends and she was Leslie's, and both were godparents to Cassidy. Whenever they were in the same space, he made it a point to not be in her presence for long.

He could clearly recall the day he'd first seen Carmen at Sloan and Leslie's wedding rehearsal two years ago. He would admit that he'd been intensely attracted to her from the first. It was a deep-in-the-gut awareness. Something he had never experienced before. He hadn't wasted any time adding her to his "must do" list. He'd even flirted shamelessly after they'd been introduced, with every intention of making out with her before the weekend ended.

Then he'd gotten wind of her bold claim that he was the man she intended to marry. Like hell! That had wiped out all his plans. He was unapologetically a womanizer, and no woman alive would change that.

Carmen wasn't the first woman to try, nor would she be the first to fail. Granted she was beautiful. Hell, he'd even say she was "knock-you-in-the-balls" gorgeous, but he'd dated beautiful women before. If he'd seen one, he'd seen them all, and in the bedroom they were all the same.

Then why was he letting Carmen Golan get to him? Why would heat flood his insides whenever he saw her, making him aware of every single thing about her? Why was there this strong kinetic pull between them? It was sexual chemistry so powerful that, at times, it took his breath away.

Over the years, he'd tried convincing himself his lust for

her would fade. So far it hadn't. And rather recently, whenever he saw her, it had gotten so bad he had to fight like hell to retain his common sense.

Although Sloan had given him that warning two years ago, Carmen hadn't acted on anything. Was she waiting for what she thought would be the right time to catch him at a weak moment? If that was her strategy then he had news for her. It wouldn't happen. If anything, he would catch *her* unawares first, just to prove he was way out of her league...thanks to Candy Porter.

Contrary to her first name, he'd discovered there hadn't been anything sweet about Candy. At seventeen, she had taught him a hard lesson. Mainly, to never give your heart to a woman. Candy and her parents had moved to Skagway the summer before their last year of high school. By the end of the summer, she had been his steady girlfriend, the one he planned to marry after he finished college. Those plans ended the night of their high school senior prom.

Less than an hour after they'd arrived, she told him she needed to go to the ladies' room. When she hadn't returned in a timely manner, he had gotten worried since she hadn't been feeling well. He had gone looking for her, and when a couple of girls said she wasn't in the ladies' room, he and the two concerned girls had walked outside and around the building to find her, hoping she was alright.

Not only had they found her, they'd found her with the town's bad boy, Sherman Sharpe. Both of them in the backseat of Sherman's car making out like horny rabbits. The pair hadn't even had the decency to roll up the car's window so their moans, grunts and screams couldn't be heard.

Needless to say, news of Candy and Sherman's backseat romp quickly got around. By the following morning, every household in Skagway, Alaska, had heard about it. She had tried to explain, offer an excuse, but as far as he'd been concerned, there was nothing a woman could say when caught with another man between her legs.

Heartbroken and hurt, Redford hadn't wasted any time leaving Skagway for Anchorage to begin college that summer, instead of waiting for fall. That's when he vowed to never give his heart to another woman ever again.

That had been nearly nineteen years ago, and he'd kept the promise he'd made to himself. At thirty-six, he guarded his heart like it was made of solid gold and refused to let any woman get close. He kept all his hookups impersonal. One-and-done was the name of his game. No woman slept in his bed, and he never spent the entire night in theirs. He refused to wake up with any woman in his arms.

Redford knew Carmen was his total opposite. He'd heard she was one of those people who saw the bright side of everything, always positive and agreeable. On top of that, she was a hopeless romantic. A woman who truly believed in love, marriage and all that bull crap. According to Sloan, she'd honestly gotten it in her head that she and Redford were actual soulmates. Well, he had news for her, he was no woman's soulmate.

When his wineglass was empty, he snagged another from the tray of a passing waiter. When he glanced back over at Carmen, he saw she was staring at him, and dammit to hell, like a deer caught in headlights, he stared back. Why was he feeling this degree of lust that she stirred within him so effortlessly?

There wasn't a time when she didn't look stunning. Today was no exception. There was just something alluring about her. Something that made his breath wobble whenever he stared at her for too long.

He blamed it on the beauty of her cocoa-colored skin, her almond-shaped light brown eyes, the gracefulness of her high cheekbones, her tempting pair of lips, and the mass of dark brown hair that fell past her shoulders.

Every muscle in his body tightened as he continued to look

at her, checking her out in full detail. His gaze scanned over her curvaceous and statuesque body. The shimmering blue dress she wore hugged her curves and complemented a gorgeous pair of legs. The bodice pushed up her breasts in a way that made his mouth water.

"Now you were saying," Sloan said, returning and immediately snagging Redford's attention.

"I was saying that maybe I should accommodate Carmen."

That sounded like a pretty damn good idea, considering the current fix his body was in.

"Meaning what?" Sloan asked.

A smile widened across Redford's lips. "Meaning, I think I will add her back to my 'must do' list. Maybe it's time she discovers I am a man who can't be tamed."

Sloan frowned. "Do I need to warn you that Carmen is Leslie's best friend?"

"No, but I would assume, given my reputation, that Leslie has warned Carmen about me. It's not my fault if she didn't take the warning. Now, if you will excuse me, I think I'll head over to the buffet table."

He then walked off. At least for now, he would take care of one appetite, and he intended to take care of the other before the night was over.

"I wish you and Redford would stop trying to out-stare each other, Carmen," Leslie Outlaw leaned over to whisper to her best friend.

Carmen Golan broke eye contact with Redford to glance at Leslie and couldn't help the smile that spread across her lips. "Hey, what can I say? He looks so darn good in a suit."

Leslie rolled her eyes. "Need I remind you that you've seen him in a suit before. Numerous times."

"Redford wore a tux at your wedding, Leslie, and he looked

good then, too. Better than good. He looked scrumptious." Carmen watched him again. He definitely looked delicious now.

She knew he was in his late thirties. He often projected a keen sense of professionalism, as well as a high degree of intelligence far beyond his years. But then there were other times when it seemed the main thing on his agenda was a conquest. Namely, seducing a woman.

Carmen knew all about his reputation as a heartbreaker of the worst kind. She'd witnessed how he would check out women at various events, seeking out his next victim. He had checked her out the same way, the first time they'd met.

She'd also seen the way women checked him out, too and definitely understood why they fell for him when he was so darn handsome. His dark eyes, coffee-colored skin, chiseled and bearded chin, hawkish nose, and close-to-the-scalp haircut, were certainly a draw.

Then there was his height. Carmen was convinced he was at least six foot three with a masculine build of broad shoulders, muscular arms and a rock-hard chest. Whenever he walked, feminine eyes followed. According to Leslie, although he made Anchorage his home, his family lived in Skagway and were part of the Tlingits, the largest Native Alaskan tribe.

Since their initial meeting two years ago, he'd kept his distance and she knew the reason why. She'd deliberately let it be known that she planned to marry him one day, making sure he heard about her plans well in advance. And upon hearing them, he'd begun avoiding her.

"Granted, it's obvious there's strong sexual chemistry between you and Redford," Leslie said, interrupting Carmen's thoughts. "Sexual chemistry isn't everything. At least you've given up the notion of trying to tame him. I'm glad about that. You had me worried there for a while."

Carmen broke eye contact with Redford and looked at Leslie. "Nothing has changed, Leslie. I'm convinced that for me it was love at first sight. Redford is still the man I intend to marry."

Leslie looked surprised. "But you haven't mentioned him in months. And at Cassidy's christening you didn't appear to pay him any attention."

Carmen grinned. "I've taken the position with Redford that I refuse to be like those other women who are always fawning over him. Women he sees as nothing more than sex mates. Redford St. James has to earn his right to my bed. When he does, it will be because he's ready to accept what I have to give."

"Which is?"

"Love in its truest form."

Leslie rolled her eyes. "I've known Redford a lot longer than you have, and I know how he operates. I love him like a brother, but get real, Carmen. He has plenty of experience when it comes to seducing women. You, on the other hand, have no experience when it comes to taming a man. Zilch."

"I believe in love, Leslie, and I have more than enough to give," Carmen said softly.

"I believe you, but the person you're trying to give it to has to want it in return. I don't know Redford's story, but there is one. And it's one neither Redford, Sloan nor Tyler ever talks about. I believe it has to do with a woman who hurt him in the past, and it's a pain he hasn't gotten over."

"Then I can help him get over it," Carmen replied.

Leslie released a deep sigh. "Not sure that you can, Carmen. Redford may not ever be ready to accept love from you or any woman. You have a good heart and see the good in everyone. You give everyone the benefit of the doubt, even those who don't deserve it. I think you're making a mistake in thinking Redford will change for you."

Carmen heard what Leslie was saying and could see the worried look in her eyes. It was the same look she'd given her two years ago when Carmen had declared that one day she would marry Redford. She understood Leslie's concern, but for some reason, Carmen believed that even with Redford's reputation as a heartbreaker, he would one day see her as more than a sex mate. He would realize she was his soulmate.

"I'm thirty-two and can take care of myself, Leslie."

"When it comes to a man like Redford, I'm not sure you can, Carmen."

Carmen shrugged. "I've dated men like Redford before. Men who only want one thing from a woman. I intend to be the exception and not the norm." Determined to change the subject, she said, "I love June weddings, don't you?"

The look in Leslie's eyes let Carmen know she knew what she'd deliberately done and would go along with her. "Yes, and Denver's weather was perfect today," Leslie said.

"Nadia looked beautiful. This is the first wedding I've ever attended where the bride wore a black wedding dress."

"Same for me, and she looked simply gorgeous. It was Jaxon's mom's wedding dress, and she offered it to Nadia for her special day."

Nadia not only looked beautiful but radiant walking down that aisle on her brother-in-law Dillon Westmoreland's arm. Both the wedding and reception had been held at Westmoreland House, the massive multipurpose family center that Dillon, the oldest of the Denver Westmorclands, had built on his three-hundred-acre property. The building could hold up to five hundred people easily and was used for special occasions, family events and get-togethers.

Carmen glanced around the huge, beautifully decorated room and noticed the man she had been introduced to earlier that day, Matthew Caulder. He'd discovered just last year that he was related to the Westmoreland triplets, Casey, Cole and Clint. It seemed the biological father Matthew hadn't known was the triplets' uncle, the legendary rodeo star and horse trainer, Sid Roberts.

It seemed that she and Redford weren't the only ones exchanging intense glances today. "You've been so busy watching me and Redford stare each other down, have you missed how Matthew Caulder keeps staring at Iris Michaels?" Carmen leaned in to whisper to Leslie.

Leslie followed her gaze to where Matthew stood talking to a bunch of the Westmoreland men. Iris was Pam Westmoreland's best friend. Pam was Nadia's sister and was married to Dillon. "No, I hadn't noticed, but I do now. Matthew is divorced, and Iris, who owns a PR firm in Los Angeles, is a widow. I understand her husband was a stuntman in Hollywood and was killed while working on a major film a number of years ago. I hope she reciprocates Matthew's interest. She deserves happiness."

Carmen frowned. "What about me? Don't I deserve happiness, too?"

"Yes, but like I told you, I'm not sure you'll find it with Redford, Carmen, and I don't want to see you get hurt."

"And like I told you, I can take care of myself."

At that moment, the party planner announced the father-daughter dance, and Dillon stood in again for Nadia's deceased father. While all eyes were on them, Carmen glanced back over at Redford. As if he'd felt her gaze, he tilted his head to look at her, his eyes unwavering and deeply penetrating.

Like she'd told Leslie, she didn't intend to be just another notch on Redford's bedpost. Their sexual chemistry had been there from the first. It was there now, simmering between them. He couldn't avoid her forever, and no matter what he thought, she truly believed they were meant to be together. She had time, patience and a belief in what was meant to be.

She would not pursue him. When the time was right, he would pursue her. She totally understood Leslie's concern but Carmen believed people could change. Even Redford. His two best friends were married with families. She had to believe that eventually he would want the same thing for himself.

Was he starting to want it now? Was that why he'd been staring tonight after two years of ignoring her? Her heart beat wildly at the thought.

When everyone began clapping, she broke eye contact with Redford and saw that the dance between Nadia and Dillon had ended. Now the first dance between Jaxon and Nadia would start. As tempted as she was, she refused to look back at Redford, although she felt his eyes on her. The heat from his gaze stirred all parts of her.

When the dance ended, Jaxon leaned into Nadia for a kiss, which elicited claps, cheers, and whistles. As the wedding planner invited others to the dance floor and the live band began to perform, Jaxon and Nadia were still kissing.

Carmen smiled, feeling the love between the couple. She wanted the same thing for herself. A man who would love her, respect her, be by her side and share his life with her. He would have no problem kissing her in front of everyone, proclaiming she was his and his only. He would be someone who would never break her heart or trample her pride.

How could she think Redford St. James capable of giving her all those things when he was unable to keep his pants zipped? Was she wrong in thinking he could change? She wanted to believe that the same love and happiness her sister Chandra shared with her husband Rutledge, the same love Leslie shared with Sloan, and Nadia shared with Jaxon, could be hers. Even her parents, retired college professors now living in Cape Town, were still in love.

People teased her about wearing rose-colored glasses, but when you were surrounded by so much love, affection and togetherness, you couldn't help but believe in happily ever after. She was convinced that everyone had a soulmate. That special person meant for them.

Unable to fight temptation any longer, she glanced back at Redford. His eyes were still on her and that stirring returned. He smiled and her heart missed a beat.

Then her breath caught in her throat as he began walking toward her.